Nicola Upson was born in Suffolk and read English at Downing College, Cambridge. She has worked in theatre and as a freelance journalist, and is the author of two works of non-fiction and the recipient of an Escalator Award from the Arts Council England.

Her debut novel, *An Expert in Murder*, was the first in a series of crime novels whose main character is Josephine Tey – one of the leading authors of Britain's Golden Age of crime writing.

Nicola lives with her partner in Cambridge and Cornwall.

Praise for Nicola Upson and the 'Josephine Tey' series:

'An ingenious concept, beautifully realised.' Reginald Hill

'Upson legitimately uses [Tey] as an avatar to meld a golden-age plot with modern frankness, and Tey's creative process mirrors her own concern about blurring fact and fiction.' *Financial Times*

'An absolute delight . . . Upson has created a fine series of cosy but intelligent mysteries . . . this tale has everything you could want: storms, murders, tea and a wonderful evocation of time.' *Catholic Herald*

'Upso   rder setting.

The portrayal of Tey herself is both sympathetic and perceptive . . . Upson is chillingly effective at showing how good intentions may lead to evil consequences . . . a fine addition to a promising series.' Andrew Taylor, *Spectator*

'Any crime aficionado whose beach reading usually consists of a bagful of crinkly old paperbacks should make room for Nicola Upson's novels in which the real-life author Josephine Tey, one of the grandes dames of the Golden Age of detective fiction, investigates murders in the Thirties.'
Daily Telegraph

By the Same Author

An Expert in Murder
Angel with Two Faces
Two for Sorrow

Fear in the Sunlight

NICOLA UPSON

faber and faber

First published in this edition in 2012
by Faber and Faber Ltd
Bloomsbury House
74–77 Great Russell Street
London WC1B 3DA
This paperback edition first published in 2012

Typeset by Faber and Faber Ltd
Printed and bound by CPI Group (UK) Ltd, Croydon, CRO 4YY

Some quotations featuring Alfred Hitchcock extracted from *It's Only a Movie* by Charlotte
Chandler, published by Simon & Schuster Ltd
Quotations from 'Women are a Nuisance', 'Would You Like to Know Your Future' and 'Why I
am Afraid of the Dark' taken from *Hitchcock on Hitchcock* © Sidney Gottlieb and reprinted by
permission of Faber and Faber Ltd

The right of Nicola Upson to be identified as author
of this work has been asserted in accordance with Section 77
of the Copyright, Designs and Patents Act 1988

A CIP record for this book
is available from the British Library

ISBN 978-0-571-24637-3

FSC
www.fsc.org
MIX
Paper from
responsible sources
FSC® C101712

4 6 8 10 9 7 5 3

For my parents, with love.

Contents

Map

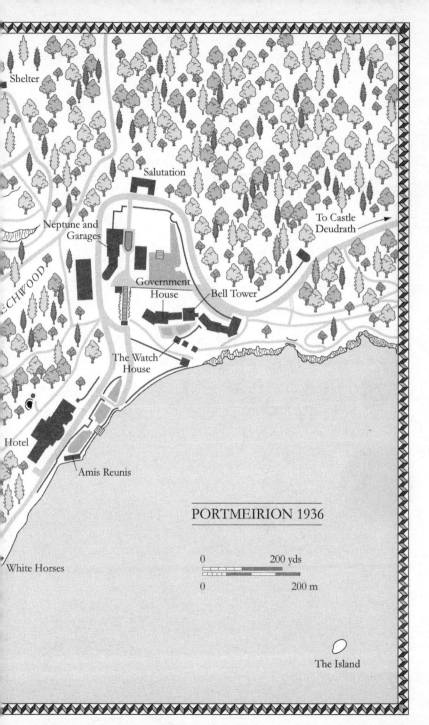

PORTMEIRION 1936

Shelter

Salutation

Neptune and
Garages

To Castle
Deudrath

BEECHWOOD

Government
House

Bell Tower

The Watch
House

Hotel

Amis Reunis

White Horses

0   200 yds

0   200 m

The Island

PART ONE

REAR WINDOW

24 July 1954, London

'Do you mind if we stop for a moment?'

'Sure.' The detective sounded impatient, but he did as he was asked and the staccato whirr of the projector gradually subsided. Archie Penrose closed his eyes, but the image of Josephine refused to go away. She sat on the hotel terrace in the afternoon sunlight, a little self-conscious in front of the camera but laughing nonetheless at something he had just said to her. He couldn't remember what they had been talking about, and that annoyed him – irrationally, because the moment was eighteen years ago now and the conversation had been nothing more than easy holiday banter; but, since Josephine's death, the gradual fragmentation of all she had been in his memory disturbed him, and any elusive detail stung him like a personal rebuke. He stood and lifted the blinds on the windows, aware that the American was watching him, waiting for an explanation. 'I didn't mean to upset you, sir,' he said hesitantly, and the lazy drawl of his Californian accent gave the words an insolence which might or might not have been intentional. 'There's worse to come in the later footage. Much worse.'

'Not for me,' Penrose said curtly, and sat down at his desk to claw back some authority from the meeting. 'A friend of mine – the woman in the film – she died.' The words sounded cold and impersonal, but he knew from experience that there was no phrase that could adequately express his sense of loss, and he had long given up trying to find one. 'So it's hard for me to look back, Detective Doyle, no matter how harmless the images seem to you.'

'You knew one of the victims personally? I'm sorry. I didn't realise.'

This time the apology was genuine, and Penrose was quick to clarify. 'No, no – nothing like that. She died a couple of years ago, after an illness. But that's why we were at Portmeirion – it was Josephine's fortieth birthday. She loved it there and we went with some friends to celebrate.'

'So you weren't part of Mr Hitchcock's party?'

'Not officially, no. Another friend of Josephine's – Marta Fox – had done some script work for his wife, and she was there for the weekend. But none of us was in Hitchcock's circle, although he and Josephine had things to discuss. He wanted to film one of her books – a crime novel called *A Shilling for Candles* which was just about to be published. She had reservations about it, but she agreed to talk to him while they were both at Portmeirion.'

'I don't remember a film of that name. Presumably it never happened, if your friend was so concerned about it?'

'Oh yes, it happened. It came out the following year, but Hitchcock called it *Young and Innocent*. It was quite a success.'

The detective shook his head. 'I still don't know it. I suppose I've only seen the ones he made since he came over to our side. Was she pleased? Your friend, I mean.'

'By the time Mr Hitchcock had finished with it, her story was no more recognisable than the title,' Penrose said wryly. 'I can recall some of the words Josephine used when she saw it, but "pleased" wasn't one of them.'

Doyle smiled. 'Then I hope they paid her well.' He took a packet of cigarettes out of his pocket and offered one to Penrose. 'Tell me about this Portmeirion – it's not really a proper place, is it?'

'It's whatever you want it to be. That's its beauty.'

'But a private village created entirely by one man? Isn't that a little strange?'

The genuine incredulity in the detective's voice amused Penrose, but he knew what Doyle meant: for anyone who had never been there, the idea of a resort designed entirely for pleasure and architectural beauty – and for those with the means to enjoy them – was difficult to grasp; for an American with, he suspected, socialist leanings, it must seem absurdly self-indulgent. 'It's remarkable, certainly,' he said, 'but strong visions often are. The village might have been created by one man, but it's founded entirely on the belief that beauty can make people's lives better. In Portmeirion, Clough Williams-Ellis found a landscape that was beautiful already and used his imagination to improve it; that's a tremendous achievement, so no – I don't think it's strange. In fact, after what the world's been through, it seems to me to be saner than ever – if a little optimistic.' He smiled, but Doyle seemed unconvinced. 'And it's not a museum – he's still adding to it. Now that the building restrictions have finally been lifted after the war, there's no stopping him. I went back recently with my wife, and he'd just started on the plans for a new gatehouse. So Portmeirion lives and breathes and changes,' he added, unable to keep a faint trace of sarcasm out of his voice, 'just like a proper place.'

'I'm surprised you wanted to go back after everything that happened there. It can't have been much of a celebration.'

'If a policeman starts avoiding places that have been tainted by violent crime, there'll come a point when he can't leave the house,' Penrose said. 'Surely you know that from your own experience?' It was an evasive answer, but rooted in truth: ironically, Portmeirion was scarred for him not by the murders that had taken place there, but by the happiness he had known during that summer – a happiness made all the more poignant by the shock of Josephine's death. He knew better, though, than to try to dull his sadness by staying away from places in which they'd spent time together: there was no logic to grief, and he felt her absence everywhere. 'At the risk of sounding callous, I wasn't personally involved in the deaths at Portmeirion, so the good memories outweigh the bad.'

Doyle shook a sheaf of photographs from a file, and unfolded a map of the village on Penrose's desk. 'Even so, something like this must be hard to forget, no matter how many cases you've dealt with in your career.' He pointed to one location after another, matching each one with its black-and-white counterpart. 'A body found up in the woods by that weird cemetery place, slashed so badly that the face was barely recognisable. Another murder on the headland, just a stone's throw from the hotel, the victim raped, strangled and strung up like an animal. These garages, right at the heart of the village – covered in blood.' He placed the last photograph in the centre of the map and Penrose looked down at the bruised and broken body, remembering the confusion and disbelief he had felt when he arrived at the scene. 'And the final death,' Doyle added. 'A very persuasive confession of guilt, which seemed to solve everything. So many locations, and so much blood. I don't know about beauty, sir – it seems to me that your architect created a playground for a killer.'

'That was hardly his intention,' Penrose said evenly. 'And Mr

Hitchcock's little games didn't help. They made things much more difficult for the police.'

'You weren't the investigating officer, were you?'

'No, it was never my case. I had to stand by and watch someone else take charge. For a moment, I was a suspect, just like everybody else.'

'That must have been quite a new experience.'

Penrose nodded. Throughout his career, he had always prided himself on a sensitivity towards those affected by murder, an awareness that – in the process of getting to the truth – many innocent lives were torn apart, but nothing could have prepared him for the ease with which people turned on each other when their own character was under question. 'Fortunately, it didn't last long. Events came to a natural conclusion, and the case seemed to be wrapped up very efficiently.'

'"Seemed to be"?'

'Suicide *is* an eloquent form of confession, as you say, but it makes cross-interrogation very difficult.'

'They tell me you were never entirely satisfied with the outcome.'

Wondering who 'they' were, Penrose said, 'It wasn't my place to comment on another force's findings. It still isn't. If you have information which calls into question the results of an earlier investigation, there are systems in place which will deal with that – but I refuse to speculate on something that was never my business. As I said, everything seemed to be resolved satisfactorily.'

The sly smile came again. 'That's the famous British diplomacy which got you here, I suppose.' Doyle looked round the office and his gaze took in the half-packed boxes and empty shelves, the striking drawing of a female nude which Penrose had removed carefully from the wall. 'Retirement's a busy time,' he said. 'The last thing you need is a stranger opening doors that were closed nearly twenty years ago.'

Penrose didn't argue. 'Detective Doyle, this is all taking longer than I expected and I'm not sure I really understand why you're here in the first place. You asked to see me in connection with some recent murders in Los Angeles, which you believe to be linked to what happened in Portmeirion in 1936, and I'm happy to tell you anything I can.' He looked at his watch. 'But you're right – it is a busy time. So perhaps we could skip the film show and get to the point. What exactly is this link you're talking about?'

'Hitchcock. Well, Hitchcock's movies. The latest one's released any minute, and that's the connection.' Penrose started to say something, but Doyle held up his hand. 'Let me explain first. The new film – it's about a photographer who breaks his leg and is confined to a wheelchair in his apartment. Because he can't do his job, he spends his time looking at people in the block opposite, imagining their lives from what he sees . . .'

'Sounds familiar,' Penrose said, thinking about one of Josephine's novels, 'but yes – I've read about it. Grace Kelly and James Stewart?'

'That's right. It's set in Greenwich Village, but filmed entirely on one huge set, built specially under Hitchcock's supervision. There were more than thirty apartments on that set, with trees and gardens down below, an alleyway leading out to the street, traffic going past, even a bar. You'd think you were looking at the real Manhattan skyline.'

'A whole borough created entirely by one man?' Penrose

said, but Doyle was engrossed in his own story and the irony was lost on him.

'Yes – amazing, isn't it? They finished shooting earlier this year, but on the morning they were due to start taking the set down, three bodies were found in one of the apartments – all of them women, all brutally murdered.'

Penrose looked at him in astonishment. 'Why haven't I heard about this?' he asked. 'It must have been all over the papers.'

'We thought it best to be discreet in the information we gave to the press.'

'And this was your investigation?'

'In a manner of speaking, but to be honest there really wasn't much investigating to claim any credit for. Someone was caught at the scene, someone who later confessed to a series of similar killings *and* to the three murders at Portmeirion . . .'

Penrose knew that Doyle was trying to rouse his curiosity by withholding any specific details about the person he had in custody, but he refused to rise to the bait. '*Three* murders at Portmeirion? You're saying that what we assumed to be the killer's suicide was actually another murder?'

'That's what it looks like. But I'm not entirely satisfied. There's obviously a lot more to what went on all those years ago, and something about it makes me uneasy. I'd like a second opinion.'

'Why mine?'

'Because you were there. Because you know the people involved. Because I've heard that the truth is important to you.'

Again, Penrose wondered who had supplied the information, but he said nothing; if necessary, there would be time to find out more about Detective Tom Doyle when the interview had finished. 'You have a confession, though – for all the murders. I really don't see what more I can add.'

'Your colleagues had what amounted to a confession, and now someone's come along to contradict that. Look, sir, if this didn't interest you, you'd never have agreed to see me – and you're interested because, in your heart, you think you only know half a story. I want to know if what I've got to show you *is* that other half, or if we're both still missing something.' He pushed a second manila file across the desk. 'In hindsight, could you believe this was your killer?'

Penrose glanced quickly at the name typed across the top. 'But that's impossible,' he said, losing his detachment for a moment. 'The suicide . . . everyone was together on the terrace when it happened.'

'And yet we have a confession for that murder from someone you say was several hundred yards away at the time. If that part of the story is suspect, why should I believe anything else I'm told? About any of the crimes?'

'You must have challenged this, if you have such doubts about it?'

'Of course, but I get the same response every time. What you said just now is the first real evidence I've had to support a hunch.'

'It makes no sense, though. Why would anybody bother to confess to an eighteen-year-old crime – let alone lie about it – when the case is closed and no one's asking questions?'

Doyle shrugged. 'That's what I hoped you might be able to help me with. To be honest, sir, I've no idea what I'm looking for, but anything you can tell me about those few days might be useful.' He seemed to sense Penrose's interest and gestured to the file. 'Would you like to read through what I've brought you?'

Penrose nodded, grateful for anything that would delay the moment when he had to look again at the film of his younger self, of Josephine alive and well. He had been shocked to see how different the real person – even a celluloid version – was from the image he carried in his mind; he had always taken it for granted that he remembered Josephine's face clearly, but he realised now that it was *just* a memory – a poor imitation, a composite of so many years and moments that none of them was quite truthful. Slowly, imperceptibly, during the months since her death, he had begun to filter her more and more through his own imagination, and that was perhaps the biggest lie of all: her image did as it was asked, whereas Josephine never had. 'I need time to study it properly, though,' he said. 'Are you staying in town?'

'Yes, at the Adelphi in Villiers Street.'

'Then come and see me tomorrow at noon. I'll answer any questions you have then.' The American stood to leave, but Penrose held him back. 'The earlier film reels from Portmeirion – they came from Mr Hitchcock, presumably?'

'From his office, yes. I thought they might help jog your memory.'

'And you said there was worse to come later in the footage. What did you mean?'

'The most recent murders – the women on Hitchcock's set. One of them was filmed as she died.' He left the room without another word and closed the door softly behind him. Penrose walked over to the window and looked down into the street, waiting for the detective to emerge. The morning was oppressive; bland, grey cloud hung low in the sky as it did so often in July, daring the summer to show itself, offering heat but drawing the line at sun. Doyle loosened his tie and opened his shirt as he ran down the steps and out onto the Embankment, his jacket slung casually over his shoulder. He waited for a gap in the traffic, then crossed the road and sauntered off towards Hungerford Bridge, looking at the river with the unhurried eyes of a visitor. Penrose watched until he was no longer distinguishable in a crowd, then turned back to the room, where the rest of his professional life was waiting to be dismantled.

Half-heartedly, he stacked a few more papers and put some photographs in a box, unable to decide whether it was the warmth of the room or a more personal lethargy that made everything seem such an effort. There was a small pile of novels on a shelf next to his desk – he had always hated offices that bore no trace of the human being who worked in them – and he started to pack them away, but stopped when he got to a copy of Josephine's final mystery, published after her death, its title page blank and impersonal. The book was barely touched, its pages as neat and new as the day he had bought it, and he still couldn't bring himself to look inside. For Penrose, reading Josephine's work had always been the next best thing to enjoying her company; it was like hearing her speak, so naturally did her voice come through in her prose. While *The Singing Sands* remained unread, it was as if there were one more conversation still to be had, one new thing to discover about her – and he wasn't ready to run out of surprises yet where Josephine was concerned. He didn't know if he ever would be.

Impatiently, he piled the rest of the books into a box with

some other bits and pieces, abandoning any pretence at a system, and threw the box onto the floor by the door, then picked up the telephone and dialled another department. 'Devlin? I want you to check all the information you gave me on Detective Tom Doyle. Find out how long he's been in England and when he's due back in Los Angeles. Talk to the Adelphi Hotel and see if he's met anyone while he's been staying there, or if he's talked to anyone else here. And give North Wales a call – find out if he's been asking questions about Portmeirion in 1936. If he has any connections at all with this country, I want to know about them.' Penrose replaced the receiver and sat down at his desk, where the only items left now were Doyle's files and a cup of coffee – cold and bitter, the only way he ever seemed to drink it. He opened the file and scanned the summary at the beginning of the report, then began to read the first few pages, astonished that – after eighteen years – he could still recall a voice that had been so brief a part of his life.

'They say you always remember your first, but I wonder if that's really true? You want me to tell you what happened, where it all began – and I'll do as you ask, because it costs me nothing. But please don't think it's a burden I've carried all these years, or that confessing it now will be some sort of relief. It hasn't kept me awake at night, and it doesn't haunt my dreams. I can bring it to mind, of course I can, but it's not forever with me in the way you seem to think it should be. Always remember. Never forget. It's not quite the same thing.

'It was summer, certainly; the air was sweet and warm and hopeful – a South of France sort of day. The headland was covered in trees, much as it is now, and they seemed to flaunt their own extravagance in a rich tangle of greens, unfolding for acres, all the

way back to the old ferryman's cottage. Even the trunks of long-dead pine trees – scattered along the shoreline, and slowly drained of their colour by the wind and sea – shone white and brilliant in the sunlight. The year had come of age, you might say – everywhere you looked, there was a tiny celebration of its beauty. We walked together along one of the paths that led up from the terrace, past the back of the old mansion house – faded and neglected then, a far cry from the rich man's toy it is now. In those days, a long snarl of depressing laurel bushes lined that path, making any view of the sea impossible, but sheltering you from the eyes of the house long before you left the grounds. It was like a tunnel between two worlds, one restrictive and suffocating, the other exotic and adventurous. "Y Gwyllt", they called it. "The Wild Place". But for me, it was the safest place on earth. When I left it – when I was forced to leave – I carried it with me in my mind, a small pocket of silence and darkness to retreat to whenever I might need it. That interests you, I suppose. I wonder what you think it proves?

'Anyway, it was a route we'd taken many times before. We both knew it by heart, and turned instinctively towards the densest part of the wilderness, deeper and deeper into the tight knot of woodland, he always a few steps ahead of me. There were some old hides in the woods, built originally for pheasant shoots, and I stopped by one for a moment to take a stone out of my boot; he looked back impatiently, and I felt a sense of power that was both daunting and exhilarating. The path grew narrower still as we moved forward, but eventually we reached the small circle of ground which they now call the cemetery. Everything was weed-choked and overgrown, a place where sunlight was a stranger, warmth an impossibility. There were only one or two graves there then, of course – or perhaps I should say only one or two that were marked. Still, the ground was covered with a carpet of fallen rhododendron petals, blood red and sinking slowly into the earth; a rehearsal, almost, for what was to come.

'Did I know what I was going to do? That's harder to answer truthfully after all these years, but yes, I think I knew. Not because I'd planned it, but because it had always been there – the violence, I mean. Let me make it easy for you: I wanted to hurt something; it didn't much matter what or whom.

'At first, he thought I was playing. I pushed him to the ground, but he twisted away and came back for more, eager to please and confident in our friendship. Then I kicked him, and I saw the first hint of confusion in his eyes, the first flicker of genuine fear. A second blow, harder this time, and he cowered in front of me, scarcely able to believe the betrayal. Looking back now, I think it was his refusal to struggle that made me so angry – somehow, it was all too easy. I grabbed his throat and slowly tightened my grip, breathing in the scent of damp leaves as I held him against the ground, scanning his face for an acknowledgement of the pain. It was over in seconds, and if the excitement had been more intense than anything I'd ever known, the disappointment was even greater. You see, it wasn't just about the killing. It never has been. It was about the fear – the fear and the pain, and later the humiliation. And you know, they never last long enough. I suppose that's what makes them precious.

'Afterwards, his body disgusted me. I just wanted it out of my sight, and I looked round for the best place to get rid of it. Then, and only then, did I realise that she was watching me. She smiled. Actually, that's what I remember most clearly of all. She smiled.'

PART TWO

THE PLEASURE GARDEN

25 July 1936, Portmeirion

I

Josephine laughed, and lifted her sunglasses for a moment to look at him. 'If that's *really* what you think, I'm amazed they promoted you at all.'

'It's all right – they'll never know.' Archie smiled and poured them both another drink, and Josephine glanced beyond him to the end of the terrace. The lawns – dry and brittle with the heat, despite the gardener's best efforts to defy the weather – culminated in a formal cascade, where water trickled lazily over rock-cut steps, exotically draped in mimosa, azalea and ferns; at the top, poised between two ornamental pillars, a man was operating an unwieldy-looking camera, and she watched him warily as he panned left to right, back from the estuary to the hotel and shoreline.

'If I'd known we were going to be filmed all weekend, I'd have gone to Bournemouth,' she said. 'Aren't there laws against that sort of thing, Chief Inspector?'

He lay back in his deckchair and closed his eyes. 'He's only doing location shots, apparently; they're not for public consumption. Anyway, don't knock it: most people would move heaven and earth to have their fortieth birthday immortalised by Alfred Hitchcock.'

'Only a man would say that,' she replied, a little tetchily. 'No woman would want forty immortalised at all – we all hope to glide quietly through it while everyone's looking the other way. But what have I got? The director of the moment closing in on every grey hair.'

'It doesn't really bother you, does it?' Archie asked, surprised. 'You barely look a day over thirty-nine.'

She laughed again, and moved her deckchair back so that Archie blocked her from the camera's view. 'No, I don't suppose it does, but I'd rather not have to talk to the man and I'm certainly not in a negotiating mood. In fact, I'm beginning to wonder what Marta's got me into.'

'How is it her fault? I thought Hitchcock approached you through your publisher?'

'He did, but only because Marta gave Mrs Hitchcock a proof copy of the book. Otherwise, *A Shilling for Candles* could have passed beautifully into oblivion like ninety-five per cent of the other crime novels published this year.'

'You must be excited, though? He wants to put your novel on every cinema screen in the country.' He lit a cigarette and looked at her in disbelief. 'Even you can't be immune to that, surely? You love films.'

'I *am* excited about walking into the Playhouse in Inverness and seeing something I've written come to life on the screen. What worries me is everything that the book and I will have to go through to get there. *The 39 Steps* was barely recognisable by the time he'd finished with it.'

'Good film, though, and I read somewhere that Buchan said Hitchcock's was a better story.' He grinned, unapologetic for being provocative. 'I know it's daunting: new opportunities always are. You've every reason to be scared.' She glared at him, but didn't argue. 'Seriously, Josephine – everything Hitchcock touches at the moment is a triumph and it won't be long before Hollywood lures him away. Think of what that could open up for you. You don't have to get involved in the nonsense – just take the money and run if you like. But this could be a wonderful adventure. Grab it while you can and enjoy every minute. It doesn't happen very often and it might never come your way again.'

'You're not working undercover for my agent, are you?' she asked. 'He's terrified I'm going to be difficult about it. I can hear the panic in his voice every time I speak to him.' She paused for a moment, absent-mindedly watching as a flock of wildfowl flew low over the water. 'You're right, though – about the adventure, *and* about my being scared. It just feels so alien. At least theatre is familiar.'

'It is now, perhaps, but it wasn't always like that. When *Richard of Bordeaux* went into rehearsals, you sat in the stalls and trembled every time Johnny looked at you. Eighteen months later, he was virtually begging you for a role and you gave it to someone else. It'll be the same with this. God help Hitchcock or any other director once you've found your feet. I don't think you'll be seeing the film in Inverness, though,' he teased, knowing how much she hated any hint of publicity. 'It'll be a London premiere with the great and the good.'

Josephine grimaced. 'Then trust me – I'll be seeing it in Inverness. There'll be chewing gum on the seats, a slightly unwashed air about the place and people talking constantly in the row behind. You can come with me if you like. It'll give Mrs McPherson something to talk about while she's selling the Kia-Ora. My solitary visits are always a disappointment to her.' She drained her glass, savouring the sharp, cold tang of the lemonade. 'Anyway, it might never get that far, and I don't want to think about it at the moment. My idea of a birthday is not to move a muscle – no, not even an eyelash – until I have to.

That's why I chose to come here: laziness is almost a requirement.'

And one that was surprisingly easy to comply with, Archie thought, glancing round at the other guests. It wasn't just the heat of late July that made everyone so reluctant to move far: there was a pleasantly languid atmosphere about Portmeirion that made it very easy to do nothing, and even he – who made restlessness an art – was seduced by it. Relaxing on the white-railed terrace with the sun on his face and the water flowing gently past, he could almost believe he was on board a transatlantic liner. 'We may as well make the most of it,' he said. 'It won't be long before our peace is shattered. I love my cousins dearly, but neither of them could be described as restful.'

Archie's cousins, Lettice and Ronnie Motley, were two of Josephine's closest friends, but she knew what he meant: although still in their early thirties, the sisters were among the most successful theatre designers in the West End, but they had a habit of carrying the drama of the stage with them wherever they went. She shaded her eyes with her hand and peered at the clock on the Bell Tower over to her left, which obliged her by striking two. 'What time are they due?' she asked.

'Lettice promised to be here for tea. They're driving down.'

'All the way from London? It's a full day's journey by car.'

'No. They stayed overnight at the Mytton and Mermaid, just outside Shrewsbury. You know – the pub Clough bought as a halfway house for people travelling here from town.'

'Yes, I've heard Ronnie mention it. Isn't there a cocktail waiter she's particularly fond of? She told me she admires his French 75.'

'Quite. So we'll be lucky if they arrive at all. What about Marta and Lydia?'

'I'm not sure now. They changed their plans to go to Stratford. Lydia wanted to catch up with some old friends of hers who have connections with the Swan. I think she's hoping to do a rep season with them in the autumn. Marta had obviously resigned herself to a long week. I never knew it was possible to sound so weary in a telegram. And you can imagine the pressure she's under to arrange an introduction to the Hitchcocks. Lydia's never quite forgiven Johnny for landing that role in *Secret Agent* and not squeezing her in through the back door.'

'Johnny might call the shots in the West End but that doesn't give him any clout at Elstree.'

'I know, but Lydia's not inclined to see reason where work's concerned. I suppose I'll know how Johnny feels when *A Shilling for Candles* comes up for discussion.'

'What role could you offer her if the negotiations go well? Christine Clay?'

'A dead actress? With friends like that, who needs agents?'

Archie laughed. 'Yes, I suppose she would be hoping for a speaking part, at least.' He held up her empty glass. 'Another?' She nodded. 'Same again or something stronger?'

'Same again. It's too hot for anything else.'

He walked back to the hotel and Josephine watched as he picked his way carefully between the tables on the crowded upper terrace, envying the way he seemed to acquire a tan by simply glancing at the sun. Across to her left was Portmeirion village, set slightly apart from the hotel but close enough to feel enclosed within the same enchanted world. The Bell Tower stood majestic as the skyline's crowning glory, and other buildings – self-contained cottages or serviced rooms which acted as an extension of the main hotel – gathered round its base, each one strikingly but subtly coloured. Not for the first time, Josephine admired the way in which the man-made buildings followed the natural contours of the rocks, as though a small pocket of Italy had been casually sewn into the Welsh landscape. She had spent a lot of time on the Continent, and the attempt to recreate it in North Wales could easily have been grotesque or vulgar, but somehow it avoided being either. Instead, Portmeirion remained unashamedly quixotic and dreamlike, partly because it refused to be embarrassed by its own romanticism, and partly because its architect, Clough Williams-Ellis, had managed to recreate the essence of Italy as well as its aesthetics: even the sun seemed to shine straight from the Mediterranean.

Uncomfortable though it made her to be involved, Josephine was not surprised that Hitchcock had decided to capture Portmeirion's beauty for the screen. The village was its own film set and had everything that a director with flair and vision could ask for: beautiful architecture, rich in eccentric detail, with an open expanse of water on one side and the statuesque splendour of the Snowdonian mountains on the other. She looked back to the camera and saw that the man had begun the laborious task of taking it down. Relieved, she settled back to wait for Archie, strangely unbothered by the way in which several complex aspects of her life threatened to collide over the weekend. Perhaps a fortieth birthday came with unexpected bonuses; if that was the case, she should have done it years ago.

2

Jack Spence looked down onto the sea-washed terrace below – the old quayside, where ships used to be built – and noticed that the elegant, stuccoed building seemed to share its guests' delight in the weather. The hotel gleamed in the afternoon sun, its white walls intensifying the heat, but all he saw was the house as it had been when he first visited, long before it was extended and opened to the public, before the name Portmeirion had even been invented: a dilapidated Victorian mansion, overshadowed by the cliff at its back. Behind him was the old walled garden, now fashioned into a small village green, with houses clustered around a tennis court and freshwater swimming pool. Only one of them had been here originally – the gardener's old cottage, neat and tidy these days, its roof and lattice windows trimmed with a bright turquoise blue which emphasised the whiteness of the stone; it was pretty, certainly, but somehow less substantial than the run-down, neglected property he had known, and its perfection faded as he looked at it, no match for the picture in his head. He opened the case at his feet, which was packed, as always, with the tools of his trade: trick glass, filters, fine gauzes with different holes burnt into them by cigarettes – artistic effects designed to distort reality, to make life more interesting. Ironic, really, that none of these optical devices was ever as convincing as his own memory.

Idly, he loaded new film into the camera, enjoying for once the chance to work at his leisure, without a director breathing down his neck. He had no idea what Hitch was up to in staging this elaborate weekend, but he didn't much care; it wouldn't be the first time that the director had demanded his complicity in a practical joke on his colleagues, and, whilst he didn't share Hitch's childish sense of humour, it was a small price to pay for working with a consummate technician. He was the only director Spence knew who never had to look through the lens to know exactly what the cameraman was seeing, a man whose visual imagination was second to none, and who was never afraid to experiment. In the years they had worked together, Spence had never known Hitchcock to raise his voice or show any sign of anger – if, indeed, he ever felt it; the director had other, more subtle, ways of manipulating people, but that was his business. Power was seductive, and Spence could understand its attraction; he could see for himself how uncomfortable some people felt in front of the camera, how easy it was to make them insecure and desperate to please. Looking around at such a peaceful, privileged retreat, he wondered who the victims would be this time.

3

Archie took a detour to his room to fetch Josephine's birthday present, then headed downstairs to order the drinks. Like most corners of Portmeirion, the hotel bar was nothing if not unusual: tucked off the main hall and known as the Cockpit, the room was constructed entirely of timber from an old warship and decorated appropriately. Nautical charts, lanterns and ropes hung from the walls and ceiling; highly polished barrels served as tables; and time at the bar was called with a magnificent ship's bell. The only jarring note was a dartboard to the right of the service hatch, which received a disapproving glance from the colourfully painted figurehead who dominated the room. The space reminded Archie of many a local pub in his native Cornwall, but it had a thoroughness which was typical of its creator: Clough was rarely satisfied with providing a flavour of something, and, were it not for the room's reassuring stability, it would have been easy for him to believe he was on board the ship itself.

The Cockpit was always popular, and even now some guests preferred its character to the luxury of a summer's day. Archie waited to be served, then ordered a pint of beer and another jug of lemonade.

'Can't help feeling we should all be drinking rum.' A pleasant-faced young man sitting at the bar gestured to his surroundings. 'This place is extraordinary.'

Archie smiled, remembering how magical he had found Portmeirion when it was new to him. 'Is this your first visit?' he asked.

'Yes. I came to Wales all the time as a kid – my parents were in variety, and they did a summer season in Rhyl every year – but none of this was here then.' He grinned. 'Anyway, I'm not sure the stuff they put on would have fitted in very well. I've only been here a few hours, but it doesn't seem to be a banjo and boater sort of crowd.'

'I know what you mean. I've been a few times and I've yet to see a chorus girl.'

'You can't have everything, I suppose.'

Archie laughed. 'No. A film party is more than enough to deal with.'

'Tell me about it.' He lifted his glass. 'That's why I'm skulking down here – Dutch courage. I've got to meet Alfred Hitchcock later and I'm dreading it. You know what it's like when you need to make an impression – you talk nonsense every time you open your mouth and trip over the carpet on your way out of the door. Thinking about it, my parents would have been proud of me.' He held out his hand. 'Daniel Lascelles.'

'Nice to meet you. Are you an actor?'

Lascelles grinned. 'Yes, although obviously not a household name.'

There was no hint of resentment in the remark, just a gentle self-mockery which Archie warmed to instantly. 'You mustn't use me to gauge your fame,' he said. 'In my line of work, we don't get to the cinema very often. Are the Hitchcocks here yet?'

'I think so. The barman wouldn't tell me, but one of the other guests saw them checking in this morning. They're staying in that cottage on the edge of the cliff, and we're all summoned to dinner at eight.'

'Then good luck – and watch that carpet.' Archie picked up the drinks and took them outside. 'I think I've found your Robert Tisdall,' he said, sitting down. 'Early twenties, charming, good-looking in that naive, English kind of way, and just the right amount of haplessness. Does the name Daniel Lascelles mean anything to you?'

'Yes, he was in *Evergreen* with Jessie Matthews,' Josephine said. 'Younger than Robert Donat, but his cheekbones aren't a patch on Derrick de Marney's.' She thought about the character in her book – an innocent man, accused of murder and on the run from the police. 'Yes, I suppose he would be good. Now we need a young female lead for Erica and a dashing Inspector Grant. Unless you'd like to play yourself? Grant is a thinly disguised version of you, after all.'

Archie didn't dignify the remark with a response, but handed her the envelope he'd brought down from his room. 'You'd better open this before everyone else arrives.'

Josephine looked at him curiously. 'You've already given me a card.'

'It's not a card.'

She slit the paper open and shook the contents out onto her lap. 'Tickets for the races,' she said, delighted. 'How fabulous! I haven't been to Newmarket for years. But these are owners' passes, Archie. Whose guest am I?'

'No one's.' He grinned, and handed her a second envelope which had been concealed under the drinks tray. 'There's someone I'd like you to meet.'

Bewildered, Josephine took out a photograph, scarcely daring to believe what he was telling her. The picture had been cut from a sale catalogue but she didn't need to read the description to be convinced of the animal's beauty. 'You can't have bought me a racehorse, Archie,' she said, trying to keep the excitement out of her voice in case she had misunderstood the gift.

It was a very poor effort at restraint, and Archie laughed. 'Actually, it's half a racehorse,' he admitted. 'He's called Timber, and you're sharing him with a trainer friend of mine.'

'I don't know what to say.' She got up to hug him. 'Except thank you. How on earth did you manage it?'

'By chance, really. You remember that case I was involved with a few years back in Newmarket?'

'Yes, although you never told me much about it.'

'They weren't the sort of details I'd want to share with you. Someone had a grudge against one of the stables there and did some truly vile things, but we got to the bottom of it and the owner was so grateful that he kept in touch.' Archie smiled. 'In fact, he sent me some remarkably good tips over the years – not that I did anything about them. That wouldn't have been right.'

'No, of course not,' Josephine said cynically.

'He died recently – he must have been well into his seventies when I first met him. His trainer's taking over the stables but on a much smaller scale, so some of the horses had to be sold off. I went up to see him and he offered to sell me a half-share in this chap because he was particularly keen to hang on to him.' Archie looked embarrassed. 'Don't ask me if he's any good or not. I don't know the first thing about racehorses, but it might be fun for you to find out. The picture doesn't do him justice,' he added as she stared at him in disbelief, 'but he's a wonderful colour – dark chestnut, with three white socks and white markings on his face. I fell in love with him when I saw him.'

'For God's sake, Archie,' she said, waving the photograph under his nose. 'A yearling colt by Cold Steel out of Crafty Alice, and you don't know whether he can run or not?'

'Is that good, then?'

'Good? It's equine royalty. When can we go and see him?'

'Whenever you like. I'll take you over there to meet Bart – that's your fellow owner – and you two can talk pedigrees while I find a decent pub.'

'You won't be so blasé about it when Timber starts to make you your money back. It's a decent bookmaker you should be looking for.'

'Don't worry – I know one or two of those.' He smiled at her. 'I'm glad you're pleased.'

'Pleased isn't the word. Really, Archie – you have no idea.

I'm so touched that you even thought of it. It's a wonderful present.'

Archie looked back towards the village, his attention caught by the silky purr of an expensive engine. 'An Alvis,' he said. 'Very nice.' They watched as the car – sleek, low built and kingfisher-blue – drove rather more quickly than was sensible down the hill to the hotel and stopped outside reception.

'Oh,' Josephine said, acknowledging a sense of anticlimax as the driver got out. 'I was expecting something rather more glamorous.' The owner of the car was a middle-aged man, tall but carrying too much weight around the waist and wearing a crumpled linen suit that made no attempt to hide the fact. 'Just shows how wrong you can be, doesn't it?' She looked closer as the driver removed his hat. 'Isn't that Leyton Turnbull?'

The man seemed vaguely familiar to Archie, but he would never have been able to summon up a name. 'I don't know,' he said, 'but I'll bow to your encyclopedic knowledge of matinee idols.'

'Fallen idols,' Josephine corrected him. 'He's never had much success since sound came in – the lisp was such a handicap. I'm surprised he can still afford a car like that.'

'He must be back in favour if the Hitchcocks have invited him for the weekend.'

'Just my luck,' Josephine said despondently. 'He's probably in line for Alan Grant. *Is* there a police rank that doesn't have an "s" in it?' She sighed. 'Have you actually seen the Hitchcocks yet?'

'No, but I know they're staying at the Watch House.' He pointed to a small, single-storey building with a pantiled roof, perched on the cliff top just to the right of the Bell Tower.

Two columns on the seaward side of the cottage cleverly transformed an otherwise undistinguished building into an attractive loggia, rather like an old Greek monastery – an impression that was enhanced by the series of steep walled steps and stone resting places that linked it to the terraces below. 'You'll know about it when they want to make their presence felt. He makes quite an entrance.'

'Have you met him?'

'Once or twice. The first time must have been about ten years ago when he was making *The Lodger*.'

'Did he want your professional advice on killers with a grudge against blondes?'

Archie laughed. 'No, nothing like that. He came to the Yard to get permission to haul a body out of the Thames, but I'm afraid I had to refuse it.' Josephine looked confused, so he explained. 'He was desperate to do a shot of London at night, something you wouldn't normally see, and he came up with the idea of dragging one of the victims out of the river against the backdrop of Charing Cross Bridge. He pestered us to let him do it – pulled every string he had and practically went to the Home Secretary. In the end, someone much higher than I was at the time let it be known that although the official answer was no, he wouldn't be stopped if he tried it.'

'I bet you were thrilled about that.'

'For a bit, yes, but I had the last laugh.'

Josephine looked curious. 'Go on.'

'The crew turned up with all the equipment: two huge vans stuck in the middle of Westminster Bridge, and God knows how many lights and cameras. They were there for hours, holding up the traffic, stopping and starting every time a tram went past, until eventually Hitchcock was satisfied that he'd got the effect he wanted.'

'So what went wrong?'

'The cameraman forgot to check the equipment. When they looked through the rushes, the scene simply wasn't there.'

'Is that *really* true, or just a showbiz legend?' Josephine asked. 'Not that it matters – it's too good a story.'

'It's gossip, obviously, but that shot certainly isn't in the finished film. I went to see it to make sure.'

'You'd better watch yourself this weekend, then. Hitchcock probably thinks you sabotaged the whole venture.'

'Oh, he doesn't remember me,' Archie said. 'He came back a couple of years later to do some research for *Blackmail* and he didn't mention it. But don't be too intimidated when you finally meet him. He might be a genius, but he's not infallible.'

'Come to think of it, Marta always says he'd be lost without his wife,' Josephine said. 'I didn't know this, but Alma Reville was senior to him when they first met. He was an errand boy at the studios, and she was already a cutter and producer's assistant. He didn't speak to her until two years later, when he had a better job than she did.'

'How very modern of him,' Archie said.

'I don't think it was like that. I get the impression that he needed to earn Alma's respect before approaching her. Their marriage is a real partnership, apparently. She's the one person he always listens to.'

'Have you seen much of Marta lately?'

Josephine glanced at him, but the casualness of the question seemed genuine. Her relationship with Marta Fox – which she still refused to categorise, even for her own peace of mind –

was the only part of her life that her friendship with Archie seemed unable to cope with. Or perhaps that was unfair: perhaps she had simply never given it the chance. Only once, just after Marta had unexpectedly come back into her life, had Josephine even tried to raise the subject with Archie, and he had reacted angrily; now, she sensed that he had begun to come to terms with his own feelings for her, but still she shied away from discussing it – and only partly to protect him. 'We've had dinner a few times in London, usually after one of Lydia's opening nights. And I went to Tagley for a weekend party in the spring, but it was a nightmare. Never again.' Much against her better judgement, she had been persuaded to stay with Marta and Lydia at the cottage they owned in Essex, but being an observer of their day-to-day life together had done nothing to ease her guilt at undermining their relationship, or to soften her own loneliness.

'How is she getting on with Lydia?'

'Fine, I think. To be honest, I haven't really asked. We haven't had the chance to talk properly.'

'Why not? I can't believe you couldn't have engineered a way of seeing her without Lydia, so what are you afraid of?' She said nothing, and he looked at her with concern. 'I'm not trying to force you to talk to me about this, Josephine, but wouldn't it help? You and Marta obviously care about each other, but you're not free to be with her and she's with someone else – that can't be easy.'

'Of course it isn't, but it's not fair of me to expect you to . . .' She was interrupted by the sound of another car coming down the hill. It came to an abrupt stop outside the hotel, dangerously close to the Victorian balustrade, and they watched as Ronnie peeled herself away from the passenger seat and struggled out of the car, recovering sufficiently to deliver a healthy kick to one of the front tyres. Josephine glanced at Archie. 'Not the most enjoyable of journeys, by the look of it.'

'No, but impeccably timed as usual.' He looked at her suspiciously. 'I'm beginning to think you pay them to turn up on cue.'

4

Leyton Turnbull stood at the front desk of the hotel, waiting to check in. He drummed his fingers irritably on the oak as the man on duty dealt in a leisurely fashion with an elderly couple's dinner reservation, and wondered where the bar was; half past two in the afternoon was no time to be sober, but he had decided against stopping for a drink on the way, cowed into restraint by the importance of the weekend. There was time for a quick one now, though, and perhaps he could hook up with someone he knew. He scoured the terraces and peered through the doorway into the main building, but could see no one he recognised.

'Good afternoon, sir. I'm sorry to keep you waiting.'

Turnbull grunted impatiently. 'I'm with Mr Hitchcock's party.'

The man waited a few seconds, then, when nothing else was forthcoming, said tactfully: 'Could you just remind me of your name, sir?'

'It's Turnbull. Leyton Turnbull.'

'Of course.' He glanced briefly down a list of names, and took a key from the board behind him. 'You're in Government

House, sir, just to the left of the Bell Tower. Your suite's on the top floor.' Turnbull followed his gesture and saw an apricot-coloured building with a red hipped roof, the largest and most normal-looking structure on the cliffside. 'I'll get someone to take you across now.'

'Don't bother – I can see where it is. Just drop my luggage off and make sure my car's parked safely.'

'Certainly, sir. The garages are back up the hill on the right-hand side, and she'll be perfectly safe there.' He picked up the keys that Turnbull had slid across the desk. 'We'll keep these here until you need them. I'm James Wyllie, the hotel's manager, and if there's anything I can do this weekend, just let me know.'

'You could start by telling me where the bar is.'

'Through the hallway and on the right, just before the stairs. If I could ask you to sign in?'

Turnbull took the pen and was fumbling in his pocket for his glasses when a young girl joined him at the desk. 'Mr Turnbull? I had no idea you were going to be here. How nice to see you.' He looked at her face – not strikingly beautiful, but warm and open in a way that made glamour irrelevant – but couldn't place it. She smiled. 'Astrid Lake,' she said. 'We worked together on *Dancing Days* but I wouldn't expect you to remember me. I was only fifteen, and hopefully I've changed a little since then.'

Certainly, the intervening years had been enough to wipe out any traces of the child he remembered from that film. Her voice no longer had the unpleasant whining quality that signalled immaturity, and the roundness was gone from her features; most importantly, she seemed to have shed the child without losing the innocence, and it was a remarkably attractive combination. 'More than a little, Miss Lake,' he said, taking her hand, 'and definitely for the better. I only wish I could say the same, but at my age another year is rarely an improvement.' She laughed politely, but hadn't yet learnt the professional insincerity which a denial would have required, and he noticed the staff at the reception desk exchange a sly smile. He had been about to invite the actress for a drink but something stopped him, something about her freshness and youth that made him feel world-weary, even ashamed. Instead, he simply asked, 'Are you here for the weekend?'

'Yes. Mr Hitchcock's office called my agent last week with the invitation. I couldn't . . .' The rest of her sentence was lost in a volley of barking from the hallway and a small Jack Russell ran into reception, trailing its lead. Astrid bent down to catch it but the dog slipped through her grasp and made straight for Turnbull's ankles. Without thinking, he kicked it away, catching the side of its face with his foot, and the girl looked at him in surprise.

'Still the same old Leyton Turnbull, I see. Preying on children and small animals.' It was the sort of voice that would have cut through any crowd, even without an insult to help it. There was an embarrassed silence, during which Astrid Lake flushed and excused herself from the room, and the staff at reception glanced nervously at each other. The only person who seemed in control was the woman who had spoken, and Turnbull turned round in astonishment.

'Bella Hutton,' he said, recovering quickly and glaring at her. 'No party's complete without the bitch.'

Reluctantly, Wyllie started to come out from behind his desk but Bella waved him back. 'It's all right. I only ever spare

37

Mr Turnbull one line at a time. It's all he can cope with, on or off screen.' She picked the dog up and caught the arm of a waitress who was passing through the foyer with a tray of dirty crockery from the terrace. 'I'll have tea in the Mirror Room,' she said. Already hot and bothered, the waitress seemed about to answer back but caught the eye of her manager and decided against it. Bella Hutton watched her go and put a hand on Turnbull's arm. 'Try that one,' she whispered in his ear. 'She's more your type.'

Angrily, he shook her off. 'Tell Mr Hitchcock I'm here,' he snapped over his shoulder as he headed for the bar. 'He'll want to know.'

Bella started to leave but Wyllie cleared his throat. 'Dogs aren't strictly allowed in the hotel's public rooms, Miss Hutton.'

She turned and beamed at him. 'And I'm not strictly in- clined to pay my bill, Mr Wyllie. Shall we both see how we feel in the morning?' The Mirror Room was next door, and Bella hesitated in the doorway before going in. It had been such a long time since she was last in this house – nearly twenty years – but she was less disoriented by what had changed than by how much had remained the same. These days, the room was used mostly for coffee after dinner. Its jade and gold decor was new and immaculately presented, if far too fussy for her taste, but – unlike much of the hotel – the fundamental structure of the space was exactly as it had always been, and its main feature was as startling and impressive as ever: the enormous, gilt-edged mirrors covered most of the walls, making the room seem much larger than it really was and filling it with light. There was no one else about and Bella walked across to the fire- place, her footsteps echoing on the polished floor just as they had on her last visit. The stone surround was elaborate and a little incongruous, with the solemn figure of a monk on either side and a frieze of cherubs and angels along the mantelpiece. She bent down to look more closely at the carving on the left and ran her finger over the damaged stone. Such a small mark for so much anger, but still there – lasting and hidden like the pain it represented. Was she the first to seek it out this weekend, she wondered, or had other fingers traced that scar, remembering?

The dog in her arms struggled to be put down, and Bella took a table by the window. She looked out across the estuary to a substantial house on the opposite shoreline, separated from Portmeirion by a mile and a half of water, but linked to the old mansion by memory. The village's distinctive skyline was reflected in the mirror to her right, but she was more interested in the image of Astrid Lake, sitting alone at the edge of the terrace. She seemed lost and suddenly very young, and Bella realised that her anger in reception had had unforeseen casualties. She remembered how she had felt when her own career was new and uncertain, how difficult it had been to maintain an air of confidence whilst desperately looking for a friend on every set, and she went outside to make amends. 'Miss Lake, I owe you an apology,' she said. 'Leyton Turnbull deserves to be humiliated, but you don't. Will you join me for tea?' Astrid hesitated, and Bella added. 'I don't blame you for thinking twice about it, but – contrary to what some people will tell you – I'm not always a bitch.'

The girl smiled. 'I'm sure there are times when you have to be and secretly we all admire you for it, so please don't disillusion me.'

'You'll risk it, then?'

'Of course.'

'Do you mind if we go back inside? I hate the heat.'

Astrid shook her head and followed Bella into the hotel. 'How's your dog?' she asked.

'Chaplin? More robust than he looks. He's like most men – never learns from past disappointments and has a rather distorted view of what he can take on, especially in hot weather.' They sat down, and the waitress arrived with the tea. 'Another cup,' Bella said without looking at her. She wiped her brow and pointed across the water to the hills in the distance. 'There's a storm coming. The sooner it gets here, the better.'

'Not for a while, surely? This heat feels as though it will go on for ever.'

'It's always like that. Then the clouds appear from nowhere, and the storm is as fierce as you'll see – biblical, almost.' She poured tea and handed the cup to Astrid. 'And there's nothing like the morning after. If you think this place is beautiful now, you should see it immediately after rain: the colours are so intense, the landscape so fresh and – well, cleansed. If I were a religious woman, I'd read something into that.'

'It sounds like you know it well.'

'We go back a long way, although I've neglected it recently.' It was ironic, she thought, that this resort – used by so many as a sanctuary from their everyday lives – should be the burden that refused to leave her. 'My family had connections with this part of the world.' She could have used a more emotive word, but she had no wish to allow a stranger into her past.

'Lucky you. It's beautiful. I went for a walk in the woods this morning and they're stunning – except for the graveyard. That strange place where they buried dogs?'

'Yes, I know it.'

'It's such a shock when you come across it unexpectedly. One of the staff told me that the old woman who used to live here started it.'

'That's right.'

'They say she was a recluse and had nothing to do with anyone except her dogs. All I could think about was her up there alone, digging those graves.' She shuddered. 'What would drive you to that, I wonder?'

The second cup was delivered, this time by a different waitress, and Bella thanked her. 'I dare say she had her reasons,' she said, pouring her own tea. The legends that had grown up around the house were well known to her and, when told in a particular way, could easily have been borrowed from the strangest of fairy tales; sometimes, though, the idea of shutting yourself off from the outside world seemed to Bella to be remarkably sane, and she saw nothing intrinsically odd in preferring the company of dogs and creating a cemetery in their honour at the heart of your land. 'Is this your first visit here?' she asked, changing the subject.

'Yes. I didn't even know where it was when I got the invitation.'

'You mean the summons,' Bella said dryly, and Astrid smiled.

'I suppose it was more like that. It's not the sort of offer you turn down, is it?'

'That depends. At your age, with so much ahead of you, probably not. It's different for me. Those days of jostling for position are over, thank God, and being old has its compensations. Not giving a damn is one of them. There's something very liberating in having nothing left to prove.'

Astrid looked at her curiously. 'You're still here, though. You didn't turn the invitation down.'

Bella smiled. 'Oh, I have my own reasons for being in Portmeirion this weekend and they have nothing to do with Hitch, as much as I enjoy working with him. I suppose you could say I invited myself.'

'And I'm sure you can have your pick of scripts. Mr Hitchcock would be lucky to have you.'

There was no calculation behind the remark, and Bella – who had reached a stage in her career when very few people were brave or generous enough to pay her a genuine compliment – was touched. 'Tell me, Miss Lake – what do you hope to get out of being here?'

'The chance to learn something,' she said, without having to consider the question. 'Obviously, I'd love to land a part in a Hitchcock film – he's the greatest director we have, and I know what that would mean for my career. But just to be around him and the people he works with, even for a couple of days – that's a fabulous opportunity.' Bella nodded approvingly. 'It's an odd sort of audition, though. To be honest, I'm not really sure why any of us are here.'

'There's no such thing as a straightforward audition where Hitch is concerned. He'll reveal his plan when he's ready. The people who get on best with him are those who can cope with that.'

'So what advice would you give me?'

'Be yourself. He'll either like you or he won't, but there's no point in *trying* to be what he likes.' She would have told Astrid to hang on to that unassuming quality for as long as possible, but it would disappear the moment she became conscious of it. Innocence was one of the few qualities that could never be faked. That was what made it so precious. 'There's something real about you, something very English, and women will like that. Women like any star who reminds them of their daughter – or rather, of the person they'd like their daughter to be – and women buy the tickets. All directors know that.' A young man walked past the window and winked when he saw Astrid. 'Of course, men aren't immune to those charms either,' Bella added with a wry smile. 'Just be careful.'

'Oh, I wouldn't . . . That's Daniel Lascelles. We've worked together a couple of times, and I was so pleased to bump into him. We both felt a bit out of our depth, but . . .'

'Look, I don't care about your honour,' Bella said, laughing. 'I know what it's like when you're young and you want to get on and everyone's telling you what's good for you and what isn't. Believe me, when I was your age, I sometimes thought I'd have more freedom to do what I wanted if I signed up with her lot.' She pointed over to the coastal path, where a nun was strolling out towards the headland. 'A film set can be worse than a convent – financers, directors, producers, all telling you what to do and what to be, and every single one of them looking out for themselves and their investment.' Astrid smiled wearily, and Bella realised that the pressures of the studios were already beginning to threaten the very qualities that gave her potential in the first place. 'You remind me of myself, a long time ago,' she said, 'and there's nothing wrong with having some fun and making your own mistakes. I'm not saying don't do it – just don't get caught. Apart from anything else, Hitch doesn't approve of fraternisation among his chosen ones, so be discreet about it.' She put her cup down and added more seriously, 'And whatever you do, stay away from Leyton Turnbull.'

'Oh, I just felt sorry for him. It must be terrible to be his age and to know in your heart that you're not as good as you used to be.'

'He was never good.'

'But he's harmless enough.'

'Don't be fooled. He once raped a girl on set.'

Astrid looked shocked. 'I'm sure that can't be true,' she said. 'Everyone would know about it if it were.'

'Would they?' Bella asked cynically. 'No charges were ever brought, of course. Nobody wanted a fuss, and we work in an industry where everything can be bought, especially a blind eye. But that didn't help the girl. She tried to kill herself – unsuccessfully, thank God, but it might have been kinder if she'd managed it. She was destroyed in so many other ways.'

'What happened to her?'

'Her career, her self-respect, her life – they were all ripped out from under her. Not surprisingly, she found that difficult to cope with, so she relied on anything that would help her to forget what had happened: drink, drugs, pills, whichever form of oblivion was closest to hand. Of course, with the way the world works, it was she who acquired the unfortunate reputation, not Turnbull. No one will touch a hysterical actress. It plays havoc with a budget.' Astrid continued to look disbelieving, and Bella added, 'I don't want to frighten you, Miss Lake, and I certainly don't want to patronise you, but can I say something?' The actress nodded. 'These are dangerous times, and they will only get worse. People can be born with nothing and transformed into gods overnight – that's the magic and the danger of cinema. Looks are important, talent less so, but ambition is what really counts. Having the taste for it. Marlene Dietrich is rumoured to have signed a deal for eighty thousand pounds for her next picture, so the money alone is incentive enough to lose any capacity to care about other people. But it's about more than money. It's about power. When people start to believe that they really *are* gods, nothing can stop them. This might sound like bitterness from a woman nearing the end of her career, Miss Lake, but please believe me when I say it's not.'

'It doesn't sound like bitterness,' Astrid said. 'It sounds like disappointment.' Bella looked at her in surprise. 'I'm sorry if I'm speaking out of turn, but it sounds like advice from a wo-man who's been let down by someone she loves.'

The comment was so perceptive that it disarmed Bella com-pletely, and she stood up to go. 'I think you'll be more than a match for Hitch, Miss Lake,' she said admiringly. 'In fact, I al-most feel sorry for him.'

5

Marta pulled the car over to the side of the road. After views that alternated between a landscape disfigured by mining and small towns packed with dark-walled chapels and tired-looking houses, it was a relief to be out on the moors. 'What are you do-ing?' Lydia asked impatiently. 'We should get on if we're going to have time to settle in before dinner.'

'We're already late, thanks to that Stratford crowd, so another ten minutes won't matter.' Marta reached across her to rummage in the glove compartment. 'I need a cigarette.'

Lydia sighed. 'That Stratford crowd is my best chance of work for the autumn. Did you have to be so rude to everybody?' She took a magazine from the back seat and began to fan herself, but there was no refuge in the open-top car from the late July sun. 'In case you hadn't noticed, I'm not exactly flooded with offers, and your Greta Garbo act doesn't help.'

'Fine. Next time, leave me at home.' Marta got out and slammed the door, ignoring Lydia's glare. The hot metal burnt her skin as she leant against the car, but, as hard as she tried to blame her mood on the heat of the day or Lydia's endless socialising, she was really only angry with herself: she had spent weeks longing to see Josephine; now the moment had come, she was so nervous that all she wanted to do was run in the opposite direction.

'Can I have one of those?' Lydia's tone was placatory, and Marta knew that she was biting her tongue, wanting to avoid a full-blown row just before they entered company. 'I'm sorry, darling, but you know how important it is to stay on the right side of people. I can't live off thin air.'

'I've got money. We don't have to spend our lives running round with people we don't like.'

'That's not the point. I need to work, Marta.' She threw the cigarette onto the ground, barely touched. 'Anyway, things might look up after this weekend. Let's just enjoy it.'

The sun emerged from behind a rare cloud, and Marta watched as the stain of light spread across the hills, transforming each shade of green into a sharper, more intense version of itself. There was no point in saying anything more: it was an argument they had had many times before and would no doubt have again, part of the settling of two lives into one, so she finished her cigarette in silence and got back into the car.

They drove for another hour before joining the main road. 'I'm not sure we were right to book into a village room rather than the hotel,' Lydia said. 'We don't want to miss anything. Where are the Hitchcocks staying?'

'I've absolutely no idea. Look, this is Minffordd – isn't that where we turn off?'

'Yes. Left at the post office.' Marta did as instructed and followed a discreet sign onto a private woodland drive. 'We can find out when we check in,' Lydia continued. 'It's not too late to change rooms.'

'I hope you're not relying on this weekend to solve all your problems,' Marta said, exasperated. 'I've got no influence with the Hitchcocks.'

'You seem to know a lot about them.'

'It's just gossip, Lydia. They enjoy the notoriety but they keep their privacy intact. No one gets through. And we could all learn a lesson from that,' she muttered, wishing she had the will power to bring a halt to the bickering.

Lydia didn't hear the final comment, or simply chose to ignore it. 'Josephine seems to have managed it,' she said peevishly. 'You obviously know Alma Reville well enough to give her a reading list.'

'That was just lucky,' Marta insisted, aware of how defensive she must sound. 'If Alma hadn't liked the book – or at least seen some potential in it – the fact that I gave it to her wouldn't have made any difference.'

'I know that,' Lydia said, as if she were dealing with an obstinate child. 'All I'm asking you to do is introduce me. I'll do the rest. Then perhaps some of that famous Highland luck might come our way for a change.' She looked impatiently at Marta. 'Can you manage that?'

Marta nodded, happy to promise anything for a quiet life. The trees cleared for a moment, long enough to reveal an extraordinary castellated building, striking rather than attractive; apart from a heavy covering of ivy, there was something playfully bogus about its Gothic façade. 'What the hell's that?' Marta asked. 'It looks like a lunatic asylum.'

'It was once, I think. Now it's a hotel.'

'Or something Bertha Mason's about to burn down. Please tell me that's not where you want us to stay.'

Lydia laughed. 'Of course not. The main hotel's by the estuary and it's beautiful.'

'Thank God, but I still think it would be nice to be able to get away from everything.'

'You make it sound like such an ordeal. What is there in a friend's birthday party to get away from?'

It was a rhetorical question but Marta could have responded with a list. 'I just thought it would be nice to spend some time together,' she said weakly, drawing to a halt by the gate which protected the private peninsula from the outside world.

'That's sweet, but we'll have plenty of time for that at home.' Lydia jumped out of the car to give their names to the man on duty, and Marta stretched in her seat, consciously avoiding the rear-view mirror; she didn't need to look at herself to know that her clothes were sticking to her and her face was red from the sun, and she hoped to God that they could get to their room without bumping into anybody. Lydia climbed back in and the man waved them through. 'We've got to check in at the hotel,' she said, 'so we might as well see if they're full. But we can leave the car in one of the garages on the way down.'

The approach to Portmeirion had given Marta no hint of what lay ahead in the village itself; after such dense woodland, she was shocked to emerge into an open space, full of light and colour. Everywhere she looked she found something magical: balconies, arches, terraces, statues and steps, all clustered together in unexpected combinations which both disoriented and delighted her. 'I knew you'd love it,' Lydia said. 'Isn't it romantic? When Josephine and I first came here, we couldn't believe what we were seeing.' Marta bit her tongue at the reminder of Lydia's long-standing friendship with Josephine and followed the single unfenced road which curved down around the central piazza. 'We're supposed to be staying in Neptune,' Lydia added. 'It's on the other side of the square.'

As the road descended, the Piazza disappeared from view behind a high stone wall which seemed to be left over from a kitchen garden. On their right, an old stable block had been colourfully converted into a shop and café. They watched for a few moments as an attractive, dark-haired woman worked on a mural above the arched windows overlooking the courtyard, then drove on to find their accommodation.

Neptune – lots of the buildings had a vaguely nautical name, Marta noticed – was a pretty yellow and white house whose leaded windows and uneven slate roof gave it an exaggerated feeling of age. Situated on the edge of the Piazza, it had good views over the heart of the village and, to the rear, of the wild, overgrown woodland which lay on the other side of the road. The ground floor was given over to garages, and Marta's temper was not improved by the three attempts it took her to squeeze the Morris into the narrow space allocated to them. 'The hotel's just down here,' Lydia said, snapping her compact shut and putting her lipstick away. 'Let's go and find everyone.'

Marta caught her arm. 'Why are we always surrounded by people?'

'We're not. But this is a party, and they do tend to involve groups of people.'

'I'm not just talking about now. It's always the same, even at the cottage: we plan a quiet weekend and you turn up with half the cast.'

Lydia shook her off. 'I'm not the one who laid down the rules on our relationship, Marta,' she said angrily. 'Surely I don't need to remind you of that? Anyway, what's wrong with having friends? I would have thought you'd had enough of isolation after your little spell at His Majesty's pleasure.'

Marta could see by the look of horror on Lydia's face that the remark was regretted as soon as it came out, but she didn't wait for the apology. 'I'm staying here,' she said, hauling a suitcase out of the car. 'You do as you like.'

6

Alma Reville sat under the loggia roof outside the Watch House, shading her eyes against the glare of sun on white stone and absent-mindedly stroking the dog on her lap. Caught on the cliff between the village and the sea, the building was part of a small enclave clustered around the ornamental Bell Tower and the houses nearby were occupied by Hitch's guests – actors he was interested in trying out, or trusted colleagues, carefully chosen because of their loyalty or technical skill and vital to the success of every film. The cottage, though small and simply furnished, more than lived up to its name: in front of her, glistening and mirage-like in the heat of the day, the Dwyryd Estuary stretched out to the sea; and below to her right, an uninterrupted view of the hotel and terraces had entertained her since lunchtime with a steady stream of new arrivals.

She heard her husband walk up behind her and waited for the familiar touch of his hand on her shoulder. 'David chose well,' he said, smiling as he took in the view. 'We can keep an eye on everything – from a distance.'

Alma took the crime novel from his other hand and looked at him questioningly. 'Well? Have you changed your mind?'

'No. I still think it's very, very bad.'

'How much have you actually read, Hitch?'

'The first fifty pages and the end.' He sat down heavily next to her, and their other dog – an elderly cocker spaniel – idled lazily out from the bedroom and collapsed on his feet. 'I have no idea what happens in the middle,' he said, a little defensive against her stare, 'but the ending's completely wrong. Not what I'd have chosen at all.'

Alma poured him a glass of orange juice and added a dash of gin, just the way he liked it. 'But you see it has potential?'

'Once you've finished with it, perhaps.' He sipped his drink appreciatively and looked at her. 'Why are you so keen on it?'

'I like the victim,' she said, without hesitating. 'She's already dead when the book opens and she never says a word, but I know exactly who she is and I understand her completely. That's quite an achievement, for any writer.'

He looked doubtfully at her. 'Victims don't make films, though. *Villains* make films, and Miss Tey's villain isn't very realistic. Fine for a whodunnit, I suppose – they're only glorified crossword puzzles. But not remotely connected to real life.'

Alma smiled. She had heard the arguments many times before and knew that the qualities she most admired about *A Shilling for Candles* were the very things that would never make it to the screen: success had placed obvious limitations on her husband's work, and already there were clear boundaries to what the public would or would not accept as part of a Hitchcock film. But she also knew that her approval would be enough to convince him, regardless of what it was based on; her instincts were good, and they both acknowledged that. 'You know as well as I do that you'll decide who the villain is,' she said affectionately. 'Just take the good bits and make the rest your own. It's what you do best.'

She had meant it reassuringly but the comment seemed to have the opposite effect on her husband. 'What? A bit of romantic interest, the car chase and a gag or two along the way?' He turned away, avoiding the sun and her concern in the same movement, but the frustration in his voice was more difficult to hide. 'You're right, of course. We all know how it goes by now.'

'That's not what I'm saying.' She took his hand and made him look at her again. 'You know it isn't. It's not what goes into the film that matters, it's the magic you work with it – and no one could predict that. There's been something new and surprising in every single movie you've made.' He raised an eyebrow. 'All right, except *Waltzes from Vienna*. And *Champagne*. And perhaps . . .'

'Don't push your luck, Mrs Hitchcock.' He interrupted her, feigning offence, and she sensed the crisis had passed, for now at least. 'I need some new blood, Alma,' he added quietly, 'and I can't keep getting it out of the same old stone.'

'I know you can't, but you don't have to. It's there for you whenever you want it.'

He nodded reluctantly. 'America will mean a big change, though. A different life for the three of us.' The dog at his feet stretched and yawned, and he reached down to stroke it. 'All right, Edward – for the five of us.'

'I could certainly get used to this weather.' Alma smiled, hoping that the apprehension didn't show on her face. Her husband had been deluged with offers from Hollywood since the success of *Blackmail* – Britain's first talkie – eight years ago, but he'd always said that he wasn't ready to move, that there were still things he could do at home; now, he was outgrowing everything the British film industry had to offer and she realised that their move to America was inevitable: the only question was when. She wasn't worried for herself or even for their daughter – they were a close family, and they could, she thought, adapt to anything as long as they stuck together – but in private she feared for Hitch: making the films he wanted to make would take courage, and she wondered how he would handle the criticism when it came. Outwardly, he relished celebrity and all it brought with it, but Alfred Hitchcock was a very different man in private – sensitive, vulnerable and full of self-doubt. She would never forget his despair when *The Lodger* was rejected at first by the studios, or the minor failures and nervous moments that had hovered over their marriage as well as their professional relationship, and she wondered how her husband's famous calm demeanour would cope with the pressures of Hollywood. In truth, any criticism of his work hurt her as much as it did him, but she had to put on a brave front for them both. 'You'll know when it's right,' she insisted, 'and in the meantime, you've got everything you need in this book to make your most exciting movie yet. Surely you found the young girl interesting?'

'Of course I did – the girl *is* the story,' he said, suddenly more enthusiastic. 'You really think it will work, don't you?' Alma nodded. 'Then that's good enough for me. You'll talk to the Tey woman? Her publisher says she's a law unto herself and we don't need her to be difficult about it.'

'Leave it to me. I'll get Marta Fox to introduce us.' She lowered the terrier gently onto the floor and stood up. 'Why don't you have a nap while I take the dogs for a walk? I want to see what the other guests are doing before they realise who I am and start acting.' She kissed the top of his head. 'We're not paying them for that yet.'

He walked her over to the steps that led down to the Piazza. 'Perhaps I will have a lie down,' he said, and Alma was relieved to see that the twinkle she loved was back in his eyes. 'I'll need to be on top form later. It promises to be an interesting couple of days.'

'What have you got planned, Hitch?' she asked nervously. 'Nothing too outrageous, I hope.'

'Oh, you know me, Alma,' he said, and then added more seriously, 'Let's face it – you're the only person who does.'

7

Branwen Erley took a tray out to the terrace and began to clear away more crockery. She had forgotten how much she hated July, but it was the same every year: Portmeirion bustled into life at Easter, when the excitement of opening and the last-minute preparations for the new season bred a hopeful camaraderie amongst the hotel staff; May and June passed quietly, with a moderate number of guests and no great test of anyone's patience; but as summer dragged on, the combination of a more intense heat and a sudden influx of people forced a change in everyone's mood. Staff bickered, guests treated them like dirt, and Branwen grew more frustrated by the day.

She moved from table to table, reaching in and out of people's conversations, picking up glasses and gossip. They acknowledged her so rarely that she could almost have believed herself to be invisible, and those who noticed her at all saw only a uniform. But she saw *them*. She saw the lies their lives were built on – the stale marriages, the mismatched affairs, the pretensions to money or youth; had it not been laughable, she would have despised them for it.

'You wanted to talk to me.' Absorbed in her own thoughts, Branwen had not noticed that Bella Hutton was behind her, and she tried not to look intimidated. For years, she had longed to speak to the actress; now they were face to face, all her carefully rehearsed questions eluded her and she stood there, tongue-tied and stupid, reading her own inadequacy in the other woman's face. 'Well?' Bella asked impatiently.

Branwen put the tray of glasses down and stared back with what she hoped was defiance. 'Like I said in my letters, I think you know what happened to my mother,' she said. 'Your family owes me. I know it's not your fault, but you're the only one here who can make amends and I think it's the least you can do.'

The actress looked at her thoughtfully, as though trying to

gauge her mettle. 'It was a long time ago,' she said, putting a full stop to all Branwen's hopes.

She turned to go, but Branwen grabbed her arm, making it impossible for her to walk away without causing a scene. 'I don't want to make trouble for you, Miss Hutton, but . . .'

She knew instantly that it was the wrong approach. Bella held up her hand. 'Let me stop you there, young lady,' she said quietly. 'You couldn't make trouble for me even if you wanted to. Better people than you have tried and failed before now, and if you follow in their footsteps you'll regret it. Do I make myself clear?' Branwen nodded. 'Anything I say to you will be of my own choosing, not because you've forced me into a corner.'

'So you *will* help me?' There was a pathetic, pleading note in her voice which Branwen despised herself for, but the show of arrogance that she used as a weapon against the pain of her mother's absence was fragile at the best of times.

'Come and see me later. I'll have dinner in my room. Make sure you bring it to me.'

'I'll be off shift by then,' Branwen said desperately. 'It's my night with the band – I can't change it.'

'I see. Fifteen minutes of glory in front of Alfred Hitchcock is more important?' Her mocking tone drew attention from some of the nearby guests; the actor who had been insulted in the foyer earlier had come out onto the terrace, Branwen noticed, and was watching her intently. 'Don't waste my time. You don't know how lucky you are that I'm even giving you the chance.'

She started to walk away and Branwen stared after her, sick and tired of being told that she was lucky. It had been the recurring theme of her life for as long as she could remember, established by her gran when she was a child and refashioned at regular intervals since. Lucky to have a job. Lucky to meet interesting people. Lucky to be her. Repeat it often enough and it might even be true. 'You wouldn't say that if you knew what my life was like,' she called angrily, and the actress turned round in surprise. 'It's all right for you – you left here as soon as you had the chance, just like she did. You didn't have to stay in that bloody town where every day's the spitting image of the one before it.' Branwen's family had lived in Portmadoc for generations, their lives seemingly interchangeable in the same houses, the same front rooms, the same boat. Families wove themselves into the fabric of those narrow streets, and each day was regulated by the sound of boots marching to work like an army to war. The men spent their nights brawling in the local pub, and violence was a third language. As a child, Branwen remembered lying on the makeshift bed downstairs, listening to her grandfather's footsteps move slowly across the bedroom, tracing their progress as clearly as if she could see the soles of his boots through the ceiling. Her mother had left that life behind at the first opportunity, abandoning a two-year-old daughter in the process; it was a courage for which Branwen both admired and resented her. 'I don't blame either of you for getting out,' she said quietly, looking at Bella. 'And maybe having a mother around wouldn't have changed things for me. But maybe it would. Maybe if she'd taken me with her, I could have had some of the chances that she must have had.' She rubbed a hand across her face, determined not to cry. 'I need to have that conversation with her, now more than ever, so if you know where she is, please tell me. Surely that's not too much to ask?'

Bella stared at her with an odd mixture of pity and respect. 'I'll see you later on tonight,' she said. 'But somewhere more private than this. As you can see, people are far more interested in our business than in their own.'

'All right. Where?'

'I'll let you know.' She walked off without another word and Branwen watched her go, scarcely daring to believe what she had been promised.

8

'They looked lovely when we left Shrewsbury,' Ronnie insisted, poking a bunch of wilted roses as if she could somehow taunt them back to life.

'Yes, but that was months ago,' Lettice said weakly, collapsing into a deckchair. 'I think *I* turned forty somewhere around Welshpool.' She leant forward and took a long drink of Archie's beer, then looked appealingly at her cousin. 'I don't suppose you could rustle me up a gin and tonic, could you?'

Archie looked wearily at Josephine. 'What did I say about a fragile peace?'

Ronnie cuffed the back of his head. 'For that, you can get me a very large Pimm's.' She pointed scornfully at Josephine's glass. 'And *she* shouldn't be drinking lemonade at her age. Go and sort us all out.' She watched him go, and added with a wry smile, 'You two look cosy.'

'And you look exhausted. Cocktails up to scratch last night?'

Ronnie was the only person Josephine knew who could blush and look more brazen at the same time. 'Let's just say that there were several new combinations on the menu which I found very much to my taste,' she said.

'And it wasn't your head they went to, I don't suppose.'

Ronnie grinned, briefly losing the mask of sophisticated cynicism. 'So are they as strange as I expect them to be?' she asked, changing the subject with a modesty that Josephine found unconvincing.

'Who?'

'The Hitchcocks, of course. Lettice and I were talking about it on the way down. She thinks he's a genius, and I'm convinced he's an overrated voyeur. Which of us is right?'

'I don't know – we haven't even seen them yet. But ask Archie – he's met Hitchcock through work.'

'You surely don't mean he's got a record?' Lettice sounded horrified, while Ronnie slapped the table triumphantly.

Josephine laughed. 'No, of course not. It was about some filming on the Thames. He had to get permission.' She repeated what Archie had told her, embellishing the story to get maximum effect from its punchline.

'He must have been devastated after going to all that trouble,' Lettice said seriously. 'But the film's still marvellous. That bit where the lodger's being chased by the crowds is so exciting.' Josephine agreed. It was several years ago now, but she remembered how the film's recreation of the Jack the Ripper case in a more contemporary London had shocked her when she first saw it, not because it dealt with a series of brutal killings but because it showed how infectious violence could be. Hitchcock's depiction of a frenzied mob, driven by fear, revenge and hysteria to take justice into its own hands, was frighteningly credible. It reminded her of the crowds that had gathered in the streets during the early days of the war: there was nothing more terrifying than a pack united by a common hatred, believing itself to be unquestionably in the right and using its fear to justify every innate prejudice. 'I did feel a bit cheated when it finished, though,' Lettice admitted. 'He's guilty in the book and it's a much better ending.'

'That's what you get for casting Ivor Novello,' Josephine said. 'Rule number one of popular entertainment: a matinee idol can never be a killer – that really would incite the crowds.' She thought for a moment, and added, 'Anyway, I think it was better that way. There's something very powerful about an innocent man being destroyed by people who think they've got right on their side.'

'It wouldn't surprise me if Hitchcock *had* been in trouble with the police, you know,' Ronnie said, returning to give her dead horse one last flog. 'There are far too many handcuffs involved in those films for my liking.' She lit a cigarette and leant back thoughtfully in her deckchair. 'It can't be a very *normal* sort of marriage, can it?'

'Is there such a thing?'

Ronnie gave her a wry smile. 'What a shame that age has made you so cynical already.'

Josephine reached for the cigarette case and took one out for herself and Lettice. 'How many so-called normal marriages can you name?' she asked. 'Normal is one of the casualties of our generation, and I knew that when I was twenty-one, so please put my cynicism down to something more creditable than age.'

'Johnny did tell us that Hitchcock has a vulgar sense of humour,' Lettice conceded. 'He said he wasn't at all sympathetic to his actors on the set and he felt very taken for granted.'

'But don't you think that's Johnny trying to excuse the fact that he simply wasn't very good in the film?' Josephine asked. 'What was it one critic said? "Bloodless, stilted and inept"?'

'I have to say, sticking Johnny opposite Madeleine Carroll and expecting sparks to fly is commendably optimistic,' Ronnie said. 'I'll give Hitchcock that, at least.'

'Exactly, so I don't think we can take Johnny's testimony as gospel.'

'It's not just Johnny who's been on the receiving end of it, though, is it? He sent Julian four hundred smoked herrings for his birthday and filled Freddie's flat with coal while he was away on honeymoon. What sort of man does that?' Ronnie sounded genuinely bewildered. 'Perhaps it's something lacking in me, but I just don't find all that schoolboy stuff very funny.'

Josephine – who had heard only professional gossip about the Hitchcocks from Marta – was growing increasingly uneasy. 'Can we change the subject?' she asked. 'If I'm going to end up working with the man, I'd rather not know all this.'

'I wouldn't take it too seriously.' Archie put the tray of drinks down on the table. 'That sort of stuff went on all the time after the war whenever any group of men got together. I doubt that film studios were any different to army barracks or a police incident room.'

'But this is eighteen years after the war,' Josephine pointed out. 'We *are* going to have to stop using that as some sort of all-purpose excuse eventually.'

'Ah, but there's another excuse on the horizon,' Archie said. 'So I think it'll tide us over.' He handed the glasses round and raised his own. 'Cheers. Did anybody know that Bella Hutton was going to be here?'

'Bella Hutton?'

Lettice looked as doubtful as her sister. 'Are you sure, Archie?'

'Positive. I nearly stood on her dog.' He glanced at Josephine. 'And Lydia and Marta have arrived – they're just checking in, but there seems to be some sort of confusion over their rooms. They'll be out in a minute.'

It was a well-intentioned warning, but Josephine wished he hadn't said anything. As it was, her behaviour on first seeing Marta was likely to be strained enough; now, robbed of the element of surprise, she could already feel her stomach tightening and the sincerity draining from her face. Resisting the temptation to glance over at the hotel, she tried to concentrate on what Ronnie was saying.

'No one ever really got to the bottom of why Bella Hutton came back from Hollywood so suddenly, did they?'

'Is this one of your famous conspiracy theories? I thought her marriage failed.'

'Yes it did, but that doesn't mean she had to throw her whole career away.'

'Perhaps being married to America didn't suit her any more than being married to an American,' Josephine suggested. 'I can't imagine Hollywood's a very pleasant place to be, and she must have made enough money from her films and the divorce not to have to work unless she wants to.'

'And she comes from somewhere round here, anyway,' Lettice added. 'So it's not surprising she should visit.'

'What?' Ronnie stared at her in amazement. 'You mean Bella Hutton's *Welsh*?'

'Bella Hutton, my dear, is international.'

She seemed about to offer further insights into the movie

star's life, but Ronnie interrupted her. 'I never thought this would last, you know,' she said, stubbing her cigarette out and peering at the hotel. Marta and Lydia were on the upper terrace, looking round for them. 'Why "rooms", I wonder?'

Josephine reached for her sunglasses, although the fierceness of the day had begun to die down. From their safety, she watched as the couple walked across the lawn. Marta wore a halter-neck top and linen trousers, closely fitted to her hips. Her skin, pale from a London summer, was burnt a little at the shoulders; her face was impossible to read. In the past, Josephine had searched for words that would adequately describe that face, but it moved so swiftly between strength and insecurity, laughter and an intense seriousness, that its essence always eluded her. Now, she took heart from the fact that Marta, too, seemed to need a mask. Even so, when she stood to greet them, it was Lydia she turned to first, Lydia whom she hugged with a genuine warmth. She had rehearsed this moment for weeks, but, when Marta was beside her, all she could manage was a perfunctory kiss and a subdued hello.

Archie looked round for two more empty deckchairs, but Lettice stopped him. 'Have ours,' she said. 'We've got to go and unpack.'

'Just a minute,' Ronnie said. 'I want to find out where Marta stands on the Hitchcock issue.'

Marta sat down opposite Josephine. 'What issue's that?'

'Is he a genius or just a strange little man?'

'Does it have to be one or the other?' She shook her hair out and retied it while Ronnie considered what was obviously a new idea to her. 'Sorry – I've only met him briefly, so I can't really help, but his wife is very sane and very clever, and I doubt she'd settle for less in a husband.'

'Mm,' Ronnie muttered, unconvinced. 'His family owns MacFisheries, though. That can't be right.'

Archie exchanged a weary look with Lydia. 'Can I get you both a drink?' he asked.

'I'm dying for a gin and tonic, but don't bother fetching it, Archie. Someone will come over.'

'It'll be quicker if I go to the bar. They're very busy out here. Marta?'

'Tea would be lovely.'

'I'll give you a hand,' Josephine offered. 'I could do with the exercise, and you've been back and forth so often they'll think you're trying for a job.'

'No, you stay here – I can manage. It'll give me a chance to see who else has turned up. Do you know Daniel Lascelles, Lydia?' he asked casually.

'Danny? Yes, he was with me in *Close Quarters*. He's a sweet-heart. Why? Is he here?'

'Yes, I met him at the bar earlier. He'll be pleased to see you – it looked like he could do with a friendly face and a bit of en-couragement.'

'Oh, I'll come and say hello now. I haven't spoken to him since he lost his father.' Archie walked with her to the hotel, leaving Marta and Josephine alone. It had been subtly done, and Josephine hoped she was the only one who had noticed.

They looked at each other for a long time without speaking. Eventually, Marta leant forward and removed Josephine's glasses. 'Hello again,' she said quietly. 'How are you?'

'Pleased to see you.'

'Are you? I thought with all the work you'd put into avoiding it that you might not be.' Her voice was gentle, the words a genuine question rather than any sort of reproach.

'It's not that I didn't want to see you. I just thought it would be better to wait a bit, that if we saw each other too soon . . .'

'I might not be able to control myself?'

Josephine flushed. 'No, of course not. I only meant that you and Lydia needed time to sort yourselves out, find out how you feel.' She stopped and bit her lip before she found something even more patronising to say. This wasn't what she had intended, and she wondered what had happened to the wise, funny, eloquent woman who had held so many imaginary conversations with Marta since they had last seen each other. She tried to think of all the things she had wanted to say, but the reality of Marta unsettled her more than ever and her mind was completely blank. In the end, all she could manage was a simple confession. 'I ran away,' she admitted. 'I'm sorry.'

She had expected Marta to press the point further, but she only nodded. 'And how has your birthday been so far?'

The abrupt change of subject floored Josephine. She had taken it for granted that, left alone, they would discuss their relationship and its future – if it had a future – but she realised now that her constant reliance on Marta to articulate feelings for both of them was childish and unfair. For the first time, it occurred to her that of all the obstacles she had placed in their way – Lydia, Archie, family commitments and physical distance – the hardest to overcome was her own selfishness. Livid with herself, she tried to find a way back, but it was too late: the moment had been missed, and they talked about Portmeirion until Archie and Lydia returned with the drinks.

9

David Franks ran lightly down the steps of the Bell Tower and emerged into the daylight, excited at the prospect of what the weekend held. The sun streaked the cobbles of Battery Square, and there were still plenty of visitors milling around at the outer limits of the village, making the most of their day before the curfew struck and they were shown politely back through the gates, leaving Portmeirion to its nocturnal guests. The character of the place changed completely after seven thirty, he had noticed: as everyone gravitated to the hotel for drinks and dinner, the village became a ghost of its daytime self, its illusions at once more rewarding and more unsettling. Without people to bring it to life, Portmeirion's essentially artificial nature was somehow exposed. Last night, returning to his suite in Government House, he had sat for a long time on a bench in the Piazza, enjoying the peace; it was exactly like being the last person left on a film set at the end of a day's shoot – so much so that, when he finally got up to go to bed, he almost felt that he should turn out the lights.

Now, he leant against one of the small cannons which had been placed in the square to justify its name, and squinted back up at the tower he had just left, admiring the way in which its architectural detail had been deliberately scaled down to make the building appear larger than it really was. There were several examples of this sort of forced perspective all over Portmeirion, and David – whose job it was to create illusions on screen – had a grudging respect for the man who managed it so successfully without the help of a camera. It was an achievement that he would have been proud to call his own had things been different.

He looked at his watch to make sure that the Bell Tower's clock was reliable: no one with any sense was late for an appointment with Alfred Hitchcock. He had ten minutes to wait, so he took a carefully timed stroll round the gardens and tennis court, and knocked on the door to the Watch House exactly as the mechanism on the old turret clock kicked into life. When he saw that Hitch was on the telephone, he offered to wait outside, but the director shook his head and waved him in, so David retreated discreetly to the balcony. There was no ethical decision to be made over whether or not to eavesdrop: Hitch's distinctive voice – gruff and deadpan, still faithful to its East London origins – carried easily across the small room, and he made no attempt to hide his part of the conversation.

'I'm not denying it's a generous offer,' he said, with a strained patience which suggested that the discussion had been proceeding along the same lines for some time. 'I'm merely pointing out to you that until I've completed the films I'm contracted to make for Gaumont British, I'm not in a position to consider *any* offer, generous or not. Forty thousand dollars a picture or four – it makes no difference.'

He fell silent again, and David waited for the next skilful deflection. Hitch turned down at least three offers a month from Hollywood, but there was a growing speculation among those closest to him that it was only a matter of time before he jumped – speculation, and an accompanying disquiet, as the people who relied on Hitchcock's career for their own jockeyed with varying degrees of subtlety for a position in the new empire. There were no guarantees, but David was reasonably confident that, after ten years of working for Hitch and Alma, first as production designer and most recently as assistant director, there would be a role for him in the Hitchcock creative circle for as long as he wanted one.

'What do you mean he's going? He hasn't said anything to me.' There was a new tone in Hitch's responses and David listened with more interest, wondering who had been reckless enough to plan a future behind the director's back. He leant over the balcony and scanned the quayside below. Two or three bathers were by the hotel pool, but more seemed to favour the small, sheltered coves which punctuated the shoreline; a couple of parties had found the energy to take out one of the rowing boats kept for idling along the coast, but most people seemed content to relax on the terraces. He picked up a pair of binoculars which was lying on the red brick and looked across to the island in the middle of the estuary, holding the glasses first in one hand and then in the other so that the scorching metal did not have time to burn his skin.

'Did you know that Selznick was trying to persuade Jack Spence to move to Hollywood?'

It took David a moment to realise that Hitchcock was talking to him. 'What? No, sir, I didn't.' It was only a half-lie. Spence hadn't actually said anything to him but they worked together closely enough for David to know that the cameraman had grown restless recently, and he was far too good for any of the major studios to baulk at exploiting that restlessness. Like David, Spence had arrived on the scene at a time when Hitchcock was just beginning to carry enough clout to make his own decisions about who worked with him, and director and cameraman had quickly developed a mutual respect. Now, that partnership seemed about to dissolve into bitter recriminations, with David caught in the middle. He admired Hitch and Alma tremendously and had learnt a great deal from both of them, inspired as much by their diligence, enthusiasm and professional courtesy as by their creativity. Even so, his liking for the couple could not blind him to a certain arrogance in the assumptions they made. Spence was a free man, not particularly ambitious but proud of his work and with no ties to hold him down; why shouldn't he try his luck in Hollywood?

There had been a long silence and Hitch was clearly expecting him to say something. 'Perhaps it's just a rumour,' he suggested, falling easily into his habitual role as studio peacemaker. 'If Hollywood can convince you that enough of your people are on the brink of leaving, perhaps they think that will encourage you to jump as well.'

He spoke persuasively, but Hitchcock looked unconvinced. Spence's timing was unfortunate: only a couple of weeks ago, Charles Bennett – another of the director's closest collaborators, who had worked on every script with him since *The Man Who Knew Too Much* – had announced his decision to go to America after one more film. To the director, it must have felt like the end of an era, as the people he trusted conspired to hasten a decision he wasn't yet ready to make. 'And what about you, Mr Franks?' he asked. 'Are you still happy with us?'

'Yes, of course,' David said truthfully. 'I'm not saying I wouldn't like to make a film of my own one day, but I've still got a lot to learn.'

Hitchcock nodded thoughtfully. 'What about the future, though? A little bird told me recently that you might draw the line at going back to America as part of your education.'

David looked up sharply. 'Who told you that?'

'Bella Hutton. Is she wrong?'

'Yes, she is. I haven't discussed my plans with her and she has no idea what's in my mind.' He made an effort to keep the anger out of his voice, but it was only partially successful. 'I'm grateful to Bella for everything she's done. She had faith in me at a time when my life could have gone in a very different direction, but these days I stand on my own feet and make my own decisions. That might be hard for her to accept, and I know she has unhappy memories of America, but they're her memories, not mine.'

'It was quite a surprise to see Bella, actually, but it plays into our hands that she's here. There's certainly no love lost between her and Mr Turnbull. Has the star of our weekend arrived yet?'

'Yes, he checked in an hour ago and he's been in the bar ever since, so we'd better catch him while he's still sober enough to listen. Do you want to brief him, or shall I?'

'Oh you do it. I can't bear the man.' Hitchcock poured them both a drink and passed David's over. 'So – run through it all with me.'

'All right, but we'll have to go outside.' They walked out onto the lawn, and David wondered how Hitch could bear to make so few concessions to the weather; true, he had removed his jacket but he was still wearing a starched white shirt and navy-blue trousers, and just looking at his tie made David's short sleeves and wide flannels feel heavy and claustrophobic. 'You see why we can't use the roof,' he said, pointing out the distance between the Bell Tower and the Watch House. 'The trajectory simply wouldn't work. No one would believe it.'

Hitchcock nodded reluctantly. 'And it would have made

such a nice scene.' He pouted, and wiped away a mock tear. 'Where do you suggest Mr Turnbull's body should land, then?'

'Over here on the gravel. Apart from anything else, it'll be easier for people to see him – those who follow us up from the hotel.'

'You'll be there to stop them getting too close, though? We don't want anyone to know it's a gag until we've had our fun.'

'Of course. It'll be easy to cut them off at the gate by the Bell Tower. Except for the steps up from the terrace, it's the only entry point to this courtyard. No one will be able to see that his bruised and broken body is neither bruised nor broken.'

Hitchcock looked sceptical. 'Unless the idiot moves.'

'I think the amount you're paying him to lie still will do the trick.'

'Good. I'll gather everyone together on the terrace at around midday. Mr Turnbull will be in the Bell Tower by then?'

'Absolutely. If he stands on the fourth level – under the bell, where the brick changes to stone, see?' Hitchcock nodded. 'If he stands there and leans out a little, he can be easily spotted from the front of the hotel, and he can see you. All you need to do is draw attention to him a couple of times to make sure everyone knows he's up there.'

'That's easy enough.'

'Then we need to make everyone believe that he's jumped. When you're ready, give Turnbull the signal.'

'Which is?'

'Oh, something simple that's plain enough for him not to miss. Why not just stand up? That's ordinary, but there's no mistaking it from a distance and it will tell him it's time to make his way down the steps and take his position outside.

When you see he's gone from the balcony and you're sure everyone's looking at you, just tell them what you want them to believe. By the time we get up there, it'll look as if everything's happened exactly as you said.'

'Turnbull *will* be there by then?'

'Yes, I've timed it. It takes two minutes to get up here from the hotel, plus an extra few seconds for the shock to register with everyone. Turnbull will be able to get down those steps easily in that time, even if he's had a couple of drinks. And the other advantage of having his body on the gravel is that no one will see him getting into position. It's a blind spot from anywhere but here.'

'Splendid. You've thought of everything.' Pleased, he slapped David affectionately on the shoulder and turned to go back inside. 'It's his most appropriate role yet, don't you think? Whoever would have imagined that Leyton Turnbull would stage such a dramatic comeback so late in his career? Bella will be livid. She's worked so hard to destroy him.' He glanced at David, trying to gauge his reaction, but David pretended not to notice; he was determined not to lose his composure again. 'And there'll be a full supporting cast for dinner?' Hitchcock asked, when he saw that David wasn't going to rise to the bait.

'Oh yes. Everyone's here now.'

'Excellent.'

'At least, everyone *I* know about.' Just because David was party to *most* of the director's jokes, it didn't rule out the possibility that there would be a little surprise or two planned for him over the weekend: Hitch was nothing if not egalitarian in his manipulation of people's lives. The director raised an eyebrow and smiled, but gave nothing more away. 'You haven't said anything about what you intend to do afterwards,' David said as they walked back across the grass towards the Watch House.

'Sit back and watch, Mr Franks. Sit back and watch.'

'But what do you hope to get out of all this? It's a lot of trouble to go to for a gag.'

'Call it an experiment in guilt and fear. Put simply, I want to know how people will behave when they think a man's death might be their fault.'

It was always a mistake to second-guess Hitchcock's motivations, but his reply genuinely surprised David. 'Why would they think that?' he asked.

'Because by the time Mr Turnbull goes to bed, he'll have been insulted, humiliated or threatened by everyone around that dinner table.'

'You can't rely on that, surely? Astrid Lake doesn't seem the type to bully anyone. Spence wouldn't think he was important enough to make the effort, and even Bella . . .'

'Yes?'

'I know she loathes him, but squabbling over a dinner table is a bit beneath her.'

'Is it? We'll see. And I'm touched by your faith in human restraint, but I'm afraid I don't share it.' He gave David a wry smile, and there was a flicker of challenge in his eyes as he sat back down under the shade of the loggia roof. 'Perhaps we should have our own little bet? That drawing you admired last time you came to dinner in Cromwell Road – the Sickert that's hanging in the hall.' David nodded. Art was Hitchcock's most expensive indulgence, and he had an enviable collection of paintings, drawings and sculpture – bought, as a rule, to celebrate the success of a particular film. 'If anyone shows the sort of self-control you credit them with tonight, the picture's yours.' He held out his hand to shake on the wager. 'Alma is exempt from the agreement, of course. A gentleman should never bet on his wife.'

'It's too easy, sir. All I have to do to win is keep my mouth shut.'

'But you won't.'

He spoke with a confidence that disarmed David. 'What do you want from me if I lose?' he asked cautiously.

'Whatever you choose to give. That's for you to decide.'

David accepted the gamble but felt strangely apprehensive as he stood to leave. 'I'd better go and find Turnbull,' he said, picking his keys up from the table. 'Just to make sure he knows what he's doing.'

'Take this with you.' Hitchcock collected a book from the bed and threw it over to him. It was a proof copy and there was no cover illustration to indicate what it might be about, but David glanced through the opening pages, intrigued by its unusual title. 'A little holiday reading for you – it looks like this will be our next project if the Madame gets her own way.' They exchanged a glance that suggested she usually did. 'You'll see it opens with a death. I've been thinking while I was sitting on the balcony, we could even do that scene here. The tide goes out so quickly once it starts. Imagine the water receding to reveal a body lying on the beach, a woman in a swimming costume, her white bathing cap picked out in the sun. There's a belt next to her, curling snakelike in the sand as the last of the water drains away – and we know immediately that it's been used to strangle her.' David looked out across the estuary, and the image was as clear to him as if he were looking at a photograph. 'Two girls come out of the hotel, dressed for an early-morning walk across to the island. It's the perfect day – carefree, hopeful, innocent. Then they spot the body, seagulls circling overhead. They open their mouths to scream, but all we hear is the frenzied screeching of those birds.'

There was nothing quite like being around Hitchcock when his imagination was given free rein, and David lived for the excitement of moments like this. No one ever really believed the director when he said that the most rewarding part of any film for him was the preparation, but it was true: a meticulous planner, Hitch put all his energies into storyboarding a picture, developing the script and conceiving the special effects; after that, the filming itself was a matter of routine, and to say he sometimes looked bored was not an exaggeration. 'Whose body is it?' David asked, already drawn into the story.

'An actress.' He pursed his lips. 'Yes, I know, there are moments when we all feel that way. But it doesn't really matter who the body is – we won't be using much of the rest of the story. There are a couple of characters worth keeping: a young girl, a wrongly accused man, a tinker. We'll have to do some work on him.'

'A tinker?'

'Yes. A tramp, a gypsy, a gentleman of the road. Whatever you want to call them.'

'You want to make a film about a wrongly accused tinker?'

David's incredulous tone seemed to amuse Hitchcock. 'No, it's not the tinker who's wrongly accused – it's the love interest. But the tramp's vital to the outcome, so we have to get him right. Do you remember how much research we did on *Black-*

mail? How we plagued Scotland Yard to get the proper proced-ures for arresting and charging a man?' David nodded. 'Well, it paid off, and this has to be the same. I might even do it myself this time. I could find out what really happens when a tramp spends a night in a hostel.' He must have seen the look of dis-belief on David's face, because he added, 'I'm not joking, you know. It might be fun to be an actor for a bit. What do you think? We could do it together, perhaps.'

'I think the genuine article might consider you a little too well fed to be convincing.'

Hitchcock roared with laughter. 'Yes, you're right, of course, and I'd never have the willpower to be credible.' He walked David to the door, and it was a relief, suddenly, to be leaving. 'Don't tell Mr Turnbull quite everything, will you?'

'Of course not.'

'And make sure Bella's invited to dinner.'

David closed the door behind him and walked back to the darkness of the Bell Tower, where he could sit for a moment without anyone seeing him. He closed his eyes and the anger began to subside. When he opened them, he saw a trickle of blood on the pages of the book and realised that he had been clutching his keys so tightly that the metal had pierced his skin.

10

Josephine walked along the coastal path, a little way behind Marta and Lydia. The well-trodden route skirted the edge of a vast woodland area and was lined on the seaward side with sloe bushes, whose fruits were just starting to form. Marta was quiet, she noticed, while Lydia chatted easily about anything that came into her head, and Josephine found her presence un-expectedly reassuring: left alone, she and Marta had behaved like strangers afraid of getting to know each other, and the distance between them hurt her more than she had ever imagined it might.

She glanced through the rich green of rhododendron leaves into the sun-streaked darkness of the woods and marvelled at the way in which – even on one of the busiest weekends of the year – Portmeirion's network of woodland paths and beautiful garden walks meant that there was always peace to be found somewhere. Idly, she picked a sloe from one of the bushes and crushed it between her fingers, glad of the time to think. Perhaps she had been wrong to avoid Marta so resolutely over the last few months. If they had seen each other more often, this paralysing shyness might never have developed, or would at least have been resolved by now. Letters were all very well but – passionate and eloquent though they were – they had allowed her to intellectualise her love for Marta, almost as if it were happening to someone else. But looking at her now, Josephine could no longer hide behind words and reasoning. Her longing for Marta was the most intensely physical thing she had ever known, and it left her feeling needy and exposed.

Marta chose that moment to turn and wait for her, and her timing was so uncanny that Josephine could almost believe that she had spoken her thoughts aloud. She felt herself blush, and Marta smiled. 'Penny for them,' she said, but the playful look in her eyes made it clear that she didn't need to pay to know what Josephine was thinking. 'And I'll go higher if pushed.'

'No prizes for guessing that one, surely,' Lydia said, squeezing Josephine's arm affectionately. 'She'll be plotting how best to tackle the Hitchcocks. Any suggestions?'

'Do it quickly.' Marta pointed up ahead, to where a small white terrier was standing belligerently in the middle of the path, barking fiercely. 'I'm sure that's one of their dogs.' They cleared the trees and walked out onto the headland that formed Portmeirion's most southerly point. 'Yes, that's Alma on the rock.'

Josephine shaded her eyes from the sun, and looked with interest at Alma Reville. She wasn't sure what she had been expecting, but it was something far more daunting than this petite young redhead, dressed unconventionally in a perfectly tailored trouser suit. Alma had a camera, and was engrossed in taking a photograph across the water. Much to Josephine's relief, the director's wife seemed far more interested in the composition of her picture than in anything going on around her. 'At least she hasn't seen us,' she said, turning to go. 'If we head back now, we won't have to speak to her.'

Lydia caught her arm. 'Why on earth don't you want to speak to her?' she asked, making no effort to hide her astonishment.

Josephine knew her behaviour was absurd, and she didn't need Lydia to point it out, particularly in front of Marta. 'Because I'm not in the mood,' she said stubbornly. 'It's far too hot to haggle, and, anyway, I don't want to have to think about it today. Being forty's bad enough,' she added, trying to make light of her nerves. 'At least let me deal with one crisis at a time.'

'Don't knock forty,' Marta said, winking at her. 'You know what they say.'

'And if you pull this one off, it'll be the best birthday present you've ever had.' Lydia turned conspiratorially to Marta. 'For God's sake, darling, talk some sense into her.'

Josephine looked defiantly at Marta, daring her to take Lydia's side. 'We could just say hello,' Marta suggested diplomatically. 'You won't be able to avoid it at dinner, and it might be less of an ordeal if you break the ice now, when she's on her own.'

'I suppose so,' Josephine admitted, although her inclination was still to put off the moment for as long as possible.

'And I honestly think you'll like her. Anyway, from what I can see, you're not bothered whether this happens or not so you've got nothing to lose. Let Alma do the running.' Marta grinned. 'Just sit back and enjoy being courted.'

'Not everything in life works like that,' Lydia muttered. 'Sometimes a little effort goes a long way.'

'And sometimes things will happen if they're meant to,' Marta countered.

'I'm not sure your blasé outlook on life necessarily applies to the film world.'

'Which you know so much about, of course.'

'Oh, let's get it over with,' Josephine said hurriedly, keen to stifle an argument which was no longer about Alma Reville. In any case, the matter had already been taken out of her hands. Another dog – a spaniel – lay at Alma's feet, offering nothing more energetic in the heat than a lazy wag of the tail; when it struggled to its feet, the movement seemed to be more noteworthy than all the terrier's efforts at attention, and Alma turned to see what the fuss was about. She waved when she recognised Marta and came over to greet them, slinging the camera casually over her shoulder.

'I'm afraid you've caught me in the middle of some shameless sightseeing,' she said, and Josephine detected the faintest trace of a Midlands accent. 'These gardens are magnificent. I don't know whether to despair or be inspired; it puts my efforts to shame.' She kissed Marta on both cheeks and waited for her to make the introductions. Her enthusiasm was attractive, and Josephine liked her instantly for her lack of affectation; most people in her position would feel obliged to play up to the role that her husband's fame had forced on her, but there was a quiet self-confidence about Hitchcock's wife which made that unnecessary and which, Josephine suspected, rarely looked to anyone else for approval.

'Miss Tey – it's lovely to meet you at last,' she said. 'And you, Miss Beaumont. My husband and I saw you in *Out of the Dark* at the Ambassadors earlier this year. I hoped I might have an opportunity to tell you how much we enjoyed it.'

Lydia looked pleased, if a little taken aback. 'You're part of quite a select band,' she said dryly. 'We only ran for a fortnight. But I'm glad you liked it.'

'Yes, very much. And we loved *Richard of Bordeaux*, of course, but there's nothing very select about that – half the country must have seen it.'

'I'm surprised you go so often,' Josephine said. 'Now that the screen is the medium of the future.'

'Ah, you read that interview.' Alma looked approvingly at her, and conceded a smile. 'Hitch and I have both been going to the theatre since we were children, and it's a very hard habit to break once it's in your blood. He has a professional interest in ringing its death knell, of course, but between you and me he sees more plays than films. In fact, he's saying no to America at the moment on the basis of our daughter Patricia, our house at Shamley Green and the fact that we can nip across to the West End whenever we like – and not necessarily in that order.' She called the terrier to heel, rescuing another couple from a barrage of barked abuse; the spaniel had never left her side, and Josephine noticed that both dogs seemed to adore her. 'Jenky's a bit affronted,' she explained, bending down to put his lead on. 'We were walking through the woods and stumbled on some sort of dog cemetery. Now he's behaving as if I were trying to tell him something. But anyway, I hope you can see a future of some sort in film, Miss Tey, because we have some business to discuss.'

'Of course. I'm here until Monday, so whenever you and your husband are free.'

'Why don't *we* talk first? If Hitch is involved, he'll launch straight into camera shots and you and I will wonder why we're there at all.' Josephine agreed, hoping her relief didn't show. 'Good. Tonight would be best. He's got something up his sleeve for the rest of the weekend, so I've no idea what will happen but it probably won't be peaceful. Shall we have a cocktail before dinner? I'll meet you in the hotel at six.' Without waiting for a reply, Alma turned to Marta and Lydia, and Josephine wondered if the rest of the negotiations were going to be any more mutual. 'And I'll see you both later, I hope. Perhaps you'd all like to join us for coffee? You never know, we might have a deal to celebrate by then.'

She turned and walked back in the direction of the hotel, and Marta quickly squeezed Josephine's hand. 'Did you tell her I was dreading this?' Josephine asked. 'I didn't expect her to be quite so gentle with me.'

'I don't know her well enough for that, but there was no need for me to say anything. She hates people as much as you do.'

'I don't hate people,' Josephine said indignantly. 'I just . . .'

'Prefer it when they're not around.' Lydia finished the sentence for her, and Josephine laughed.

'Yes, something like that.'

'Actually, that's not fair on Alma either,' Marta said as they headed back to the village. 'I've heard she's a fabulous host, but she chooses her friends very carefully – and his. I suppose she has to.'

'It should be an interesting evening,' Josephine said, surprised to find herself looking forward to it.

'Yes, although I think someone might have to put a muzzle on Ronnie,' Lydia said. 'Whatever progress you make with Alma could all be undone the first time she opens her mouth.'

'That's a head-to-head I'd pay to see.' The path narrowed slightly, and Josephine allowed the other two to go first. 'Alma's younger than I expected,' she added. 'When people have the sort of reputation that the Hitchcocks have got, you automatically expect them to be older than you. It's quite sobering when it turns out to be talent rather than experience.'

'Get used to it, darling,' Lydia said with feeling. 'It's all downhill from here.'

11

An experiment in fear and guilt, he had called it, but an exercise in control would have been more accurate. Staging a joke, like making a film, was a way of holding on to the power, and

Hitchcock had discovered long ago that the manipulation involved in both helped him to forget his own anxieties and doubts. It suited him if people thought him childish, if they underestimated him as a result; behind the grinning schoolboy, there was someone smart enough to realise that people were most truly themselves when they were disoriented, frightened, exposed – and he had important decisions to make. There had never been a more important time to know whom to trust.

He had lost track of how many times people asked him if he enjoyed watching his own films. The answer was always the same: his work was laid out scene by scene in his mind, and he had no need to go to a cinema to see it. It had been the same for as long as he could remember: his past, like his career, was made up of pictures; memories were visual rather than verbal, like a very young child's. The older he got, the more fervently he wished he could storyboard his future, plan it out day by day and get rid of this paralysing fear that his life was in someone else's hands. By going to America, he knew he would be setting in motion something that was bigger than he was, and it terrified him.

Still, he would do it for Alma. Everything he did, he did for that moment when they went home together in the evening and he could see the pride in her eyes, another memory for their old age. It was the best of who he was, the only reason for doing anything. Hitchcock got up from the bed and walked over to the balcony, impatient for Alma to come back. It was never the same without her. He hated being alone.

12

Bridget Foley stood on a stepladder outside the Salutation Restaurant, putting the finishing touches to the mural that had occupied her for the past ten days. It had seemed an insurmountable task at the beginning, but she knew by now that the trick was to treat it as a game of patience, mentally dividing the wall into grids and concentrating on one small square at a time, working her way inch by inch across the hot stone without any thought for the picture as a whole. She engrossed herself in her work each day, following the branch of a tree or the path of light on water as if it were the only image that concerned her; now, when the mural was almost complete, patience became less important than faith – and if art was anything, it was an act of faith. She had learnt long ago that creating one thing did not necessarily mean you had a God-given right to do it again, and – successful as she was – a blank space still frightened her as much as it had when she had first begun to paint; more so, in fact, because the fearless arrogance of youth was such a distant memory that she sometimes wondered if it had ever existed.

There was something very satisfying in continuing a tradition that was as old as humanity itself. As a child, she had been fascinated by the medieval wall paintings which dominated the churches that her father preached in – terrifying lotteries of judgement and salvation that stretched from the chancel arch to the timbers of the roof. A sense of honouring the past made the first few strokes of the brush even more nerve-racking than usual, especially when every movement was under public scrutiny; out here, she didn't have the protective shell of a studio, where mistakes could be destroyed before they saw the light of day. She hated being a public spectacle, but Portmeirion forced a choice between solitude and fine weather: its fertile, almost tropical climate meant that it was impossible to find a dry wall except at the height of summer. Fortunately most people were happy to watch quietly while she worked. Only a few were rude enough to offer a constructive comment or two along the way, and she had perfected a smile which dealt with them effectively. Crowds were never really a problem: even now, with Portmeirion's increasing popularity, the village still felt like an island, unthreatened by an influx of people and cut off from the outside world. To deter too many visitors, daily admission charges altered according to the privacy needs of its residents and had hit an all-time high with the arrival of the Prince of Wales a couple of years ago; Alfred Hitchcock, she noticed, was a couple of shillings cheaper.

The sky was the lightest part of the painting, pale blue at the top, fading down through white and yellow; Bridget stretched cautiously up to her right to add some warmer tints just above the treeline. The ladder wobbled precariously, much to the delight of two small boys who were standing nearby, threatening to have some fun with the tantalising array of paints that she had laid out on the floor, and she sent them scuttling back to their families with an unnecessarily vigorous stroke of the brush. There was a great sense of freedom in working here: Clough's 'home for fallen buildings', as he affectionately referred to it, was a continual experiment in form and colour. Nothing was considered too bizarre, and the shades of the buildings mirrored the flowers and plants which filled the woods behind the village, bridging the gap between the natural and the man-made, the real and the illusory. In all her life, even among artist friends who were notoriously selfish, she had never known anyone to do exactly what he wanted in the way that Clough did – and yet that single-mindedness was such a benevolent gesture, an assurance that here, at least, trees would always be trees, streams would continue to tumble into the sea, and rocks would stand unthreatened. It was no longer the fashion in art to glorify a property or a landlord, but it made what she was doing more important, somehow, if she thought of it as a tribute to his sense of beauty and permanence.

She had known Clough for most of her life. Her father had met him at Cambridge and presided over his marriage to Amabel Strachey, and the families had remained friends – part of a circle of influential writers, artists and political activists which had enriched her childhood with its ideas and eccentricities. As a young girl, she had spent most of her summers in North Wales, staying in one of the farmhouses near Clough's family home. It was long before Portmeirion existed, but, even then, the love that she developed for the landscape was tempered by an awareness that families like hers were not welcomed by the local people. She felt the same resentment these days from some of the older staff in the village, though she couldn't fault them for it: there was precious little housing for them and their families, yet extravagant buildings sprang up at Portmeirion each year to be played in during the holiday season then left empty and useless over the winter months. Not everyone blessed Clough the way she did.

Bridget swapped to an old decorator's brush, conscious that she was running out of those cowardly finishing touches which served to put off the moment of truth. She had painted a carved arch to frame the mural, and she added some darker tones at its edges to give it a more solid look, using the roughness of the surface to create a mottled effect and subtly ageing her painted stone until it resembled the wall around Portmeirion's original kitchen garden. Knowing that she risked ruining the whole image if she added anything else, she got down from the ladder and walked a few steps back from the building, picking her way carefully through the detritus of her work. Her body ached from another day of bending and twisting at odd angles, but she was quietly excited: when her work was going well, it was almost as if she were uncovering what was already there rather than creating something from nothing. She turned round and saw with relief that her excitement was justified: she had created a fine illusion, worthy of its place in a village where nothing was quite what it seemed. Her mock arch enclosed a woodland scene, a glorious profusion of trees, rhododendrons and ferns with a lake in the foreground; the mural brought the wild gardens of Portmeirion into the heart of its ordered piazza, and, if you glanced at it quickly, you would believe you were looking through the wall of the restaurant into the woods beyond.

But it was missing something – a bird in the trees, perhaps, or a sign of life on the lake. She reached for some white paint, then changed her mind and picked up the black; like many of her brushes and artist's materials, she had inherited it from a friend who had died too young, and she had found herself using the paint sparingly, wanting to create as much as possible with it to compensate for what had been destroyed. The swans she had in mind would need all that was left, but somehow that was fitting. She sketched the outline, making sure that the figures were balanced within the overall composition. As the birds began to take shape, she smiled.

Satisfied at last, she decided to call it a day. The café had shown no sign of dwindling in popularity as the afternoon wore on, and she was glad to leave the families behind and head for her own small cottage on the southern boundary of the village, just beyond the hotel. White Horses, so called because waves had been known to beat at its door and flood the property, was unique among the buildings of Portmeirion in that it was neither available for hire by the public nor simply decorative. Formerly a fisherman's cottage, the building had been variously used by Clough as a storeroom, a workshop for weaving and dyeing and temporary lodgings for builders and craftsmen employed in the village. She made her home there whenever she was at Portmeirion, feeling comfortable in that final category and using her dogs as an excuse to fend off repeated invitations to stay at the hotel. While she appreciated Clough's hospitality, Bridget had no liking for a life governed by other people's routines.

The lower terrace seemed quieter, so she chose that route past the hotel, conscious that a woman in paint-splashed overalls carrying a stepladder wasn't the illusion of perfection which most of the clientele paid for. Up ahead, moored at the quayside, the *Amis Reunis* – a graceful old trading ketch from Portmadoc, used now as a houseboat – shone proudly in the sunlight, giving the wharf a deceptive air of seafaring activity which always made her smile. As she drew closer, she noticed a man standing alongside the boat and hesitated when she recognised him, instinctively calculating how many years it must have been since they last saw each other. He was filling a pipe, and she watched as he packed the tobacco into the bowl, remembering how he had always given even the simplest of tasks his full attention. It was one of the things she had loved most about him, that intensity which relaxed so easily into laughter whenever she teased him about it, like the sun breaking suddenly through a cloud. Looking at him now, she was pleased to see that she had been right: the face she had drawn so often – still young then, if aged prematurely by war – had grown leaner and stronger in the intervening years and was now more attractive than ever.

'You never could get that damned thing to stay alight.'

'Bridget!' He looked at her in astonishment, and she was touched to see how quickly delight followed surprise. 'What on earth are you doing here?'

She glanced down at her paint-covered clothes. 'I would have thought that was fairly obvious,' she said, trying to transfer everything she was carrying to one hand in order to hold out the other. The stepladder defeated her, but it was an oddly formal gesture anyway, and he pre-empted it by bending to kiss her.

'I learnt a long time ago never to take anything about you at face value,' he said with a wry smile. 'It's always sensible to check.'

Bridget laughed. 'And how often did I tell you that sensible is overrated?' She dumped her bags on the quayside so that she could embrace him properly. 'Here, give those to me,' she said, taking the matches out of his hand. 'We could be here all day.' She held the flame up to the bowl, surprised at how easily the first traces of pipe smoke erased twenty years, and nodded to the *Amis Reunis* sign on the ship's bow. 'Looks like this old lady's very well named. How are you, Archie?'

'I'm fine,' he said, 'and I don't need to ask how *you* are.

Whatever you've been doing, it suits you.' He gazed at her, and she brushed the hair away from her eyes, unusually self-conscious. 'You've hardly changed at all,' he said, and flushed slightly at his own cliché. 'It's the first time I've ever said that truthfully, although the paint could be hiding a lot – is there *any* on the canvas?'

'On the walls,' she corrected him. 'I've been doing some work for Clough up at Salutation. He fancied a mural to liven up the café terrace. Every now and then, he gets bored with a wall or ceiling and decides it needs Cloughing up a bit.'

'Your phrase or his?'

'Neither. I think someone used it in a novel and not necessarily as a compliment. He doesn't mind, though – he always says he'd rather be vulgar than dull.'

'I'm sure his mural's neither. Is he pleased with it?'

'He hasn't seen it yet. He's off in Flintshire, saving a vaulted ceiling that no one else can find room for. God knows where he'll put it if he gets it.'

'Somewhere ludicrous, no doubt. We'll all say he's off his head and then marvel at how good it looks once it's in place.' He nodded at her paints. 'Is the mural finished?'

'Just about, although I'll probably see a hundred things I don't like about it when I go back tomorrow.'

'But it's safe for me to look?' Bridget nodded. Funny, she thought, after all these years, that he should remember how much she hated people seeing her work before it was finished. 'I'll go up there later then. I haven't been that way today, and it was getting dark when we got here last night.' The 'we' hung awkwardly in the air between them for a moment, as she resisted the temptation to ask and he avoided seeming overanxious to explain. 'It's a friend's fortieth birthday,' Archie said eventually. 'That's why I'm here – a few of us have come over for the weekend.'

'I see.' She didn't, but was determined not to flood him with questions when they had only just met. In any case, it made no difference to her with whom Archie had come to Portmeirion; they had never had that sort of relationship, and she was surprised to find herself more curious now about his life than she had ever been when they were young.

'How are your parents?' he asked, and the clumsy change of subject made her burst out laughing, even though she could see that it hurt his pride. Embarrassment made him irritable, and he added tetchily, 'I don't see what's so funny. It was a straightforward question.'

'Oh, Archie – you were always so polite,' Bridget said, still laughing. 'I'd quite forgotten what good manners you have.' She looked at him affectionately. 'They're both very well, thank you.' He smiled grudgingly, and she took his arm. 'Come on – you can help me get this lot home. I'm staying at White Horses.' It was late afternoon, but the heat still shimmered over the estuary, blending with the ripples on the water until it was hard to tell where one ended and the other began. 'You're not connected with this film circus, then?' she asked as they walked along.

'Not really, no.'

'When I first saw you, I thought the Yard might have been called in to take care of Mr Hitchcock.'

He stared at her in surprise. 'How did you know I was a policeman?' he asked. 'Please tell me it's not obvious.'

She laughed. 'Of course it isn't. I wouldn't be walking along here in daylight with you if it were. No, I've just seen your name in the paper a few times. It beats the wireless, you know. Inspector Penrose of the Yard – he's quite a hero.'

'Chief Inspector now, I'm afraid.'

'Good God, that's even worse.' The combination of admiration and gentle mockery in her tone was unfamiliar, and she tried to think of someone else she used it for. 'Actually, it makes me realise what a lucky escape I've had. All that effort I've put into bucking the trend and being radical, only to end up on the long arm of the law. It takes a lot of discipline to be a free spirit, you know. What would Dover Street think of me?'

'Whatever the most fashionable critic told them to, I suppose,' Archie said cynically. 'Anyway, I'm not the only one in the newspapers. Your retrospective had the reviewers falling over themselves to compliment you.' He grinned at her, making the most of having the upper hand for once. 'And not without good reason.'

She stopped. 'You went to see it?'

'Of course I did – several times. I thought about leaving you a note, but you didn't need any kind words from me, not with Augustus John singing your praises.'

'They would have meant more coming from you.' She smiled. 'Although Augustus John earns me more money.'

'Tell me about it. It's a lot to find on a policeman's salary.'

'Jesus, Archie – I can't believe you bought one. What on earth were you thinking of?'

'Grantchester Meadows in 1915.' He looked serious for a moment, and for once she didn't want to shake him out of it. 'It's beautiful – more so because I thought that time had gone for ever.'

Bridget nodded, pleased. 'I was sorry to see that picture sold, actually, but not any more. You should never have bought it, though. I'd happily have given it to you if I'd known you liked it so much.'

'And I'd happily have paid twice as much to own it.' She smiled. 'Have you any idea how strange it is to walk into a gallery and see a portrait of yourself on the wall?' Archie asked, opening the gate that led from the terrace to the coastal path. 'I see that one's in somebody's private collection. I hope I've got a good home.'

'Mine, of course. I don't know if you'd call it good, but it's never dull.'

'You kept it?'

She looked out across the estuary, turning her face away so that he couldn't see the colour rise in her cheeks. 'Who else would want to look at you, Archie?' she said, a little too glibly. 'And they certainly wouldn't pay me for the pleasure.' He was about to say something, but she cut him short by pointing further down the path; three women – two walking arm in arm and the other slightly apart – were heading in their direction. 'Somebody's waving to you. You didn't tell me the birthday party was such a female affair. I'm not surprised you look so revoltingly pleased with yourself.'

'Believe me, it's not what you think,' Archie said, and there was something in his tone that made her look at him curiously, but there was no time to probe any further. 'Bridget – this is Josephine,' he said, beginning the round of introductions, then added rather weakly, 'It's her birthday.'

They shook hands, and Bridget wondered what the appraising full-length glance told Archie's friend about her. 'Congratulations,' she said, resisting the temptation to apologise for her clothes, her hair, her very existence. 'I went to bed for a week when I was forty, but you soon get over it.'

To her credit, Josephine laughed, but Bridget guessed that Archie would not be forgiven quickly for revealing her age. 'And Marta Fox and Lydia Beaumont,' he continued, oblivious to his breach of etiquette.

Marta smiled warmly at her. 'We saw you working on our way in,' she said. 'You were up a ladder, but I recognise the paint on your trousers.'

'Bridget's an artist,' Archie explained redundantly to Josephine. 'She painted the oil of Grantchester in my flat. Well, she didn't paint it *in* my flat, obviously – I meant the oil that's hanging on the . . .'

'I know the one.' Josephine looked at Bridget again, but this time there was a glint in her eye which suggested that they might share an amused solidarity in Archie's discomfort, and Bridget revised her first impressions. 'You didn't tell me you knew the artist, though,' Josephine continued. 'No wonder you were so delighted with it.'

'Where *is* it hanging, Archie?' Bridget asked. 'Just out of interest.'

'It's in the bedroom.'

'Do you live near Portmeirion, Bridget?' Lydia asked brightly, while everyone else looked at each other.

'No, in Cambridge most of the time, but I have some friends in Hampstead so I stay with them whenever I need to be in town.'

'Oh, whereabouts? We're in Holly Place.'

'Redington Road, not far from Clough and Amabel.'

'Then you must come for supper some time.'

'And bring Archie,' Marta added. 'It would be lovely to see you both.'

'We must go,' Josephine said, looking at her watch. 'I have to decide what to wear for cocktails with Mrs Hitchcock, God help me.' She smiled at Bridget. 'Will you have dinner with us? I haven't seen that painting of Grantchester since Archie first bought it, but at least I could get to know you a bit better.'

It was an exceptionally eloquent white flag, Bridget thought, and something told her that it was not aimed exclusively at her. 'I'm sorry – I have to work tonight,' she said, 'but I'll gladly accept a drink tomorrow when I've had a chance to assess everything that's wrong with the mural. You're here for the weekend?'

'Yes.'

'Good. I'll look forward to it.' Bridget watched them go, noticing how often Marta glanced across at Josephine. 'Well, that's all very difficult,' she said.

'It's fine, honestly – she just wasn't expecting to see me with anyone.'

She laughed and hit his shoulder. 'You men – you always think it's about you, don't you? I meant those three. Call it a peril of the job, but I can spot an awkward composition a mile off. God knows, I've been involved in enough of them myself.' He smiled, but she could see that he was trying to work out if the comment referred to her work or to something more personal. 'The only thing dividing my affections at the moment, though, is a pair of border terriers, both of whom will leave me if I don't get back and take them for a walk.' She kissed his cheek. 'So I'll be free for a drink later on. Come and find me at the cottage.'

'I thought you were working?'

'Give me a reason not to.'

He smiled, and shook his head. 'If anything, you've got worse over the years and I never imagined that was possible. What time shall I come over?'

'Whenever you like. If I'm not there, I'll only be walking the dogs, so make yourself at home.' She raised an eyebrow. 'And I'll be needing you to explain why you've kept me quiet all these years, even with your closest friends.'

He looked uncomfortable. 'I haven't deliberately kept you quiet, Bridget, but you're not very easy to explain. I never quite understood what we were.'

'We were lovely, Archie,' she said, turning to go. 'What is there to explain?'

13

The bus from Portmadoc to Harlech was late, and it was five o'clock by the time Gwyneth Draycott put her shopping away in the kitchen and went up to the attic. Weary from the heat and the effort of leaving the house, she used the banister to haul herself up the final flight of stairs, marking her progress with a series of prints on the wood from palms that refused to stay dry. Her clothes were sticking to her, and she was glad to kick off her shoes and settle down by the window; even with the casement flung wide, there was very little air at the top of the house, but the chance to sit still was something to be grateful for. The weather would surely break soon. Over the past few hours, she had felt the pressure tighten like a wire around her throat, threatening the storm that carried with it so many memories. When it came, she knew that each flash of lightning would illuminate the past, and she dreaded it. Anxiously, she shifted in her chair and reached behind her to remove the toy monkey which dug at her back. The mohair made her feel hotter than ever, but she looked fondly down at its black button eyes and felt ears. Its arms and legs moved, although Taran had always carried it by its tail; the repairs she had made to the monkey's hands and feet were nothing compared to the crisscross of neat stitching which almost obliterated its face, patching the tears where its nose had bumped and dragged along the floor. Taran. Thunder, in her native language. She had always loved the name, and what it represented. Now, it was the hollowest sound she knew.

For Gwyneth, trying to describe how she felt in the days and weeks that followed Taran's loss was like struggling with a foreign language, looking for words which simply did not exist in her vocabulary. The one emotion that she could identify with any certainty was resentment: she felt cheated. She had been a good mother during the brief time allotted to her, watching the cot as her child slept and keeping a careful eye on playtime in the garden of the old house; she kept Taran by her while she worked, always away from the stove, always within reach, always safe. So many innocent dangers carefully negotiated, only to be let down by a horror beyond her control. Gwyneth had tried not to lay blame or wish her suffering onto others, but there was no common ground between reason and grief. All around her, women started to take greater care of their children, learning from her mistakes. She saw the guilty relief in their eyes and knew exactly what they were thinking: there but for the grace of God. It would have taken a better woman than she not to despise them for what they still had.

As news of Taran's disappearance spread, suspicion scarred the whole community, breathing new life into age-old prejudices and obliterating any impulse to reason or compassion. It was an unthinkable crime, the abduction of a child, and the locals responded in the only way they knew, turning instinctively on the outsider – even though he had lived quietly among them for years and no child's body was ever found to justify their conviction that he had killed one of their own. Anger spread, as swift and as sudden as the tide that covered the estuary sands, surrounding Gwyneth and leaving no possibility of escape. Other people's rage suffocated her until she felt there was no room for her own, and, in that way, Taran was taken from her for the second time: as the newspapers spoke of a collective tragedy and a community's loss, the child she wept for became somebody else's. Their violence had terrified her, not least because it was done in her name, but she understood now that it was inevitable. In those fragile years that followed the war, her grief had become a focus for everything that was lost, for the children of a nation who had disappeared in their thousands.

The irony of it all was that she had never seen herself as a mother. She knew from her own family what a burden children could be and had sworn to herself long ago that one generation's pain would not be replicated in the next. She married for security, because passion frightened her and she had never expected love, and, in that joyless, ill-judged compromise, husband and wife had learnt first to exploit the shame and disappointment of the other and then to find what they needed elsewhere. When they parted, Gwyneth would have danced for joy had Henry Draycott not left her with a living scar of their marriage. She had denied the pregnancy for as long as possible, even praying that what was growing inside her was a tumour rather than a child, and then, when the baby could be ignored no longer, had done everything she could think of to get rid of it, half killing herself in the process. But Taran had proved too strong for her, worthy of the name she eventually chose, winning her round day by day with that smile and those eyes and the most forgiving nature she had ever known. A gift rather than a curse.

The air smelt of rain, and Gwyneth stood to close the window, ready to go downstairs. Her foot brushed against one of the toys on the floor, a wooden Noah's Ark whose elaborate arched windows made it look more like a house than a boat. Its paint was chipped now, and the palm trees that stood on either side had faded from green to brown, as though they were as vulnerable to the seasons as their less exotic counterparts. She reached down and lifted the lid. All the tiny animals had seen better days: both elephants had lost their trunks; one of the giraffes was reduced to three legs; and the zebra's stripes were so pale that it could easily have been mistaken for a surplus pony. None of them was a specimen that Noah would have chosen to ensure the earth's future, but Gwyneth knew that it would have been pointless to try to replace them with other toys, even if she had wanted to. Taran had loved those creatures and played with them constantly, finding an infinite number of ways to arrange and rearrange them. She was always coming across the figures, stowed away two by two in a pocket or under a pillow. The dogs had been missing from the set now for eighteen years. At first, she had harboured a foolish belief that they might somehow keep Taran safe, but that was a very long time ago, and Noah's world remained as incomplete as hers. Incomplete, and reliant on a miracle simply to stay afloat.

PART THREE

RICH AND STRANGE

25 July 1936, Portmeirion

There was a queue at reception. Impatiently, Leyton Turnbull leant over the desk and removed his own car keys from the hook, ignoring an apologetic smile from the harassed woman on duty. He found the Alvis in the garage allocated to him and drove quickly out of the village, allowing the familiar sense of power and control to calm his temper.

The breeze against his skin was a relief after the oppressive heat of the hotel, but the sunshine was uncomfortably strong, even through dark glasses. His sight was a casualty of the primitive studio conditions in the 1920s, when the lights were noisy and generated too much heat; staring into them for long periods of time had damaged his eyes, and the heavy make-up – which made the actors look and feel ridiculous – had aged his face. The psychological scars of his profession were less obvious: his career had fizzled out as the industry had left him behind, and he had struggled to relearn his craft. Making films with sound was alien to him. He had put up with the indignity of diction coaches, the arrival of new studio personnel and the pressures of more demanding production schedules, but it had all been in vain: those at the top of the pile were back at the beginning like grateful newcomers, and he had known it would be so from the moment he heard Al Jolson open his mouth and sing. Turnbull was filled with an immense sadness whenever he thought back to that brief period in his life, when what he wanted to be and what he was were less at odds. It wasn't about the money. He had found other ways to make that – more, probably, than he would ever have got from legitimate cinema. It was about shame, and what he had sunk to: Hitchcock's stooge and thankful for it, beholden to a much younger man.

At the Minffordd junction, he turned right and took the road that had almost tempted him on his journey down. In the end he had decided against it but, as he stood on the hotel lawn, staring at the house across the water and troubled by Bella's unexpected arrival, the pull of the past had proved too strong: he was curious to see if, in the past twenty years, bricks and mortar had fared better than flesh and bone. He crossed the estuary by the toll road, surprised by how familiar the route still felt to him, and slowed down as he entered Talsarnau. The house he sought was at the end of a lane. He pulled onto the verge before he reached it and parked in the shade of some trees where his car could not be seen from the windows. Across the estuary, Portmeirion shone in the late-afternoon sun like a child's colourful drawing, extreme in its invention, yet vivid enough to be real. From here, it seemed so far away, but its distance was an illusion: the journey had only taken him twenty minutes, and it was still not quite five o'clock. He sat in the car, trying to peel back the layers from the landscape he had once woken to every day, then got out and shut the door behind him. Quietly, he walked through the copse of silver birch until he was within a few yards of the garden wall.

At first, the house had seemed unchanged; now he was upon it, he could see that his former home had given up on itself, like a woman shrinking from the truth of a harsh mirror. The bars attached to some of the downstairs windows were red with rust. One of them – his old study – had been bricked up; the rest stared out, blank-eyed. Deep cracks in the brickwork zigzagged down from under each sill and disappeared into the ivy which clung to the walls and crawled into gaps where the wooden window frames had rotted. Turnbull imagined it working its way through the building, curling round the banisters and down the staircase. He remembered how the hallway used to be bathed in colour and how, at a particular time of day, the sun had shone through the fanlight over the door directly into the room where he worked; now, the glass was so thick with dirt that it was barely distinguishable from the cast iron which divided the panes, and even a day as bright as this would find no way in. Several slates had fallen from the roof and lay uncollected on the path around the house, nestled in long grass. The garden, for want of a better word, was gloomy, too – unkempt, and defined by absence: no plants in the greenhouse; no dog in the kennels; no birds in the dovecote. Deprived of their function, the outbuildings looked faintly ridiculous. What was there left of him inside, he wondered? Did Henry Draycott – the man he had once been – still exist here? There was no way of knowing. The house remained now as it had been then: secretive and unwelcoming, the shell of all that was private in a life, a physical embodiment of his darkest fantasies. A fortress of sorts, and that was what he had loved about it. He had been sorry to leave, and, for a moment, he wondered if the melancholy he sensed here was in the brick at all or if he had brought it with him. Things could have been so different. If he had made other choices at each crossroads, he might never have arrived at the point where there *was* no choice.

Behind him, he heard the rhythmic creaking of a badly oiled bicycle. A girl was pedalling along the road towards him, and he noticed her glance curiously at the car as she passed, but she seemed in too much of a hurry to linger. To Turnbull's surprise, she braked when she was level with the house and leant the bicycle against the hedge. He thought she looked familiar, then recognised her as the waitress he had seen talking to Bella on the terrace of the hotel. She was pretty in an obvious sort of way, with carefully curled brown hair and a full figure that she carried well. She looked older in her green cotton dress and hat than she had in a uniform – early twenties, he guessed, but it was so hard to tell with women these days; they copied their make-up from the faces on the screen, had their hair done to look old before their time, and all because they saw fame in the cinemas, read about it in the magazines and thought they could taste it in their own mouths. How did she know Bella, he wondered, and what was she doing here? He moved further back into the trees and watched, uneasy, as the girl opened the iron gate and walked up the path to the door, pushing the overhanging branches away from her face. She seemed familiar with the place, and he half expected her to get a key out of her bag and let herself in, but she stood on the step and pulled the bell instead. When there was no response, she tried again, then left the door and walked over to one of the downstairs windows. The curtains were drawn but there was a gap between, and she peered through, cupping her face with her hands to block out the sunlight. She knocked on the glass – more in frustration, it seemed, than in any real hope of attracting attention – and walked full-circle around the house, repeating the process at every window. Eventually, she returned to the front door and took an envelope out of her bag, ready-written as if she had not expected to find anyone at home. She put it through the letter box, retrieved her bicycle without bothering to close the gate behind her, and cycled away. Her expression, Turnbull noticed, was that of a disappointed child.

It was time he followed suit but he took a last look at the house before turning away, doubtful that he would ever come here again. He glanced up at the windows in the attic and saw Gwyneth's face. She was staring down the road after the girl, unaware that she, too, was being watched, and something in her stillness reminded Turnbull of how badly he had wanted her, how he had put up with her moods and her absences, how she had teased and pushed and laid down the rules of their marriage until he could bear it no longer. He knew that he should go now, that to look at her for a moment longer would make him vulnerable to everything he had ever run from, but still he stood there. Quite unwittingly, Hitchcock had invited him to be a guest in his own past, and now he found he couldn't walk away.

2

Josephine left her room twenty minutes early, hoping that punctuality would give her the advantage of choosing where the meeting with Alma took place. She was surprised by how quickly she had warmed to the director's wife, but realised, too, that her friendliness held its own agenda: Hitchcock might control things in front of the camera, but it was already obvious to Josephine that Alma's role in the couple's success was just as important, if far more subtle, and she was determined not to let herself be charmed into an agreement that she would later regret.

The wide, elegant staircase led down to a series of elaborate interiors which suggested that the old house had enjoyed an eclectic architectural history even before its present owner arrived. The terraces and Cockpit bar were busy, and Josephine noticed Lydia and Marta outside with Daniel Lascelles and an attractive young girl who looked vaguely familiar, but there was no sign of Alma Reville. Of all the downstairs reception areas, the library was the quietest, and she settled herself there, relieved not to be distracted by anyone she knew. It was an odd sort of room, finished with intricately carved doorways and a fireplace which was supposed to have come straight from the Great Exhibition, and it was by no means her favourite part of the hotel – but she felt comfortable in a place devoted to the written word and looked on the library as a silent ally in the conversation that lay ahead. She scanned the shelves while she was waiting and took down a copy of *England and the Octopus*, Clough's book on architecture.

The French windows opened onto the lawn, and she walked over to a table, but stopped awkwardly when she realised that Bella Hutton was already seated there, her figure hidden by the armchair's high back. As familiar as Josephine was with actors and actresses, she could not help but be struck by how strange it felt to be face to face with a real movie star. Bella was staring across to the other side of the estuary, deep in thought, and although she must have heard Josephine approach, she did nothing to acknowledge her presence. The table in front of her showed no sign of drinks or afternoon tea, and Josephine guessed that she was here simply for the peace. She hesitated, reluctant to intrude but loath, too, to make a hasty, embarrassing exit. In the end, the problem was solved for her. 'It's all right,' Bella said. 'Come and sit down. The room's big enough for both of us.'

She spoke without looking round, a weary note in her voice, and Josephine knew that she must be sick to death of seeing rabbits in headlights wherever she went. Her own fame was tiresome enough, but Bella Hutton's was a level of celebrity that must make any attempt at a normal life impossible. 'Thank you, but I'll go somewhere else,' she said. 'You've managed to find some peace and quiet, and I don't want to be the one who disturbs it. Mine might not be a very restful conversation.'

'Is there such a thing?'

'Probably not if it involves talking terms with Alma Reville.'

The name brought a reaction, but not the one she was expecting. Bella looked at her for the first time. 'Are you Josephine Tey?'

'Yes. How did you know?'

'Oh, there's always gossip about Hitch's next project, and they've let it be known that it involves the author of *Richard of Bordeaux*. You're a versatile lady. Not many people mix historical plays with crime fiction and do both of them well.' She smiled. 'I shouldn't prejudice your negotiations, but they seem to think they've bought you already. Discreet enquiries have been made with my agent.'

'I don't know whether to be flattered by their enthusiasm or offended by their cheek.'

'I'm impressed you've noticed there's a choice. Most people gravitate towards them like moths to a flame at the slightest encouragement. Haven't you heard it?' She paused and pretended to listen. 'The walls here echo to the sound of people panting, and it has nothing to do with the heat.' Josephine laughed. The wisecrack was typical of the series of smart, resilient women Bella Hutton had played on screen – always a step ahead and in touch with the modern age, and actually far better suited to the harsher Depression era than they had been to the sweetness of the 1920s. Unlike most of her contemporaries, Bella's professional reputation had improved as she aged.

'What did they offer you?' Josephine asked, trying to think of a role in the book that would suit her.

'The heroine's aunt.'

'But she hasn't got an aunt.'

'Not in your version, no. I noticed that when I read it.' Bella saw the expression on Josephine's face. 'Sorry. I didn't mean to put you off before Alma even gets here.'

'You haven't. I'm just cross I didn't think of it first. If I'd known you were a possibility, I'd have given Erica an aunt myself.'

Bella smiled. 'Sadly, I've had to decline. The timing doesn't work for me. It's a shame, because I like what you do very much.' She gestured to the chair opposite. 'Please, Josephine – join me while you wait for Alma. She'll be ten minutes late. She always is.'

Josephine sat down, surprised by the sudden familiarity and feeling a little like Pip on his first visit to Miss Havisham. There could only be ten years or so between them, but Bella's long career, sophisticated image and formidable reputation made her feel like an awkward child in comparison. 'If being late is a ploy to soften me up, I'd like to think it would take longer than ten minutes, but I couldn't guarantee it.'

'Ten minutes is good by Hollywood standards. You obviously haven't spent much time in America.'

'I've never been.'

'So you didn't see *Richard of Bordeaux* on Broadway?' Josephine shook her head. 'Probably just as well. It wasn't a patch on the West End production. But the play of yours that I really loved was *The Laughing Woman*.'

Josephine was surprised and pleased. The play she had written about the sculptor, Henri Gaudier-Brzeska, had been the least successful of her West End productions, but it was the one she was fondest of, if only because it had had very little interference from a producer and still felt like hers when the curtain went up. There was a lesson about pride in there somewhere, but not one she cared to think about so close to her meeting with Alma. 'I'm glad you liked it,' she said. 'It was important to me.'

'Did you know him?'

The vision of herself as a sophisticated teenager swanning around the sort of artistic circles that Bella Hutton must have moved in amused Josephine, but she didn't disillusion her by making that obvious. 'No. I based it entirely on other people's memoirs, and picked the brains of a sculptor friend of mine in Primrose Hill. Actually, I made the mistake of taking her to see it one night and she spent the whole performance laughing at the clay head they had on stage. I was quite relieved when he smashed it.'

'He smashed a lot of things, I gather,' Bella said. 'Perhaps he might have been more careful if he'd known how little time he had left to create a body of work. If I think my life's gone by in a flash, how must he have felt?' The question had a melancholy note to it which seemed personal, but it was rhetorical, and Bella moved on before Josephine had time to consider what it might imply. 'I met him once, you know – at a dinner party very much like the one you describe in the play. As far as I can tell, you and your actors did him a great service. That's the film Hitch should make.'

'I don't think tormented artists have quite the same box-office appeal as murdered actresses.'

'No, you're right, and there's a perverse comfort in that, I suppose. Good news for someone that I'll still be making money when I'm dead. Perhaps I should take a leaf out of your murdered actress's book and leave it all to charity.' As a stranger, Josephine found it difficult to read the expression on Bella's face but the bitterness in her voice was unmistakable. Too shy to probe further, she changed the subject. 'You started out on the stage, didn't you?'

'Yes, but only briefly. My training, if you can call it that, consisted of understudying at the Vaudeville for a few months.' Josephine listened, captivated, as the movie star talked about her early days in London before moving to America. It was easy to see why Bella Hutton was one of very few actresses who had successfully made the transition from silent films to modern movies. Most stars – Leyton Turnbull, for example – had lost work because their own voice was so unlike the one the audience had imagined for them over years of devoted viewing; there was nothing worse than hearing the epitome of virility speak in a high-pitched voice or with a speech defect. Women faded from view and leading men became villains overnight, but Bella's distinctive voice – strong and low-registered, Americanised to a carefully judged degree – suited her essential toughness and had enabled her to transform herself over and over again. 'Then I was spotted by Maxwell Hutton on one of his trips to London, and he whisked me off to New York and got me in as a player at Vitagraph. The rest, as the lawyers say, is alimony.' She smiled sadly. 'The theatre was a happy time for me, though – the first taste of freedom. Sometimes I wish I'd never left it, but he was a very difficult man to turn down.'

'He certainly knew how to shape your career.' Bella's marriage to the maverick producer had been one of the legendary show-business partnerships, generously giving the movie magazines all they could ask for, from unlikely love story to acrimonious divorce. 'Apart from nearly killing you on the *Titanic*, it seems to me he didn't put a foot wrong.'

Bella threw back her head and laughed. 'No, I don't suppose he did. That trip was his engagement present to me. It was sup-posed to be my grand farewell to England before we married. I always used to tease him about knowing it was going to sink, because in spite of all the hard work it really *was* that story that made my career. Up to then, I'd done a good crowd scene in *A Tale of Two Cities* and that was about it.'

It would have taken a better woman than Josephine to cham-pion discretion over curiosity in this case, and her one conces-sion to decency was to keep the sensationalism out of her voice. 'What was that night really like?' she asked.

The sun, lower now in the sky, had crept in under the top of the French windows, and Bella leant forward to feel it on her face, closing her eyes as she talked. 'We were in my cabin when it hit. We'd been for a walk on deck, but we didn't stay out for long because it was so cold. All the nights had been like that – crisp, clear skies full of stars, the air fresh and exhilar-ating. The sort of weather that goes well with a new life, I re-member thinking. It was a jolt, that's all. Neither of us really thought much about it until we noticed the silence. The hum of those engines had become so familiar, and suddenly they weren't there. Max went out to see what was happening, and one of the crew told him we'd grazed an iceberg. We were to go up on deck with our lifebelts on, but it was just a precaution. No one was the slightest bit concerned, even when they unroped the lifeboats.' She shook her head in disbelief. 'They dropped the boats down until they were level with our deck. I had to leave Max then because the men stayed behind, but it still didn't seem like a big deal – the ship was fine and everyone was calm. The first time I felt any fear at all was when we were being lowered into the sea. It was the size of the thing, I suppose. It would have been so easy to be sucked under. Anyway, we got away to a safe distance and looked back, and this is going to sound strange but it was one of the most beautiful things I've ever seen.'

Josephine could believe it. As a fifteen-year-old, she had watched enthralled as the newsreels showed the *Titanic* pulling out of Southampton, and it had never entirely lost that sense of grandeur in her own mind, even as she had pored over the artists' impressions of the ship going down. 'Then the lights went out, and we realised that the decks had been gradually filling with water all the time,' Bella continued. 'No one spoke. We just watched in silence as that huge silhouette tilted straight on end. She stayed like that for about five minutes, and all you could hear was the roar of machinery sliding down through the hull. It was like watching a silent film, now I think about it – one where the music's not quite right. There were women all around me with their mouths open in a scream, and all I could hear was the tearing and crashing of metal. The soundtrack from Hell, you might say. Just when I thought it couldn't get any worse, the ship disappeared; one quiet, slanting movement into the sea, and she was gone. And then you could hear the screams – not us on the boats this time, but the poor devils in the water. It was so cold, Josephine, and we couldn't do anything but watch them die. And you know what? We had empty seats in that lifeboat. It was all so random, like some kind of judgement being played out in front of you.'

It was an extraordinary account, and the storyteller in Josephine admired the quiet, evocative way in which Bella told it. 'When did you find out that your husband was safe?' she asked.

'Not until much later. The *Carpathia* picked the survivors up and took us to New York, and we found each other on board. He'd managed to get a place on one of the last rafts off.'

She expected Bella to add something about her relief at the reunion, but the actress was quiet. 'I'm surprised you ever crossed the Atlantic again. I'm not sure I'd have been able to set foot on another ship if I'd been through that.'

'I didn't for a long time. But things happen, life moves on, and people force you into facing things you'd rather avoid.' Josephine remembered what Ronnie had said about Bella's sudden return to Britain and considered asking her about it, but she hesitated and the moment was lost. 'It's probably just as well that they do, and it's second nature to me now.' A knowing smile transformed her face. 'Anyway, a star's fee begins on the day she leaves home, so it pays to take your time. The bigger the cheque, the faster I forget.' She paused, then spoke more seriously. 'But Max knew so much more than how to shape my career, Josephine. I've never loved anyone the way I love him.' The present tense jumped out at Josephine, although Bella seemed oblivious to having used it. 'That trip was the most romantic thing you could ever imagine, and it was so typical of him. It should have told me something when the damned thing hit an iceberg, though, shouldn't it? It's not what you see that matters; it's what lurks below the surface. A sharper girl would have learnt from that.'

Normally, Josephine would not have dreamt of asking anyone she had just met about a failed marriage, but she reminded herself now that Bella Hutton was hardly conventional company. 'What did he do to hurt you so badly?' she asked.

'He disillusioned me. He turned out to be just like all the rest: a powerful man with smart clothes and dirty hands. In fact, now I think about it, no man in my life has *ever* turned out to be the person I thought he was. And doubt chokes love. There's no going back from there.'

'Do you wish you'd never met him?'

'Ah, what a good question. No, I've never quite managed that. I just wish I'd been right about him.' She stared out of the window, and Josephine waited for her to decide how much more to say. 'It's funny, isn't it, what we'll give up for love? It never makes any sense. I was thinking about that this afternoon – being in the Prince of Wales suite gave it a certain irony.' She noticed Josephine's questioning glance. 'Sorry, I forgot – nobody here knows that we're about to lose our king to an American divorcee, do they? The papers are so beautifully discreet about it. I'm afraid journalists in the States lack their sense of restraint. It must be a defect in the republican genes.'

'What on earth do you mean?'

Bella seemed to relish her astonishment. 'The King, by all

accounts, is taking things a little too far with his mistress. Some say he'll give up his crown for her.'

'Why would he do that? He can have both – there's no need for him to be so ridiculous about it. No,' she added, beginning to feel a little naive in the face of Bella's certainty, 'he'll never let go of the throne.'

'Oh, he will. I've met her. But what I can't understand is why we're so in awe of his dilemma. All of us make that choice at some point in our lives. It's a very lucky man who doesn't pay for what he loves.'

'It doesn't usually cost a kingdom, though.'

'Not in reality, no – but doesn't it always feel like that?'

It was Josephine's turn to give an ironic smile. 'I'm not sure I can answer that. Ask me again in six months.'

'Not possible, I'm afraid.'

There was a finality to the way she said it that signalled more than the unlikelihood of their meeting again. 'Is six months really so long?' Josephine asked quietly.

Bella looked at her appraisingly, and seemed to make a decision to trust her. 'I'm dying, Josephine. There's nothing they can do, and it's weeks rather than months.' The words were spoken with a lack of emotion which would have been completely alien to any screen performance she had given, as though Bella were merely discussing an inconvenience to her daily routine. She moved on quickly, deliberately making a response impossible, but if she had had all the time in the world Josephine would have found it hard to know what to say. The sudden, profound sadness that she felt, a mourning for more than the woman in front of her, could not be adequately articulated by the usual expressions of regret. 'What did I tell you?

It's the thing you can't see that always gets you. And I don't suppose I'll be able to keep it a secret for long, but I'd appreciate it if you didn't tell anyone. The insurance alone will be such an inconvenience to the studios.'

The darker subtext that she had felt so strongly in some of Bella's words now made perfect sense to Josephine. 'Of course I won't say anything.' It was an easy promise to make; in Bella's position, she would want nothing more than to keep her illness as private as possible and come to terms with the end of her life in her own way.

'Thank you. Dying isn't easy when you're famous – people act very differently when they realise they've only a limited amount of time to get what they need from you.' She looked shrewdly at Josephine and said, 'Usually, I'd feel the need to apologise for my cynicism, but I get the impression from your book that we view celebrity in much the same way. There's a lot of truth in the way your character talks about fame, and somehow I don't think you got *that* from other people's memoirs. It doesn't sit well with you, does it?'

'No, it doesn't,' Josephine said truthfully. 'I don't like the way it encourages people to think they know you when they don't.'

Bella nodded. 'And to compensate for that, you end up becoming someone you don't always recognise yourself.' She treated Josephine to a world-weary glance, straight out of one of her films. 'And you'll understand now that I found Christine Clay's death strangely prophetic when I read your book. I imagine people will react to mine in much the same way – pity, dismay and horror, but very little real grief.'

'What about your family?' Josephine asked. 'Is that why you've come back – to be with them?' Bella looked so surprised that Josephine suddenly doubted Lettice's information. 'I'm sorry – I thought you were born here?'

'Yes I was, but I always forget how much people know. I suppose even I could learn something about my life if I read enough newspapers.' It wasn't an accusation, but Josephine reproached herself for being guilty of the very thing that she had claimed to despise in others. Bella pointed across the estuary. 'I grew up in that house over there. My family name was Draycott, and there were four children. I was the middle of three sisters and we had an older brother called Henry. He wasn't a nice man. Once he inherited the house from my parents, the rest of us couldn't wait to get out.' She took an exquisite art-nouveau cigarette case from her bag and offered it to Josephine. 'Do you know Portmeirion well?'

'I've been a few times.'

'Then you'll have heard about the eccentric old woman and her graveyard for dogs?' Josephine nodded. 'Well, that was Grace, my older sister – except she wasn't really old, and she wasn't really eccentric. She rented this house for many years, but she didn't deserve the reputation she seems to have. She was no fairy-tale witch, just a gentle woman who took in strays and mourned them when they were gone.'

Intrigued, Josephine said, 'It must upset you to come back here and listen to strangers talking about your own sister.'

'It feels disloyal to sit there and say nothing, but I'm too tired to argue, Josephine. Is that cowardly of me?'

'I imagine it preys more heavily on your conscience than it does on hers.' She smiled. 'I don't have the sunniest reputation in my home town, although I've only got myself to blame for much of that. But it doesn't really bother me now, and I certainly wouldn't want my sister to lose sleep over it when I'm dead. Would Grace have cared what people say?'

'No, probably not. She'd be too busy laughing at the thought of the heir to the throne having slept in her bedroom. Anyway, compared to the rest of the family, her eccentricities are fairly tame.'

'Oh?' Josephine said encouragingly, hoping that Bella would have time to finish her story before Alma Reville joined them.

'My younger sister, May, ran off with one of the Gypsies who passed through every summer – much to the moral outrage of all the people round here, of course, but she knew her own mind. And *she* really *didn't* give a damn about what people thought of her. I suppose she must have had the romantic streak of the family.'

'Are you telling me that Hollywood isn't romantic?'

'Only from the outside looking in. When you see it up close, it's got more cracks in it than the House of Usher. But May's romance was very real. Tobin was the love of her life and a good man by all accounts, although I never really knew him. I was too busy with my own life. Not that love did her any good in the long run. She died having their second child, little more than a kid herself.' There was a restrained anger in her voice. Josephine guessed that it was half grief and half guilt at her absence during her family's sadness; she knew, too, that there was nothing she could say to make Bella feel any better. 'So no,' the actress said matter-of-factly, 'there's no one left here to grieve for me, even if I wanted them to.'

'What about your brother?' Josephine asked. 'Is he still alive?'

'Sadly, yes.'

'But he doesn't live here?'

'No. He ran off with a married woman from Portmadoc – his wife's best friend, actually. Loyalty was never something that either of them aspired to. His wife still lives there,' she said, nodding to her family home, 'and I think she was glad to see the back of him. As I said, not a nice man, but nothing he does ever seems to come back to haunt him like it would in a just world; he simply moves on and blights someone else's life. He certainly won't be shedding any tears on my account, any more than I would for him.' She spoke dispassionately, as if she were recounting the plot of her latest film, then lowered her voice and added with more feeling, 'Thinking about it, that's another thing I seem to have in common with your Miss Clay – a healthy capacity for hatred, particularly where our brothers are concerned. Sometimes, Josephine, I wonder if it's actually hate which is eating me up inside and not cancer at all.'

'Have you been to see his wife?' Josephine asked, wondering if the intensity with which Bella had been watching the house when she first came in was down to a human connection or simply an attachment to the bricks and mortar of home.

'Gwyneth? No. I haven't seen her for eighteen years. She hides herself away from everyone as much as she can, and I'm not surprised. What happened to her isn't the sort of thing you just get over.' Josephine looked curious. 'Just after Henry left her, Gwyneth found out she was pregnant,' Bella explained. She never told him because she didn't want him back, but she adored that child, and Grace took her in for a while and helped her as much as she could – not out of family duty, but because she genuinely liked Gwyneth and she had the kindest heart of anyone I've ever known. Three years later, Taran went missing and was never seen again, dead or alive. It destroyed her – the loss, and then the uncertainty. So the house has become an obsession with her, something she's terrified to leave in case Taran is still alive and doesn't know where to find her. She cut herself off from everything and everyone the day that child disappeared.'

'Doesn't she have *any* idea what happened?'

'No. There was talk of an abduction, and the locals turned on an outsider – out of desperation, I hasten to add, rather than knowledge.' She looked down. 'That was the worst part for me. The outsider was May's Gypsy.'

'But surely he didn't . . .'

'Of course not, but violence and prejudice don't work according to reason, do they? Remember the mob scene in *The Lodger*?' Josephine nodded. 'It was just like that, except Tobin wasn't as lucky as Mr Novello. Nobody remembered to write him a happy ending.'

'What happened?' Josephine asked.

'They killed him. There used to be an old cottage in the woods, and they cornered him there like an animal. It was all conveniently brushed over, of course. There was a long and bitter history between the Gypsies and the men from the town – fights every summer when the camp arrived, accusations of vandalism and theft on both sides, rows over women. But the locals stuck together on this one, and the police weren't exactly diligent. As far as they were concerned, one less Gypsy in the world was a public service. Anyway, no one could prove who was ultimately responsible, and they could hardly arrest the whole mob.' She gave a heavy sigh. 'Grace was devastated, but at least May was dead by then. She never had to see it.'

'Surely the police could have worked a bit harder to find out who *was* to blame?' Josephine said, thinking about Archie and the personal responsibility he took for every case he worked on. 'You can't turn a blind eye to someone's death just because it's difficult.'

Bella was quiet for so long that Josephine began to wonder if she had finally overstepped the mark; the story, though freely told, was not hers to comment on. 'No,' the actress said eventually, but her tone was wistful rather than resentful. 'No, I don't suppose you can.'

Another couple sat down at the next table, and Josephine watched as the girl made a less than subtle gesture towards the film star. 'It must be difficult to try to make peace with your ghosts in the middle of a busy hotel.'

'It's probably the best thing that could have happened to the place. When something's too dark, covering it with glamour and glitz is the only way. Hollywood depends on it. I've done it all my life. But you're right – there are ghosts everywhere.' She leant forward and surprised Josephine by taking her hand. 'Thank you,' she said. 'I didn't realise it until you sat down, but I needed to talk to someone – someone who, sadly, I'll never meet again. You've been very kind, and you've helped me make my mind up.'

'Can I ask what about?'

Bella shook her head. 'No, I've said enough, and, if I'm right, you'll soon find out.' She looked up and withdrew her hand. 'Anyway, the power behind the throne has just arrived, and there's not a chance in Hell of an abdication there.'

'Miss Tey – I hope I haven't kept you waiting.' Alma Reville had changed into a rust silk-crêpe evening dress which emphasised the auburn shades of her hair, and its formality, together with a perfect make-up, made her look older than she had at first seemed. Bella raised an eyebrow and subtly tapped her wrist, and Josephine couldn't resist a quick glance at her watch. It was precisely ten past six. 'What would you like to drink?' Alma asked. 'Shall we start with a Martini?'

'Why not? We can switch to something stronger later if I need it.'

'I hope you won't. Bella? Can I get you something?' The offer was formal, and Josephine noticed a cool civility between the two women. Alma seemed relieved when the actress declined and left them to it. She beckoned a waiter and ordered their cocktails with an authority that suggested she was used to having people at her command, and a warmth which told Josephine that she never took it for granted. She nodded at the book which Josephine still held in her hand. 'Not much time for reading when Bella's around.'

'No, but I probably do too much of that anyway,' Josephine said, matching the subtlety of the probing in the way it was deflected. 'It's always easier to read other people's books than to write your own. I used to justify my time by calling it research. Now I'm just shameless about it.'

'I suppose I'm lucky. We're always looking for new projects, so I could call anything work and get away with it. I'm afraid it takes me for ever to read a novel, though. I can't pick one up without imagining every camera angle, or dramatising every scene and piece of dialogue.'

The comment was friendly enough, but that only made it more irritating. 'How interesting,' Josephine said before she could stop herself. 'Most authors rather imagine they've saved you the bother.'

To her credit, Alma looked embarrassed. 'I'm sorry. That

must have sounded very rude, but it wasn't intended to be. All I meant was that it's my job to see a story in pictures. I've been doing it since I was a teenager and it's a very hard habit to break.' She thought for a moment, choosing her words more carefully this time. 'A film can't just be a visual record of a book or it will never have a life of its own,' she said. 'You saw *The 39 Steps*?' Josephine nodded. 'And you must have read the book, so you'll know that most of the things that made it a great movie were entirely Hitch's invention – the love interest, Mr Memory, the scene at the London Palladium. It's those things that a film audience responds to, but none of them would have been possible without the book.' Josephine's scepticism must have been written all over her face, because Alma added, 'It's like any marriage, I suppose. The two things *can* coexist if they're both good in their own right, and it doesn't have to be one at the expense of the other.' She smiled. 'I know what you're thinking: that's easy for me to say when it's not my book which is being vandalised. I can understand why you might feel protective.'

'Overprotective, probably, but that's only because this particular marriage is so uneven – when people start making books out of films, authors might relax a little.'

'And film-makers will bring a whole new meaning to the word indignation. Hitch hates it if a producer makes the slightest alteration to the way he's filmed something.' Their drinks arrived, and Alma picked the glass up gratefully. 'Can we start again?' she asked. 'I know how hypocritical it all must sound, but it's important that I'm honest with you from the start. If you allow us to base our film on *A Shilling for Candles*, changes will have to be made.'

'Such as?' Josephine asked, aware of how carefully the last sentence had been phrased.

'It's too early to say in any detail, but some characters will have a much bigger role and others will go altogether. Your plot won't necessarily be our plot, and you might be surprised at how quickly our storyline diverges from the one you've written. Some of the changes you'll hate; others – I hope – you'll understand, and even like.'

Josephine admired her frankness, even if she was a little unsettled by it. 'And I dare say none of those changes would be detrimental to the book's sales,' she said wryly. 'Or to the box-office receipts.'

Alma raised her glass. 'That much we *can* agree on.'

'Tell me – if your husband wants to use so little of my story, why don't you just go ahead and write your own? Surely that would save you the trouble of consulting anyone?'

'Because the idea is yours, and it seems right to recognise that – financially and creatively. We could just develop the movie from it in our own way without giving you or the book any credit whatsoever. I've seen that happen, but it's not how we do things.'

It was an honourable attitude, although Josephine couldn't help thinking that the other way might be kinder in the long run. She noticed how naturally Alma referred to the work as a joint endeavour, and began to understand the extent to which when people spoke of a Hitchcock film they were unconsciously referring to a partnership. 'How do you choose which ideas to work on?' she asked, genuinely interested.

'We read the review pages, see new plays in the West End, wade through manuscripts.' She smiled. 'And sometimes we get a nudge in the right direction. Miss Fox did us a favour. When she gave us your book, we were rather stuck.'

'Oh?'

Alma hesitated, and Josephine sensed she was gauging how honest she could be without causing offence. 'To be quite frank, Miss Tey, we were hoping for another John Buchan, but he was far too busy being Governor General of Canada even to see us.'

Josephine laughed and finished her Martini. She looked directly at Alma. 'Does either of you actually *like* the book, Miss Reville?'

'My husband sees its potential,' she said diplomatically, but then spoke far more warmly. 'And I like the book, Miss Tey. I like it very much, and I'd be delighted if you'd consider working on it with us.'

'Oh, I don't know about that. Other than a twice-weekly visit to the cinema, I know nothing about the film world. As you say, it's very different from writing a novel.'

'But not so different from writing a play. A lot of the best screenwriters come from the theatre and we'd be lucky to have you, so don't dismiss it.' She accepted a cigarette and leant forward to have it lit. 'I often think I'd like to write a novel, you know, if only because I could do that on my own.'

It was the first time that Alma had hinted at a professional ambition which existed independently from her husband's career, and it surprised Josephine. 'I got the impression that the partnership was as important to you as the work,' she said. 'Wouldn't you miss that?'

'Of course, but it can't go on for ever and I'll need something to take its place.' She signalled for more drinks, and answered

127

Josephine's questioning glance. 'Don't get me wrong: I love being part of a team, but it's not always like that now. The team is becoming an organisation, and organisations are always about power, even if their business is a creative one.' She sighed, and absent-mindedly twisted her wedding ring. 'I'll always support Hitch, of course I will. He involves me in everything he does, and my opinion is invariably the one he listens to, even at the expense of his own, but it's the sort of support that a wife gives a husband. If – when – he goes to America, there'll be no place for me as his equal. Not in other people's minds, anyway.'

'If it were me, I'd resent that.'

'I don't know how I'll feel,' Alma said honestly. 'And I won't until it happens. Back when we started, we didn't think about the future. It was just a case of muddling through together, trying things out and doing the best we could. Film wasn't really any older than we were, so there were no rules. That sense of adventure isn't there any more; we all have to pretend we know exactly what we're doing.' She smiled. 'It's been replaced by other excitements, of course, and by opportunities which we could only dream of back then. Still, I miss it.'

'How *did* you start?' Josephine asked. 'Marta told me that you were involved in cinema before your husband.'

'Yes, I was about four years ahead of him,' Alma said, although there was no hint of competitiveness in her voice. 'When I was young we lived in Twickenham, just round the corner from the London Film Company studios. My father worked in the costume department there, and he used to take me to work with him. I fell in love with it the moment I first walked on a set, and that hasn't changed.' Josephine could understand that: she had never been inside a film studio in her life, but the magic of the cinema had captivated her since she was a child, and she would never forget the first time her mother had taken her to see something. It was just the two of them, one of those precious times which she guarded jealously as a privilege of being the oldest daughter, and back in the days when films were shown in converted shops or halls rather than designated cinemas. She had no idea which picture they had been to see, but it didn't matter; it was the sudden connection to a more adventurous, more romantic world that had excited her, a sense of escape which stayed with her to this day. 'As soon as I could, I got a job there,' Alma continued. 'I started right at the bottom and made myself useful by doing every odd job I could find. It was the best way to develop the technical skills I needed to get on.'

'You weren't tempted to try the other side of the camera?'

'What teenage girl wasn't? But I soon realised that there was far more security as a technician than as an actress, and I've always been blessed with a practical streak.'

'But it was still very glamorous, I suppose.'

'Yes and no. The job itself was very tedious and very precise, and these have paid the price for it,' she said, pointing to her eyes. 'You don't cut and splice films by hand for a living if you want to hang on to your eyesight, but I wouldn't have had it any other way.'

'Did your husband work his way up in the same way?'

'Yes, he started by designing title cards. The first time I set eyes on him, he was carrying an enormous package of them under his arm. He was very confident, even then.' She smiled, more to herself than at Josephine. 'The studio was like a second home to me. I loved watching people's first reactions to it – the lights and the cameras and the noise of technicians shouting at each other. It intimidated most people, but not Hitch; he just walked calmly across the floor to the production office like he'd been born to it.'

'And that impressed you?'

'To be honest, I thought he was a bit snooty. His first words were a job offer, and I was grateful for it: the studios had made a lot of people redundant by then and I'd been out of work for months. I suppose you could say it worked. We've been together ever since.' Her warmth had a wistful quality to it, but Josephine could still sense the enthusiasm she felt for those early days and the excitement that such a partnership must have inspired. 'We had no inkling of what was to come,' she added, more cynically this time. 'No thought of sound or colour. Or of money, and how a business can make and destroy people.'

'You're not selling it to me,' Josephine said doubtfully. 'I think I'll stay on the outside.'

Alma laughed. 'Don't let me put you off. We're by no means typical. It doesn't have to be your life, and plenty of people manage to keep it in perspective. Marta, for example. The work she's done on *The Passing of the Third Floor Back* has been excellent, and she doesn't seem to have suffered for dabbling in a murky world. Just the opposite, in fact.'

'I know she enjoyed it.'

'I got the impression it was more than that. She needed it. Or, rather, she needed the satisfaction it gave her to do it well.' Josephine looked at her and realised that she never missed a thing. It was true: Marta's life had been unsettled for years, but Josephine knew from her letters that she had gained a new confidence from the work that Alma Reville had offered her. 'Of course, it's harder for women in film these days. Back in the

1920s, when everyone thought it was an adventure that was going nowhere, there were plenty of opportunities; now there's money in it, the men are suddenly taking themselves very seriously and those chances are fewer. But Hitch is different.'

'You make sure of that, I imagine.'

'I do my bit.' She winked conspiratorially. 'Whatever its faults, there's a lot of satisfaction in the work. Perhaps I shouldn't have given you an insider's view.'

'It's not just that. I'd miss the magic of it if I got too close. I don't want to see the nuts and bolts of how a film is made, the friction and the egos and the jealousies. Selfishly, I don't want it spoilt.'

'Do people disappoint you, Miss Tey?'

The question came from nowhere, and Josephine was taken aback by it. 'What a strange thing to ask,' she said.

'Not really. I was thinking about the murder victim in your book. For a dead woman, she speaks very eloquently and I rather thought there was a lot of you in her.' As Josephine hesitated, she added, 'Perhaps what I really mean is there's a lot of me in her. We seem to have a great deal in common, and not just being born into a Nottingham lace family.'

'In what way?' Josephine asked, but she was still considering Alma's question. It was the second time in half an hour that she had been compared to Christine Clay. Now she thought about it, it was true: a lot of what she had put into that character *did* reflect her own attitudes, but she was surprised it was so obvious to strangers.

'It's what someone says about her going from Nottingham to the top of the film world and how fame propels you through such different social spheres so quickly that you lose sight of who you are. I think you likened it to a diver coming up from a long way down and continually adjusting to the pressure?' Josephine nodded. 'You don't use an image like that unless you know how it feels. And I suspect that keeping people guessing is your shell, just as it was hers.'

'I suppose so, although clearly that shell isn't as protective as I thought it was.'

'Oh, I don't know. From what we've been able to find out about you, it's reasonably effective – no interviews, nothing personal in the public domain, in fact. My husband calls you a Theodora.' Josephine shrugged, and Alma explained. 'She's a character in a Capra picture who writes a best-seller which is scandalous to the society she moves in.'

'I'd hardly call a detective novel scandalous.'

'Of course not, but it sets you apart from what you were born to. Does your family really like what you do? Does the town you grew up in celebrate your success, or resent you a little for it? Can you be yourself there?' Alma took Josephine's smile to mean she was right. 'I know how that feels,' she said, 'and it's bound to affect you in some way. At least America will be an improvement in that sense: there's no class system like there is in England.'

'You're surely not telling me that Hollywood doesn't have its own hierarchies?' Josephine asked. 'America might be too new to call it class, but there'll be something set up by now to keep everyone looking over their shoulders.' The more personal turn which the conversation had taken would normally have made Josephine uncomfortable, but she found she liked Alma more for her honesty and it made her want to respond in kind. 'In answer to your original question, yes – I suppose people do disappoint me. Perhaps it's the times we've lived through, but we seem very good at destroying each other, and not just through wars. We wear each other down all the time through little acts of jealousy or cruelty or greed. I look at people's faces in the street, and so very few of them are happy; mostly they're tired or worried or angry – or just bewildered.' She ran her finger around the rim of her glass, thinking. 'When was the last time you stood in a crowd and felt contentment?' she asked. 'Not in a theatre or cinema – we go there to escape, so they don't count. I mean a crowd of ordinary people doing everyday things like shopping or queuing for a bus?' This time, it was Alma's turn to have no answer. 'And most of all I disappoint myself,' Josephine admitted, thinking about her feelings for Marta and how they threatened her friendship with Lydia, not to mention her own integrity and peace of mind. 'We all like to think we're above that, but sooner or later we meet someone who shows us what we're really capable of. That's never a very comfortable realisation.'

'No. No, it isn't.' Reluctantly, Alma looked at her watch. 'I must go and get Hitch for dinner,' she said, 'but perhaps we can continue this conversation later. And whatever you decide about working on a screenplay with us, I hope I haven't put you off a film of your book altogether.'

'Of course not, but I'll need some time to think about it.' Alma nodded, and they walked out onto the terrace together. 'Would you involve Marta in the adaptation?' Josephine asked, glancing over to where she sat with Lydia.

'I'm afraid not. She'd never be ruthless enough with your work. You have quite a fan there, but I'm sure you know that already.' Josephine felt herself blush and looked away. 'It's a shame. She'd have made an excellent job of it. But I suppose the benefits of friendship outweigh a decent script. As my husband would say, it's only a movie.'

'Aren't you worried that it will affect your marriage?' Josephine asked. 'The fame, I mean, and Hollywood. Do you ever worry that you might be on the receiving end of that ruthlessness one day?'

'All the time, and I've no doubt it will happen sooner rather than later. But we love each other, Miss Tey, and more importantly we understand each other. We were both lonely children, unpopular at school, solitary within our own families. Hitch often says that's where he gets his imagination from: he was forced to live in it for so long. In a sense, we've given each other the life we never thought we'd have, and that's a very strong bond. I'm confident it can withstand most of the challenges we throw at it.'

What Alma brought to the partnership was obvious to Josephine, but what she received in exchange was less clear. 'What's the most important thing about your marriage?' she asked. 'The thing that prevents it from being one of you at the expense of the other?'

There was no hesitation about the response. 'In the ten years we've been together, my husband has never once bored me, Miss Tey.' She smiled and held out her hand. 'How many wives can say that?'

3

Branwen had known the journey would be a waste of time even before she set out. As she hurried to her room to change at the end of her afternoon shift, she thought about the miles and hours she had clocked up going to that house only to be greeted by drawn curtains and locked doors, and there was no reason to suppose that today would be any different. But still she had gone, because the victory was hers and she needed Gwyneth Draycott to know that all her secrecy had been in vain. Gwyneth wasn't the only one who knew what had happened to Branwen's mother, and Branwen couldn't care less where the truth came from as long as it was told. She had spent years pretending that it didn't matter. Only in that second when Bella Hutton had agreed to talk to her could she finally admit to herself that it *did*, that her life so far had been entirely defined by her mother's absence, a life of half-truths and silence and wondering.

With her message safely delivered, Branwen cycled back to the hotel, grateful that most of the return journey was downhill. Her dress stuck to her skin, and she took first one hand and then the other off the handlebars, trying without much success to wipe the sweat off her palms. She was too preoccupied with the heat and the evening ahead to concentrate much on where she was going, and, as she rounded a bend on the wrong side of the road, she had to swerve quickly into a passing place to avoid a car coming the other way. In her panic, she braked far too sharply, and the bicycle skidded from under her on some loose stones, sending her crashing to the ground. She lay there for a moment, dazed, until the angry hooting had faded into the distance and all she could hear was her front wheel spinning uselessly in the air, then got gingerly to her feet. Her stockings were torn and her left leg badly grazed below the knee where it had taken the brunt of her fall. No wonder it hurt so much: some idiot had left a broken beer bottle behind, and small shards of glass mixed with dirt had embedded themselves in her skin. Wincing, she bent down and removed the worst of it, but was dismayed to find that her bike had fared even worse than she had: the back tyre was completely flat, punctured by the neck of the bottle, and she still had two miles to go. Blinking back tears of frustration, Branwen started to half wheel, half carry the offending machine along the road, but she hadn't got far before she heard another car coming up behind her, the expensive one that had been parked over near the Draycott house. The driver pulled in to the side when he saw her, and she recognised him as the film star who was staying at the hotel.

'You look as though you could do with some help,' he said, getting out.

Branwen smiled. 'It's not my lucky day, I don't reckon. Those nylons cost me a week's tips.'

'Never mind the stockings. That looks nasty.' He took a handkerchief from his top pocket and put it to his mouth to wet it. 'Here – it needs bathing.' She thought he was going to pass it to her but he knelt down to do it himself. 'This might sting a bit. Be brave.'

'Quite the hero, aren't you?' Branwen said, looking down at him. 'On screen and off.' His frown confused her for a moment, then she noticed the lines under his eyes and the grey at his temples and realised that he thought she was making fun of him. 'When I was a kid, I used to want to be Mae Murray just so I could dance with you,' she added. 'Can't say I've grown out of it.'

Her sincerity seemed to convince Turnbull. 'You obviously

have me at a disadvantage,' he said, and she struggled to associate the voice with the face she knew from the screen. 'What's your name?'

'Branwen.'

'Well, Branwen – can I give you a lift back to the hotel? If that's where you were going, of course.' He looked doubtfully at the bicycle. 'We can probably fit this in the back.'

'Oh, don't worry. It's my day off tomorrow and I can come and pick it up then. No one's going to pinch it in that state, are they? Come to think of it, I might just leave the damned thing where it is for all the use it's been.' She smiled at him and ran her hand approvingly along the side of the car. 'I'd be ever so grateful for a lift, though. I can't afford to be late this evening, and this looks like it'll get me back in no time. Feel like a real movie star, I will.'

He lifted the bicycle over the hedge where it couldn't be seen from the road and opened the door for her. 'What's so special about tonight?' he asked, pressing the starter. 'Business or pleasure?'

'Bit of both, I suppose. I sing with the band sometimes. Nothing special about that – I've been doing it for years – but it's not every night you get Alfred Hitchcock in the audience.'

'No, I don't suppose it is.'

His response was half-hearted, and she put it down to his familiarity with everything she found so exciting; even glamour must fade eventually, she supposed, although he should try doing her job for a few days if he wanted to know what boredom really was. 'I suppose you can afford to be blasé about it when you're one of them,' she teased. 'The rest of us have to grab our fun when we can.' She settled back into her seat, enjoying the smell and feel of the leather. 'So what's Mr Hitchcock like, then? You must know him well.'

'Hitch? I've known him for years.' That wasn't quite the same thing, Branwen thought, but she didn't interrupt him. 'I knew from the first time I met him that he was bound for great things: he was always such a talented boy.' She half listened while he reminisced about his early days in film, mentioning a lot of names she vaguely recognised but telling her very little about Alfred Hitchcock. 'And I have to say, it's nice to be working with him again. I'll introduce you if you like. He's always pleased to meet a talented young lady.' He glanced quickly across at her and added, 'Unless Bella Hutton's already offered? I saw you talking to her earlier.'

'You don't miss much, do you?'

'Can't afford to in my business. And Bella is so rarely nice that one tends to notice when it happens.'

He smiled at her, but there was a bitterness in his voice which made her wary. She hadn't come this far only to ruin everything by making Bella Hutton think that she couldn't be trusted. Anyway, having spent years speculating about her mother with anyone who would listen, Branwen found that the prospect of knowing the truth was something so precious that she wanted to keep it to herself; to talk about it before it actually happened would be to tempt fate. 'No, she didn't mention Mr Hitchcock,' she said truthfully. 'And I'd love to meet him. Thank you.'

She tried to change the subject, but, for someone so self-absorbed, Turnbull was remarkably persistent. 'So what pearls of wisdom *was* Bella sharing with you?' he asked.

'It was nothing like that. She was just talking about how different Portmeirion is now from how she remembers it.' It was only half a lie: Bella Hutton had made it clear by her attitude that she considered her time there to be a different life altogether, but that had nothing to do with a changing landscape. 'She's a bit of a heroine for us local girls. We read about her in the magazines and just for a minute we think her story could be ours. I suppose that sounds daft.'

'Not at all,' he said, then added mockingly: 'Especially if you marry well and divorce in style.'

He slowed the car down as they entered Minffordd village and turned left at the post office. 'You're not local as well, are you?' she asked curiously.

'Good God, no,' he said, laughing. 'What on earth makes you think that?'

'Just that you seem to know your way round, and I saw your car parked out by the old Draycott house.' He shrugged; the name seemed to mean nothing to him. 'It's that big place by the water, over on the other side.'

'I didn't really take much notice of it. Someone told me how magical the village looks from the other side of the estuary and I wanted to see it for myself. They were right: it's breathtaking. But now you mention it, that house does look like it's seen better days.'

'You're right there. The same woman's lived there for years and she hardly ever leaves the place. God knows what it's like inside.'

'Seems like a big house for one person to rattle around in.'

'She's got her ghosts, I suppose. Mad as a badger, Gwyneth is – everyone says so. My grandmother always said it ran in the family.' It wasn't all her grandmother said: Branwen could have filled a book with what she had heard about the Draycott family while she was growing up, and none of it good. 'Can't say I blame the woman, mind. A Gypsy ran off with her kid, so it's not surprising if she's not the full shilling, is it?'

'What?'

He looked at her, astonished, and Branwen basked in the safe attention of someone else's scandal. 'They say she thought she couldn't have kids, then some bastard takes the one she does have. Where's the justice in that? And they never did find the poor little sod. Vicious lot they were, those gippos. They'd have anything if you took your eye off it long enough.' Listening to herself, it was like having her dad in the car with them, speaking over her shoulder; she hadn't realised until now how deeply his prejudices had been absorbed into her own soul, and it shocked her. 'I wouldn't be surprised if they'd buried the kid up there with the dogs in that cemetery. Here – watch it!' Turnbull had taken his eyes off the road, and she reached over to grab the steering wheel and pull them back on course. 'You'll get us both killed if you're not careful.'

'When did all this happen?'

Branwen looked at him, surprised by the intensity of his interest and worried that she had already said too much. Her grandmother had always forbidden her to talk about the incident because of the part her dad had played in the Gypsy's death. 'Twenty years ago, near as damn it – towards the end of the war,' she said cautiously. Her dad was dead and gone now, and she didn't see what harm it could do, but her gran still frightened the living daylights out of her. She tried to think of something to change the subject, but Turnbull wouldn't let it go.

'Was the child a boy or a girl?' Branwen shrugged, deciding that ignorance was the safest tack. 'Come on – you must know.'

'Look, I was only a kid myself. What's it to you anyway?'

'Nothing. Nothing at all. I was just shocked by what you said.' He backed off after that, and Branwen was relieved when they arrived at the entrance to the village. The man on the gate let them through, and the expression on his face when he recognised her was priceless. She smiled brazenly at him. 'Shall I drop you at the hotel?' Turnbull asked, his composure apparently restored.

'That'd be perfect.' Branwen was determined to make the most of her entrance; staff were not allowed to fraternise with the guests, but there wasn't a thing anyone could do about it while she wasn't on duty. She took her lipstick out of her bag and refreshed her make-up, then straightened her stockings as best she could.

Turnbull obliged her by pulling up right outside reception. He hopped out to open the door for her and smiled apologetically as she got out. 'I'm sorry, Branwen. I shouldn't have lost my temper like that. It must be the heat. Please forgive me.'

'Nothing to forgive. It's like water off a duck's back round here, and if it's not the guests, it's the boss.' Out of the corner of her eye, she noticed the restaurant manager watching her from the terrace and kissed Leyton Turnbull provocatively on the cheek. His aftershave was musky and expensive, she noticed, and she was surprised to see him blush. 'See you later, I hope.'

'Of course. And I look forward to hearing you sing.'

Branwen slipped quickly through reception and headed for the staff quarters. Glancing back over her shoulder, she noticed that Leyton Turnbull was still watching her. The expression on his face was impossible to read.

4

'Same again?' Astrid Lake nodded, and Danny walked back across the lawn to the hotel.

Lydia watched him go, trying not to be too cynical about his obvious affection for the young actress. The sliver of envy that reared its ugly head whenever she met someone with her whole career ahead of her had not prevented her from liking Astrid as soon as they were introduced, but she was less sure about Danny's ability to compete – romantically or professionally – in the future that lay ahead of the girl. From what Lydia had seen on screen, Astrid had the sort of radiance that character-ised the young female stars of the silent generation but none of the old-fashioned, rosy-cheeked romanticism; hers was a more sophisticated sexuality, appropriate to a different decade and all the more compelling because it seemed so unselfconscious. Lydia could just about remember what that sort of innocence was like. It made you brave, simply because you were too naive to realise there was anything to be frightened of, and that was a very desirable commodity. 'Have you known Danny long?' she asked.

'Not really. Our paths crossed on a couple of jobs, but I didn't get to know him properly until a few months ago. We were working together on *Looking for Trouble* when he got the news about his father, and he needed someone to talk to.'

Marta waved a wasp away from her drink. 'What happened to his father?'

'He committed suicide, and Danny blamed himself for the fact that they were estranged at the time.' She must have noticed the question in their eyes, because she added, 'I don't know what they fell out over – he won't say – but it must have been serious because they hadn't spoken for years.'

'Miss Lake? Sorry to interrupt, but I just wanted to say hello and make sure you have everything you need?' The man at Astrid's side was tall and broad-shouldered, but it was his smile that was most noticeable. Lydia guessed that he was around thirty, but he had a combination of earnestness and boyish charm which could have placed him five years either side. 'I'm David Franks,' he said. 'I work with Mr Hitchcock.' Had Hitchcock himself been present, 'with' would almost certainly have been changed to 'for', Lydia thought to herself, but she admired Franks's confidence. 'Are you the Marta Fox who's been working with Miss Reville?' he asked, when Astrid introduced them. Marta nodded. 'It's lovely to meet you. She's mentioned you often, but I didn't know you were going to be here.'

He looked Marta approvingly up and down as they shook hands, and Lydia mentally revised her use of the word 'boyish'. God help Danny if Astrid was Franks's type. Marta, on the other hand, was more resistant to charm than anyone else she knew. 'It's a coincidence,' she said. 'We're here for a friend's birthday party.'

Lydia looked at her with a mixture of pride and irritation. She knew that Marta was being modest about the impression she had made with her first attempt at screenwriting, but why did she have to be so casual about everything? If she could only bring herself to be a little more ambitious, life might be easier for them both. Fortunately, Franks didn't seem to have noticed any coolness. 'With a boss like mine, it's always best to double-check the arrangements,' he said. 'He has a talent for surprises.'

'What is it you do for Mr Hitchcock?' Astrid asked.

'Depends what the film is – all-purpose dogsbody, special effects, production design, even a bit of direction. I've had more titles than I can remember, but I suppose the word "assistant" is the common theme.' He grinned, and accepted the invitation to sit down. 'At the moment, I'm just trying to make sure his weekend runs smoothly.'

'You must have your work cut out.'

'Oh?' He feigned an expression of anxiety. 'Don't tell me there's trouble already. I hoped we might at least get as far as dinner.'

Astrid laughed. 'I only meant that it's a lot to organise. Although, now you mention it, Leyton Turnbull and Bella Hutton obviously aren't the best of friends.'

'Those two go back a long way. It's a love-hate relationship.'

'I didn't see much of the love.' She opened her mouth to add something but seemed to think better of it.

'Believe me, the time to worry is when they're *not* squabbling. I know Bella very well. I have her to thank for just about every stroke of luck I've ever had.'

'One Dry Martini.' Danny set the drink down and nodded to Franks.

'Have you two met?' Astrid asked.

'Yes, at the top of the Bell Tower.' He grinned. 'I was having a look round and I didn't realise that David was already up there. He made me jump out of my skin.'

'I think we're quits,' Franks said. 'It's not the most comfortable feeling to be at the top with nowhere to go and suddenly hear footsteps you're not expecting.'

'You were just telling us how you know Bella Hutton,' Lydia reminded him. It wasn't strictly true, but she was intrigued by the relationship between the film star and Hitchcock's protégé, and Franks didn't seem to mind being nudged into an explanation.

'My parents died when I was young and I got into some trouble. Bella hauled me off to Hollywood with her, out of harm's way, and showed me there was more to life than being a difficult teenager.' Lydia suspected she was not the only one who was dying to ask what sort of trouble, but nobody said anything. 'The film set was a safe place to be dangerous, I suppose – a fantasy world with no risks. Bella knew I loved it, so, when she came back here to work, she pulled more strings and got me a job on *The Lodger*. That's when I met the Hitchcocks.'

'What's he like to work with?' Lydia asked.

'Brilliant. I worked on a few films for the studios, his and other people's, mostly on models and miniatures and the kind of stuff I'd learnt in the States. I didn't even know that Hitchcock had noticed me until he invited me down to his cottage for the weekend. They were so kind to me, both he and Alma. In hindsight, it was the most subtle job interview I've ever had. Before we went back to London, he handed me the script of a play and asked me what I thought of it as a movie idea. They must have liked what I said, because the next thing I knew I was working on *Blackmail*.'

'So what's the most important thing you've learnt from him?' Astrid made her question sound like a challenge, but

Lydia suspected that she was wisely doing her own research, gleaning all she could from an insider in the Hitchcock camp.

'That you have to be able to do everything if you want to direct – camera, lighting, design, script, even promotion,' Franks said without hesitation. 'And to be brave. I see in Hitchcock what I love about America and admire in the German directors – that sense of freedom and imagination, the courage to try things out.'

'I suppose you'll go with him if he moves to America?' Danny asked. 'It'll be easier for you, as you know the place already. Less of an upheaval.'

'Oh, I'm used to upheaval. My family travelled around a lot when I was a kid.'

'So did mine. That's why I hate upheaval.'

Franks laughed. 'I can understand that, but opportunities like moving to Hollywood with Alfred Hitchcock don't come along very often.'

'Well, when you put it like that . . .' Danny smiled and finished his drink. 'In the unlikely event that it's a decision I'd have to make, it would probably take all of ten seconds.'

'From what you say, it'll be a shame for the Brits if we lose him,' Lydia said.

'Yes, but it's going to happen sooner or later. The most exciting opportunities are in America at the moment.' He looked at Marta. 'And not just for directors. Lots of the best British screenwriters are thinking about moving or have already gone.'

Lydia didn't trust Marta not to break her silence by making it clear how she felt about receiving career advice from a stranger, so she said quickly, 'It's better now, surely? I remember a time when we only made the terrible second features that you had to sit through to get to the Hollywood film, but it's not like that any more.'

'No, it's not.' He smiled. 'Not all the time, anyway. Have you ever been interested in films, or are you happy with the stage?'

Feeling faintly patronised, like someone who misguidedly prefers cheap wine to champagne, Lydia said, 'I've considered it, but I'm not sure it's an easy transition to make.' She was going to say 'at my age', but thought better of it. 'A friend of mine was in *Secret Agent*. I suppose everybody's experience of working with Hitchcock is different, but it wasn't the happiest job he's ever had.'

'You mean John Terry?' Lydia nodded. 'He made it too obvious that he thought film was beneath his dignity as a stage legend,' Franks explained, 'and that's never the way to go with Hitch. He cares deeply about what he does, and a film director doesn't want to feel like a poor relation any more than a stage actress does.' She was treated to the smile again, irresistible because it came from his eyes. 'Sorry. I didn't mean to offend you. It was a clumsy way to ask the question.'

'I read an interview in *Film Weekly* where Hitchcock said that women didn't act as well as men,' Astrid said. 'Was that exploiting publicity or does he actually mean it?'

Franks laughed. 'A bit of both, probably. Some people have a hard time with him, some adore him, but there are men and women in both camps.'

'So he doesn't exploit women? I was talking to Bella Hutton earlier. She didn't mention Hitchcock – she obviously likes him – but she seemed to think that film in general favoured men and allowed them to get away with too much.'

'How does that make film different to most other professions?' Franks asked, turning to Lydia. 'Is the stage any better, Miss Beaumont? Have you never had to play up to a male producer to get a part you want?' Lydia felt Marta's eyes on her and gave what she hoped was a non-committal smile. 'It depends what you mean by exploitation. All film is voyeuristic to some extent. It's an excuse for people to sit in the dark and live out their dreams – privately, with the person on the screen. And that's not a male prerogative. The women in the audience are just as possessive over their matinee idols.'

'I don't think that's quite what Miss Hutton meant,' Astrid said, a little impatiently. 'She was talking about what happens when the lines between reality and fantasy get blurred.'

'What do you mean?'

She hesitated when faced with a direct question, and Lydia wondered what Bella Hutton had said to her that she was reluctant to repeat. 'That some people are powerful enough to get away with anything, no matter who gets hurt.'

Franks nodded thoughtfully. 'That's probably true. But in the States, one of the most powerful people in film is a woman who runs a mobile unit for dirty films in Chicago – all completely illegal, of course, but she's worth a fortune. And she asks things of her female stars that Hitch would never dare mention, even if he wanted to.' He smiled and continued more diplomatically. 'Bella's quite influential herself. I doubt she's ever been exploited in her life – it would be a stupid man who tried it. But don't listen to gossip where Hitch is concerned. Keep an open mind and decide for yourself.' He looked at his watch. 'If you'll excuse me, I've got to check that everything's in place for dinner.'

Lydia watched as he walked away. 'Why does good advice always sound so damned condescending?' she asked with a wink at Astrid. 'He meant well, I suppose.'

'There's Josephine,' Marta said, looking over to the hotel entrance. 'She's with Alma – I wonder how she got on?'

'Which one's Mrs Hitchcock?' Danny asked, and Marta pointed her out. Against her better judgement, Lydia glanced at Marta's face as she watched Josephine, and wondered how little of her heart she would be willing to settle for.

5

Josephine was hesitating over whether to join Marta and Lydia, when Archie came downstairs. 'You look lovely,' he said, bending to kiss her. 'And relatively unscathed. How did your meeting go?'

'Well, I think. She's not at all what I expected, but I liked her. You might be on for that premiere after all.'

'She managed to talk you into it?'

'It was odd, really. She has a knack of getting what she wants by being honest – about herself and the whole process. The more she said, the more sceptical I became, but by the time we parted I knew that I was going to say yes. You're right, Archie – it's a once-in-a-lifetime chance. I'd be stupid not to take it.' He smiled at her, genuinely pleased. 'I don't think I want to be closely involved, though. She made it sound like a nightmare. I just need to accept that it's a different medium entirely, another version of my story. There'll always be the book, no matter what they do to it.'

'I'll remind you of that when we go and see it. Are the others about yet?'

'I haven't seen Ronnie and Lettice, but Marta and Lydia are out there.'

'Do you want to join them?'

'In a while. First I want you on your own so you can tell me about Bridget.' They found a quiet table at the other end of the terrace and ordered some drinks. 'So – who is she?'

'We met in Cambridge during the war.'

She waited for him to continue and, when he didn't, said, 'I've been accused of some lazy plotting in my time, but even I can see that's only half a story.'

He laughed. 'Give me a chance. It was when I came back from the Front for the first time. September 1915.'

'I remember. You wrote to me from hospital. You'd been hit in the shoulder.'

Archie nodded. 'That's right.' He was still wary of discussing the war with Josephine, as it held ghosts for them both, but there was no other context in which he could talk about Bridget. 'They sent me to a hospital in Cambridge. I say hospital, but it was a makeshift affair. The military had taken over Nevile's Court in Trinity, and there were beds all round the cloisters. I came round one day, and there was a woman sitting by my bed, drawing. She didn't say anything – just smiled, as if it were the most natural thing in the world – and I drifted off again before I could make any sense of it. When I was more myself, I half thought I'd dreamt it. But she came back and brought the drawing with her. I still have it.'

'I'd like to see it.'

He reached inside his jacket and removed a folded piece of paper from his wallet, creased and discoloured now from years of wear and tear. 'I kept it with me all through the war,' he said. 'It was a small pocket of stillness and sanity amid the chaos.'

Josephine unfolded the image of his younger self, a sleeping soldier on a narrow bed. Even now, Archie could still remember the peace it had brought him. He watched as she traced the outline of his face on the paper, and found himself instinctively removing the years from her, too, trying to remember her as she was when he had first known her. 'Was that really twenty years ago?' she asked, as if reading his thoughts.

'I'm afraid so. Goes quickly, doesn't it?'

'Yes. Far too quickly.' She handed the drawing back. 'I can see why it's so precious to you.'

'It's exactly how I remember that time in Cambridge,' he explained. 'The extraordinary sense of calm – gentle nurses, ordered beds and safety. It was such a contrast to the hell of those first few weeks in France. As I began to get better, it was almost impossible to face up to the fact that I was going to have to go back there. I thought I was going mad – despair is so much worse than fear. And it was Bridget who got me through that.' He saw Josephine looking at him intently, and guessed that she was wondering why she had never known this about someone to whom she was so close. 'I had some leave when I was well again, but I couldn't face going home to Cornwall. It wasn't long after my parents died, and I didn't want to be somewhere that reminded me of them wherever I turned, so I stayed in Cambridge and we spent some time together. Even there, you couldn't quite get away from the war. We'd cycle out into the countryside and lie on the grass by the river, and listen to the dull throb of the guns in France. It seemed extraordinary to hear them there, amongst all that innocent green. I might have thought they were in my head if she hadn't heard them too.'

'You forget how far it spreads, don't you?'

'Yes. Cambridge was a place we both loved, but it was unrecognisable by then, and in a funny sort of way that made us closer. There were soldiers and military vehicles everywhere. The college courts were empty, and the pace of life was slow and dull. I'll always remember something Bridget's father said to me – Cambridge was nothing without its youth.'

'You got as far as meeting the parents, then?'

'Yes. He was vicar of St. Edward's at the time.'

'Good God. I know I've only met her once, but I wouldn't have had her down as a daughter of the cloth!'

'No. I got the impression it hadn't always been an easy relationship, but they were still close.'

'What happened when you went back to the Front?'

'She went back to the Slade and continued her art training.'

'And you haven't seen her since?'

'No, not until today.'

'She's beautiful,' Josephine said, and he noticed that her voice had a wistful quality to it. 'There's something very free about her. You know instantly that she'll do whatever she likes, and that's always irresistible.'

'Haven't you got enough on your plate?' He made the joke without thinking and wondered for a second if he'd gone too far, but she only laughed, and he sensed that they might at last be ready to talk honestly with each other about their lives. 'Do you love her?' he asked quietly.

'I've only just met her, Archie. It's far too early to tell, but I'm a fool for an Irish accent.'

'I meant Marta.'

'I know what you meant.'

'And?'

'I'm not sure.'

'Of course you're sure. Don't play that game.' His frustration with her evasiveness was obvious, and he tried to soften it. 'The answer might come with complications but the question's very easy. Do you love Marta?'

'Yes.' It was less a declaration than an admission, and Archie wondered if her hesitation signalled a need to come to terms with her own feelings or a desire to protect his. 'Yes, I love Marta.'

'And have you told her?' She shook her head. 'Then do it now, Josephine. For God's sake give her some hope.'

'How will that help? As you say, it's complicated. We can't be together, so telling her how I feel will only make it worse.'

'Shouldn't you let Marta be the judge of that?' he asked gently. 'She's not stupid. I've learnt that to my cost in the past, and I get the feeling that she knows exactly what she's taking on by loving you.'

'You make it sound like such a trial.'

'Well, it is. Not many people would put up with your nonsense.'

'I'll ignore that, but only because you've bought me half a racehorse.'

'If it means I can be truthful with you, I'll buy the other half as well. Honestly, Josephine – have you any idea how infuriating you can be? Sometimes *I* want to pick you up and shake you, so I can only begin to imagine how Marta must feel.'

She tried to glare at him, but didn't make a very good job of it. 'I think I preferred it when you two hated each other. This uneasy truce you seem to have come to makes me feel very vulnerable.'

The rebuff was half-hearted by Josephine's standards, and he guessed that his words reinforced something she had just realised for herself, or at least had only recently allowed herself to acknowledge. 'Well, love can force some strange alliances,' he said, matching her tone, and then added more seriously, 'Knowing how *you* feel might at least make Marta believe that there's a point to it all. You know what it's like when you're trying to guess how someone *really* feels about you – it tears you apart. You become obsessed by it until you lose sight of yourself completely.'

'You're not talking about Marta, are you? You're talking about us.'

He ran his finger idly up and down the stem of his champagne glass while he decided what to say. 'I've been doing a lot of thinking lately,' he began, 'and I suppose I've realised that worrying too much about what someone else thinks can also be an excuse not to look too deeply at your own feelings. It's time I looked at my life and what I want from it.' He caught her expression and smiled. 'Not because of Bridget; because of me. And you need to do the same. Be honest with yourself about what you want, and find a way to make it work.'

She put her hand on his cheek. 'When did you get so wise?'

'Somewhere around forty,' he said. 'With a bit of luck, it should hit you at any minute.'

6

Bella sat at the desk in the royal suite and sealed an envelope, obscuring the mermaid who decorated Portmeirion's distinctive letterhead. Without warning, the door crashed open behind her, startling her as it knocked over a chair, and she turned round angrily to see who it was. Her brother stood in the doorway. The barely contained anger in his face jarred sharply with the quiet of the room. Without acknowledging him, Bella turned back to the desk and calmly addressed the envelope.

Her silence only provoked him more, as she had known it would. Even when they were young, she had been able to wind him up to breaking point, and old habits died hard. 'Why didn't you tell me I had a child?' he demanded furiously, slamming the door behind him. 'You must have known.'

It wasn't the question Bella had been expecting, but she hid her surprise well. 'Of course I knew. Grace told me.'

'Did it never occur to you to mention it?'

'You made it clear to me that you'd left here for good, so what would have been the point?'

'I had a right to know, that's the point.' He walked over to the desk and looked down at her. 'God, you're a cold bitch. I don't know why I'm surprised that you should side with Gwyneth. You're two of a kind.'

Bella smiled. 'There was never any love lost between Gwyneth and me, but she didn't deserve you, and she wouldn't have thanked me for sending you back when she'd finally managed to get rid of you. Anyway, a marriage is private, and it wasn't for me to interfere.' She stood up so that her face was level with his, determined he should never know that, deep down, she had always been a little afraid of him. 'It's a shame you didn't respect that when you came crashing into mine.'

'Change the record, Bella. How is your failure of a marriage my fault? Maxwell Hutton was making his money out of dirty films long before I met him.'

'But I didn't know about it, goddammit.' She slammed her hand down on the wood. Talking about Max and her illness had left Bella vulnerable to the darkness that coloured her thoughts more each day, and she struggled to regain her composure, helped by the sly smile which crept across his face when he saw she was upset. 'And what you don't know can't hurt you.'

'So not telling me that my child is buried up there in those woods like a dog was an act of kindness, was it?'

'Buried in the woods?' Bella stared at him. 'Who told you that?'

He seemed to think her astonishment was an act and brushed her comment impatiently away. 'Come off it. That waitress you're so friendly with told me she thought Gwyneth's missing kid was in the cemetery.'

Bella had no idea if that were true and wouldn't have told him if she had. 'There's a certain irony in that, don't you think?' she said quietly.

A satisfying flicker of fear crossed her brother's face, and his tone became suddenly more placatory. 'Tell me about the child, Bella. What happened to him? Or her? Christ, I don't even know if I had a boy or a girl.'

'It's Gwyneth you should be talking to,' she said. 'Why don't you go and ask her?' He hesitated, and she added, 'You won't get anything out of me, so you might as well leave.'

'Why *were* you talking to that girl?' he asked. 'Were you

telling her not to say anything to me? Because if you were, you're wasting your time. I know how to get round her sort.' She saw his eyes travel down to the desk, trying to read the name on the envelope. 'What else don't I know about my own life, Bella?'

She threw back her head and laughed. 'Dear Henry. You never were the brains of the family, were you?'

'Don't call me that,' he snapped. 'Especially not here. My name is Leyton Turnbull now. I left Henry Draycott behind a long time ago.'

'Oh, don't worry. I'm no keener for people to know we're related than you are.' She shook her head in disbelief. 'You really don't know who she is, do you?'

'What do you mean? She's a waitress with a mouth on her. What else is there to know?'

'That's you and women all over. Try looking *above* the waist, Henry. Look at who she *is* rather than what she can do for you. That girl's been writing to me for years, begging me to help her find her mother.'

'I don't understand. Why would she do that?'

'Because she's Rhiannon Erley's daughter, and she thinks her mother abandoned her to run off with my brother.' She watched, satisfied, as the realisation finally sank in. 'Except she didn't, did she? Rhiannon Erley never left here at all.'

'Of course she did. I told you what happened.'

'It was a pack of lies. You killed her, Henry.'

The certainty in her voice must have told him that it was useless to pretend any longer. He walked over to the bed and sat down, and she knew as clearly as if she were watching a film she had seen many times what his next move was going to be. 'It was an accident,' he said, word-perfect with the script she had roughed out for him.

'And that makes a difference?'

He shrugged. 'It makes a difference to me. I'm not a killer, Bella.' He waited for her to speak, but she said nothing, and he asked instead, 'How do you know what happened?'

'It doesn't matter *how* I know. It's what I'm going to do with the information that counts.'

'You wouldn't. The scandal would ruin you. Anyway, what do you care about Rhiannon or her daughter? You couldn't get away from your own family quick enough, so don't start banging the drum for someone else's. You only think of your precious career: that's why you'll keep quiet.'

'You're right in one sense,' Bella admitted. 'I don't give a damn about you or your slut, and if you'd learnt your lesson then I might be happy to leave it alone now. But you didn't, did you? You carried on, dirtying everything and everyone you touched, and you're still doing it. That girl needs to know what happened to her mother, and as you've never been capable of one decent thing in your life, the job seems to have fallen to me.'

'You haven't got any proof.'

'No?' She glanced down at Chaplin. The dog obviously remembered his encounter in reception because he kept a wary distance. 'I thought Chaplin and I might take a walk up to the cemetery later. He loves these woods. You know how it is – dogs and their bones.'

'You wouldn't dare.'

'Try me. Perhaps we'll look for your child as well.'

From nowhere, he lunged towards her and pushed her roughly to the wall, his hand around her throat, his body pressed hard against hers. The attack took her completely by surprise, and, in her panic, she cursed herself for underestimating him. Chaplin forgot his fear, but he was kicked easily away, and Bella smelt her brother's aftershave, mixed with sweat and stale whisky; his physical proximity was abhorrent to her, worse even than the tightening in her throat and the pain in her breasts and back as he crushed her body with his own. As she struggled in vain to breathe, she felt herself losing consciousness – and suddenly, in her fear, she realised that this was the answer to everything; at least this way her death would count for something. She forced herself to meet his eye and smiled, willing him to squeeze harder, but for once he showed some self-control; just in time, he took his hand away and left her doubled over in pain, gasping for air.

'What the hell's going on? Bella? Are you all right?'

She looked up as David Franks hurried across the room, horrified that he should see her like this. He put a hand on her shoulder, but she shook it off and somehow managed to speak. 'What do you want, David?'

'Don't act as though nothing's wrong,' he said, glaring at them both. 'What are you playing at?'

'A bit of rivalry got out of hand.' From somewhere she found the strength to walk across the room and calm her frightened dog. 'That's enough, Chaplin. The gentlemen are just leaving.' She looked questioningly at David. 'Well?'

'Hitch asked me to invite you to dinner.'

Bella laughed. 'That's very kind of him but I don't have much of an appetite.'

'Let me stay with you. I'll have something brought up.'

'Don't pity me, David. For God's sake, after everything that's happened, at least spare me that. Now get out – both of you.'

Her voice was calm, but it invited no argument. Reluctantly, David turned to go, but her brother lingered, his eyes resting on the note to Branwen. 'Come on, Turnbull,' David said, ushering him out of the room. 'I don't know what this is about, but you've done enough damage.'

Bella watched the two men leave, then sank exhausted onto the bed. She stared at her image in the dressing-table mirror and put her fingers to her throat, where the imprint of her brother's hand – red and livid against her pale skin – lay like a gauntlet of shame. 'You should have put me out of my misery, Henry,' she said softly. 'But you couldn't even do that, could you?'

7

'That bloody shower! First I couldn't get it to work at all, and then it only had two temperature variations: hot or scalding. I had to sit on my bed for half an hour before I could come down. Otherwise, I'd have lit up the restaurant single-handedly.' Ronnie sat down next to Archie, and Josephine noticed that, despite her protestations, she was the only person on the terrace whose elegance remained unaffected by the heat. 'Anyway, Bella Hutton was having a blazing row with someone in the next room and I had to wait to find out who it was.'

'And?' Lettice asked.

'Leyton Turnbull. I couldn't hear the details,' she admitted, anticipating her sister's next question. 'And I was hardly dressed to go and loiter in the hallway. But I did happen to poke my head round the door as he was leaving, and he seemed in a terrible state. There was another man with him, too – very good-looking but I didn't recognise him.' She accepted a glass of champagne and smiled round at everybody. 'What have I missed?'

'Nothing much,' Lettice said nonchalantly, stabbing at an olive. 'Josephine's all but signed a deal with the Hitchcocks. Archie's rekindled a lost love from twenty years ago. And I've talked Bella into letting us handle the wardrobe for her next five movies.' She paused, enjoying the expression on Ronnie's face. 'That last point is a lie, by the way. Relax and enjoy your drink.'

If anything, Ronnie looked even more incredulous. 'You mean the other two are true?' She pointed at Josephine. 'I'll deal with you in a minute. What lost love, Archie?' she demanded, poking him hard in the leg. 'Why don't I know about this?'

Archie looked uncomfortable, but made a gallant effort. 'Sorry,' he said. 'Stupid of me, but I didn't realise that I had to run my love life by you. Anyway, Lettice is exaggerating. It's just someone I knew during the war. I bumped into her earlier. She's an artist, and she's doing some work for Clough.'

'She seems very nice,' Marta said, winking at Josephine.

'Yes, I thought so, too.'

'Actually, her name sounded familiar,' Lettice continued, 'but I couldn't place it. Don't we know a Bridget Foley?'

'Bridget Foley?' Ronnie's eyes widened and she stared at her cousin with a new respect. 'We know *of* a Bridget Foley. Does yours live in Cambridge?'

Archie nodded defensively. 'Yes, but she's not *my* . . .'

'Don't you remember, Lettice? It was while we were there

in the spring, doing the costumes for the Ibsen at the Arts Theatre. Everyone was talking about it.'

'Yes, of course. Bridget Foley! Fancy your knowing her, Archie.'

Josephine was dying to find out what was so memorable about Archie's old flame, but it would have been unfair of her to ask in front of him. Instead, she tried to think of something sufficiently interesting to lure Ronnie onto another subject, but she was saved the trouble. Lydia came back from the cloakroom and sat down next to Marta. 'Why on earth is there a nun at the Hitchcocks' table?' she asked.

'A nun?' Josephine echoed her astonishment. 'Are you sure?'

Lydia gave a wry smile. 'They're quite hard to mistake.'

'I didn't mean are you sure it's a nun. I meant are you sure it's their table?'

'It must be. It's the only one apart from ours that's set for more than four people. Unless the Hitchcocks are dining in a private room and we're sharing the restaurant with a Catholic convention.'

Lettice got up to see for herself, taking an unconvincingly casual stroll across the terrace to peer through the dining-room windows. 'Well, it's definitely a nun,' she confirmed. 'A Sister of Our Lady of Sorrows, if I'm not mistaken.' She caught Josephine's bemused expression and explained: 'We designed *Measure for Measure* recently, so I know what their costumes are like – it's all to do with the wimple. I've no idea what she's doing there. She must have sat down at the wrong table.'

Ronnie smiled. 'She's in for a shock, then.'

'They *are* Catholics,' Marta said. 'Alma converted to marry him.'

'Even so, you don't take your religion on holiday, do you? I'm a well-brought-up Church of England girl, but if I took the vicar of St Martin's off to the South of France with me whenever I fancied it, he'd never have time to deliver a sermon, let alone write one.'

There was a queue to take issue with Ronnie's claim, but Archie got in first. 'If you took a vicar to the South of France, he'd be in no position morally to do either,' he said, smiling sweetly at his cousin. 'You're a menace, even to the most spiritually certain among us.'

'Just because I don't wait twenty years between romances...'

'Perhaps Hitchcock has insisted on fancy dress,' Josephine suggested. 'From what you were saying earlier, that's just the sort of thing he'd find funny. The next time we look, we'll probably see a vicar, a tart and someone dressed as Dracula.'

Marta looked over to the next table, where an unattractive middle-aged man was leering at a waitress, delivering a monologue which she seemed professionally obliged to endure. 'I think one or two of them have arrived already,' she said. 'It's like something out of *Nightwood*.'

'What?'

'It's an American book that's just come out. All misfits, lost souls and wretchedness.'

'Sounds charming,' Ronnie grumbled.

'Talking of America, we had an interesting conversation earlier,' Lydia said. 'We were having a drink with Danny Lascelles and Astrid Lake...'

'*Obviously* her real name,' muttered Archie.

Lydia smiled. 'We don't mention it. Anyway, we met David Franks. He's Hitchcock's production designer and assistant director, and he's organising their weekend. He spent some time in Hollywood in the twenties, and he suggested that Marta should think about going out there to work – she's been quite a hit with Alma, apparently.' She looked proudly at Marta, oblivious to the bombshell she had just dropped. 'I knew you were being too modest. Just think how exciting America would be.'

'What do they do when they're working on a screenplay, Marta?' Archie asked, looking at Josephine's horrified face. 'How would Hitchcock go about adapting *A Shilling for Candles*?'

Marta smiled at him, apparently grateful not to have to pick up Lydia's thread. 'Well, first they find a property,' she said.

'You make it sound like buying a house.'

'It's not dissimilar, actually. I've known people choose a home with less fuss.' She glanced quickly at Josephine, and, if she was trying to gauge the effect of Lydia's words, Archie guessed that she would not be disappointed. 'When they've found what they want to work with, they reduce it to a bare outline and talk about the characters – who they are, how they would behave in a given situation. From that, they produce a more detailed scenario, plotting the action scene by scene.'

'When does Hitchcock get involved?'

'From the start. That sort of visual storytelling is what he does best. It's Hitchcock, Alma, and the flavour of the moment is Charles Bennett. I'm sure he'll do *A Shilling for Candles* if Josephine doesn't want to have anything to do with it.' She paused, while Lydia lit her cigarette. 'When they're happy with what they've got, they call in people like me to write the dialogue. We're the lowest of the low, because Hitchcock doesn't really think that dialogue is important. He'll have to change his habits if he does go to America, though. He won't get that kind of independence in Hollywood.'

'I dare say America will prove *very* popular when the war comes,' Josephine said, finishing her drink.

Lydia glanced sharply at her. 'Possibly, but people can't be expected to put their careers on hold for fear of seeming unpatriotic.'

'Can't they? What about for fear of *being* unpatriotic?'

Alfred Hitchcock defused the tension as unwittingly as he had brought it about. The appearance of such a familiar figure on the terrace stopped the conversation at every table, and Lettice was one of many diners whose desire to move through to the restaurant became suddenly more urgent. For once, Archie was relieved to follow suit. Judging by the expression on Marta's face, he wasn't the only one.

8

Hitchcock handed the menu back to the waiter. 'I'll have the steak-and-oyster pie,' he said, 'but kindly remove the oysters.'

'Certainly, sir.'

'And bring some more wine.'

He smiled round at the table, and wondered who, if anyone, would be brave enough to question the purpose of the evening. So far, each of his guests was behaving more or less as he would have expected: Turnbull had drunk too much and was saying very little; Astrid Lake and Daniel Lascelles were both nervous, watchful for an opportunity to impress but too eager to please when it came; Spence was as detached from the conversation as usual, revealing nothing of himself except a wry amusement in the whole charade; and Alma sat by her husband's side with that air of patient resignation which was as integral to their public relationship as her love and guidance were to their private life. Only David Franks surprised Hitchcock: he seemed preoccupied, his habitual friendliness replaced by a quiet unease, and several times Hitchcock caught him looking nervously at Turnbull. Bella would have livened things up considerably, but, in hindsight, it was just as well that she had declined his invitation; she was one of the few people he knew with a personality as dominant as his own, and he wasn't in the mood to be eclipsed.

Every now and again, someone glanced curiously at the stranger in their midst and then at the rest of the party, but no one dared to say anything. In the end, it was the nun herself who broke the silence. 'Don't I know you from somewhere?' she asked, peering across the table at Leyton Turnbull. Hitch frowned at her; he was used to people doing what they were paid to do and no more, but she seemed oblivious to the warning. 'We've met before, surely? I never forget a face.'

Spence shook his head in mock admiration. 'Started on the convents now, have you, Turnbull? Is no woman safe from your charms?'

Turnbull ignored him. 'I'm an actor,' he said to the nun. 'You probably recognise me from a film.'

Hitchcock was amused to see that he could still manage a note of pride in his voice as he spoke. 'Don't be so modest, Mr Turnbull,' he protested. 'You're looking at one of our finest leading men, Sister Venetia. He can rise to anything.'

There was a snigger from down the table, but the nun was either oblivious to the innuendo or chose to ignore it. 'I don't watch films,' she said firmly. 'Murder, adultery, the worshipping of false idols – I can't think of anything that manages to break God's laws quite as effortlessly as the cinema.' Her eyes remained fixed on Turnbull as she added, 'It corrupts the soul.'

'I can't help thinking you might be happier at another table, Sister,' Franks suggested.

'You really have made a mistake,' Turnbull insisted, and Hitchcock noticed that the attention was beginning to make him uncomfortable. He settled back in his seat to enjoy the entertainment, forgetting his irritation; he had no idea where David had found this woman, but he had to admit she was good.

'It will come to me eventually,' she said, and there was a barbed promise in the words which belied the smile they were delivered with. 'You've changed, but I definitely know you.'

'He hasn't changed that much,' Spence said. 'I saw you dropping that girl off earlier, Turnbull. Old habits die hard.'

'I was only giving her a lift back. She'd had an accident and her bicycle was damaged. What was I supposed to do? Drive past and let her walk?'

'Mr Turnbull has quite an eye for the ladies, Sister,' Spence explained conspiratorially. 'That's his latest, over there.' He pointed to a dark-haired girl who had just joined the band on stage. Everyone turned to look at her, and Hitchcock noticed a flicker of recognition cross Lascelles' face.

'Ignore my colleague,' Turnbull said. 'His imagination runs away with him. It's a casualty of the industry we work in. And we really haven't met,' he added firmly, trying to close the conversation once and for all. 'I'd remember if we had. Anyway, to what do we owe the pleasure of your company?'

Hitchcock cut in before the nun could answer. 'Sister Venetia takes care of my daughter's education,' he explained. 'Alma and I wanted to bring her up as a good Catholic girl, and the sister runs an excellent school in Cavendish Square.' He paused. 'The only trouble is, she drinks.'

All eyes turned to the nun in astonishment. Her hand hovered over the glass she had been about to pick up, but she withdrew it and lowered her head. There was an uncomfortable silence as her shame touched everyone but the director. Eventually, Astrid made an effort to change the subject. 'Are you making plans to go to Hollywood, Mr Hitchcock?'

Hitchcock looked at her and smiled. 'You'll have to ask the Madame,' he said, winking at Alma. 'She does continuity.'

'If I had my way, Miss Lake, we'd be leaving for the plane in about ten minutes.'

Everyone laughed. Although Hitchcock knew that his wife's comment was a subtle warning rather than a joke, he chose to ignore it. The waiter arrived with the wine, and, as the nun leant to one side to allow him to fill her glass, Hitchcock held up his hand. 'Nothing more for her.' He glared at her, and tried to keep any telltale trace of amusement out of his voice. 'You know what happens when you drink. Don't you remember St Moritz? You were lucky no one pressed charges. Now show some respect.'

'Please . . .'

'Absolutely not. You're embarrassing everybody. Just be quiet.'

Hitchcock smiled apologetically at the other guests, and saw to his satisfaction that embarrassment was an understatement; no one knew where to look. Out of the corner of his eye, he noticed that tears were now falling quietly down the nun's face, and he marvelled again at her performance. She continued to cry softly as the waiters served dinner, and eventually it became too much for Astrid Lake. 'Are you all right?' she asked gently.

Sister Venetia looked at her gratefully. 'If I could just have a drop of...'

Hitchcock slammed his hand down hard on the table, knocking over a glass of wine in the process. 'That's enough,' he shouted. 'You're ruining our whole evening and I won't have you taking advantage of my guests. I should never have invited you. Go to your room.'

The nun stood and left the restaurant without another word. David got up to follow her, but Hitchcock put a hand on his arm. By this time, the embarrassment had spread to the rest of the diners, and the band's cheerful rendition of 'No One Can Like the Drummer Man' was an incongruous backdrop to the tension. With all eyes on him, Hitchcock summoned a wait-ress to clear up the mess and calmly carried on eating. He knew without looking that Alma was staring at him with a mixture of curiosity and weariness; one day she would hit him for a stunt like this, if someone didn't beat her to it. As the other diners tried to gauge if they could safely resume their conversations without missing anything, Jack Spence began to applaud. 'It's a gag,' he said, and a ripple of nervous laughter ran through the restaurant, although several of the guests seated at Hitchcock's table seemed unconvinced. 'You're a gag, too,' Spence contin-ued, pointing at Turnbull. 'Always have been, always will be. One of these days, you'll meet a woman who gives as good as she gets.'

'I'm not sure what gives you the right to lecture me on how

to treat a woman,' Turnbull snapped. 'It's hardly your area of expertise.' He drained his glass and looked defiantly at the other guests. 'Women are there to take direction. Don't you think so, Hitch?'

'Oh, nothing pleases me more than to knock the ladylikeness out of chorus girls,' Hitchcock said cheerfully, knowing that Turnbull was too far gone to notice the irony in his voice, or to realise that he was being encouraged to hang himself. Astrid Lake frowned; it was only a matter of time before she joined in, and he raised his glass to her with a wink. Across the table, David Franks smiled and shook his head in admiration.

'Beautiful women think they're too clever,' Turnbull continued. 'People will overlook lack of talent for a pretty face, but only for a while. After that, they have to think of other ways to get themselves noticed.' He leant across Lascelles and put his hand on Astrid's leg. 'You've got a *very* pretty face, Miss Lake. What sort of films do you have a mind to star in?'

Danny stood up, his fists clenched, and for a moment Hitchcock thought he was going to use them, but Astrid put a hand on his arm and shook her head. 'Watch your mouth, Turnbull,' Lascelles warned as he sat down. 'One more crack like that and she won't be able to stop me.'

'Is it true that you take what you can't get, Mr Turnbull?' Astrid's voice was low and even, but she was obviously livid. 'I hear you like to continue the action long after the director shouts cut.'

'No prizes for guessing who's been pouring poison in your ear.'

'Is she lying?'

'Bella would say anything to slur my reputation,' he insisted, and looked to Franks for support. 'Tell them, David. She's always been out to get me.'

'Just leave it, Turnbull. You've caused enough trouble with Bella tonight.'

'Why do you always take that bitch's side?'

'I'm not taking her side, but I won't side *against* her. She's been too good to me.'

'And will continue to be, no doubt, unless you step out of line.' Even Hitchcock was surprised by the hatred in Turnbull's eyes as he talked about Bella Hutton, and it occurred to him that if the actor had been capable of showing such pure emotion on screen, his career might have been very different. 'She's no fucking saint, David, so grow up and find yourself another idol to worship. Bella looks out for herself, just like we all do, and she doesn't care who she hurts in the process. One of these days, you'll wish I hadn't stopped myself tonight.'

Hitchcock caught Franks's eye. 'Don't forget our wager, David,' he said, but his assistant scarcely seemed to care whether he won or lost.

'And what sort of role model would you have been, I wonder?' Franks asked, smiling innocently at Turnbull. 'Perhaps things turn out for the best after all.'

9

'Well, this has been considerably more engrossing than any of his films,' Ronnie said.

The hotel's beautiful curved dining room, which added a bold modernist touch to the original Victorian architecture, was as elegant on the inside as it was distinctive on the out:

rich walnut walls blended effortlessly with a blush-rose ceiling and a floor of light polished oak, whilst the glazed, open frontage ensured that the restaurant was flooded with light for most of the day. Tonight, though, the surroundings paled into insignificance. All eyes were fixed on the Hitchcocks' table, and Josephine pitied the musicians who had been booked to provide the official entertainment: their set – no matter how good – was bound to seem bland by comparison. She had watched on and off, intrigued more by the subtle dynamic between the Hitchcocks than by the histrionic reactions of their guests; Alma seemed smaller than ever next to her husband, but Josephine noticed how often he looked to her for a reaction to something he had said and was genuinely touched by the way his face lit up whenever she spoke. She had read somewhere that the director was shy, but to her he seemed watchful and quietly self-confident, able to express himself with ease and humour when he wished but just as content to stand back from the conversation and observe. As he drained his glass and stood up to leave the table, Alma whispered something in his ear, and he glanced in their direction and nodded. 'Oh God, he's coming over,' she said, nudging Archie. 'Just when I thought we'd got away with it.'

'Shouldn't that be "God *is* coming over"?' Archie said acidly. 'It's how they've been behaving all night. No wonder the nun had to leave. It must have been quite confusing for her.'

Lettice frowned at him. 'Don't be such a killjoy. It's so exciting.'

'How do I look?' Lydia asked, fumbling in her bag for a mirror.

Marta snapped the bag shut and affectionately brushed Lydia's hair back from her face. 'Perfect. Margaret Lockwood's better-looking sister.'

'Better-looking *younger* sister, I assume.'

'Naturally.'

For a large man, Hitchcock wore his clothes well; despite the fractious dinner, he looked elegant and unruffled as he walked across the restaurant. He smiled at them all, nodded to Marta, and held out his hand to Josephine. 'Miss Tey, my wife tells me the opening skirmishes have been satisfactorily negotiated and we might even have reason to be optimistic?'

Feeling a little railroaded, but seeing no point in playing hard-to-get now that she had made up her mind, Josephine nodded. 'Yes. As long as we can agree on the terms, I'd be very happy for you to work on *A Shilling for Candles*.'

'Splendid. I'm so glad.' His acting was almost as good as his directing, Josephine thought; if it had not been for Alma's frankness, she would never have guessed that Hitchcock's attitude to her novel was at best lukewarm. 'We're shooting *Sabotage* in the autumn,' he added, 'so we'll be keen to get started on a new project as soon as possible after that.'

'Good. I'll be interested to see what you do with it.'

'You intend to take a back seat in the adaptation process, then?'

She detected a note of relief in his voice, and didn't blame him: there must be nothing worse for a director than an author clinging to her novel with white knuckles, and she knew it would make it easier for both of them if she just took the money and ran. If she didn't like the results, she didn't have to do it again, and she might as well learn her lesson with the most successful director of the moment. Much to her surprise, she trusted Alma to find a compromise that would satisfy both her husband's ambitions and the integrity of the novel. 'I think I'll stick to books and the theatre,' she said with a smile. 'Adding another string to my bow might be pushing my luck.'

He nodded. 'You're wise to stick to what you enjoy most, and the stage is lucky to have you.' He smiled briefly at Lydia, acknowledging the part she had played in making *Richard of Bordeaux* such a success. 'Perhaps you'd all like to join us in the Mirror Room for a nightcap to celebrate?'

Lettice stood up as Josephine shook her head. 'Thank you, but no,' she said firmly, feeling Lydia's eyes in the back of her neck. 'We haven't finished here, and your evening looks complicated enough.'

There was a twinkle in his eye as he said, 'Ah, you noticed. Please don't let that put you off. I'm about to conduct an experiment which might interest you. After all, we both deal to some extent in fear and guilt.' He paused when he saw her surprise. 'Professionally speaking, of course. There's no hurry: just come through when you're ready.' He turned to go, then stopped and looked at Archie. 'Have we met before?'

'Yes. At Scotland Yard.' It was a good line, and Josephine admired the restraint with which Archie gave it the timing it deserved. 'You wanted to know how to arrest a man,' he explained, 'and I was the detective inspector who told you.' He held out his hand. 'Archie Penrose.'

'Chief inspector now,' Lettice added proudly.

Hitchcock looked surprised, and Josephine could see that it was the last thing he had expected: nobody looked less like a policeman than Archie in black tie. He recovered well but seemed a little uncomfortable as he walked away, and she wondered if he regretted having unwittingly invited a senior detective to witness his experiment, whatever it might be.

'God, I thought you'd blown it there,' Lydia said.

'What makes you think she hasn't?' Ronnie lit a cigarette. 'We should have made a run for it as soon as he stood up. Now we're stuck with them.'

'Sorry, but he didn't leave me much choice.'

Marta drained her glass and shook her head as a waiter stepped forward to refill it. 'I think I'll give coffee with the film crew a miss,' she said.

'Are you all right?' Lydia asked. 'You've been quiet all evening.'

'I'm fine – just a bit tired from the drive and not really in the mood for that.' She nodded towards the hallway.

'What will you do?'

'Oh, go and finish unpacking or something.'

'I could give you a hand.'

Lydia looked torn. Marta smiled and gave her a kiss. 'Go and dazzle the Hitchcocks. You know you want to.'

'Are you sure you don't mind?'

'Of course not. I'll see you all later. You can tell me about it then.'

Josephine watched her go, trying to ignore how flat and colourless the evening had suddenly become. If she felt like this when Marta left the room, what effect would her leaving the country have? 'Let's go,' she said reluctantly. 'The sooner we get there, the sooner we can make our excuses and leave.'

Coffee and brandy were already laid out for them when they sat down in the extraordinary sitting room which adjoined the hotel's lounge. Hitchcock had wasted no time in getting under way. He acknowledged their arrival with a brief nod and carried on talking, making the most of a captive audience. 'Ten years ago, film was still the poor relation of the stage. We clung to its material and idolised its stars.' Josephine sighed, wishing she had been firmer. 'But the world has changed. The only thing a play can do that a film can't is bring those actors into the same room as their audience.'

'Good to know we count for something,' Lydia muttered.

'These days, people expect realism, not unconvincing rooms full of cheap stage props.' Ronnie cleared her throat, ready to say something in defence of her profession, but Lettice glared at her and she thought better of it. 'And the same is true of conversation,' Hitchcock continued. 'Film allows us to deliver dialogue more effectively than a stage ever could.' It was Josephine's turn to feel indignant. She wondered if he had set out to be as rude as possible, or if it just came naturally. It was inconceivable that he didn't realise how offensive he was being, and she sensed that it was only a matter of time before he steered his insults closer to home: the people who knew him best were looking apprehensive rather than smug. 'But sound mustn't make us lazy. We can't simply film someone talking. By cutting to whoever is listening, we give each word more meaning by showing its effect.'

'You could always just turn your head slightly and look at the other actors on stage,' Josephine said, and for once she made no effort to keep the comment under her breath. Archie laughed, and even Alma threw an amused glance in her direction.

'But the craft of making movies is a subject for tomorrow. Tonight, I thought we'd get to know each other better, and, to my mind, the best way to do that is to share our deepest fears.' He paused and looked round the room. 'What frightens a man is fundamental to who he is, to who he has always been: the things that frighten us now are the things that frightened us when we were children – and I must confess that I am easily frightened. When I was four, I woke with a start. The house was plunged into darkness and completely silent. I sat up and I began calling my mother. No one responded because no one was there. I trembled with fear. However, I was able to find enough courage to get up. I came to the kitchen, which was illuminated in a sinister fashion. I trembled more and more. At the same time, I was hungry. I opened the kitchen buffet, in which I found some cold meat, and I began eating and crying. I couldn't calm down until my parents came back. The sense of isolation and abandonment that I felt that night has never left me. To this day, I avoid being alone wherever possible, and I fear the dark – or rather, what the dark may hold.'

'I don't know about you, but this is pretty close to one of my worst nightmares,' Ronnie whispered loudly, glaring at Josephine. 'I can't believe you've got us into this.'

'I don't remember being the one who broke my neck to get a seat,' she retorted, gesturing towards Lettice and Lydia. 'Right now, being alone would be my idea of heaven.'

'My wife will tell you that I'm frightened of authority.' Hitchcock turned and spoke directly to Archie. 'Policemen terrify me. English policemen, especially, because you're always so polite. When I was five, I did something very bad,' he continued, and Josephine suddenly had a terrible feeling that they were going to explore his fears year by year. Could any man have that many neuroses, she asked herself, and decided that this one probably could; if that was the case, it was going to be the longest weekend of her life. 'I don't recall what it was, but my father wanted to punish me. He made me go to the police station with a letter and they locked me up – only for a few minutes, but the noise of the cell door is something that I'll never forget. It terrified me.'

As the director began to talk about a fear of embarrassing himself in public – without any great sense of irony as far as Josephine could see – she looked out of the window and wondered what Marta was doing. The sky seemed at war with itself, and a ribbon of dark blue touched the hills on the other side of the water, threatening the gentle summer evening which had descended on Portmeirion; during a rare pause in Hitchcock's monologue, she thought she detected the distant rumble of thunder. Outside on the terrace, the nun walked quickly past the window, rounding the corner in the general direction of the hotel's reception. Josephine waited to see if she would rejoin the party, but no one appeared, and she turned her attention reluctantly back to Hitchcock's speech. 'But my greatest fear of all is to know the future. A movie director can *predict* the future, of course: in making a film, he takes an imitation slice of life in his hands and arranges it just the way he wants it. He knows, in the first scene, what is going to happen in the last. But the stuff the movie director is working with isn't real. In real life, we can plan and take precautions, but we can never be sure – and to know the future without any semblance of control would be a peculiar kind of hell. To see the pain along with all the beautiful things ahead, the misery, the death – that would be terrible. The loss of those we love is something we should not be asked to know about too soon. When God keeps the future hidden, He is being merciful, and He is saying that life would be unbearable without suspense.' He sat down and smiled expectantly at his audience. 'Who'd like to start us off?'

'Have you left them anywhere to go, Hitch?' Alma's easy teasing of her husband made the atmosphere in the room instantly more relaxed, and everybody laughed, but Josephine noticed that she had distanced herself from the exercise, making it clear that she had no intention of taking part. 'You've probably spoken for most people here.'

'We'll see. How about you, Mr Lascelles? If I've touched a nerve, feel free to elaborate on it, or take us in a different direction altogether.'

He seemed to have picked on the shyest person in the room, and Josephine wondered if that was deliberate. The young man cleared his throat nervously and took a healthy swig of brandy before saying, 'Injustice, I suppose. When I was a boy, I was accused of something I didn't do and I've never got over it.'

Hitchcock nodded sympathetically. 'Shame is a terrible thing. How did it make you feel?'

'Devastated. It was just a childish prank, but it felt like the end of the world. I grew up that day, and there was no such thing as innocence any more – not because I felt guilty, but because I realised then that the truth doesn't always matter. It's what people *think* that determines how the world works. And that made me so angry.' Listening to him speak, Josephine was astonished that strangers were prepared to open themselves up to such public scrutiny, but the writer in her could only admire the skill with which Hitchcock manipulated people, directing their private emotions as effortlessly as he presumably did their professional ones. Even she was caught up in the game now, aware of a certain shameful voyeurism in her attitude but implicated nonetheless by her fascination with what was to come. 'No one believed me,' the actor continued, 'not even my parents, and it made me feel so helpless because there was absolutely nothing I could do about it. It was as if I were talking a completely different language. In the end, I almost began to doubt myself. That's what frightened me, really – not the idea of being punished for something I hadn't done.' He smiled, trying to make light of what he had said. 'I suppose I've always been too concerned about what people think of me. Bad choice of profession, I know.'

He looked round the room, made vulnerable by having been the first to speak and keen that someone else should join in. It was Astrid Lake who offered solidarity. 'For me, the greatest fear is rejection,' she admitted, unprompted. 'I'm adopted. My parents gave me up when I was too young to remember anything about them, and no matter how happy my childhood was in the end, or how often I tell myself that there must have been a good reason for it, I can't quite get over the fact that they gave me away.' She smiled at Lascelles. 'Like Danny, I seem to have chosen a profession which thrives on what I'm most afraid of.'

'You'd be surprised by how quickly you develop a thick skin.' The words were cynical, but they were delivered with a genuine kindness and offered as advice rather than criticism. Josephine looked round and saw Bella Hutton standing in the doorway. She walked over to the fireplace and put her brandy down on the mantelpiece. 'Don't let me interrupt,' she said, with the confidence of someone whose arrival in a room made normal conversation impossible. 'You were talking about rejection.'

The girl glanced at Hitchcock, but he showed no sign of resentment at Bella's intrusion into the conversation; on the contrary, he seemed more interested than ever. 'Yes. I was going to say that I feel it to a certain extent whenever I finish a film,' she explained. 'For a while, it's like being in a family: there are roles and hierarchies, people you get on with and people you don't, but personalities don't matter because you're stuck with them and you make the best of things. What counts is that you have a place, no matter how small, and you know exactly what it is. You can rely on it. Then everyone moves on and you have to start again, doing whatever's necessary to fit in. I suppose that reminds me of things I'd rather forget.' She looked at Bella. 'I don't know if the idea that I might become too tough to care about that makes me feel better or worse.'

Hitchcock waited to see if Bella intended to respond, but she said nothing so he continued his way round the room. 'You've been very quiet since dinner, Mr Turnbull. Is there anything you'd like to share with us?'

Leyton Turnbull seemed to have drunk himself sober. The erratic behaviour of earlier had vanished, and, when he spoke, his voice was calm. 'I'm afraid you're right,' he said quietly, unable to meet Hitchcock's eye.

'Sorry? I don't understand.'

'Everything you said at dinner, what you all think of me. I'm afraid it's true. I've seen him very clearly tonight – the man I've become.' He laughed, but there was no mirth in it. 'And I can see my future very clearly, too. You're right, Hitch. It's terrifying.' He pushed his chair back and stood up.

'Look, Turnbull, I'm sorry for what I said.' Daniel Lascelles caught his arm as he walked past, but he shook it off and walked out of the room with more dignity than he had managed all night. They watched him go. David Franks looked nervously at Hitchcock, whose expression remained inscrutable. Astrid Lake seemed genuinely upset.

Archie leant forward and whispered in Josephine's ear. 'How much of this is genuine, do you think?'

She shrugged. 'I don't know, but I get the feeling that he's only just started. If this is going on all weekend, perhaps we should decamp to Bangor.'

Hitchcock's manner suggested she was right. 'How about you, Mr Franks?' he asked, without any hint of awkwardness. 'What makes you tremble?'

'Fire,' Franks said, without a moment's hesitation. 'When I was fourteen, my father was burnt alive and I watched it happen. I wake to his screams every morning of my life.' The room was silent, and Josephine looked at Archie in horror. For the first time, Hitchcock was thrown completely and stared half accusingly at his colleague, as if the game were the biggest victim in what had just been said. Alma seemed genuinely devastated. She reached across and covered Franks's hand with her own. 'I'm so sorry, David,' she said quietly. 'We had no idea. It must have been horrific for you.'

'Yes, it was.' He bowed his head, and no one spoke. When he looked up again, he was grinning. 'Only joking,' he said, squeezing Alma's hand apologetically and winking at her husband. 'My father's alive and well and living in a nursing home in Croydon.'

For a moment, Josephine thought Hitchcock was going to hit him; instead, he walked over to Franks's chair and slapped him heartily on the back. 'Very good, David,' he said, but his expression changed. 'Let's just pray there are no fires in South London tonight. If one should break out now, think how you'll feel in the morning. Now, do you want to tell us what *really* frightens you, or shall we move on?'

Alma looked worried. 'Maybe we should leave it there, Hitch. I think we all know each other well enough by now, and some dancing might be a better idea.' Josephine glanced hopefully at her friends and saw her own discomfort reflected in their faces; even Lettice and Lydia seemed eager to get out of the room.

'It seems a shame to stop now, just when things are getting interesting.' Bella smiled at Alma, although she seemed as unsettled by Franks's joke as everyone else. 'And I've missed a lot of the fun. I don't even know if you've shared your darkest fears yet?'

Having shown no interest in taking part, Alma suddenly seemed intent on rising to the challenge, and Josephine wondered what issue existed between the two women to make Alma so reluctant to back down. 'Crowds,' she said simply. 'When I was a child, my parents took me to see the King's funeral.' She smiled wryly. 'I was very small and I lost hold of my father's hand. There was a sea of people, and it was impossible for me to stand my ground. I ended up being dragged through the crowds, and since then I've been very claustrophobic. The thought of not being able to breathe terrifies me.'

Bella nodded. 'Although there's more than one way to suffocate someone.'

The man whom Marta had pointed out to Josephine as Hitchcock's cinematographer hadn't said a word since they arrived, but there was something in the way he stood up now which expressed his disgust with the evening as eloquently as any speech could have done. His movement distracted the director from whatever he had been about to say to Bella. 'Are you leaving us already, Mr Spence?'

'I've had enough of this, Hitch. I need some fresh air and I'm not in the mood for games.'

'I'm not sure I can allow you to leave without telling me what I want to know, Jack.'

'I'm not sure you can stop me.'

The two men stared defiantly at each other, and Josephine got the impression that their conversation was not simply about the evening. In the end, Spence sat down again, but it was far from an act of submission. 'All right. I'll tell you what frightens me. Gallipoli in 1915. They sent me out there to take photographs. Before the war, I'd never seen a dead body. I knew that was about to change, but I never knew how bad it would be.' He looked at Hitchcock. 'People will tell you that reality is never as bad as your imagination, but they're wrong. The first thing we saw when we got off the boat was a big tent, like one of those marquees you get at a village fete. We went over to open it. I don't know what we thought we were going to find, and the smell as we began to unlace the sides should have told us something, but none of us was prepared for a pile of dead Englishmen, hundreds of corpses lying on top of each other, their eyes wide open, starting to rot.'

Hitchcock pushed the decanter across to him but Spence ignored it. 'We started to bury them, but there were so many. You don't think about that, do you? Having to find somewhere for the dead. You cling on to decency and dignity for a bit, but it soon defeats you. We pushed them into the trenches, but it was impossible to keep them all covered. We lived with the dead. Their arms and legs taunted us, sticking out of the earth like they'd just rolled over in bed. The soil was soft and springy underfoot because of the bodies, like autumn in the woods, when you know you're walking on decay.' He paused, and changed his mind about the drink. As he poured brandy, Josephine looked at Archie, but he had bowed his head, and she wondered what fugitive images had found their way back to him thanks to Spence's words. 'So we buried them, but they kept coming, more each day. And we found ways to deal with it. If a hand came out of the soil, we'd shake it as we went past. It wasn't disrespect, it was a way to cope. We all did it. Then one day I grabbed a hand and it held on. We'd buried him alive, for Christ's sake. We were so tired and so used to death that we could no longer tell the difference.' He shook his head in disbelief. 'I scrabbled in the dirt as if I were insane, scraping it off his face until I heard him moan and saw his eyelids flicker. When I was sure I'd found him in time, I started to cry with relief. I began to haul him out, but that wasn't what he wanted; he wanted me to finish it there and then. He clutched at my clothes, pleading with me to kill him. I didn't have a rifle with me, and I couldn't leave him on his own, so I put my hands round his throat and choked him, and this time I made sure. And do you know what? He looked grateful.'

There was a sudden division in the room between those who were too young to understand the war, and who were shocked by Spence's story, and those for whom his words were an extreme version of a familiar sadness. 'What you did was very brave and very merciful,' Hitchcock said quietly.

'Perhaps, but I wonder how many weren't so lucky? He can't have been the only poor bastard we buried alive. You didn't serve in the war, did you, Hitch?'

'No. I was excused on medical grounds.'

'He enlisted in the volunteer corps of the Royal Engineers,' Alma added protectively.

Spence held up his hand. 'I'm not questioning your courage or your loyalty. I'm only saying that when you talk about fear, when you show death on screen, it's just a game – like the one you're playing now.'

'Would you be happier if we did it for real?' Franks asked.

Spence ignored him. 'But I'll go along with it, and those are my answers: I'm afraid of dying, and I'm afraid of killing. I have nightmares about both.' He stood up and looked at Franks. 'And I'm not joking.'

This time, he left the room without any opposition. 'Well, who's still to go?' Bella asked, unnerving Josephine by looking directly at her.

'We're just observers,' Archie said diplomatically. 'And it's time we were going.'

'Just a second, Chief Inspector,' Hitchcock said, and his emphasis on the rank drew one or two surprised glances from his guests. 'Won't you stay until the game is over? I think Bella may be about to deliver the sort of exit line we all love her for.'

The actress didn't disappoint him. She stubbed out a half-smoked cigarette and walked to the door. 'I've always thought that there can be nothing worse than to know the manner of your own death,' she said, choosing her words with impeccable timing. 'And now I know that to be true.'

10

'What the fuck was that all about?' Ronnie asked when they

186

were safely back in the restaurant. 'Next time, remind me to stick with Marta. She's got more sense than the rest of us put together.'

'I wonder what Bella Hutton meant?' Lettice asked.

'Perhaps she's ill,' Lydia suggested. 'Although if that's a typical Hollywood evening, anything terminal would be a blessed relief.'

'Have you gone off the idea, then?'

Lydia looked at Josephine, and a guilty smile flickered across her lips. 'Let's just say I'll scuttle back to my dressing room at the Adelphi with a new-found humility. More drinks, everybody?'

Ronnie and Lettice followed her enthusiastically to the bar, and Josephine lingered behind with Archie to watch the band, whose first set was just drawing to a close with a subtle rendering of an Ivor Novello song. 'Isn't that the waitress who was on duty this afternoon?' Josephine asked, pointing to the singer.

Archie looked more closely. 'Yes, I think so. Amazing what lipstick and a posh frock can do for a girl.'

'Posh-ish,' Josephine corrected him ungraciously. 'And not so much of the girl. She won't see twenty again.' She ignored a look which had the word forty in it, and was forced to admit, 'Actually, she's very good.'

'Why do you say that so grudgingly?' Archie asked, laughing.

'Oh, you can just tell she's a little madam. I was watching her earlier, when she was serving tea to the table next to ours. It's all in the colour of her eyes: exactly the same as the girl who works in the shop for my father. I've never known that shade of blue to mean anything but trouble.'

The waitress-turned-singer took her applause and left the

small stage. She made her way across the dance floor to where Hitchcock and Alma were talking, and lingered by the director, waiting for a chance to introduce herself. Without looking at her, he held out his empty glass so that she had no choice but to take it. Mortified, the girl flushed and left the room, and Archie noticed some of the waiting staff snigger. 'Nothing like being brought down to earth with a bump, is there? Do you want another drink?'

'Only if you're having one.' She glanced round the room. Mercifully, there was no one she recognised; except for Alma and the director himself, Hitchcock's party seemed to have other plans.

'Why don't you go and find her?'

She looked embarrassed. 'Am I that transparent?'

'I'm afraid so, but probably only to me. I'm going to get changed and have that drink with Bridget. If we leave together now, they'll think we're going for a walk.'

'Are you offering me an alibi, Chief Inspector?'

'Yes, but only if you'll do the same. I can live without any more words of wisdom from Ronnie.' He looked across to where the Motleys and Lydia were already deep in conversation with another couple. 'I don't think we're going to be greatly missed. Is there *anybody* those three don't know?'

'I doubt it. Not in a place like this.' They went over to make their excuses and were just leaving when Lydia caught Josephine's arm. 'Do me a favour while you're out, darling. Pop in on Marta and make sure she's all right.'

PART FOUR

MURDER!

25–26 July 1936, Portmeirion

I

There were many paths to the dog cemetery, but Bella chose the route that rose up from behind the old stable block, simply because it was the one she knew best. While Grace lived here, these woods had been more like a jungle – wild and impenetrable, so much so that the way had had to be cleared by woodcutters before the hearse could pass through to collect her body. Even now, the land had an untamed and untameable quality about it: the maze of narrow pathways which ran back and forth across it were not man-made, it was said, but had been cut by a lone stag which appeared on the peninsula shortly after Grace's death. Bella had no idea if it were true or not, but the paths remained long after the stag had moved on, and the tale was one of the kinder myths that had been spun around her sister's isolation. It saddened her to hear Grace scorned by strangers: her privacy, her desire to honour the animals she had loved, her refusal to allow any living thing, beast or plant, to be destroyed on her land – these were codes that seemed oddly out of kilter to a generation that accepted cruelty and waste as natural and inevitable, although Bella could not help feeling that the eccentricity lay not with her sister but with the world.

The route she had chosen also had the advantage of being the most direct, and, with the light dwindling and rain threatening, she was anxious to spend as little time in the woods as possible. Chaplin ran ahead of her, excited by the novelty of an evening walk, and Bella was glad of his company. A sharp right-hand bend in the path led her away from the village and deeper into thick woodland, and she realised that the open spaces around the hotel had fooled her into underestimating how dark it would be among the trees. In a matter of seconds, the lamplight from the Piazza and the comforting silhouette of Portmeirion's skyline vanished as completely as if they had never existed. But daylight was no good for what she needed to do, and she couldn't risk being interrupted. Resisting the temptation to turn back, she fumbled in her bag for the torch she had brought with her and shone its beam determinedly onto the path ahead.

She longed for the release of the storm. The air was heavy and suffocating, closing in on her as she walked, and already her dress clung uncomfortably to her body. It was a relief when she reached a crossroads and the trees cleared, allowing the sky back in for a few precious moments. The cemetery lay a short distance ahead. She moved forward, but a rabbit shot out of the bushes, startling her, and Chaplin gave chase before she could stop him. She called the dog back but he ignored her, and Bella had to change direction to find him. A dark silhouette rose up ahead of her, and she stared at it in horror. For some reason, she had taken it for granted that the cottage was long gone, razed to the ground when the land was sold, but its shell was still there, a reminder of past obligations unfulfilled. She had turned away from so much of her family's grief and a sense of justice had never burned strongly inside her unless it was personal; now her home had pulled her back, and she was shocked by how strongly she felt an emotional bond with the people she had left behind and a physical connection to the earth which held them – a physical connection made more intense by the knowledge of her own mortality.

Unsettled, she clipped Chaplin's lead onto his collar and dragged him sharply away from the ruins, then retraced her footsteps to the crossroads. The luxury of the clearing was short-lived: when nature reasserted itself, the shadow of the trees was worse than ever, and, in the darkness, the woodland's age and lush profusion seemed menacing and other-worldly. The path narrowed again, forcing its way through old firs and rhododendron bushes, then climbing steeply as if daring Bella to reach her destination. She could only have been walking for ten minutes or so, but it felt much longer; the illness that she had refused to acknowledge was making itself known now with alarming regularity, and she paused to get her breath, leaning against a tree for support. Chaplin seemed to sense her anxiety; he stared into the blackness of the undergrowth, ears pricked, tail taut and quivering, straining at his lead to go back the way they had come. Gently, she pulled him on, but they had not gone far before she stopped again and looked back over her shoulder. Had she heard footsteps? She coiled the leather round her hand a couple of times, instinctively wanting the dog closer, and listened carefully, but the woods were silent and she blamed her imagination.

As soon as she moved on, she heard them again, and this time they sounded very close, mirroring her movements, stopping and starting when she did. She longed to switch off her torch, knowing that it placed her firmly in the sights of whoever was behind her, but she needed the light to find her way, even if it made her vulnerable. Willing herself to stay calm, she quickened her pace, but the noise quickened too, and, just as she was about to sink to the ground in despair, something in its rhythm told her how stupid she was being. The path was dry and hard from a long summer, and all she could hear was the echo of her own footsteps. It wasn't surprising that her mind was playing tricks, aided and abetted by the gloom of the woods and the knowledge of what she had come here to find. She walked on more confidently, but – now that it had been awakened – the instinct to fear could not be entirely dispelled. Ridiculously, because it was something she never did, she began to hum quietly to herself.

When she saw the old pheasant hide, she knew she was close to the cemetery, but she had forgotten quite how suddenly it appeared. Her torch picked out the wooden carving of a dog which stood at its entrance, as still and lifeless as the companions it guarded. Chaplin whimpered and stared at her reproachfully, sensing that this was a place of death, and Bella had a pang of guilt at having brought him here. 'Don't worry, honey,' she said, crouching down to reassure him. 'I wouldn't do it to you.' She looked around her and shivered. So much loss, so many friendships cut short – and now, so much guilt. The cemetery had always spoken to her of desolation, not comfort or solace. It was the last place in the world that she would ever want to leave someone she loved; better that they should burn in Hell than lie cold and alone in such unforgiving soil.

The rich scent of pine and the melancholy sound of birds roosting served only to darken Bella's mood. Reluctantly, she hooked Chaplin's lead around the wooden dog, sparing him from any more distress, and walked alone into the circle of graves. She moved slowly, avoiding the tangle of twigs and branches which crawled at head height through the air. The summer growth had become so densely entwined that very little rain could find its way between the leaves, and the groundcover was dry and brittle underfoot. A branch snapped as she stepped on it, holly scratched at her face, and, in her mind, Bella imagined bones breaking, felt fingers touching her skin. She shone her torch round to identify the grave she had been told about, the tangible proof of her brother's guilty secret, but something in the cemetery's defiant peace made her hesitate. After all these years, what good would it do anyone to discover the truth behind Rhiannon Erley's disappearance? Then she saw the marker in front of her – a mound of rough stones, more like a cairn than a traditional memorial, and its poignancy gave Bella her answer. As she knelt down to examine its careful formation, the dank, fetid smell of earth rose up to greet her.

The second time she heard it, there was no mistaking the sound, no blaming her imagination. Footsteps circled the cemetery – slow and predatory, making no attempt at secrecy, and it was this very openness that frightened Bella most: it told her that any hope of escape was already lost to her. She stood up and swung her torch round defiantly, desperate to put a name to the evil that threatened her, but its beam was too weak to reach the edge of the burial place, and, without thinking, she threw it away from her in frustration. Deprived of any definite form, the footsteps became more sinister than ever, crawling insidiously into her mind and fashioning horror after horror. Behind her, Chaplin growled, then began to bark furiously, but the barking stopped as suddenly as it had started. Fearful that her dog had been hurt, she went to retrieve the torch to look for him but, before she could pick it up, the light from the beam went out.

And then she felt it. A presence, unbearably close. The terror that had so far failed to overwhelm her did so now with a dreadful, all-consuming force. Blindly, she turned to run, but the panic disoriented her, and she had no idea how to find the path out of the cemetery. Something moved to her left, and she stumbled in the opposite direction, but it must have been a trick of the shadows because she realised immediately that she had in fact moved towards the danger. A hand reached out to her face. She ducked to avoid it, and the holly scratched her cheek again, deeper this time, its prickles sharper than she would ever have imagined possible. She tripped and fell, and her exhausted body longed to stay where it was and submit to the earth, but the primeval instinct for survival was still strong enough in her to force her to her feet. She wiped the damp, rotting soil from her skin, sickened by the smell of death that clung to her so stubbornly, refusing to be brushed away, and a sharp pain shot down her cheek as she rubbed it. Her hand came away wet with blood. Only when she saw the knife flash towards her face again did she realise that what she had believed to be a holly tree was something far more deadly.

With a scream, she broke free for the final time, but she had lost all control now and crashed against the nearest gravestone. On her knees, she began to crawl like an animal through the undergrowth, but all the time she was aware of someone walking behind her, taunting her with the possibility of escape whilst waiting for the moment to strike. At last, the game was up and hands grabbed her ankles and dragged her roughly back to the middle of the graveyard. Her face scraped along the ground, rubbing dirt and leaves and pine needles into the open wound. The agony was almost enough to make her faint, but her body refused her the oblivion she craved. Out of nowhere, she heard a mournful, pathetic whimpering; just for a moment, she allowed herself to hope that Chaplin was alive after all, but the noise was too close, and it did not take her long to realise that it came from her own throat.

And then the knife was there again, driven with force through her hand so that she was pinned to the floor. Instinctively, Bella yanked her arm upwards, but the sight of the blade piercing her flesh made her gag, and the drag of the knife through her skin as it was pulled slowly out left her weak and defenceless long before the pain had time to register. The knife passed back and forth across her body, cutting rather than stabbing, to prolong her agony, indiscriminate in where it landed and moving so swiftly that she barely felt it touch her skin. Sobbing, she rolled over onto her back, wanting the knife to strike where it mattered, offering herself to its deadly caress if only it would do its work swiftly. Still the torture continued, but there was a different, frenzied quality to it now, as if her submission were an incentive to even greater violence. The knife was thrust repeatedly into her stomach, deep enough for her to feel the hilt against her skin. Her body jerked in some terrible, violent dance, as if she were possessed, and she felt her life seeping away in the warm trails of blood which mapped the blade's path. As the knife worked its way systematically upwards, reaching her chest and neck, she heard a gurgling sound coming from her throat but it was the last thing she was aware of. She had closed her eyes for good long before the knife sought them out.

Glad of some air and some peace, Josephine slipped away from the hotel and found Neptune in darkness. She knocked softly on the door, thinking that Marta might simply have fallen asleep after a long day, but all was silent. Perhaps they had missed each other and she was already back at the hotel with Lydia, but Josephine was reluctant to go and find out; tired of dancing around her own feelings and other people's, she wanted Marta on her own or not at all.

The strong scent of roses and lavender drew her further into the Piazza, and she sat down on one of the benches. This was her favourite part of Portmeirion, particularly during the evening. The glamour of the hotel was exciting in small doses, but there was something about the village itself that appealed more to her imagination. The visitors had gone, leaving the imprint of their day in the air and the promise of return in the neatly stacked chairs and clean café tables, and a few of the residents were taking a stroll after dinner. Their voices sounded deceptively clear across the peace of the square, making them seem closer than they really were, and it interested Josephine that Portmeirion played tricks with the ear as well as with the eye. The atmosphere reminded her of solitary walks at dusk through small French towns, when the character of a place seemed to reveal itself more honestly, freed from the confines of tour guides and history books. Or perhaps it was simply that *she* had felt free.

She smelt the cigarette smoke before she felt Marta's hand on her shoulder. 'Running away from your own party?'

Josephine smiled. 'Age must have some privileges.' She took

Marta's hand and pulled her down onto the bench next to her. 'Anyway, I was looking for you. Where have you been?'

'Just for a walk. It was far too hot inside. Sorry.'

'Don't apologise. Sitting out here is exactly what I need after coffee with the Hitchcocks.' She kissed Marta's cheek, noticing the faint scent of gardenia on her skin. 'And you're worth waiting for.'

'I'm glad to hear it.' The words were playful, but Josephine knew that they had each said exactly what the other wanted to hear. 'So was Hitch's cabaret as awful as you expected it to be?'

'Worse, if that's possible. He delivered some sort of definitive lecture on fear, then wound everyone up and watched them go. It was good to see him squirm when it turned nasty, though,' she admitted. 'I thought Archie was going to have to get his notebook out.'

'Didn't Alma rein him in?'

'She had the sense to stay out of it until Bella Hutton turned up. Is there an issue between those two?'

Marta shrugged. 'I don't know, but I can see why you're out here. Where's everyone else?'

'Back at the hotel, except Archie. He went to have a drink with Bridget.'

'Ah. Leaving his notebook at home, presumably.'

'Quite.'

Marta stubbed her cigarette out on the floor. 'Do you mind?'

'No,' Josephine said truthfully, taking the packet out of her hand. 'For what it's worth, I liked Bridget.'

'So what *were* you so deep in thought about just now?'

'Nothing very original, I'm afraid.' She paused while Marta

lit her cigarette. 'I promised myself I wouldn't start taking stock of my life at every big birthday, but that's exactly what I was doing. Forty obviously matters more than I thought it would.'

'You must be pleased, though? You've got a Hitchcock movie, a string of stage hits and another book about to be published. Oh, and half a racehorse. That's not bad for forty.'

'But I haven't got you.'

Her directness seemed to take Marta by surprise. 'Why do you say that?' she asked. 'I'll move heaven and earth to be with you, Josephine, whenever you ask me to. I don't know how to make that any clearer.'

'It's not you I'm doubting,' Josephine said, looking out across the square. 'But that sort of life isn't real, is it?' Her eye fell on a bust of Shakespeare, perched playfully on one of the balconies that linked the two buildings on the southern side of the village and convincingly lifelike from a distance. 'We're like one of Clough's tricks, you and I: it's beautiful and intense and exciting, but if you look at it for long enough you see straight through it.'

'You told me not to ask any more of you,' Marta said quietly. 'You said that's how you wanted it to be.'

'No. I said that was how it *had* to be. It was never a matter of choice.' Josephine took Marta's face in her hands, wanting her to understand that this frustration was only with herself. 'But there are times when I'd swap intense and exciting for something more normal, for what you and Lydia have. You're not continually analysing your own relationship. You laugh, you bicker, you look out for each other and make plans.' She paused. 'You talk about moving to Hollywood together.'

'Is that what this is about?' Marta asked, exasperated. 'I don't want to go to Hollywood, Josephine. It isn't an option.'

'No, you're probably right. I think this evening put Lydia off any travel plans she was tempted to make, at least for now.'

'Not just for now. I'm not going anywhere. There's no way that I would ever . . .'

Josephine cut her off with a kiss. 'Please, Marta – don't look that far ahead. It's tempting fate, and I don't want either of us to make promises we might not be able to keep. Things change. People change.'

'I didn't know you felt like this. I thought it was out of sight, out of mind the minute you crossed the border.'

'Don't think I haven't tried, but I can't do it any more. I can't be content in that other life because part of me is always with you.' Such thoughts were a familiar part of the hours she spent alone, but Josephine had never intended to speak them aloud; suddenly, though, there seemed little point in keeping anything from Marta. 'Sometimes, just for a minute, I let myself think about what it would be like if you and I were free to do whatever we wanted,' she admitted. 'I imagine you in my house, in my bed; going shopping or walking over the sands at Nairn. And then I have to stop because it hurts too much and I can't bear all the things I don't know about you, the things you only find out when you're with someone all the time.' The quiet of the square conspired with Marta's silence to make Josephine feel vulnerable and uncertain. 'Because I'm *not* free, Marta. I have people who expect things from me. A father to keep an eye on, a house and a reputation to look after, sisters who take things for granted now because there was a time when it suited me to let them. I could never drop everything and go to Hollywood with you, even if you wanted me to.'

'And neither could Lydia. Have you met her mother?'

Josephine laughed. 'Once was enough. But that's what I mean by normal. I could never share my whole life with you in the way that Lydia does. I have to keep it all in compartments and remember to be someone slightly different in each one. Lydia's always Lydia. All right, she flirts with the odd producer if it'll get her a part, but pretending to be someone else is her job. It shouldn't be mine.'

'So what are you trying to tell me?'

Josephine heard the fear in her voice and wondered how she had managed to stray so far from what she really wanted Marta to understand. 'That I love you,' she said, trying again. 'I love you and I'm scared – scared that I won't be able to do all the things I want to do in the time I've got left. Scared because there's another war coming, and people will disappear and the joy will go out of everything. Scared because I'm trapped by my own decisions and I might never be able to find a way back. That's *my* fear – running out of time before anything changes. And you're the only person I can say that to. The only person who makes it go away.'

Marta let her hand rest gently on Josephine's cheek. 'And you don't think that's real?' she asked softly. 'Come on – let's go somewhere more private.'

Josephine stood and turned towards Neptune, but Marta caught her arm and nodded in the opposite direction. They left the square and took the steps down to the beach, using the lights from the hotel to guide them, and then, as they faded, a torch which Marta had brought with her. 'You came prepared,'

Josephine said dryly, wondering where Marta was taking her. 'I wouldn't have thought you were the Girl Guide type.'

'And you'd be right. I can't say uniforms have ever been my thing.'

The tide was out, and they followed the headland round until they reached a stretch of coastline dotted with tiny coves. The path narrowed and Marta slowed down to let Josephine walk in front. Up ahead, she could see a faint light coming from one of the small caves; it was further inland than the rest and, as she crossed the sand to reach it, she realised that it was filled with candles, tucked into crevices in the rock where they were sheltered from the night air. The floor was covered in blankets and cushions, and a picnic hamper stood waiting on a makeshift table. Josephine stared at it in astonishment. 'This is what you've been doing?'

'Happy birthday.' Marta stood close behind her and kissed the back of her neck. 'We're just in time – it's not even midnight.' She put her arms round Josephine's hips and spoke softly into her hair. 'I know it's hard, but you don't always have to imagine it.'

Josephine turned and looked at Marta for a long time. 'I once asked you not to change anything about my life, didn't I?' Marta nodded. 'Well, now I'm begging you not to leave it as it is.'

3

The weather was threatening to compete with the outbursts that had been a feature of the evening so far, but Archie was glad to be outside. Hitchcock's gathering had brought together the sort of people he most despised, people whose personalities he would never understand, and he was relieved to have an excuse to leave them behind in exchange for something more familiar. He laughed to himself as he left the hotel, amused by the irony of his situation: never, as a young man, could he have imagined himself turning to Bridget for sanity and a world that made sense, and he wondered what had made the difference – whether it was wisdom, as Josephine had suggested, or simply a happy acquiescence.

White Horses formed a gateway between the hotel grounds and the headland, and seemed to Archie to act as mediator between the civilised world of the village and the miles of untamed woodland that surrounded it, ensuring that the values of one did not encroach too far on those of the other. It was a simple, single-storey building and its whitewashed walls shone proudly in the lantern light, as if pleased to offer a contrast to the more elaborate style of the rest of the village. A lamp was on in the window but there was no answer when he knocked, so he waited a couple of minutes and let himself in. The cottage was small and seemed designed for a solitary lifestyle – a contemplative life, he would have said, were it not for the thoroughness with which Bridget had made herself at home. His job had trained him to read people's lives from where they lived, usually in the most tragic of circumstances, but there was no need here for either his professional expertise or his personal knowledge: any stranger would know instantly that the room's occupant was happy with her own company, and that was exactly what Bridget had always been. It was one of the things he admired most about her: the ability to stand on the outside without ever seeming detached, to mix without letting anything of herself be compromised, and it was true of both her life and her art.

The two mingled easily here, although the basic necessities of eating and drinking played a secondary role. He walked over to the central table, which most people would have reserved for dining, and looked affectionately at the clutter of paper, pencils and half-finished sketches, at the mug used to wash brushes and the plate which had become a makeshift palette, and felt a sudden connection to his past which was both welcome and unsettling. The battered old box which Bridget used to store her paints was, he noticed, the same one that she had carried twenty years ago. He unclipped its lid and ran his finger across the row of small tubes, variously shrunken and misshapen with use, reading the names of the pigments: cerulean, chrome yellow, crimson alizarin. He had always loved the words she used, a secret language of colours and techniques which punctuated her everyday speech and made her inseparable from what she did; the words were not his, and yet they had become familiar to him, an important part of his life, signposts in their conversation. Now, he was surprised to discover how directly they still spoke to him.

He heard footsteps and laughter outside, and, when Bridget opened the door, he was surprised to see her with Hitchcock's cameraman. Like him, Spence had changed into something more casual since dinner, but neither of them could hold a candle to Bridget for informality; she was wearing the paint-stained overalls he had seen her in earlier, and not an inch of the dark-blue material seemed to have escaped unscathed. They were in the room before he had a chance to close the box, but, if she felt any irritation at having caught him looking through her things, she didn't show it. 'Archie!' she said, dumping a large bag on one of the chairs and letting two overexcited dogs off their leads. 'I didn't expect you so early. How nice.'

The words were genuine, and the awkwardness which Archie felt was of his own making, but that didn't help to ease his embarrassment. 'Sorry,' he said, 'but you told me to make myself at home. I didn't realise . . .' He tailed off, hoping that the disappointment didn't show in his face and angry with himself for assuming that he and Bridget would be on their own. It had been a casual meeting, after all, and the offer of a drink was made on the spur of the moment; she had probably been regretting it all evening.

She dismissed his apology with a wave of her hand and deftly moved one of the border terriers off the remaining chair. 'Do you know Jack Spence? He's here with those film people.'

Archie couldn't help smiling at the way in which she made film sound like a dirty word. 'We haven't been formally introduced,' he said. They shook hands, and he noticed that Spence didn't seem any more comfortable than he was. 'But we've shared some difficult moments thanks to Mr Hitchcock.'

'You were there too? Well, I'll let you get to know each other better while I have a quick shower. I won't be a minute.'

She left the room, shadowed by one of the terriers. 'That was a very eloquent parting shot,' Archie said to Spence when they were alone. 'And a very moving one. I rather got the impression that your boss's evening backfired on him.'

Spence shrugged. 'I've no doubt he'll make me pay for it sooner or later. Usually I don't mind being his pawn, but occasionally it grates.'

'Does he make a habit of games like that?'

'All the time.' He sat down, and the other dog jumped onto

his lap; Archie tried to ignore the suggestion of familiarity and how much it piqued him. 'I've sat through dinners where the food was blue, had a loan repaid to me in farthings, and looked on while he smoked Elsie Randolph out of a telephone box. At the wrap party for *The Farmer's Wife*, he hired a bunch of actors to play the waiting staff, just to see how long it would take us to notice. Some of his stunts are funnier than others, but they're all designed to keep us in line.' He leant forward and accepted a cigarette. 'It doesn't take a genius to see that film is his way of controlling people. A set is his doll's house, and we're his dolls.'

'So Portmeirion is his set for the weekend?'

'Oh, this is just a rather peculiar audition for the people who haven't worked with him; for those of us who have, it's a test of our loyalty ready for the big move.' He spoke the last three words as if they were capitalised. 'We're all under scrutiny, and he won't miss a thing. What gets past him certainly won't get through Alma's net. They're quite a team.'

'Don't you resent having to perform all the time? People who choose your side of the camera don't expect that.'

'It's tedious, and sometimes it gets out of hand, but we accept it because he's brilliant.' Spence must have seen the scepticism on Archie's face, because he added, 'Hitch really is that good, you know. Most people would tolerate far worse to work with him. For every stroke of genius the audience sees, there are two or three more behind the scenes.' He grinned. 'Anyway, I get off lightly because I'm *almost* as good as he is.'

'As modest as ever, I see.' Bridget sat down on the arm of his chair. She had changed into a sleeveless white linen dress, and her skin shone deep brown in the lamplight. From where he sat, Archie could smell the subtle scent of jasmine.

'What's wrong with that? I said almost.' Spence stubbed out his cigarette. 'We're all schoolboys at heart, I suppose. It's just that most of us try to hide it and Hitch chooses to make it a feature.'

It was the same line of defence that Archie had used with Ronnie but, now that he had seen Hitchcock's sense of humour in action, he couldn't help feeling that she had been right after all: behaving like a schoolboy was a dangerous trait in someone who wielded that sort of power. He said nothing, though, and asked instead, 'Are you part of the big move?'

Spence shook his head. 'No. I have other plans.'

He didn't elaborate on what they were, and Bridget stood up. 'I'll get us some drinks. What will you have?'

'Not for me, thanks,' Spence said, gently moving the dog from his lap. 'I'd better be going. I'll catch up with you over the weekend.' He raised his hand to Archie and kissed Bridget's cheek.

'Let me know how you get on,' she said, and Spence nodded. On his way out of the door, Archie was sure he saw him wink. 'Ever the soul of discretion,' Bridget added wryly when he was gone.

'I'm sorry. I didn't mean to interrupt your evening.'

'You didn't. We just bumped into each other in the woods. He was angry about something but that's always his way: he's got a terrible temper, but it blows itself out as soon as it arrives.' She peered out of the window. 'Let's hope this storm will do the same when it finally gets here.'

'Do you know him well?' Archie asked casually.

'Jack? As well as you can ever know someone like him, I suppose. We go back a long way. His family was part of the set that used to mix with Clough's, here and in London, so we met each other as kids and then ended up at the Slade together. I often see him when I'm here.' Archie felt someone nuzzle his hand, and he reached down to respond. 'That's Carrington, by the way,' Bridget said, and he was touched that she should have named her dog after the painter; their friendship stretched back to art school, and Dora Carrington's suicide in the early thirties must have devastated her. 'And this is Lytton.' She indicated the dog who had remained glued to her side. 'Ironically, he's a one-woman kind of chap. That would have made her laugh.'

'You must miss her,' he said, hoping that the tenderness in his voice would make up for the inadequacy of the words.

'Yes, every day. It was such a shock, and so inevitable.' She crouched down and scratched the dog's head, and he looked adoringly up at her. 'She was never going to carry on after Lytton died. It was a loneliness too far, and nothing had a point to it without him. Even painting was meaningless, because he wasn't there to see it. I can understand that. We all need someone to impress, someone who matters.'

He wanted to ask who mattered for her, but didn't trust himself to be gracious with the answer. In any case, he sensed she wanted to talk about something else, so he picked up their earlier conversation. 'I thought Jack Spence was only here because of Hitchcock. Does he come back often?'

'Whenever Clough adds a new building. They're very close, those two. It took Jack a while to get back on his feet after the war, and Clough gave him some work to help him out. Architectural photography, mostly – nothing as glamorous as what he's doing now, but easier on the eye than the things he had to cover abroad. No dead bodies in sight.' Her voice took on the cynical, ironic tone that had become second nature to their generation as they struggled to find new ways to distance themselves from the horror of war. 'He photographed this headland as it was when Clough bought it, and he's recorded its transformation ever since. Not that he needs the work now, but I think he has a great affection for it.' Archie nodded, and she laughed. 'Don't look so uncomfortable. I told him you were coming, but I didn't expect you to leave your party so early.' She kissed him and let her hand linger on the back of his neck. 'I'm flattered. And wine, too.' She rinsed a couple of glasses in the sink and looked for a corkscrew among the debris on the table.

'I would have let it breathe but I wasn't quite sure about your – uh – system,' he said, amused.

Bridget ignored the comment, then found what she was looking for and made an expressive gesture with it. 'You have to leave your systems at the door with me, Archie,' she said. 'Surely you remember that?' He nodded and passed her the bottle. 'Let's take it outside,' she suggested. 'It's hot in here, and we can keep an eye on the weather. I don't want to start that damned mural from scratch.' The back door of the cottage led to a private inlet with its own tiny rowing boat; there was a pretty walled area with a small table and chairs, lit by lanterns and well shielded from the public footpath. Bridget sat down and smiled at him. 'So how did you get caught up in Hitchcock's foreplay?'

He laughed. 'That's an interesting description.'

'Jack's term, not mine. He senses worse to come over the weekend. Did Josephine's cocktails go well or badly?'

'Well, but we were wrong-footed by the invitation after dinner. Hitchcock's a hard man to refuse. Did Jack tell you about it?' She nodded. 'At least we weren't expected to take part, but it was bad enough as a spectator sport.'

'Jack said it was all about fear.'

'That's right. If it hadn't felt quite so voyeuristic, it might have been interesting. I'd never realised that what you're afraid of says so much about who you are.'

'So what *are* you afraid of? If it's not a professional sin for a policeman to admit to fear at all?'

'Being wrong.' She looked at him disbelievingly, and he tried to explain before she teased him for his arrogance. 'That's not as egotistical as it sounds. I mean being wrong professionally. There's too much at stake.'

'Accusing the wrong man, you mean?'

'Or missing the right one. People are badly served either way, and it's not a mistake you can put right.'

'I would have thought knowing that was half the battle,' Bridget said seriously. 'And from what I remember, you're not short of compassion or understanding. I doubt you're often wrong.' She grinned. 'Professionally speaking, anyway. If I were in trouble, I'd want you on my side. But isn't the law infallible?'

'Oh yes. Just like we learnt our lesson from the war, and this government will be more effective than the last.' His wryness matched hers. 'You'll be pleased to know that the older I get, the less faith I have in my systems.'

'Now that can't be a bad thing.' She raised her glass. 'To the wisdom of age. Shame we have to wait for it.'

'I'm not so sure about that. Hitchcock talked about his greatest fear being a knowledge of the future. It was the most sensible thing he said all night, actually; knowing what's in store for you and not being able to do a thing about it would be terrible.' He drained his glass and watched as the first flicker of lightning split the sky across the water. 'A bit like having another war waiting in the wings, I suppose. It's hard to believe that it could have been worse, but the knowledge of what we were heading for would have made it so. This time, some of us won't have the luxury of ignorance.'

Bridget was quiet. He knew she was thinking back to that time in the hospital, when – with kindness, patience and understanding – she had slowly talked him back to sanity. 'You must have nightmares about going through it again.'

'Yes, and about what we might put up with as a nation to avoid it. But even on a day-to-day level, there'd be no point in hoping or striving for anything if you knew the future, no sense of discovery. You'd know how every painting was going to turn out before you picked up your brush. And as far as people are concerned, you'd miss out on all the joy, all the excitement, all the love, because you'd be obsessed with counting the days. You'd blunt your emotions to stop yourself getting hurt. Of course, some of us do that anyway.' Bridget looked at him curiously, but he didn't give her the chance to ask. 'What about you? What are you frightened of?'

'Losing my . . .' She stopped and took longer to consider her response. 'Not being able to express myself, I suppose,' she said at last. 'Having a vision that I can't communicate, either because I'm not talented enough or because of some physical disability. You never quite get the painting you set out to create, but to have a sense of beauty and not be able to share it in some way, or a demon that you can't exorcise somehow through your work – that would be a form of madness for me, I think.' Her face had a childlike earnestness when she was trying to understand or explain something; with a smile, like the one she gave him now, it crinkled into life and was completely transformed. 'Of course, some critics would say I'm there already.'

He couldn't have explained it, even to himself, but Archie's curiosity about Bridget's life became suddenly more urgent. Impatient to chip away at the distance that twenty years had created, he asked, 'What about the good things? Are you happy?'

The question sounded absurdly simplistic but she didn't treat it that way. 'Yes, Archie, I'm happy. Most of the time, anyway. There's not a day goes by when I don't want to work, and how many people can say that? It hasn't always been easy being a . . . well, being a painter isn't the most secure of jobs. Unlike some people, we don't get promotion.' He smiled, and listened as she talked about Cambridge and her friends, noticing that she spoke generally rather than about one specific person. All those years ago, that was how their feelings had begun – unconsciously, as friendship. They had got to know each other slowly, without the urgency of love, but the discoveries seemed richer for being leisurely. She had expected nothing from him, had made it clear that he was to do the same – and, because their time together was free of the pain of love, he realised now that he had carried it with him happily. He thought of Bridget without bitterness, regret or any of those other small betrayals that a more intense attachment can breed. And for that reason, she held a unique place in his life. He tried to put his thoughts into words, but she stopped him almost immediately. 'You think I didn't love you?'

Archie was taken aback by the question. Bridget looked at him, half teasing, half serious, and he remembered how he had always struggled to work out what those eyes were saying – but he had never minded. Something in her calm, relaxed ability to accept life as it was and at the same time grab all it offered was the antidote to his own need for precision and direction, and, for a while, it had made his life richer. 'Of course I loved you, Archie,' she said, taking his hand. 'Just because I didn't want to make a lifetime of it doesn't mean it was less than that. People are so funny about love. It always has to lead somewhere, as if it's only the beginning of something and never enough in itself.'

The storm, which seemed to have been prowling around the headland, looking for a way through Portmeirion's defences, finally found its way in, and thunder cracked loudly above them. Bridget laughed as the first big drops of rain fell onto the table between them. 'Wonderful timing,' she said. 'Now I've got to go and secure that mural. It's not dry enough to withstand this yet.' She stood up and pulled him to his feet. 'You can come and help me while you think of something to say.'

4

'You're angry with me, aren't you?'

'No, Hitch. I'm just tired. Don't worry about it.' Alma smiled unconvincingly at her husband's reflection in the dressing-table mirror and carried on removing her make-up. 'It's been a long day.'

'And you're angry.'

She sighed and turned to face him. 'I just don't understand why you do it.' He sat on the end of the bed, his face flushed from the wine and the heat of the room, and she could see from his expression that he didn't know either. She worried about his health more and more these days: his weight had always fluctuated but he was heavier now than he had ever been, and recently he had even begun to take short naps on set; it would only be a matter of time before someone mentioned this in an interview, and rumours would go round that his best was behind him. Alma recognised the streak of cruelty that entered her husband's jokes whenever he was undergoing a personal crisis. She had seen it several times already in the course of their marriage: when *The Lodger* was shelved, for instance, or when *Blackmail* failed to win over American audiences. This time, the intensity of it frightened her, and she had to make him see that. 'I think you went too far,' she said.

'Blame David. He invited them.'

'Only because you told him to. And sending him after Turnbull with a bottle of single malt doesn't suddenly make everything right.'

He looked defensive. 'How was I to know they were going to behave like that?'

'You couldn't have known, and that's exactly my point. It isn't a film set, Hitch. You don't get to decide what happens. People have emotions that didn't start in your head. They have jealousies and attachments and grudges that you have no idea about. We all do.'

'Oh yes?' He winked at her and tried to soften her mood, a sure sign that he knew he was in the wrong. 'And what might those be, Mrs Hitchcock?'

'I was talking generally,' Alma said firmly, remembering her brief exchange with Bella Hutton, out of character for both of them but symptomatic of the way in which petty jealousies could escalate. 'And don't try to joke your way out of this.' She walked over to the bed and kissed the top of his head, then sat down next to him and took his hand. 'There's already enough in our life that's unsettled, Hitch, things that are beyond our control. Why go out of your way to make trouble?' It was his chance – one of several she had given him lately – to talk honestly about everything that was worrying him: the colleagues he was losing; the mounting financial crisis at Gaumont which threatened them all; his disappointment with the response to his last film and his doubts about the one that was scheduled for release at the end of the year. Even though she knew he was only doing it to protect her, it hurt her when he hid his anxieties from her, internalising his darkest fears just like the characters in his films. More than anything, she wished that he could shrug them off as easily as he pretended to.

'Things will work out.' It was no more convincing now than the last time he had said it. 'And we *can* do something about America.'

Alma nodded, although she sometimes wondered if she had the energy to start all over again, when the pressure would be so much greater. If Hitch were to succeed in the States, he would need to command a salary which covered their taxes and enough respect to fight a system which placed power in the producer's chair, not the director's – and to do those things, he had to have another hit here as soon as possible. But that wasn't why she wanted this particular project so badly, and, having met her, Alma guessed that she would have got Josephine Tey's approval much faster if she had simply been honest. It was too personal, though – almost too personal to admit to herself. She saw in *A Shilling for Candles* the possibility of a different sort of film, one through which Hitch could rediscover a boyish delight in the simplest of things, a film of sunshine and innocence and tenderness – all the qualities that she loved about him but which had been lost somewhere along the way. For months now, Alma felt as though they had been fumbling about in the dark, playing a game of blind man's buff with their lives and their careers, and she mourned a more carefree time. She wanted her husband back. For very different reasons, they both needed this film to work.

5

Branwen stood at the edge of the coastal path and watched as forked lightning ran down the sky. The flash lit up the great mass of cloud that had gathered ominously over the estuary during the course of the evening, a declaration that the rain was likely to continue for some time now that it had started, and she was glad that she had had the foresight to bring an umbrella. There was an old stone hut behind her, marking Portmeirion's most southerly point, but she was reluctant to take shelter inside for fear of missing her rendezvous with Bella Hutton. As it was, she cursed the weather. This meeting was important to her and to her alone, and she doubted that anyone with less of an incentive would venture out at all. But still she waited, her hand clutching the note in her coat pocket as if her faith in it could bring her what she wished for. Her bond with her mother consisted of one fragile memory, an image of a young woman bending over her to say goodbye. Branwen had no idea if it was the final goodbye or simply an everyday parting, but she knew that her mother had been wearing bright red lipstick, that her clothes and hair had seemed somehow different. It was a fleeting impression, and she had played it through so often now that there was no way of knowing for certain how much of it was real and how much her own invention, but it had spread like a dye over the blankness of the years before and since, colouring her life without ever really giving shape to it.

'Hello?' At last, she thought she heard someone coming. She called out a second time, less tentatively now, but the rain was pounding down on the umbrella and she could barely hear her own voice. The lightning darted into the water again, and Branwen waited for the thunder to respond, counting the seconds to judge the storm's distance just as she had when she was a child. She got to three before someone grabbed her from behind and she felt a man's hand over her mouth, his arm around her waist. The umbrella clattered uselessly to the ground and rain stung her face like a thousand tiny needles. Too shocked to resist, she allowed herself to be dragged roughly backwards. By the time they reached the hut, the intensity of the downpour and her own growing panic had combined to bring her to her senses, and she clung to the sides of the doorway, dreading what might happen to her if she let her attacker pull her inside, away from any hope of rescue. The pain as he slammed his fist into her fingers was almost unbearable, and she let go instantly, but at least he had had to remove his hand from her mouth to do it, and from somewhere she found the strength to cry out. It was a pathetic, half-strangled sound, muffled even more by the enclosed space, and Branwen knew she was deluding herself if she thought anyone was nearby to hear her.

The hut was dark and claustrophobically small, the sort of place that an animal crawled to die. She struggled to get away, sickened as much by the damp, fetid air as by his presence, but he swung her round and pushed her against the back wall, holding her there with the weight of his body while he tied a blindfold over her eyes. The slate was cold and rough against her sunburnt cheek, but she struggled to speak: 'Please don't hurt me. I'll do whatever you want. It doesn't have to be like this. You'll hurt the . . .' Angrily, he grabbed her hair and jerked her head backwards to stop her talking, but there was no longer any need: shame and fear were powerful anaesthetics. He forced her legs apart and her body froze as she felt him pulling up her skirt, tearing at her underclothes, his hands all over her, hurting her again and again and again as the tears ran silently down her face.

When it was over, she was too frightened to move. For what felt like an age they stood locked together in a parody of the peaceful embrace that follows love; Branwen closed her eyes, trying to blot out the shame of his body against hers. Eventually, he pulled away from her, and she heard him readjusting his clothes. Without saying a word, he stroked her hair as though he were sorry, and she tried not to flinch at his touch, wary of angering him again by showing how much he disgusted her. His manner was calm now – affectionate, almost. Only when she caught the faint scent of leather and felt the strap tightening around her throat did Branwen realise that her suffering was far from over. It was actually just beginning.

6

When Gwyneth came round, it was already dark outside. She lay on the first-floor landing, listening to the rain pounding against the windows on every side of the house, and tried to work out how she had got there. Her aching head told her what her memory would not. She put a hand to her face, and winced with pain when she found the tender places on her jaw and cheekbone. Then she remembered Henry, standing at the edge of the trees in the afternoon sunlight, staring up at the attic window. At first, she had thought her mind was playing tricks on her, had closed her eyes to get rid of the image – but he was still there when she opened them, and this time he was moving towards the house. Terrified, Gwyneth had run to the stairs to check that the ground-floor windows and doors were locked, even though she never left them any other way – but she must have tripped before she got there, and now, hours later, she couldn't be sure. What if Henry had found a way in after all? What if he was still there?

A clap of thunder shook her from her indecision. She dragged herself to her feet with the help of the banister and hurried down the landing, trying the lights in one room after another, but there was no electricity at all in the house, and, as the storm arched its back and roared, it seemed to Gwyneth that every bit of energy had been absorbed into its fury. As if to taunt her, a streak of brilliant white sizzled down the sky. Mesmerised by its power, she stood at her bedroom window and watched as the black, swirling storm made a stranger of the landscape she knew so well, obliterating the silhouette of the mountains opposite and giving a dark, unearthly quality to the water below. The thunder came again, impossibly close this time, and a second crash followed before the first had even died away, then a third and a fourth. She put her hands over her ears, but the noise spoke straight to her heart, shaking her whole body with its force. Not to be outdone, the lightning flashed more vividly than ever, piercing the gap in the curtains and shining directly onto Taran's face. Gwyneth picked up the photograph from her bedside table and clutched it to her chest, speaking softly to her child as she had always done at the first sign of trouble. She locked herself in and cowered by the bed, longing for it to be over, but it was hard to say now which she was more frightened of: the undeniable force outside, or the possibility of an intrusion from her past. The house felt suddenly vulnerable to both.

Eventually the storm was exhausted. Its outbursts became less violent and more sporadic, and, with a final shudder of thunder, it crawled away to sleep, leaving the landscape to recover quietly from its rage. Gwyneth opened the door and stood at the top of the stairs, listening for the telltale footstep or creak of floorboard which would confirm her worst fear, but there was nothing. The electricity chose that moment to return and, as the landing filled with a comforting light, she caught sight of herself in the full-length mirror on the far wall and stared at the madness and fear in her own eyes, the striking family resemblance which she had tried so hard to ignore. Quickly, she lunged for the light switch, wanting nothing more now than to hide from herself.

7

Astrid pulled the garage door open and went inside, dragging her umbrella behind her without bothering to close it. Bad luck, in this case, meant getting even wetter than she was already. It was barely a two-minute walk from the hotel, but the wind had blown the rain in under its defences, and the water gushing down the steep incline had soaked her shoes and splashed her dress. Perhaps it was God's way of telling her that meeting a stranger at midnight with an important day ahead of her was not the most sensible idea she had ever had, but Astrid had never set much store by God's rules, and the evening had left her feeling troubled and lonely. Danny – although she didn't know him very well – was the nearest thing she had to a friend, and spending an hour or two with him couldn't do any harm. Too honest to let herself get away with that, Astrid smiled; the more she saw of Daniel Lascelles, the more attractive she found him, and friendship was only part of it. The invitation to meet him somewhere private in the middle of a storm had not taken much consideration.

She was a few minutes late, but everything was in darkness. The garage smelt faintly of oil, rubber and wood, that peculiarly masculine combination, and she wondered why – of all places – he had suggested they meet here. Folding the umbrella and leaning it against the wall, she was surprised by how acutely the scent took her back to the suburbs of London where she had grown up. Her adoptive father had owned a series of unreliable cars, each boasting something more seriously wrong with it than the last, and he seemed to spend most weekends alone in the garage of their semi-detached house, trying to make something roadworthy. On rainy afternoons, when she was bored and the day seemed to stretch out in front of her, she would wander in and watch him, silently absorbed in his task. He was a kind, shy man – not an easy talker, even with his wife – and he had no idea, really, how to engage a child, but he never gave up trying. He'd smile at her, and she would do her best to follow what he was doing so that the two of them had something in common, as if by learning where each small piece of metal went and what it did she could somehow teach herself how to fit into their lives.

Hurried footsteps outside brought her back to the present, but they were accompanied by voices and laughter, and they carried on towards the hotel. Wondering where Danny had got to, Astrid fumbled for a light switch and eventually found it by the door. She flicked it, but nothing happened. Impatiently, she switched it on and off repeatedly as if she could trick the light into working, but it refused to pander to her bullying. Just as she had decided that no man was worth sitting in the dark for, she heard more footsteps outside – along the side of the building from the Piazza this time, and slower. They stopped, and she thought for a moment that whoever it was had turned right up the hill towards the stable block, but then she heard the twist of the door handle and, through the chink of moonlight, saw the silhouette of a man slip quietly inside and close the door behind him. 'Danny?' she whispered, instinctively moving further back into the garage.

'I'm sorry I'm so late.' When she heard his voice, she sighed with relief and cursed herself for allowing her imagination to get the better of her. 'I went for a walk after dinner to clear my head and got caught in the storm. I had to go and change.'

'It's all right. I haven't been here long myself, and I suppose it *is* difficult to know what to wear for a garage rendezvous. I'm not sure there's a recognised etiquette on the subject.' She heard him laugh and relax a little. 'It's an interesting choice of venue.'

'But at least it's private.' There was an awkward silence, and Astrid guessed that he was blushing. 'Is there a light switch?' he asked.

'Near where you're standing, but it doesn't work.'

He tried it anyway, and she smiled at the typically male refusal to accept a woman's assessment of anything mechanical. 'Hang on a minute.' She waited while he felt his way round to the front of the car, then opened the driver's door and switched on the headlamps. The room – if hardly flooded with light – was now at least navigable, and she noticed that what looked like an individual garage from the outside was actually a larger space for two cars, divided down the centre by stone pillars and accessed through separate entrances. Danny pointed to the ceiling, where the light flex hung impotently down, stripped of its bulb. 'I would have thought this place attracted a better class of clientele than that,' he said. 'Cutlery and crockery I can understand, bathrobes are worth it if you've got the nerve, but walking off with the light bulbs smacks of desperation.' He walked over to the other car, an open-top Morris, and flicked on its lights. 'That's as good as it gets, I'm afraid. Dingy or moody. Take your pick.'

'Moody. I'm the glass half-full type.' In fact, the understated lamplight was not unpleasant. Objects hanging down from the rafters – ropes and metal cans for petrol, tools and other paraphernalia used by Portmeirion's gardeners – cast larger-than-life shadows on the ceiling, but the yellow glow from the headlamps was strong enough to give the room a welcome warmth. She cast her eyes admiringly over the sleek lines of the Alvis. 'Which is more than Leyton Turnbull will be in the morning when he finds out he's got a flat battery.'

'I think that'll be the least of Turnbull's troubles, don't you? If it were me, after what went on at dinner, I'm not sure I'd even hang around until the morning.'

'Yes, it's been a strange evening. After all the unpleasantness, it was nice to get your note.'

Danny looked confused. 'I didn't send you a note.'

'Of course you did. I picked it up from reception.'

'No. I picked *yours* up from reception. Look.' He put his hand in his breast pocket and passed her a piece of blue paper.

'I don't understand,' Astrid said. 'Except for the signature, this is exactly the same as the one I had.' She took her own from her bag to compare. 'See – the handwriting, the wording – they're identical. "Meet me in Garage No. 1 at midnight. I'll bring the champagne."' They looked at each other. 'It's obviously someone's idea of a joke, but I can't imagine what it means.'

'It means we've got no damned champagne,' Danny said matter-of-factly. 'I'll go and get some from the hotel.'

'No, Danny, it's fine. You can't go racing about for champagne in this weather.' The joke seemed harmless enough, but Astrid was reluctant to be left alone when someone obviously knew exactly where to find her. 'Look, as neither of us seems to be particularly attached to these garages after all, why don't we go to the hotel and have a drink there?'

'Or we could go back to my apartment,' Danny said. 'I've got some brandy.' Astrid hesitated, remembering what Bella Hutton had said. Danny was staying in Government House, just a stone's throw from the Hitchcocks' apartment, and she didn't want to be seen. He sensed her dilemma and began to apologise. 'I'm sorry, Astrid. I wasn't suggesting . . . of course you don't want to do that.'

His embarrassment won her over. She put a finger to his lips and said, 'It's fine, Danny. I know you didn't mean anything by it. Let's go.'

'Are you sure?'

'Yes, I'm sure.'

He grinned and went over to the door. Astrid walked round to switch the car's headlights off, but hesitated when she heard him swearing under his breath. 'What's the matter?'

'The door won't open.' He put his shoulder to the wood and pushed harder, but still it resisted. 'It's jammed with something. I'll try the other one.'

She watched him walk over to the other side of the garage, but something told her that he wasn't going to have any more luck there. 'I don't believe it,' he said angrily, giving the door a kick. 'I didn't have any problem getting in, did you?'

She shook her head. 'No, but somebody's idea of a joke obviously doesn't stop at sending us bogus notes.'

'You think someone's done this deliberately?'

'Of course they have, and don't you think it smacks of our host? He's been having a laugh at someone's expense all night, and now it's our turn.' She cast her eye around the garage, then looked inside Turnbull's car. 'There you go. I knew it.' On the back seat was a large parcel, extravagantly wrapped and half hidden under a blanket. 'Doesn't that look too precious to be left out here overnight?' she asked, reaching for the label. 'See?

It's got our names on it.' Danny watched, bewildered, as she bent down to listen. 'And it seems to be ticking.'

'What the hell are you doing?' he asked, but Astrid was already ripping the box open. When she turned round, she was holding a toy dog with an alarm clock tied to its collar.

'I have no idea what this is about,' she said, making an effort not to smile, 'but the look on your face was priceless. Our champagne's here, too, and caviar, chocolates, cigarettes: everything you could possibly need if you're locked in a garage with a stranger.'

Relieved, Danny laughed and joined her by the car. 'Hang on – there's a card.' He took it out and read it in an exaggerated impersonation of Hitchcock's voice. '"Well, boys and girls, time is ticking and the audition has begun. Good luck."' The card was signed with the director's familiar caricature of himself.

She smiled. 'Perhaps Hitchcock doesn't object so strongly to fraternisation after all.' He looked questioningly at her. 'It was something Bella Hutton said to me: he doesn't like his stars to get too close to each other.'

'Could have fooled me. What else did Bella tell you? I noticed you talking to her.'

'Oh, just that Leyton Turnbull destroys young women, so nothing new, really.' He didn't laugh as she had expected him to, so she added, 'She may be as wrong about that as she is about Hitchcock, though. It seems to me that he positively encourages fraternisation – unless this is a test, of course.' She smiled. 'Perhaps we're supposed to scream the place down in moral indignation until someone rescues us.'

'Is that what you'd like to do?' She shook her head. 'Then make yourself at home, Miss Lake.'

He gave a mock bow and held the door of the Alvis open for her, and she climbed into the passenger seat, noticing that the lamps on the Morris were already beginning to fade. 'I bet this is down to David Franks,' she said. 'No wonder he gave me such a cheery goodnight.'

Danny got in beside her. 'What do you make of him?'

The question was expressed casually as he opened the bottle, but Astrid knew that he was more interested in her answer than he cared to admit and she considered it carefully. 'I think he's dangerous,' she said, holding out her glass. 'Just from that conversation out on the terrace, you could tell he was the type to bleed people dry and move on, whether it's Bella Hutton and her connections or Hitchcock and his expertise.'

He poured his own drink in the dwindling light and stood the bottle on the floor. 'There goes our ambience,' he said as the Alvis followed the other car's example. 'Nice while it lasted. Cheers.'

'Cheers.'

'Franks has surely met his match if he's going to take Hitchcock on, though?'

'Probably, but I'm not sticking up for him either. Schoolboy stuff like this is all very well, but some of the things he did tonight were completely out of order.'

'I know what you mean. I dropped in on Turnbull when I went back to change, just to see if he was all right and apologise again for what I said, but he was either out or just not answering.' Astrid was quiet. She had been shocked by her conversation with Bella Hutton, but had also seen a different side to the actress later which reinforced her original instinct to trust only herself. Film wasn't an industry that took any prisoners: at dinner, as everyone – herself included – responded to Hitchcock's goading, she had felt dirty all over. As if the thought had transferred itself, Danny said, 'Thanks for speaking out tonight. I began to think that Hitchcock had set me up to be the only one to talk.' It was true, Astrid realised: the whole evening had been geared around encouraging people to turn on one another, leaving each of them isolated in their own way. 'I didn't know you were adopted,' Danny continued gently as she said nothing. 'All the time I spent during that last film complaining about my relationship with my father, and you never had the chance to know yours at all. I'm sorry. It was selfish of me, and you were so kind, but you should have said something.'

She ignored his apology because to acknowledge it would have meant talking more about her own life than she cared to. 'The thing you were wrongly accused of,' she said, deflecting the attention back to him. 'Is that what you and your father fell out about?'

He said nothing, and she thought at first that he was avoiding the question, but he put his finger to his lips. 'I think I heard the door,' he whispered. 'Someone's coming in.'

Instinctively, they slid down in their seats, hoping not to be caught. They were in luck: rather than coming right into the garage, the visitor stayed at the back of the car, and, after several attempts, eventually managed to unlock the boot. 'It must be Turnbull,' Astrid whispered. 'You don't think he *is* leaving, do you? What are we going to do?'

Danny shrugged. 'Sit tight and blame Hitchcock if we're caught.' There was a noise that sounded like the zip being drawn back on a bag or suitcase, and then the lid of the boot was firmly closed. 'Perhaps he's just packing his career away,' Danny said softly, and Astrid had to struggle to contain her laughter. Anxiously, they waited for footsteps to come round to the front of the car, but there was nothing. Instead, they heard the creak of the garage door again, and then silence.

'Christ, I thought we'd had it there,' Danny said when he was sure it was safe to speak. 'All that moralising I did at dinner, only to be found taking advantage of a helpless young woman in someone else's car.' He wound the window down and looked back towards the entrance. 'He's left the door ajar, though. Rescued just when it was getting interesting. That's my luck all over.'

'There's no hurry,' Astrid said. 'We may as well finish the bottle while we're waiting for this rain to stop.' He smiled and refilled her glass. 'So are you going to tell me what it was, this childish prank you mentioned at dinner?'

Danny held up his lighter and took longer than was necessary to select a chocolate from the box. 'That was a lie, I'm afraid,' he admitted, still avoiding her eye. 'It was rather more serious than that. I told you my parents were entertainers?'

'Yes. You said you were virtually brought up on the road.'

'That's right. We went from one set of digs to another, each dingier than the last. I could write a guidebook on miserable guest houses in miserable towns. There's scarcely a resort in England where I haven't picked the pattern off a candlewick bedspread.' She smiled, but didn't interrupt him. 'It was music-hall stuff, very old-fashioned and virtually obsolete after the war, but it was all they knew, and they clung to it, even while the audiences dwindled along with their fees. It's funny, but I never noticed how faded everything had become. At the time, it was all still magical to me, but I can see now that the coming of film was the final nail in the coffin.' He sipped his drink thoughtfully. 'Every summer, they'd do one of those seaside end-of-pier jobs because there was still a market for that. For some reason, people seem to enjoy things on holiday that they can't stand at home. Must be the sun.'

'Oh, I don't know. There's a lot to be said for a bit of Punch and Judy. Not everyone would want all this, even if they could afford it.'

'No, I suppose not. Anyway, it was the summer of my fifteenth birthday and we were in Rhyl. I'd seen their act a thousand times, and the days when they kept me safe by strapping me to a chair at the side of the stage were long gone, so I went off on my own, and I met a girl. She was about the same age as me, or so I thought. We spent the afternoon together on the beach, and I arranged to see her again the next day, but she never turned up. I waited in the same place for three days, just in case, and after that I got the message. The first time you're stood up is always the hardest, isn't it?' He smiled. 'But what would you know about that?'

'You'd be surprised. So *did* you see her again?'

'No. Not then, anyway. But at the end of the week, just after my parents had finished their act, this man forced his way backstage and began beating seven bells out of me. My father dragged him off, so he started on him instead.'

'Who on earth was he?'

'The girl's father. She told him I'd forced myself on her and gone too far.'

'She accused you of raping her?'

'She said I'd tried, and that was enough for my father. He looked at me with such disgust, Astrid. I'll never forget it.'

'He didn't believe you hadn't done it?'

The unquestioning acceptance of his innocence was not lost on Danny, and he looked at her gratefully. 'No, he didn't. I don't think my mother did either, although she never actually said as much. The man threatened to go to the police, so my dad paid him off. It was all he could think of. I begged him to let me prove my innocence instead, but he said no one would accept my word over hers. He was probably right. She was the butter-wouldn't-melt sort. They'd probably pulled the same trick all over the country.'

'Was it a lot of money?'

Danny nodded. 'Yes. He gave up all their savings, then borrowed to keep them afloat. When he ran out of lenders, he tried his luck at gambling.'

Astrid took the cigarettes out of the box and lit one for both of them. 'You said keep *them* afloat; did they throw you out because of what had happened?'

'Oh no. We stuck together for about a year after that. Anything else would have made their sacrifice even more senseless than it was already. And in fairness to them, they never mentioned it again. My father said he didn't want to hear another word about it, and he meant it. But that was worse for me because convincing them I hadn't done anything wrong was never an option. In the end, I couldn't stand it any longer. I left them a note when we were in Lowestoft and hitched a lift to London to make my own way. I've never been so lonely in my life.'

It might have been romantic, Astrid thought, had it not

been so unfair, and ultimately so destructive. 'Wasn't there any-one else for you to turn to?' she asked.

'No. We had some relatives in the business, but family was out, for obvious reasons, and we never stayed anywhere long enough for me to make friends. Anyway, I wanted to get on and work. It was the only way I could think of to get my father out of debt and gain his respect back. But perhaps that was too much to hope for. Going into film was a mistake, for a start. It was as if I'd shamed him even more by hammering that coffin nail in myself. But it was the future, and I needed the money.'

'Couldn't you explain why you were doing it?'

'He wouldn't have listened. And I thought it would be better to get my first hundred pounds and send it to him, let the money do the talking that I wasn't able to.'

'But he killed himself before you had the chance.'

'Yes.' Danny downed the rest of the glass and said bitterly, 'I was nearly there, too. Just four quid short.'

Astrid tried in vain to think of something to say that would make him feel better, but everything sounded either patron-ising or naive. Instead, she asked, 'What about the girl? You said you didn't see her again *then*, so have you bumped into her since?'

He nodded. 'This afternoon. I wasn't sure at first. It was a long time ago, and she looked different in a uniform. But to-night, when she'd tarted herself up to sing with that band, I knew beyond a shadow of a doubt that it was her. And God help me, Astrid, but I wanted to take the little bitch by the throat and show her what pain feels like, how much it hurts to lose someone.'

'And that's why you disappeared so quickly.' She took his

hand and gently unclenched the fist, waiting for his anger to pass. 'I'm so sorry, Danny,' she said eventually. 'I'm surprised you even considered coming back to this part of the world. It hasn't exactly been lucky for you, has it?'

He shook his head sadly. 'No, it hasn't. But if you must know, when I agreed to come I thought Portmeirion was in Cornwall.' They both laughed, and he looked at her gratefully. 'Thank you,' he said. 'You've done it again, when I wanted to talk about you.'

'There's always that brandy,' Astrid suggested. 'I'll take my chances with the umbrella if you will.'

Danny smiled. 'There's just one thing I need to clear up first, though,' he said as he walked round to open the door for her. 'That bit about being stood up – I don't believe a word of it. You *can't* know what it's like, surely?'

'No,' she admitted, 'but only because I don't take the risk. Like I said, nothing frightens me as much as rejection.' She looked away, embarrassed at having been made to talk about herself for a change. 'I suspect I'd be a very needy lover, and that's never an attractive quality.'

'Oh, I don't know,' he said, running his fingers through her hair. 'I can think of worse.'

8

Marta and Josephine threw the blankets over their heads and ran back to the village. The rain drove in with twice the force for having been made to wait, and, by the time they reached the shelter of the narrow passage that divided Neptune from the neighbouring cottages, they were soaked through. 'I'm sorry we were driven out with so little ceremony,' Marta said when she had got her breath back, 'but how was I supposed to know the fucking tide would come in so quickly?'

In the darkness, she heard Josephine laugh and felt her hand against her cheek, cupping her face. 'At least it had the decency to wait.'

Marta turned her head to kiss Josephine's palm. 'But not long enough.' She drew Josephine towards her, breathing in the smell of the rain on her skin, feeling her shiver as the blanket fell to the floor. 'Come up with me now. We need to get out of these clothes.'

Josephine hesitated. 'Are you sure? What if Lydia's looking for you?'

'She won't be. Lydia and I . . .' Marta faltered, aware of her own hypocrisy in being happy to betray Lydia by deed but not by word. 'It's not . . .'

Josephine sensed her difficulty and stopped her, apparently as relieved to avoid the subject as Marta was. 'You don't have to explain. You and Lydia – it's not my business.'

'Come inside, though. I haven't given you your present yet.'

'Are you sure about that?' Marta felt herself blush like a schoolgirl. She led the way up the steps, precarious now in the rain, and found her key. As she fumbled for the lock, a flash of lightning obliged her by illuminating the whole of the square, distorting the buildings and briefly transforming Portmeirion's magic into the twisted stuff of nightmares. She braced herself for the response; in truth, she had always been a little afraid of storms, and, as the thunder cracked above her head, she was glad to get inside, where its violence was at least muted.

She switched on a lamp and stared at the half-unpacked suitcases and piles of clothes and books which seemed to cover every surface. 'Sorry about the mess,' she said, wishing she had bothered to tidy up. 'I could pretend it was a burglary, but I'd never get away with it.'

'You don't believe in travelling light, do you?' Josephine glanced round the room. 'I can count seven pairs of trousers from here.' She walked over to the bed while Marta bundled some clothes into a drawer, and picked up a book from the pillow. '*Nightwood*. This is the novel you were talking about?'

Marta nodded. 'It's brilliant. You'd hate it.'

'How do you know what I'd hate?' She opened the book and read the first few pages. Marta watched her, amused by her defiance, getting to know her moods as well as she had begun to know her body and glad that their trust in each other was nurtured by the physical intimacy which seemed so important to both of them. The evening had surprised her, and she realised now that she had been foolish to assume that – of the two of them – her commitment to this relationship was the greater. She should know by now to take nothing for granted where Josephine was concerned, especially her toughness. When they made love, she sensed a need every bit as great as her own, and it frightened her; it was one thing to accept your own vulnerability in a relationship, much harder to assume responsibility for someone else's, and as the bond between them grew stronger, Marta was forced to consider where it would lead and who might get hurt in the process. After a couple of minutes, Josephine looked up and smiled sheepishly. 'You're right. I'd hate it.'

'You'll like this more, I hope.' Marta took a flat parcel out of one of the suitcases and handed it over.

Intrigued, Josephine unwrapped the paper and looked down at the charcoal drawing of a female nude. The figure seemed to be walking away from something, one arm behind her head, the other gesturing back to where she had come from; she was glancing over her shoulder, oblivious to the gaze of the artist; her expression was impossible to read, and all the more intriguing for its ambiguity. There was no signature but Josephine did not need one to recognise the artist. 'It's a Gaudier-Brzeska. Where on earth did you get it?'

'I'm not sure I should tell you after tonight, but Alma gave me the name of a dealer in London. She and Hitch have got an amazing collection of art, including some Gaudier-Brzeska nudes in the bedroom, apparently, and I was talking to her about your play. Do you like it?'

'It's beautiful, Marta. *She's* beautiful, but it's more than that. It's the physicality of it. I can't believe I'm holding something he's actually touched. This must have been in that squalid little room in London; he and Sophie probably argued over it.'

Marta looked at the drawing and knew what Josephine meant: there was something very personal and immediate about the marks on the paper, the areas where the artist had deliberately smudged the shading with his finger to emphasise the softness of the woman's skin, and it gave the work an intimacy over and above its subject matter. 'I know how proud of that play you are,' she said. 'I'm sorry she *isn't* laughing but that could just about be a smile.' She squinted over Josephine's shoulder. 'In the right light.' A few drops of rainwater fell from her hair onto the glass as she leant forward. 'None of us are dressed very suitably for the middle of the night, are we? Pour us a drink and I'll run a bath.' She grinned. 'I assume you don't mind sharing?'

'Have you forgotten I went to a physical training college? I used to shower with thirty other women every day, so it's not something I'm likely to be shy about now.'

Marta turned on the taps and drew the curtains in the bathroom, noticing that the character of the storm was somehow different on the other side of the village; away from the buildings and the people, rain slanted against the dark mass of trees with a primeval power which suggested that it belonged there, that sunshine was the aberration, and she was glad to shut it out. Josephine handed her a glass of wine and Marta smiled as she propped her birthday present up against the mirror. 'You don't take long to make yourself at home. Moving your art in already?'

'With all your luggage, the only space left is on the walls.' She sat down on the side of the bath and tested the temperature of the water. 'I was talking to Bella Hutton earlier.'

'Said very casually for someone who's supposed to be shy.'

'It was more like having an audience with her, I suppose,' Josephine admitted, 'but I liked her. I liked her very much.' She told Marta what the actress had said about *The Laughing Woman*. 'She met Gaudier-Brzeska, apparently, and she said something very interesting – that he might have destroyed less of his work if he'd known he was going to die so young.'

'I'm sure that's true, but I wish you'd stop talking about running out of time and dying young. I hope you're not going to be like this every year on your birthday.' She looked intently at Josephine and asked more seriously, 'You're not keeping something from me, are you? You'd tell me if you were ill?'

'I'm not ill.' Josephine slipped out of her clothes and climbed into the water.

'So why the sense of urgency?'

'Oh, I don't know. I suppose it's because my mother was still so young when she died. Fifty-two is nothing, is it?'

She was quiet for a moment, and Marta guessed she was thinking about the twelve years that stood between her and the same age. She got into the bath and Josephine lay back against her. 'It was cancer, wasn't it?' Marta said gently.

'Yes. I'd only just started to find out who she really was – you know how that relationship changes when you grow up and you start to become friends.'

'In theory. I was never that lucky with my mother, but it sounds like you had a lot in common.'

'We liked the same things, I suppose. It's her fault I love the cinema so much – she took me all the time when I was young. I used to crawl under the seats, and I remember her hauling me onto her lap and reading the difficult words on the title cards so I understood what was going on.' She smiled at the memory of it. 'It must have all been very primitive then, but I know I went to *The Great Train Robbery* when I was about seven or eight and thought it was the most exciting thing I'd ever seen.' Marta listened as she talked about her childhood, gently tracing the contours of Josephine's face with her hand, touching her brow, her cheekbones, the line of her jaw, committing them to memory as a safeguard for the weeks apart. 'When I left home, I'd write to her about the films I'd seen and she'd do the same. Then gradually her letters changed. There was no magic in them any more. It took me a long time to find out that it was because she was too ill to leave the house.' She paused to kiss Marta's fingertips as they reached her lips. 'Too ill, or too ashamed.'

'Why ashamed?'

'People don't talk much about cancer now, but they certainly didn't then. There was a stigma to it, like having a drunk in the family or someone who was mentally ill. It's the same with any illness: cancer, depression, epilepsy. People treat it as a disgrace, as though you're somehow to blame, and as much as you know that isn't true, some of it sticks and you start to believe it yourself.'

'I know what you mean,' Marta said quietly. There had been a time when she had suffered from depression, and when – committed to an institution for falling pregnant with a child who wasn't her husband's – she had begun to believe everything about herself but what she knew to be true.

Josephine reached up and pulled Marta gently down into a kiss. 'Of course you do.'

It was, Marta knew, as close to prompting her as Josephine would go. One day, if she ever found the courage to talk properly about that part of her life, it would be Josephine she turned to, but she was still too afraid of it. She felt somehow that the despair was still inside her, waiting to return, and to speak it out loud would be to allow it back into the light. 'That must have been hard for your mother,' she said, shifting the conversation away from herself.

'As soon as her body started to give her away, she retreated into herself,' Josephine said. 'I don't know what would have happened if she hadn't had my father to deal with the outside world for her. She made him put a brave face on it, and I think it nearly killed him. I used to hear him crying at night when she'd finally fallen asleep, but he never let that mask slip in front of her. At least not when I was around.'

'How long ago was it?'

'Thirteen years now. I was nearly twenty-seven, but I felt like that small child crawling around in the dark again – lost without her, resentful of what her death meant to our family and my role in it, and terrified in case the same thing happens to me. From that moment . . . well, I was like her in so many ways.'

'I think she'd forgive you for making an exception.'

Josephine smiled. 'Yes, I suppose she would. And for someone who's obsessed with time, I've just wasted too much by a long and rambling answer to a very straightforward question.'

'It was hardly straightforward.'

'No? You should have met my grandfather: "If there's anything you want to do, do it now. We'll all be in little boxes soon enough."' She laughed at the expression on Marta's face. 'Perhaps it's a Scottish thing – you languid English wouldn't understand.'

It was a weak attempt to make light of her grief, and Marta cut straight through it. 'I'm sorry your mother didn't live to see what you've achieved. She'd have been so proud of you.'

Josephine picked up her glass and spoke more seriously. 'I suppose that's what made me decide to do this film in the end: for her. She would have been so excited. The books and the plays – she'd have been pleased for me, even if she didn't necessarily like them all. But a film, even though I'll have had nothing to do with the finished results – that's something she'd genuinely have loved.' She gave a wry smile. 'And something she could show off about in Inverness.'

'You're not going to get involved in the script, then?'

'No. I mustn't make the mistake of turning everything I love into work, and I don't want to know the reality of it. I once read a rather snide article about Betty Compson in a film magazine which said that she was incapable of registering emotion without the help of a three-piece orchestra; apparently they had to churn out 'Mighty Like a Rose' for her to cry real tears. I know you think that's funny,' she added as Marta began to laugh, 'but I was absolutely devastated. It was like being told there's no Father Christmas, except I was a grown woman.'

'It's just one contradiction after another with you, isn't it?' Marta said affectionately. 'For someone so cynical, you're such an innocent.'

'I know. Don't tell anyone.' Josephine reached for a towel and went through into the bedroom to fetch the bottle. 'I asked Alma if she'd let you do the script,' she said, refilling Marta's glass, 'but apparently you wouldn't be ruthless enough.'

'Bloody cheek. My devotion to you does have its limits, you know.'

'Does it?'

Marta grinned at her and got out of the bath. 'No, damn you, I don't suppose it does.'

Josephine took a towel and wrapped it round Marta's shoulders, drawing her close. 'I'm serious, Marta. I need to know what I can hope for and what I can rely on. It's not only artists who can be reckless, and I don't want to destroy this by expecting too much from it – or too little. You love Lydia, don't you?' It was a statement, not an accusation, and Marta nodded. 'And you're building a life together, one that suits you both.'

'You said you didn't want to talk about this.'

'I lied.'

Marta saw the anxiety in Josephine's eyes and searched for the words to reassure her. 'Do you remember when we first met, and we sat on that station platform and talked about my mess of a life?'

'Yes, of course.'

'And I told you that what counted was coming first with somebody.'

'Yes. You were explaining that what came first with Lydia was her work.'

'Well, that hasn't changed, Josephine. Lydia always has and always will love her work above all else, and there's nothing wrong with that. What's different now is that you come first for me. When you were telling me about Hitchcock's charade and running through everyone's worst fears, all I could think of was how strange it was that no one had mentioned the love of another person and what it would mean to lose them. That's my fear – a life without you. Yes, Lydia and I care about each other. We enjoy each other's company, and you were right in what you said earlier: it's sane and it's normal and it gives us a stability which we both need. But Lydia gets what she needs *most* in the world from an audience; I get it from you. We're both selfish in that way, and whatever companionship we share comes a very poor second. She knows that as well as I do.'

'But the longer I'm not free, the more I risk . . .'

Marta took Josephine's face in her hands. 'What is this business about being free? You're free now in the way that matters.

It's not about sharing a house or being together all the time, and I'm not going to turn up at Inverness Station with a suitcase asking for directions to Crown Cottage if I don't see you for a month. It's what happens when we *are* together that counts, and how we feel when we're apart. Your absence doesn't make me doubt you. I don't get this kind of love from anyone else but you, emotionally or physically, and I don't try.' She saw the joy and understanding in Josephine's eyes, and for a moment the world seemed to shrink to include just the two of them. '*We* come first. Is that what you wanted to know?'

'Yes,' Josephine said. 'Yes, it is.'

9

David Franks stood beneath the canopy of a Welsh oak tree and looked down across Portmeirion as if it were a map laid out before him. A stranger to the place, standing at ground level, would never know that there was a path up here at all, but from where he stood he could see the lives of the whole village played out in miniature below: a figure moved across the balcony from Dolphin to Government House, its progress inside marked by the switching on of successive lamps; a car horn sounded cheerfully near Salutation, bidding farewell to an invisible companion before its tail lights disappeared around the sweep of the drive and out of the village; above the garages, in the house they called Neptune, a woman drew the curtains and her silhouette moved slowly over to the bed. David watched, unseen and unsuspected, completing each fragmentary story in his mind as a distraction from the narrative of his own life.

The rain stung his face as he left the shelter of the tree. He walked the short distance to the burnt-out shell of the cottage as quickly as darkness would allow and stopped a few yards away, his hand resting gently on the trunk of an enormous fir. It was a magnificent specimen, and, as a child, he had stood here often, looking up through the blue-green needles until its height and the strong scent of pine made him dizzy. The tree must be nearly a hundred years old now; when the camp returned each summer, it had always been one of the first things that David sought out, a treasured symbol of stability in a drifting, rootless life. Reluctantly, he forced his eyes to focus on the shadow in front of him, a sudden, searing reminder of pain. There was no need for daylight here. The image from eighteen years earlier was quite literally emblazoned into his memory, as powerful and intense as if the building's scorched walls still held their heat: his father's murder, burnt to death by a brutal lynch mob when David was only fourteen years old.

He remembered how frightened he had been, although 'remembered' was the wrong word because the fear had never left him. Hatred and rage had spilled out of their mouths, sharpened by years of suppressed prejudice. He saw their fists clenched tightly around their own anger, heard boots trampling through the undergrowth. Men too old to fight, women, boys even younger than he was – an army of self-appointed heroes, denied a real war but marching to one of their own making. They hurled half-bricks, bottles and stones at the cottage – makeshift missiles, mostly, although some had come prepared, battering at the door with coshes or waving chair legs wrapped in barbed wire. He heard the crash of broken glass and saw his father's frightened face appear briefly at the damaged window. Their eyes met, and, for a moment, David was convinced that his father believed him to be one of the mob, a defector to the settled lifestyle which he had, in his heart, always longed for. The crowd pushed him to the ground, called him a child killer's son and promised he'd be next. He smelt the smoke before he saw the flames, and realised too late that the odour he had detected on their hands and clothes was petrol.

The fire took hold quickly, and he noticed one or two members of the crowd glance anxiously at one another, wondering if they had gone too far but unable now to stop the rush of blood – in each other, or in themselves. Then he heard his father's dying screams, echoing his mother's agony as she had tried to push a dead baby from her body, filling the years of his childhood with one long cry of pain. David had no idea now what had made him mention his father that evening, except a devilment which sometimes overcame him, a need to push his luck, to find out if anything would make him care. Impatiently, he shook off the memory of Alma's hand on his: it was a sympathy he did not deserve, because his father's death was his own fault and he had not been able to stop it. He had run away and fled back to the old mansion house – to fetch help, he had told himself, but help from whom? From a frail old woman and a pack of dogs who had been taught to expect only kindness? No, he had run for his own safety. Shut up in that room like a dog himself, while other people decided his future, he had cried and shouted and railed against his own cowardice, almost as if he had absorbed the anger from each and every member of that mob and turned it in on himself.

His mother's grave was not far from this spot. There was no stone, nothing to indicate to a stranger where she was buried, but everyone who mattered knew where to find her. Even though she had not been of Gypsy blood, his father had insisted that the ancient rites be observed to the letter, and, after the funeral, he had packed everything she owned into their wagon, poured in paraffin and set it alight. When the fire had burned itself out, the leftover metal was raked away and buried safe from thieving gorgio hands; her animals were slaughtered, her young dog killed, and David was left with nothing but a bewildering sense of how transient a life could be. Later, when his father died, the ashes from that terrible fire – ashes of bricks and bone and hate – had been buried here too. He turned away from the ruins and headed back to the village, thinking of how ironic it was that his parents should be so rooted now while he wandered from place to place, picking up camp and moving on. Always restless. Always moving on.

10

Bridget and Archie had managed to tie the tarpaulin tightly to the roof of Salutation so that it hung down to protect the paintwork against the storm, and Bridget took advantage of the shelter it offered to check for any damage to the mural. He watched as she shone the torchlight onto each individual section, gently touching the stone with a cloth to absorb the rain without smudging the image. She had always been completely at one with the building she was working on, as though she possessed an intuitive understanding of its life before the present moment and could sense its nature with her hands, just as she had seemed to sense his joy or his pain through his body whenever they were together. He remembered how he had loved to watch her work, even though he was rarely allowed to see the results until she was satisfied with them. For Bridget, the sharing of that very private world was as trusting and intimate a gesture as the sharing of her bed, and Archie had never taken either for granted.

Eventually she stood back, satisfied. 'It's a makeshift job, but it'll do,' she said, and he had to strain to hear her over the drumming of rain on canvas at their backs. 'This storm will have died down long before the morning anyway.' She hadn't bothered to bring a coat and her long dark hair, only half-heartedly tied back, hung loose over her bare shoulders. As usual, she was quite unconscious of how beautiful she looked, and he leant forward to kiss her. The moment had been inevitable from their first greeting, and yet it surprised him; he had expected the kiss to be familiar, a return to a known if distant past, but her touch felt new to him, and he drew her body into his with all the fear and excitement of a stranger.

'That's what I hoped you'd say.' She laughed softly and put her hand to his cheek, and Archie saw his own uncomplicated happiness reflected in her eyes. 'I think it's time we found somewhere more comfortable.'

She gathered up the knife and the rest of the rope that they had used to secure the tarpaulin and they headed back to White Horses. The Piazza seemed to offer more shelter from the storm than any other route, and they hurried across the tennis court, Archie holding Bridget close under an umbrella. It had been designed for a more temperate rain than the deluge that Portmeirion saw fit to offer up, and they were soaked again in seconds, but neither of them cared. They cut between Neptune and Mermaid, the pretty blue-and-white cottage which was one of only a handful of buildings not to have sprung from Clough's imagination, and were about to take the road to the hotel when Archie noticed Leyton Turnbull standing by the small freshwater pool. He had just been joined by David Franks, and their body language suggested that they were having a heated discussion. He paused, and Bridget stared at him. 'What on earth are you playing at, Archie? It's not the weather for sightseeing.'

There was a handsome iron canopy built onto Mermaid's southern gable and Archie pulled her in out of the rain. 'Over there – it's Leyton Turnbull.'

'So?'

At any other time, her complete disregard for celebrity would have amused him, but he was curious to see what was going on between Turnbull and Franks. The sort of tension he had witnessed earlier in the evening could easily get out of hand, and, although he would cheerfully have banged their heads together at dinner, he wasn't happy to stand by while they did it themselves. 'It looks like there's going to be trouble.'

Bridget glanced at the two men. 'He's drunk, Archie. What are you going to do? Arrest him for disorderly conduct?' She took the umbrella from his hand and made him look at her. 'Do I really have to remind you that you've got other things to think about than being a policeman?'

Turnbull chose that moment to lurch drunkenly at Franks, but he missed his footing and stumbled forward into the pool. Franks did his best to haul him out, but he was no match for the indiscriminate strength that comes with too much whisky, and Turnbull stayed on his knees in the shallow water, hurling abuse into the wind.

'He needs a hand.'

'But does it have to be yours? David Franks is with him. Let them sort it out between themselves. You've got other plans.'

'It really won't take a minute. Wait here.'

Bridget sighed and followed him out into the square. As she had predicted, the storm was dying down already, and the rain was considerably less brutal now. 'Jesus, look at the state of him,' Archie said. Turnbull's clothes were dishevelled and soaked through. He was wearing a light mackintosh over his dinner clothes, and the front was covered with mud, as if he had fallen; as they got closer, Archie could see that there was blood on his face which had not been washed away by the rain. 'You never told me about this,' he was yelling at Franks. 'You brought me here for this charade, David, and you didn't even warn me.'

'Can I help?'

Franks turned round quickly and looked surprised, then grateful. 'You certainly can. I don't seem to be getting very far on my own.' He smiled at Bridget. 'Whoever said there's never a policeman around when you need one?' Between them, they managed to drag Turnbull to his feet and out of the water. 'We need to get you cleaned up, old chap,' Franks said, 'but the pool's not really the place for it. Look at you: you're in a terrible mess.'

'I've been in the woods,' Turnbull said, as if that explained everything. 'I wanted to go to the cemetery. It was so dark, though. I lost my way.' He slumped down onto the low wall and looked up at Franks, and there was a desperation in his eyes which surprised Archie. 'What have I done, David?' he said quietly. 'My God, what have I done?'

He seemed oblivious to anyone else's presence. 'What's he talking about?' Archie asked.

'Oh, it's something to do with Bella. They had a falling out earlier. It's a long story.'

'That bitch,' Turnbull said aggressively. 'All of this is her fault.'

'What's that got to do with the cemetery, though?'

Franks shrugged. 'Come on, Turnbull, let's get you back to your room. You're not making any sense and you need to sober up. You've got a big day tomorrow. You'll never know how hard I've worked on Hitch to get you here at all; if you let me down now, we'll all be for the high jump.'

Wondering what Hitchcock had got planned for the next day, Archie asked, 'Where's he staying?'

Franks nodded towards the large set of buildings on the other side of the square. 'Government House.'

'Come on then. I'll give you a hand.'

'It's all right. I'll do it.' Jack Spence had appeared from nowhere, and Archie looked at him in surprise. 'Leave him to David and me. We'll see him safely home.'

'Don't argue, Archie.' Bridget smiled gratefully at Spence. 'Thanks, Jack. I owe you a favour.'

'I'll let you know when I need it.'

Archie and Bridget watched while they half carried, half dragged Leyton Turnbull across the square and up the steps to Government House. 'You recognised David Franks,' Archie said. 'How do you know him?'

'He was at the hotel a couple of weeks ago with Jack. They were having a look at the place for Hitchcock ahead of this weekend, but I've seen him here before.' Archie was furious with himself for succumbing to the same spark of jealousy that he had experienced earlier, when Bridget and Spence returned from the woods together. 'Jack likes the boys, Archie, just in case you were wondering.' He attempted a look that said it made no difference to him either way, but it was less than convincing. 'I know because I threw myself at him when we were at the Slade. It was quite the nicest rejection I've ever had, but there was no room for negotiation.' She pulled him towards her and they kissed. 'Now is there anyone else you'd like to call in on, or can I take you home?'

Archie smiled, and answered by turning towards White Horses. As he held the gate open for her, he glanced back towards the village and noticed that all the lights were on in the top floor of Government House. Bridget followed his gaze and spotted Leyton Turnbull slouched at his window. 'There you are,' she said, squeezing his hand. 'No need for a police presence tonight.'

Spence and Franks saw Turnbull, too, as they walked together to the hotel bar, where they would sit and drink into the early hours, and Danny raised a hand to him as he took Astrid back to his room to make love to her. On the lawn in front of the Watch House, Alma Reville found solace in the fresh night air while her husband slept, and looked up just in time to see the butt of the evening's jokes stumble back into his room. Only one of them felt more than pity, because only one of them knew that Leyton Turnbull would die the following day. And across the water, as the final hours of her husband's life drifted past in a haze of self-recrimination, Gwyneth Draycott nursed her fear and watched the lights go out one by one in Portmeirion.

PART FIVE

SUSPICION

26 July 1936, Portmeirion

I

When Bridget opened her eyes, it was just beginning to get light. She lay still, enjoying the warmth of Archie's body curled around her own while the world came to life outside, and then, as the sun rose above the hills, casting tentative fingers over a new day, she slipped quietly from the sheets, hoping he wouldn't stir.

His shirt was the first piece of clothing that came to hand; she put it on, knowing that too much movement would bring on a volley of hopeful barking from the sitting room next door and destroy any chance of peace. The sketchbook was on the floor next to the bed and she picked it up, pleased by the way the light flooded in through the window onto his face. Asleep, Archie was entirely at her mercy, with no self-consciousness or shy protestations, no elaborate poses or distracting conversation. She drew freely and quickly, searching out the contours of his body with each line, resisting the temptation to embellish with memory and accepting only what she saw in front of her – the hand resting on the pillow, the graceful curve of the neck and shoulders, the sheet draped across narrow hips. His body was beautiful, more so now that it had lost the artificial perfection of youth, but it was the strength in his face that moved Bridget and filled her with an unexpected longing; for all the fuss she had made about remaining independent, beholden only to her work, it was a strength she would have welcomed during the past twenty years, more often than she cared to acknowledge.

There were things she should have told him about her life,

255

things he had a right to know. Last night, she had convinced herself that there was no need; it was a chance encounter, miraculous in its way but fleeting, and if they were unlikely to meet again, she wanted to part sure of his good opinion. But that was last night. This morning, she was reluctant to let go of the joy they had found in each other but knew that honesty would destroy it. Her past was not something for which Archie would be able to forgive her: he was sensitive and compassionate, but he had an instinct for right and wrong which ran deeper than his job – and what she had done *was* wrong. The longer she stayed silent, the harder it would be to explain. She put the charcoal down before she destroyed the drawing by adding too much, and looked up to find that he had been watching her.

'The shirt suits you, but not yet.' He slipped it from her shoulders and looked at her, hoping to find a mirror of his own happiness. Bridget smiled. It wasn't Archie's fault that all she really wanted to do was cry for mistakes which, once made, could never be undone.

2

Josephine sat down to breakfast on the terrace and marvelled at the beauty of the morning. Portmeirion had been restored to its proper state after the aberration of the night before, and the only lingering sign of the storm was a rich, moist air which gave a freshness to everything. There was just enough breeze to move fragile wisps of cloud across a brilliant blue sky, and the village shone with a new lustre, its lines more exuberant, its colours more intense. A flock of oystercatchers rose up from the estuary sands, peeling off erratically into the air like ashes from a bonfire, and, where pools of water had been left behind by the tide, the reflection of the sun was too bright to look at. She smiled, remembering its moonlit counterpart, the rain on Marta's skin, and wondered how much of the day's magic was down to the weather and how much to her own happiness.

'Good God, you look exhausted,' Ronnie said, joining her at the table. 'Did the storm keep you awake?'

'Something like that.' Josephine beamed at her. 'And thank you for getting my forty-first year off to such a complimentary start.'

'It wasn't meant as a criticism, just an observation.' She glanced knowingly at her sister, and Josephine could feel the rings around her eyes darkening under their combined scrutiny. Lettice was one of the few people who knew something of her feelings for Marta, but her discretion could be taken as read; Ronnie, on the other hand, could usually be relied upon to back the wrong horse. 'Isn't Archie down yet?' she asked, running true to form.

'I haven't seen him,' Josephine said, reaching for her sunglasses.

A waiter brought toast and coffee, and took their orders for breakfast. 'We'll be as quick as we can,' he promised, 'but we're a bit short-staffed this morning.' He nodded conspiratorially to the Watch House on the cliff. 'As if we haven't got enough to worry about.'

'It's fine,' Josephine said. 'We're not in any hurry.'

'Darling, you *are* in a good mood!'

'So what did you two get up to last night after we'd gone?' Josephine asked, ignoring Ronnie's smirk.

'We had a few drinks with Lydia, as you know, and then a couple of Hitchcock's people drifted back in, so we got talking to them. The band was fabulous, wasn't it, Ronnie? There was a bit of a kerfuffle when the singer didn't turn up for her final set, but they managed beautifully without her.' She cast a sly glance at her sister. 'Ronnie was on her feet until the early hours.'

'And on her back after that?' Josephine seized her chance to give as good as she got. 'Which waiter was it this time? No wonder they're short-staffed.'

'It wasn't a waiter.'

Lettice was coy rarely enough to make Josephine genuinely curious. 'Oh?'

Lydia came out onto the terrace and sat down at their table. 'You look lovely,' Lettice said, distracted for a moment from her story. She looked the casual elegance up and down with a professional eye. 'Isn't that a Maggy Rouff?'

'Yes. It's such a beautiful day that I thought I'd make an effort,' she said, and the cynic in Josephine couldn't help wondering if the effort was for Marta or for Hitchcock. 'First things first: marks out of ten for Mr Franks?'

'Eight, but I'm holding the other two in reserve.'

Josephine looked at Ronnie in astonishment. 'You spent the night with Hitchcock's sidekick?'

'I most certainly did not. David was the perfect gentleman.' She grinned at Lydia. 'We're just trying to establish if the same can be said about Archie. He seems to have kept the birthday girl up *very* late.'

'Really? I thought I saw him out walking with his Irish eyes, but I must have made a mistake.' She smiled at Josephine. 'It was difficult to tell who was who in that rain last night, with umbrellas and blankets everywhere.'

The waiter made a timely arrival with three full Welsh breakfasts and looked enquiringly at Lydia. 'Same for you, madam?'

'Yes please, and will you bring a smoked haddock as well? And plenty of coffee. Marta's joining us in a minute,' she explained, buttering some toast. 'She's just getting dressed. No sign of the Hitchcocks yet?'

'Perhaps they've packed up and gone,' Josephine suggested hopefully.

'I doubt it. Round two is supposed to be taking place on the terrace. Jack Spence said they'd all been summoned after breakfast. We should have a ringside seat.'

'Not if I can help it.' Over Lydia's shoulder, she saw Archie strolling along the coastal path from White Horses. 'Nice walk?' she asked mischievously as he kissed her and sat down.

'Lovely, thanks. It's done me the world of good. How are you?'

'I couldn't be better.' She poured him a cup of coffee and smiled. 'You were absolutely right.'

Ronnie had eagle eyes but her ability to add two and two left a lot to be desired. She drew a deep breath, ready to launch into a lengthy interrogation of Archie's whereabouts, but Lettice jumped in before she could start. 'Is that a parrot?' she asked, peering towards the village.

Josephine was grateful for the effort but would have preferred a more credible change of subject. Then she saw a bright green bird swooping down from the Bell Tower and circling over the estuary before settling on the balustrade further down the terrace. 'That's Agatha, madam,' the waiter said. 'She belongs to the hotel's general manager. They've both been with us for years.'

'She reminds me of Hephzibah,' Ronnie said thoughtfully.

Lydia laughed. 'In what way exactly?'

'Didn't you hear what happened at Regent's Park this year? She's only just had the stitches out.'

They were so engrossed in Ronnie's story that they almost missed Hitchcock's arrival. He walked across the lawn with his cameraman and, as he passed their table, raised his voice: 'Don't worry about the blood. I'll wash off what's left and get rid of the knife.' He pretended to notice Archie for the first time and faked a look of horror. 'Ah, Chief Inspector. I didn't see you there.'

Archie laughed. 'A word of advice,' he said. 'It's virtually impossible to wash it off completely. You should *always* worry about the blood.'

'I'll bear it in mind.' Spence moved on to another table, but Hitchcock drew up a chair to form a triangle with Josephine and Archie, effectively forming a separate party. 'A famous crime novelist and a chief inspector of Scotland Yard should be able to answer a question that has always puzzled me,' he said with relish. 'Why are the English so fascinated with murder?'

'I can't speak for the English,' Josephine said, with a mild exaggeration of her accent. 'I just hope it lasts.'

'But seriously – do you think it's because our crimes are more exciting?'

'The papers try to make them seem that way,' Archie said, 'but only a small percentage have anything shocking about them. Most crimes, even murders, are drab domestic affairs or sordid squabbles about money, and there's nothing intriguing about that – it's all depressingly inevitable.' He smiled at his own cynicism. 'Having said that, murders are rare. Your industry and Josephine's thrive on distorting the numbers: you'd have us believe that there's a corpse round every corner, but compared to somewhere like America we're extremely lazy when it comes to homicide. Perhaps that's why we take more notice when it happens.'

'Is that true, David? You'll have to speak for our American friends.' Josephine had noticed that, like his wife, Hitchcock rarely missed a thing, but he would have needed eyes in the back of his head to see Franks coming across the terrace without turning round; then she realised that they were seated outside the Mirror Room, and the director had deliberately positioned himself at the right angle to watch everything. Not for the first time, she acknowledged a grudging respect for his shrewdness. 'The Chief Inspector tells me we value our murderers for their novelty value.'

'Don't you think it's more a sort of shameful admiration?' Franks suggested. He winked at Ronnie, and to Josephine's astonishment she blushed like a virgin. 'A murder here is worth so much more than in America. Kill someone in California and you have miles of desert to get rid of the body in; try it in London, and your best options are a cellar or the left-luggage department of a railway station. No wonder we idolise anyone who has the courage to risk it.' He smiled and drifted off to join Spence; Ronnie stared after him, reverting to her usual indifference only when she noticed Josephine watching her.

'I think there's something in that,' Archie said. 'The attention they get puts murderers on a warped pedestal. It's invariably *their* names we remember, not the victims.' He paused to pour more coffee. 'And the wheels of justice turn more quickly here. Sentence to execution in three clear Sundays: even the British can't lose interest in that time. America's appeal system would bore us to death. Our sense of justice never burns that brightly.'

'A sceptic as well as a policeman,' Hitchcock said approvingly. 'I knew Edith Thompson's family, you know. They lived round the corner from us in Leytonstone. Her father taught me ballroom dancing. I imagine *his* sense of justice would have stayed the course if it could have saved his daughter from the noose.'

Archie nodded. 'Yes, I imagine it would.'

'I still think there's something inherently dramatic about the famous English reserve, though,' the director insisted. 'We have a tendency to bottle our emotions up, so when they emerge, they're liable to do so in a more extreme fashion.'

'That's a stereotype, surely?' Josephine argued. 'It certainly doesn't account for Lizzie Borden. Or Belle Gunness. Or Amy Gilligan.'

'So what do *you* think keeps people glued to the trial reports, Miss Tey?'

'Apart from a natural inclination to revel in the misery of those less fortunate, you mean?'

He smiled. 'Apart from that, yes. Why do we love a good murder?'

'Because we're all capable of it,' Josephine said, thinking of Marta and how they had met. For her, there was no inherent contradiction in knowing that the woman who knew her more intimately than anyone else had once wanted to destroy her; Marta's was a grief of which she had no experience, but she knew what darkness was and understood the temporary insanity of hatred. 'Things get out of hand very easily. We fall in love with the wrong person, make a mistake and then another one to cover it up, feel so much pain that there's nothing left to lose and rail at the injustice of it all. From there, violence isn't such a very big step. So when we read about those crimes in the papers, it isn't admiration we feel; it's relief – relief that it wasn't us.' She smiled. 'This time, anyway.' Hitchcock nodded thoughtfully, and Josephine decided that she liked him much better away from his audience. 'What fresh hell have you planned for everyone today?' she asked. 'It's too beautiful a morning to carry on where you left off, surely?'

The director laughed. 'On the contrary,' he said. 'Fear of the dark is natural, we all have it, but fear in the sunlight, perhaps fear in this very restaurant, where it is so unexpected – *that* is interesting.' He gestured to the hotel and added with a wink, 'Being somewhere like this takes the sting out of any unpleasantness, don't you think? Murder can be much more charming and enjoyable – even for the victim – if the surroundings are pleasant and the people involved are ladies and gentlemen.'

A young man had been hovering at the French windows for some time; at last, he managed to pluck up the courage to approach Hitchcock for an autograph, and the director welcomed him with a genuine warmth which surprised Josephine. 'Doesn't that sort of attention bother you?' she asked, as the fan disappeared back into the hotel with a broad smile on his face.

'Not at all,' he said. 'I couldn't do what I do without it. Ah – here comes my wife.'

Alma's progress down the hill was hastened by an overexcited terrier, who seemed to resent the confines of his lead on a day that promised such adventure. Marta was with her, looking relaxed in a sleeveless white cotton blouse and red linen trousers, and the two were deep in conversation. 'Are you sure it's not too much trouble?' Alma asked as they walked across the terrace, and Marta shook her head.

Hitchcock kissed his wife and led her off to a table for two, and Marta sat down next to Lydia. 'We've got a friend for the morning, I'm afraid,' she said. 'I've promised Alma we'll look after Jenky while she makes some calls in peace.'

'I hope he's got his sea legs,' Lydia said. 'The girls and I were thinking about taking a boat out and rowing over to the island.'

'I'd rather tire him out with a walk first,' Marta said, looking doubtfully across at the terrier. 'She adores that dog. If he goes overboard, I'll never work again. Couldn't we get a boat after lunch instead?'

'The tide will be out by then,' Lettice said, and Marta's smile would have been subtle had she not been wearing a lipstick to match her trousers.

'Why don't you take the boat along the shoreline instead?' Josephine suggested. 'We can walk up to the headland and meet you there. If you think you can row that far,' she added provocatively, looking at the Motleys.

'Bloody cheek,' Ronnie said. 'Lettice was the most popular girl in the Saltash rowers when she was young. They were devastated when we moved to London. We'll be there before you two have changed your shoes.'

'That sounds like a challenge,' Lydia said with relish. 'What's it to be, Archie? Land or water?'

'Neither,' Archie said. 'It's all far too energetic for me. I think I'll just sit in the sun and read the papers.' He glanced over to the Hitchcocks' table. 'I doubt there'll be a shortage of entertainment. Apart from anything else, I want to know what happened to the nun.'

'Perfect,' Lettice said, getting up. 'You can bring us up to date over lunch.'

3

Rhiannon Erley knocked softly on the bedroom door. There was no reply, but she knew that Gwyneth would not be asleep. She opened the door and walked quietly over to the bed, where Gwyneth lay on her side, looking out across the estuary. Her face was hidden, but Rhiannon could picture its expression all too well: that look of longing, sadness and fear was as familiar to her as her own features. She sat down on the edge of the mattress and put the cup on the table. 'Are you all right?' she asked. Gwyneth nodded. 'I'm sorry I wasn't here when you needed me.'

'You can't be with me all the time, I know that.' She searched for Rhiannon's hand with her own, never once taking her eyes off the horizon. 'But you're here now.'

'I've brought you some tea.'

Gwyneth sat up and sipped the drink, but Rhiannon knew that she was doing it to please rather than out of any genuine enjoyment. She looked at her friend's exhausted face, haggard in the morning sunlight and drained of any colour except for the bruising around her eyes, and felt as though she were trying to revive a ghost. 'He came to look for me,' Gwyneth whispered, her voice so low that Rhiannon could barely make out the words. 'When I heard your car, I thought it was him again. I thought he'd come back to finish what he started.'

'Henry can't hurt you now,' Rhiannon said, surprised by the confidence in her own voice. 'You believe me, don't you?' Gwyneth looked searchingly into her face, and must have found the reassurance she needed because she smiled. 'You're shattered, Gwyn. You know you have to rest.' The routine was second nature to her. She encouraged Gwyneth to lie down again, and gently stroked her hair until she slept.

4

'Lydia knows all about last night. I'm sure of it.'

Marta frowned. 'What *can* she know?'

'That I didn't spend it with Archie and you didn't spend it on your own.' After the public performance of breakfast it was a relief to Josephine to be able to talk to Marta alone, free from the worry that her face would give her away. 'She made a comment about blankets and confusing people. She must have seen us.'

They were beyond the hotel grounds now, and Marta bent down to let the dog off his lead. He barked gratefully at her and scampered off into the woods. 'I don't know why you're worried. Lydia knew you were coming to see me last night. You said she told you to call in.'

'Call in, yes. Not run around Portmeirion in the rain like a lovesick teenager.' Marta raised an eyebrow, and her obvious amusement provoked Josephine into continuing a subject that she might otherwise have dropped. 'She came to see you this morning, didn't she?'

'She came to fetch me for breakfast, but I wasn't ready,' Marta said calmly. 'There's nothing unusual about that. Lydia knows by now that early mornings and I don't mix. It's fine, Josephine. Trust me.'

'And I didn't leave anything behind?'

'Nothing tangible, no. You were impressively thorough in your departure.' She made Josephine look at her and spoke more seriously. 'Don't do this. There's no need.'

Oddly, Josephine found Marta's confidence less reassuring than the solidarity of a shared fear, but the thoughts running through her head belonged to the sleepless hours of a long night, not to a day that shone with promise, and she tried to brush them aside. The trees and shrubs that graced the shoreline were not as exotic as some of the species found elsewhere on the peninsula, but were no less beautiful for their familiarity. A sandy path cut deep through sweet-smelling gorse, whose flowers gave the sunshine a run for its money, and clusters of pink, white and purple-blue hydrangea grew in such profusion that the heads seemed almost too heavy for their stems. All along the water's edge, a thin ribbon of rocks covered in wild thrift provided a subtle but welcome relief to the dark green mass of woodland. Alma's dog ran ahead, alert to the slightest rustle of a leaf, and they watched as he danced playfully around a border terrier; Bridget appeared from the opposite direction and reclaimed her dog with an apologetic wave, but she turned away into the woods before they had a chance to speak.

After five minutes or so, they came to a promontory where the path forked, with one strand following the line of trees and the other going down onto the sands. There was a curious circular building on the headland, small and rough like the bottom of a tower that someone had forgotten to finish; a black umbrella was caught in the low-hanging branches of the tree next to it, an incongruous reminder of the previous night's storm. 'Let's wait down there while Jenky tires himself out,' Marta said, pointing to an outcrop in the rock. 'I'm afraid I don't have his energy this morning.'

They sat down on the springy turf, enjoying the strong scent of the grass which was, for Josephine, pure summer. 'No sign of a boat yet,' she said, shading her eyes and looking back towards the hotel.

'Perhaps Lettice is a bit rusty.'

'Or perhaps they're waiting for Ronnie to change. She's the only person I know who wears a designer dress to a village cricket match, and I can't imagine that taking to the water will be less of an event. Anyway, it would be just like those three to bump into someone else they know and forget about the boat altogether.'

'Don't knock it. Just enjoy the peace while it lasts.' Marta lay back and closed her eyes, her hand resting casually on Josephine's leg. 'Have you decided what you're going to start work on next? You said your publisher had asked you to write a biography.' She smiled mischievously. 'Some Scottish bloke I'd never heard of. McTavish, or something like that.'

Josephine laughed. 'Said with typical English ignorance. I think you mean Claverhouse. Or John Graham, First Viscount Dundee, to give him his full title.'

'Well, it was close.'

'I can tell you went to the sort of school where no one has to learn anything unless they want to.' Marta refused to rise to the bait. 'I suppose not knowing who he is does him less damage than most historians have managed,' Josephine conceded. 'He's either Bonnie Dundee or the bastard who drowned two old women in Galloway.' She brushed a lock of blonde hair gently away from Marta's forehead. 'Are you asleep already? That doesn't bode well for the sales.'

Marta opened her eyes. 'Of course I'm not asleep. I'm just listening to your voice. It was the first thing I loved about you.' Josephine smiled and leant forward to kiss her. 'So, are you going to take the commission? You obviously feel strongly about the man.'

'I don't know. I'm not sure how I feel about writing a book which is someone else's idea. And anyway, non-fiction's such a lot of work: all that research and objectivity, no nice chunks of dialogue or convenient coincidences to get you out of a hole. I'd rather lie in the sun and make something up.'

'You could write it as a novel.'

'Mix fact and fiction?' Josephine asked, and Marta had to laugh at the disapproval in her voice. 'How would that help restore the reputation of a much-maligned man? No one would know what was true and what wasn't.'

'Exactly. That's the fun of it. And a biography would only be your interpretation. At least calling it fiction is honest.' Before Josephine could argue, there was a tirade of barking from just above their heads. 'Being a dog owner isn't very peaceful, is it?' Marta said. 'I don't believe for one moment that Alma had any calls to make; I think she just wanted a rest.' She called the dog but he sat belligerently at the top of the rock, refusing to come any further. 'Oh God, is that a shoe next to him?' she asked, squinting against the sun. 'I'd better find out what he's up to.'

She climbed back to the path, and Josephine watched as she collected the shoe and looked round for someone to apologise to. Then she disappeared from view and the barking stopped. After a couple of minutes, Josephine followed her up the rock to see what was happening. She found Marta leaning against the small stone structure, looking as though all the strength had been drained from her body. Her face was deathly white, and she was plainly in shock. She had clipped Jenky's lead back on, and the dog seemed as subdued as she was. When she saw Josephine, she came forward to meet her, anxious to stop her going any further. 'Don't look in there,' she said, but Josephine ignored her, hell-bent on sharing whatever had shaken Marta so badly.

She stood slightly to the side of the narrow entrance to avoid blocking the light and lowered her head to look inside, noticing how effortlessly the smell of decay – hoarded year after year – could overpower the sweetness of a single summer. It was immediately obvious to her – from the dress rather than from the girl's bruised and beaten face – that she was looking at the waitress from the band, and her words to Archie came back to haunt her: whether the girl had looked for trouble or not, it had found her in the cruellest of ways. Her body had been positioned to be found: anyone continuing along the path instead of going down to the sands as she and Marta had done would have seen her instantly. A shaft of morning sunlight shone directly through the doorway, as if deliberately placed to illuminate every vile detail of her degradation, and Josephine found it hard to imagine a more perfectly composed scene of horror.

Inside, the curious lookout point resembled something halfway between a hermit's cell and a medieval torture chamber. The girl was slumped against the wall opposite, arms outstretched, wrists tied with her own stockings to two of the old iron rings which were set at regular intervals into the stone. Her dress was torn and pushed up to her waist, and there was blood all over her thighs and matted in her pubic hair – such a lot of blood that Josephine wanted to weep, not just for the violence of the attack but for the inhumanity of how the body had been left. It took every ounce of self-restraint she had not to go over to the girl and cover her shame. A dog's lead was wound around her neck and the leather cut deeply into the skin, embedding itself so thoroughly that it could only just be seen; in places, there were scratch marks on her neck where her fingers had clawed frantically at the ligature. A pair of lace knickers had been stuffed into her mouth, a grotesque and humiliating gag, and her lips were dark and swollen. Small, circular areas of bruising were visible on her shoulders and chest, and Josephine tried in vain to close her mind to the realisation that they were bite marks. The belt from a raincoat acted as a blindfold for unseeing eyes, and she was struck by how effectively that one act removed all traces of the girl's personality. In a final gesture of mockery, someone had drawn a clumsy, grotesque smile around her mouth with lipstick.

She had looked on death only once before: then, it had surprised her with a peace which she had always believed to be a cliché designed to give solace to the living; here, it was a violent wrenching from the world, a scream of pain and humiliation which endured long after the final breath was taken. She felt Marta's hand on her arm, and allowed herself to be pulled away. 'It's the waitress from the hotel,' she said.

'Yes, I recognised her.' They stared at each other in silence, and Josephine saw her own impotent fury looking back at her. The pure, melodious song of a blackbird filled the air, and she wanted to scream at it to stop. 'Go and get Archie,' Marta said quietly. 'I'll stay with her.'

Josephine shook her head. 'I'm not leaving you here on your own. We'll both go.'

'We can hardly leave *her* on her own, either,' Marta snapped. 'It's not right.' Instinctively, she wiped the lipstick from her own mouth. 'The world and his wife will be along here when the village opens, and she's been humiliated enough.'

'I know, but if you seriously think I'm going back to the hotel without you when whoever did this might be sitting in those trees now, watching us, you must be mad.' Josephine struggled to rein in the fear that had made her react more angrily than she meant to. 'Of course it feels wrong to leave her, but she's beyond help. I won't let you put yourself at risk.'

'You don't have any choice.'

Josephine sighed and took the lead from her hand. 'Fine. You go back to the hotel and I'll stay here with the dog.' Marta began to object, as Josephine had known she would. 'Come on,' she said gently. 'It'll only take us a few minutes.' Still, Marta stood rooted to the spot. Josephine saw the expression of grief on her face, and realised that it was only in part for the stranger whose body she wanted so badly to watch over. Marta's own daughter had been murdered two years ago, and her stubbornness now, Josephine guessed, was a reaction to having failed to keep her safe. 'You're thinking about Elspeth, aren't you?' she asked quietly.

Marta nodded. 'Is that how she looked?'

'I don't know, Marta. I didn't see her.'

'But Archie must have said something.'

During their time together, Marta had pressed her over and over again for every detail of Elspeth's death, always suspecting a darker truth than the one she was being told. 'He told me that she lost consciousness almost immediately,' Josephine said, imagining what torment that small word 'almost' must be. 'She would have known very little about it. I promise I'd tell you if it were different.'

'So she wasn't hurt like that?'

'You know she wasn't.'

'I don't though, do I? I don't know anything about her because I wasn't part of her life.' Josephine held her close, waiting for the tears to subside. Eventually, Marta said, 'I'd give anything just to be told that she was never alone, Josephine. Does that sound ridiculous?'

'No, it doesn't sound ridiculous. And I can't argue with it.' Reluctantly, she handed the lead back to Marta. 'I won't be long.'

5

Archie finished reading about the uprising in Spain and dropped his newspaper onto the grass, glad to put the world down with it. He had moved to one of the deckchairs by the swimming pool; from there, he could watch the antics on the terrace without any danger of being caught up in them. The only new arrivals from Hitchcock's party were Danny Lascelles and Astrid Lake, who had come down from the village within a couple of minutes of each other and made a great show of saying good morning. Archie wasn't surprised that the gathering was incomplete: Bella Hutton didn't seem the type to breakfast in public; and, after what he had drunk last night, Leyton Turnbull deserved the sort of head that would keep most people in bed until noon. In fact, there were very few people about now that the girls had made a move, and once or twice he caught Hitchcock looking anxiously around at the remnants of his weekend, wondering where his audience had gone.

Archie watched, amused, as his cousins and Lydia chatted down by the quayside, making elaborate preparations to take to the water without actually getting into the boat. Josephine and Marta would be halfway to Harlech before anyone caught up with them, but he guessed that they wouldn't miss the company. He wondered how he would have felt when he saw Josephine's happiness at breakfast if he had not been marvelling at his own, then put the thought from his mind; it was far too early to start relying on Bridget for his emotional welfare, and not fair on either of them.

The clock in the Bell Tower chimed the half-hour. He settled back in the sun and closed his eyes, and was just drifting off to sleep when he heard his name being called. Bridget was on her way across the lawn with Lytton and Carrington, and he got up, delighted to see her; his smile faded when he noticed how upset she was. 'Archie – thank God you're here. I didn't know what else to do.'

'What's the matter?' She seemed to struggle for words. He sat her down and said calmly, 'Bridget – tell me what's happened.'

'There's a body in the dog cemetery. I think it's Bella Hutton, but it's hard to tell.'

'Hard to tell?'

'Yes. Her face . . .' She stopped and made an effort to control her voice. 'She's been killed, Archie. I didn't go right up to her; her dog was upset, and I didn't want trouble with these two. Anyway, to be honest, I wasn't in a hurry to go any closer. But I saw enough.'

'And you're sure she's dead?'

'Jesus, Archie, nobody's make-up is that good.' Her sarcasm was defensive, an antidote to fear and shock. 'What a stupid question. Don't you believe me?'

'Of course I believe *you*,' he said, remembering Bella's parting shot last night and what Hitchcock had said about murder. 'I just don't trust that anything around here is quite what it seems this weekend.' Would the director really pull a stunt like that? he wondered. Probably, but he doubted that Bella Hutton would collude in it. The nun was a possibility: he didn't believe for a moment that she was genuine – no one with heels like that was holy – and if she was on the payroll, she could just as easily turn up today as a corpse. He was torn between going to the cemetery first to see for himself or acting immediately on Bridget's word. In the end, he chose the latter: if this turned out to be an extreme practical joke, it would do Hitchcock good to be charged with wasting police time. 'Go into the hotel now and find James Wyllie,' he said. 'Tell him in confidence what's happened. Get him to call the police and close the village on my authority.' He looked at his watch. 'They open the gates at ten thirty?' Bridget nodded. 'With a bit of luck, not many people will have come in yet. Make sure James understands how important it is that he keeps this absolutely private. Nothing to his staff or any of the guests. If word gets out that there's a murdered Hollywood star in those woods, we'll have the press and the public trampling through them in no time, and all hell will break loose. What's the quickest way up there?'

'There's a path that runs behind the hotel.' She outlined the route for him and put her hand to his cheek. 'You will be careful, Archie?'

'Of course. Don't worry. And make sure you stay at the hotel until we have a better idea of what's going on.' She nodded. Touched by her concern, he found the track she described and set off. It took him less than a minute to be grateful for Bridget's succinct directions: the maze of pathways through the woods was bewildering, and it would be impossible for a stranger to be sure of his bearings or find the same route twice. Before long, he spotted the distinctive Scots pine she had told him to watch out for, tall and straight with a hundred years of growth behind it, and he turned right into the densest part of the wood. Even at such a brisk pace, the exuberant mass of fuchsia trees, ferns, camellias and old rhododendrons was breathtaking, and Archie thought about how his father – who had been a botanist himself – would have admired planting like this, so natural and yet carefully considered at every turn. Then he saw the pheasant hide which Bridget had offered as a sign that the cemetery was imminent. He slowed down and looked inside, noting the empty whisky bottle and cluster of cigarette butts on the ground by a rough wooden bench, then drew a deep breath and moved forward.

Bridget had done her best to describe what he would find here, but the essence of the place was in its atmosphere, not its physical layout, and he was utterly unprepared for the sense of isolation that hit him from the moment he found the entrance.

The circular burial ground was forty or fifty feet in diameter, although its boundaries were difficult to determine after years of neglect. Branches tumbled everywhere, fighting for light and space, their progress through the air mirroring the ramble of their roots underground. For a moment, he wondered if they had been trained deliberately at head height to deter casual intruders from entering a place of peace. But he was no sightseer, and he knew instinctively now that this was no longer a place of peace.

There was an ancient feel to the cemetery which belied the fact that, as far as he knew, it was less than fifty years since the first dog was buried there. It was easy to tell which were the original graves: they stood close together, slabs of dark slate inscribed with texts from the Bible, or simple granite pillars, covered in moss, which gave no indication of what or whom they marked. The tomb in the very centre was larger than all the rest and flanked on either side by two smaller stones, a silent guard of honour. Bella Hutton's body lay on top of it, her hands folded across her chest, as lifeless as the carving on a sepulchre, and Archie dismissed all thoughts of a practical joke. Death held its own muted reverence, and it could never be faked.

He hesitated before moving closer. The actress's Jack Russell cowered by the grave, watching him warily, and it occurred to Archie that there were few things more unnatural in a living world than an animal that showed such fear. He crouched down slowly and began to talk to the dog in a low, even voice, reassuring him until the persistent growling softened, then ceased altogether. Archie looked round for a lead, but there was nothing. He walked slowly over to the grave and reached out his hand, hoping that the animal wouldn't fly at him. It didn't take him long to realise that any aggression was unlikely: one of the dog's front legs was injured, but from what Archie could see of his owner, the Jack Russell had got off lightly. He stroked the dog's head and received a lick in return. 'It's all right, boy, we'll soon get that leg fixed,' he promised. 'But first I need to have a look at your friend.'

Archie was no stranger to knife wounds: stabbing was the most frequently used method of murder in Britain, common in both domestic disputes and street brawls; he had seen victims attacked with anything from kitchen knives, scissors and razors to chisels, fire-irons and even an ice pick. But nothing like this. Bella Hutton's clothes, made of thin silk, had been torn to shreds. Although the canopy of trees overhead had protected her from the full force of the rain, enough had penetrated the leaves to wash some of the blood from her wounds, making it easier to see the pattern of death on her skin – livid red on white, running the length of her body with the uniform thoroughness of flowers on a dress. It would have been impossible to count the number of injuries: forty or fifty at least, perhaps more. Several of the cuts were long rather than deep, made with a swiping action and suggesting to Archie that the assailant had wanted to prolong Bella's agony as much as possible; some of the deeper wounds on her stomach and breasts showed a bruise on the surrounding tissues where the knife had been plunged in as far as the hilt. The actress had obviously put up a fight: her forearms were covered in classic defence wounds from a vain attempt to ward off the attack, and he could see loose flaps of skin on her palms and fingers where the blade had sliced through her hands as she tried to grab hold of it. From the soil and imprint of undergrowth on her body, Archie guessed that she had, at some point, been forced face down onto the ground; almost certainly, a pathologist would find further damage on her back. As it was, there were so many variations in the size and shape of her injuries – cuts where the knife went in and out cleanly, gashes where it had been moved back and forth while still inside her body – that it was pointless for Archie to speculate at the type of knife used: that would have to wait for the post-mortem.

The heat had begun to build again, and he raised his hand to wave away a fly. Bella's body had obviously been moved after death and placed deliberately on this tombstone, and Archie wondered if there was any significance to that. Everything else about the murder seemed frenzied and out of control, but it was not unusual for a sense of calm and purpose to take over once the killer's work was done. He could identify where the worst of the attack had taken place: a few yards to the right there was an area of damaged vegetation and scattered stones which showed signs of a struggle; again, although the rain had been sufficiently strong to wash some of the blood from the stones, dense foliage had prevented it from being completely obliterated. But none of this told him what a Hollywood movie star – a woman in her fifties – had been doing here late at night. Surely she would not have chosen to walk her dog somewhere so bleak and lonely? And if she had been brought here by force, the dog would have been left behind. Had she known her life was in danger? he wondered. Was that dramatic exit line a warning to someone else in the room, someone whom she later came here to challenge? He glanced down at the Jack Russell, wishing the dog could speak.

And then he forced himself to look at her face. Bridget was right: it was barely recognisable. He tried to bring to mind the woman he had seen in the hotel last night, but all he could remember was her image on the screen, the face that had articulated the joys and fears and pain of a generation. That was how people would remember Bella Hutton when the actress's death was announced, and he envied them their illusion, their memories safely couched in black and white; what Archie would see from now on was a blaze of hatred delivered in merciless colour. Her head was tilted slightly towards him, as if she were waiting to be found. One eye stared blankly upwards, the other was impossible to make out amid a mass of blood and swollen tissue; the left-hand side of her face had been stabbed repeatedly until the skin hung loose, revealing the cheekbone underneath. Nothing of her character remained, and Archie wondered who had wanted to obliterate that spirit so brutally. He longed to believe that Bella had fallen victim to a chance attack by a stranger, but he knew in his heart that her killer had woken to the sun of Portmeirion.

Nature had already begun its relentless collusion in the killer's work, and he watched an ant crawl over what remained of Bella's lips. Sickened by what he had seen, and desperate to feel the sun on his face again, he gathered up the Jack Russell gently in his arms; the animal whimpered and tried to resist, reluctant to leave the body he had loved, but Archie turned and carried him slowly away. The dog's grief, he suspected, would not have a human equivalent, and he wondered sadly what that said about Bella's world.

6

Hitchcock sat on the terrace outside the Mirror Room and saw the reflected image of two police cars driving down the hill to the hotel. They pulled up outside, and, as he watched the uniformed men get out and disappear into reception, he felt the familiar constriction around his heart. For a moment, he was back in that cell again, thirty years older but still the same little boy, terrified of being thought bad, already irretrievably cast as the innocent man accused. He remembered the indiscretion that had got him there, the fury in his father's eyes and the voice of the policeman as the cell door clanged shut behind him: 'This is what we do to naughty boys.' He would have that on his gravestone.

Turning away, he caught sight of his own reflection in the glass – his body rigid with fear, palms sweating, eyes staring ahead – and the mirror seemed to act as his conscience. He had no idea why the police were here, but their presence unnerved him more than ever, coming so soon after Alma's disapproval of the night before. What if he *had* gone too far? What would she do? Her absence seemed to underline his anxiety.

He had always felt the need to prove himself to his wife and had never, in his heart, believed himself to be worthy of her; one day, she would see that for herself, and the idea that he might lose her terrified him. It was the only thing that he would never be able to share with her. For all his talk, he knew that the greatest fears were the ones you never admitted to, in case the very act of speaking them aloud made them come true.

7

Marta lit her third cigarette with the dying embers of the second. There was a noise from further along the path, and, for all her bravado, she felt a sudden sting of fear. She pulled the dog closer and considered moving down onto the sands, but she had left it too late to hide; the footsteps were almost upon her. When Archie emerged from the trees with a uniformed policeman, she could have cried with relief. 'Is Josephine all right?' she asked anxiously.

'She's fine. I've left her back at the hotel with Bridget. It wasn't easy to stop her coming with me, but I promised I'd keep you safe.' He put his hand on her shoulder and looked at her with concern. 'It's never right that it has to be anybody, but I'm so sorry it was you.'

Marta shrugged unconvincingly. 'It's made me realise that for someone who's been to prison as an accessory to murder, I'm embarrassingly ill acquainted with the subject.'

It was a feeble attempt at humour, but Archie smiled any-way, more at the expression on the other policeman's face than at the joke itself. 'I'm afraid we're all going to be more familiar with it after last night. A second body's just been found in the woods. Bella Hutton.'

Marta looked at him in disbelief. 'What on earth's going on, Archie? Does Josephine know?'

'Yes.'

'She met Bella last night. They talked. Did she tell you?'

'I didn't really give her the chance. I came straight here when she told me you were on your own.' He glanced over to the stone hut where the girl's body lay, and scowled. 'What the hell do you think you're doing, Constable Powell? You can't go in there.'

The policeman moved away from the entrance, apparently unruffled by the reprimand. 'It's the Erley girl, sir,' he said. 'Just like I thought.'

There was a note of satisfaction in his voice which Marta found despicable; judging by the expression on Archie's face, she wasn't the only one. 'Does she have a first name?'

'Branwen. I could have told you she'd come to no good.'

'And would you mind telling me how you arrived at such an enlightening prediction?' Archie asked, making no effort to hide his irritation.

'She's a chip off the old block, sir, just like her mother. She couldn't keep herself out of trouble either.'

Marta opened her mouth to speak, but Archie got there first. 'Let's get this straight, Constable. What has happened to Branwen Erley wasn't determined by her genes. Rape and murder are not part of any inheritance I've ever come across. Neither has she brought this on herself, no matter who she was or what she's done. The fault for this lies entirely with the culprit, not with the victim. Do I make myself clear?'

'As crystal, sir.'

'Good. Because if you ever say anything like that in my hearing again, I'll have you off the force faster than you've moved in your life.'

Marta watched Archie's face as he looked at Branwen Erley's body. She had expected his to be a purely professional view, devoid of any emotion, but she was wrong. He must have been called to so many scenes like this, but a day-to-day familiarity with violence did not seem to have hardened him to the individual tragedy of this death. As he looked at the body, taking in every detail, his face held a genuine sadness for the victim, and she liked him all the more for it.

'Right, Powell, I'd like you to stay here with Miss Erley's body until forensics arrive,' he said when he had seen enough. 'Don't go any closer than you are now, and, should anyone else pass by here, I don't want them straying from the path. Take their names and send them straight to the hotel. We can't have people wandering around these woods at the moment.' Powell gave a grudging assent, and Marta suspected that his resentment had less to do with being ordered around than with being ordered around in front of a woman. 'But first you can tell me what you know about Miss Erley and her family. And I'll have it without the personal commentary this time.'

'They lived over in Portmadoc,' he said. 'Gareth Erley – that's her father – was a quarryman at the slate caverns in Llechwedd. Decent sort of bloke, but he had a lot to put up with from his missus. That's the price you pay for marrying a looker, I suppose. He never quite knew who was as cosy with his wife as he was, if you know what I mean.'

'And where are Branwen's parents now?'

'Her dad died a few years back. I don't know where Rhiannon ended up. She left him when the kid was little more than a baby. Did well for herself, you might say. Ran off with the lord of the manor.'

'What do you mean?'

'The Draycotts had the money round here. They really thought they were something, looking at each other across the water in their grand houses, having nothing to do with the likes of us.' He saw Archie's face and got to the point. 'Henry Dray-

284

cott lived across the estuary, one of the big places off the Harlech road. He liked the girls from the town, and marrying one of them didn't stop him keeping up with the others. Rhiannon Erley must have worked a real number on him because he ended up taking her abroad. Neither of them ever came back here. Can't say I blame them: her old man would have killed them both.' Archie resisted the temptation to interrupt his story by asking, in that case, what his definition of 'decent' was. 'I don't expect Gwyneth Draycott was too happy about it, either,' Powell added. 'She was pregnant when they left, and Rhiannon was her closest friend.'

'So Branwen was brought up by her father?'

'By her gran, really. His mother. She still lives over in Portmadoc.'

'And she would be Branwen's next of kin.'

'I suppose so, unless you can find Rhiannon. Branwen wasn't very close to her gran, I don't think. As far as I know, she'd been working here pretty much from when it opened. I suppose she thought it was glamorous, but I wouldn't let *my* daughter anywhere near the place. All them queers and arty types.' Powell gave a shudder. He looked at Archie and added slyly, 'I don't think you mentioned why you were here, sir?'

'Do you know if Miss Erley had a boyfriend?'

'Always, sir. No one specific.'

He left the implication hanging in the air. 'And what about Mrs Draycott? What did she do after her husband left her?'

'She shut the house up and came over here with the child for a few years.' Archie looked at him questioningly. 'Her sister-in-law rented the house – that's what I meant about them looking at each other across the water. Then when Grace Draycott died

285

and they turned it into a hotel, Gwyneth moved back home. She still lives there.' Archie glanced at the house across the water and saw it properly for the first time, even though he had been staring at the same view all weekend. 'She's not all there, though, by all accounts. Half her family died in the loony bin up the road. I don't blame her husband for wanting to get away. Her kid was probably better off out of it, too.'

'Why? What happened?'

'The poor little sod was killed by one of the Gypsies who used to come here for the summer.'

'You were on that case?'

Powell nodded. 'We never found the body.'

'So how do you know what happened?'

'It stands to reason, doesn't it?'

Archie stifled his automatic response and asked, 'Did you get a confession?'

'We didn't get the chance. The gyppo died in a fire before we could ask him.'

As tempting as it was to give Powell a few thoughts on his style of policing, Archie resisted; he needed to get back to the hotel. 'Thank you,' he said, signalling to Marta that he was ready to go. 'You've been very informative.'

'And as for Bella Hutton,' Powell began, but Archie held up his hand.

'That's enough for now. I'm very grateful for your local knowledge, but I think there'll be enough gossip and speculation about Bella Hutton without any encouragement from us.'

The man gave an insolent smile and shrugged. 'Whatever you say, sir. Glad to have been of help.'

8

The news of Bella Hutton's death refused to feel like anything other than a sick joke to Josephine as she sat on the top lawn with Bridget, trying to make sense of the past hour. At Archie's request, the guests had been asked to return to their rooms or wait in one of the hotel's public areas until the murder sites had been secured, and, as more police began to arrive from the surrounding towns, she noticed how the character of Portmeirion changed instantly: the glimpse of a dark-blue uniform at the foot of a pathway or the door of a building turned its secret beauty into something more sinister and threatening, taking its toll on guests and staff alike. No one had been told any details yet, but the carefree, live-and-let-live attitude of the morning had gone, and everywhere Josephine looked people were suddenly watchful, suspicious, afraid. Only Lydia and the Motleys seemed oblivious to the change in atmosphere: she had made several attempts to beckon them in from the water, but they were too far out now to recognise the urgency in her greeting, and in the end she had given up.

'What's the worst thing Archie's ever forgiven you for?' Bridget asked. The question came from nowhere, and Josephine looked at her in surprise. 'I'm sorry, that was too personal. I wasn't trying to pry into your life, just to find out if Archie is still as understanding in his old age as he was when I knew him. He was always so kind.'

'He still is.' Josephine took a sip of coffee, and its temperature reminded her that she had never wanted the drink in the first place. 'I don't know that I can really answer your question,' she said, pushing the cup away. 'The worst thing I've ever *done* to Archie is to fall in love with someone else, but you'd have to ask him if he's forgiven me or not.' She could see from Bridget's expression that her response had satisfied one of the questions that remained unspoken between them. 'And it's not really the sort of thing I'm very good at discussing with him. Not in so many words, anyway.'

'But you're still friends.'

'For want of a better word, yes.' Of all the qualities Josephine had expected to find in Bridget, uncertainty wasn't one of them, and it intrigued her. 'What are you worried about?' she asked more gently. 'Forgiveness is a very big word.'

Bridget smiled. 'And don't I know it?' She sighed, and reached down to check on the injured Jack Russell who lay quietly in the shade under her chair, diligently licking his paw. 'I wouldn't know where to start with that one, Josephine, even if I could trust you not to tell Archie. And you would tell him, wouldn't you?'

'Of course I would. Unless I was absolutely sure you'd do it yourself.' She watched as Alma came out onto the terrace and looked round for her husband. It was obvious from their body language that they had no idea what was going on, and, ironically, the suspense seemed to be something that Hitchcock found difficult to bear. Alma put a reassuring hand on his arm as they went back into the hotel, and Josephine wondered if she should seek them out and have a discreet word, but Archie's instructions had been very clear, and he wouldn't thank her for interfering. In the end, her dilemma was solved for her: Archie and Marta came round the bend of the coastal path, and only then, when they were tempered with relief, did Josephine allow herself to acknowledge her worst fears. She stood to go and meet them, but was stopped by the strange combination of concern and longing in Bridget's eyes as she watched Archie. 'You obviously want to see him again,' she said.

'Yes, very much.'

'Then I don't think you have a choice. Whatever it is will destroy you if you keep it from him. It's started already.'

'You make it sound very simple.'

'Meddling in someone else's life always is. That's why so many people do it.' She smiled, and nodded towards Marta and Archie. 'For what it's worth, the odds are in your favour. It's a long story, but ask Marta how understanding Archie can be. I think you'll be pleased.'

9

James Wyllie met Penrose at reception and took him discreetly to one side. 'The local force have sent as many men as they can,' he said, 'but the officer in charge will be another half an hour at least. An Inspector Roberts, apparently. He's coming from Colwyn Bay.'

'You don't know him?'

'No. I can't say we have much call for the police here as a rule.'

The comment was sober rather than defensive, and Penrose understood what a black day this must be for Wyllie, both personally and professionally: the stain of murder would have serious consequences for Portmeirion, particularly if the killer turned out to be connected with the village, and the manager had been here for several years now, freeing Clough from day-to-day concerns and coming to love the place almost as much as its creator. Wyllie seemed to read his thoughts. 'Funny, isn't it, how hell is always so much worse if it's once been heaven. *Is* the other body Branwen?'

'Yes, I'm afraid it is.'

'I'm so sorry. She was only in her twenties, and yet she must have been here longer than anyone.' He paused, then asked reluctantly, 'Does it suggest that whoever did this is more likely to be one of us?'

'It's far too early to say. Did Miss Erley live in?'

'Yes. There are some staff rooms at the back of the hotel. She had one of those.'

'Would you make sure it's locked?'

'Of course. I've secured Miss Hutton's suite as you requested.'

'Good. I'll need to examine both, but I want to talk to everyone first. It's not fair to keep them in the dark any longer.'

Wyllie gave a knowing smile. 'I think Mr Hitchcock would agree with you there. They're all waiting for you in the Mirror Room, but I can't say they went very gracefully.'

'I can imagine. I assume you're all right with my handling this for now until Roberts arrives?'

'Of course.' He turned to go, but Wyllie called him back. 'I'll have to tell Clough,' he said. 'He'll be devastated, but he'd never forgive me if he heard it from someone else.'

'Fine. Telephone him now but . . .'

'Ask him to keep it to himself. Don't worry,' he said, smiling at Penrose with a hint of his usual charm. 'Discretion is one thing we *do* know about here.'

As he walked into the Mirror Room, Penrose couldn't help feeling that his life had been wound back twelve hours; Hitchcock's guests had, for the most part, chosen the seats that they had occupied the night before, an instinctive attempt to find order amid chaos. To save time, he had asked Josephine to join them so that she could share her conversation with Bella Hutton; Marta had very sensibly elected to stay outside with Bridget and wait for Lydia and his cousins to return to dry land. The only person who hadn't yet arrived was Leyton Turnbull. Penrose didn't blame him for showing a reluctance to come back into the company that had so recently torn him to shreds, but he hoped that there wasn't a more sinister explanation for his absence. 'Where is Leyton Turnbull?' he asked, turning to Hitchcock.

'We haven't seen him this morning. I imagine he's nursing his hangover.' The director looked anxiously at David Franks, and Penrose guessed that a silent instruction had passed between them.

Franks stood up, confirming his suspicions. 'I'll go and find him for you. He's probably still in his room.'

Penrose had no intention of allowing the director to slip into his usual role. 'No, it's fine. Please sit down. If he's not here by the time we've finished talking, I'll go and look for him myself.' The tone of his voice left no one in any doubt as to who was in charge. Franks did as he was told, glancing apologetically at Hitchcock.

'Is this about Bella?' Everyone, including her husband, stared at Alma Reville. 'It's just that she's the only other person who isn't here, and you don't seem surprised by that, Chief Inspector.'

With a grudging respect for her intelligence, Penrose nodded. 'There have been two murders overnight in Portmeirion, and I'm afraid that Miss Hutton is one of the victims. Her body was found in the woods this morning.'

David Franks stared at him in disbelief. 'You're lying. You must be.' Penrose was used to news of a violent death being met with such ardent denial, but he had not expected that reaction from anyone here, and he looked at Franks's devastated face in surprise. 'Is this another one of your gags?' Franks shouted at Hitchcock. 'Something you've dreamt up to keep us on our toes this weekend? Because if it is, you've gone too far.'

'Of course it's not a joke, David.' Alma tried to console Franks but he pushed her away. 'You wouldn't do that, would you, Hitch?'

Penrose was interested to see that it was more a question than a statement, but he gave Alma the backing of which her husband seemed incapable. 'Miss Reville is right. I'm afraid there's no doubt about it.'

'What happened?'

'She was stabbed in the dog cemetery,' Penrose said, thinking how little justice his words actually did to the actress's fate. Even so, out of the corner of his eye, he saw Astrid Lake shudder. 'We'll know more when the forensics team has had a chance to examine the scene.'

'I want to see her.'

'I'm afraid that's not possible at the moment.'

'Try and stop me.' Franks turned away and began to walk out of the room, but Spence was too quick for him. 'Let me go, damn you,' he yelled, struggling to get past.

'Not until you've calmed down.' Penrose noticed how gently Spence held Franks until his anger began to subside. When he sensed it was safe to do so, he relaxed his grip and squeezed

Franks's shoulder affectionately. 'The Inspector's right,' he said quietly. 'You can't do any good by going up there now. Bella wouldn't want you to see her like that. You know what she was like.'

'What was your relationship with Bella Hutton?' Penrose asked.

Franks sat down and made an effort to pull himself together. 'She was my mother's sister,' he said. 'My mother died when I was eight; my father followed her six years later. Bella and Max took me to live with them in America. They got me a job on a film set – between them, they knew just about everybody in Hollywood, so it wasn't hard – and they kept me out of trouble. I was a very angry young man after my father's death, and they showed me how to channel that into something more creative than I might otherwise have chosen. When their marriage broke up, I came back here with Bella, and she vouched for me with the studios until I could prove myself all over again in England.'

The details of Franks's family connections to Bella Hutton seemed to be news to everyone except the Hitchcocks and Jack Spence. Penrose noticed that Josephine, in particular, was looking at him curiously, and he wondered why. 'I'm sorry,' he said. 'If I'd known you were so close I'd have handled things rather differently.'

Franks shrugged. 'How were you to know? Anyway,' he admitted, 'we hadn't been as close recently. I may as well tell you that before someone else does.'

'Why was that?'

'Bella was used to guiding my career, and she found it hard to accept that I wanted to make my own decisions, even if they turned out to be the wrong ones. I wanted to stand on my own two feet.' He smiled sadly. 'I suppose I'll have plenty of time to do that now.'

Astrid Lake spoke up for the first time. 'You said two murders. Who else is dead?'

'One of the hotel's waiting staff,' Penrose said. 'Her name was Branwen Erley. She was the young woman singing with the band last night, and her body was found at the lookout point on the headland this morning.'

The actress looked across at Daniel Lascelles but he refused to meet her eye. 'Was she stabbed as well?'

'No.'

She waited for him to expand and, when he didn't, asked angrily, 'So what does that mean? Is there more than one killer, or is he just versatile?'

'It's far too early for me to speculate like that. When both bodies have been thoroughly examined, we'll have more evidence to go on. In the meantime . . .'

Hitchcock interrupted him, unable to control his temper any longer. 'Then shouldn't you be out there gathering that evidence, Chief Inspector, rather than wasting time in here pretending you're Hercule bloody Poirot in the final chapter?' He glanced accusingly at Josephine as he delivered the insult, and Penrose found it hard to decide whether her affronted expression was on his behalf or if she simply resented the association. 'I don't see what a maniac on the loose in those woods has to do with any of us.'

'What makes you assume it was a maniac?'

'What makes you assume it wasn't?' It was a reasonable retort, but Penrose wasn't prepared to admit as much. 'Surely someone had a grudge against this waitress? Bella probably saw something she shouldn't have and was killed because of that?'

Anything to deflect attention from your fun and games this weekend, Penrose thought. 'I can assure you, sir, you're not getting any special treatment.' It was an ambivalent phrase, and he scarcely cared whether Hitchcock took it as a warning or a comfort. 'All the staff and guests will be questioned in due course, and I appreciate your theory, but as Miss Erley was almost certainly strangled with the lead from Bella Hutton's dog, and as her clothing suggests that she was alive later, when the night grew cold, it seems logical to me to assume that Miss Hutton was killed first.' It had the desired effect: Hitchcock's bluster collapsed like a house of cards, and he sat down meekly next to his wife.

'I think they knew each other, Archie. Bella Hutton and Branwen Erley, I mean.'

Penrose looked at Josephine. 'What makes you say that?'

'They were talking on the terrace yesterday afternoon. I don't know what they were saying, but it didn't look like a waitress and guest conversation. The girl seemed upset. Then Bella said something to her, and she smiled.'

'Do you know anything about that?' Penrose asked Franks.

He shook his head. 'No, but Bella was always a generous tipper. A lot of staff smiled when she was around.'

Penrose turned to Hitchcock. 'Did you invite Bella Hutton to join you here for the weekend?'

'No,' the director said, clearing his throat and looking round for some water. 'We were friends. I've known her for about ten years, but I didn't realise she was going to be here until yesterday.'

'And when was the last time you saw her?'

He looked frightened to death by the continued questioning, and Alma answered firmly for both of them. 'At coffee last night. Neither of us set eyes on Bella again after she left this room. We went back to the Watch House at around ten thirty,' she added, offering Penrose the alibi he hadn't yet asked for. 'And we were there until breakfast this morning.'

'Did anyone else see her after she left here?' Everyone looked at each other but nobody spoke. 'What about her parting remark? She said that her greatest fear was to know the manner of her own death; that's a very peculiar thing to say hours before you're murdered. Can anyone explain what she meant by that?'

'I think I can.' All eyes in the room turned to Josephine again. 'Bella had cancer. She told me she only had a few weeks to live, but that's plenty of time when all that's ahead of you is pain and misery. I imagine that's what she meant. It must have been terrifying for her.'

'It was,' Franks agreed. 'She kept her illness very private, though. She didn't want anyone to feel sorry for her.'

'But you knew about it?'

'She told me most things. At least I thought she did, but perhaps your friend will prove me wrong.'

He looked at Josephine, almost challenging her to do so. 'I doubt that,' Josephine said. 'It was a very brief conversation. But she'd obviously been weighing up her life, which is probably what we'd all do in her position. I caught her at a time when she needed to talk but I'm sure she wouldn't have done it if I hadn't been a stranger.' She glanced apologetically at David

Franks. 'You don't burden someone you love with your own fears, do you? But an outsider is different.'

Penrose knew Josephine well enough to understand that she would not have been untouched by her meeting with Bella, no matter how much of a stranger she was. 'Tell me what she talked about,' he said gently. 'Everything you can remember, no matter how insignificant it seemed at the time.'

She hesitated, and he knew that she was reluctant to discuss it in front of an audience, but he wanted to see how the others reacted to what she had to say. 'She talked about her early career and meeting her husband. From what she said, it was obvious that she still loved him; it seemed to me that he'd hurt her very badly, though.'

'She didn't like the way he ran his business,' Franks explained. 'For someone who had spent so long at the top of her industry, Bella could be very naive about the deals that were done and the way money was made. She thought he exploited people, and I suppose he did, but Max could never understand why that made a difference to her or to their marriage. He loved her every bit as much as she loved him. I remember being caught in the middle when it started to go wrong. God, those two could fight.'

'And he's still in America?'

'I don't think he was prowling the woods last night, if that's what you mean.'

'I mean he'll need to be informed of her death,' Penrose said evenly, although the thought had crossed his mind.

'Oh, I see. Yes, he's still in LA. Sorry.'

'What else did Bella tell you?' Penrose asked, turning back to Josephine.

'She talked a lot about her family and what had happened to them after she moved away from here.'

'Here? You mean Portmeirion?' He listened as Josephine explained, furious with himself for dismissing what Constable Powell had been about to say just because the man irritated him. 'Her older sister created the dog cemetery, and her younger sister died in childbirth.' She paused and looked at David Franks. 'That was your mother?' He nodded. 'So it was your father . . .'

'Who was murdered by a pack of dogs, metaphorically speaking? Yes, it was.' He didn't give Penrose the chance to ask for an explanation, but described the circumstances of his father's death with a calm matter-of-factness which was undermined by the anger in his eyes.

'So what you said last night wasn't a joke? You really did watch your father burn to death?' The compassion in Alma's voice was as strong as it had been the night before, even though she had been lied to.

'Yes, but I don't know why I said that. It was out of order. I'm sorry.'

'There's no need to apologise, David,' Hitchcock said, looking at his wife. 'Sometimes a joke is the only way to get through.'

'Bella took me away because Grace begged her to,' Franks continued. 'It was dangerous for me here: I was frightened and angry, and the mob would have found a way to get to me, too. There's no stopping violence like that once it starts.' He looked round the room. 'It's ironic, but this was where Bella told me that I was leaving with her. If you look carefully, you can still see the mark where I threw a doorstop at the fireplace. I didn't want to go.'

'The child who went missing was related to Bella,' Penrose said, piecing the details together with what the policeman had told him. 'Her brother's child. Is that right?'

Franks looked surprised. 'Taran? Yes. He was only three at the time. How did you know?'

'One of the local officers told me. He also said that Bella's brother never knew his son because he ran off with another woman. Branwen Erley's mother, to be precise. That's how she and Bella were connected. Did you know that?'

'Yes.'

'And were you going to mention it?'

'No, but only because I was trying to protect someone.' His honesty was disarming, and Penrose looked at him in surprise. 'What's the point now, though? You're going to find out anyway. Bella's brother – it's Leyton Turnbull. He changed his name when he left here.'

It was obvious that this was a revelation to everyone in the room, including Josephine. 'Why didn't you tell me this before?' Penrose asked.

'Because he's all I've got left, dammit.'

Penrose left the room for long enough to control his temper and find James Wyllie. 'Will you take one of these officers to Leyton Turnbull's room and find out if he's there? If he is, bring him down here but don't tell him what it's about.' He went back to the Mirror Room and sat down opposite Franks. 'Right. Tell me everything you know about Leyton Turnbull.'

'He turned up in America about eighteen months after I got there. He'd spent some time in Europe – Denmark first, then Germany after the war ended, and he'd had a few small parts in terrible films. By that time, Bella was very famous and very rich, and he wanted to cash in on her success. He arrived at the studios one day, completely out of the blue.'

'With Branwen Erley's mother?'

'No. That can't have worked out because he was on his own when he got to us. Bella was horrified, but he hit it off with Max straight away. He found Turnbull some work on the production side. That didn't go down very well with Bella.'

'But she put up with it?'

'As long as there was never any acknowledgement that they were related. She didn't want anything to do with him. Then Turnbull pushed his luck too far, Max refused to rein him in, and Bella had had enough. She filed for divorce and came back to England.'

'Was that when he raped an actress?' Astrid asked. 'Bella told me he'd destroyed a young girl's life. Did the boys stick together and turn a blind eye?' She looked at Penrose. 'Had Branwen Erley been raped?' He said nothing. 'She had, hadn't she?'

'Jesus Christ, what about Bella?' Franks demanded. 'She hadn't ...'

'No,' Penrose said. 'There's no sign of a sexual assault on Miss Hutton.' He chose not to add that it was about the only atrocity that had not been performed on the movie star's body.

'Turnbull was with that waitress last night, Archie,' Spence said quietly. 'He brought her back in his car at about seven o'clock and dropped her off at reception. I saw them when I was walking down to the hotel. She kissed him goodbye, and her stockings were ripped.'

'Obviously begging for it, then,' Astrid said sarcastically.

'That's not what I meant,' Spence said impatiently. 'For Christ's sake grow up. People have died.'

'You've been very quiet, Mr Lascelles,' Hitchcock said, his confidence seemingly restored by the growing antagonism in the room. 'I couldn't help noticing that you were quite interested in Miss Erley last night while she was singing for us. Is there anything you'd like to share?'

Danny flushed, as he had the night before when Hitchcock had picked on him. 'I was looking at her because of something Turnbull told me.' He caught Penrose's eye. 'He said he'd fuck her one way or the other before the night was out. You heard him, didn't you, Astrid? He offered me a bet on it.'

Astrid ignored him and continued to glare at Jack Spence. 'Why is Turnbull here this weekend?' Penrose asked.

'I told him about it,' Franks admitted. 'We kept in touch now and again. He begged me to get him an invite, and Mr Hitchcock needed someone to play a certain role, so it seemed to kill two birds.'

Penrose didn't bother asking what that the role was: Hitchcock's games had ceased to be important. 'He didn't come because he knew Bella was going to be here?'

'I don't think so, but I couldn't swear to that.'

'So it's not impossible that he could have known and seen an opportunity to settle the score with her? From what Miss Lake says, she was spreading allegations about him quite liberally, and he must have wanted to stop that?' Franks hesitated. 'Is that why they were arguing in her room last night?'

'How did you know that?'

Ronnie had her moments, Penrose thought, but he didn't explain. 'Was that the reason?'

'No. At least not entirely. Turnbull only found out yesterday that he'd had a child. Branwen Erley let it slip – he told me he'd picked her up on the Harlech road, said she'd had an accident on her bike and had to abandon it. She didn't know who he was,' he added, anticipating the next question. 'She was just telling him the local gossip, oblivious to the damage she was doing. He was livid with Bella for keeping it from him.'

'And was he angry with you? You didn't tell him either.'

'I know, but he was too busy with Bella to think about me. It was wrong of me not to say anything, but I didn't want to have to admit that my father was involved in the disappearance of his son.'

'But your father was an innocent man,' Josephine said. 'Bella made that very clear.' Franks remained quiet, and she looked at him curiously. 'You think your father did it, don't you?'

'I'm not sure what to believe. I don't think he meant to hurt Taran, but I think he might have taken him.' He rubbed his hands wearily across his eyes. 'He'd done it before, you see, in another part of the country, somewhere we were just passing through. After my mother died he was sick with grief, for her and for the baby; he didn't know what he was doing. Everyone else in the camp looked out for him, but this time no one could help him. It all happened too quickly.'

'You mean they set fire to that cottage with the child alive inside?' Josephine asked, horrified. 'Surely they would have looked?'

His expression showed his contempt for her naivety. 'Have you ever been near a mob when it smells blood?' he asked. 'Nobody stops to check. Not until it's too late. The fire took hold so quickly that I think even they were surprised, but when I looked up at the window I thought I saw the boy in my father's arms. Maybe they realised later what they'd done. That would explain why no one tried harder to find Taran's body.'

'You've never told anyone this?' Penrose demanded angrily. 'It didn't occur to you that you could have saved Taran's mother from the pain of waiting and wondering?'

'At the expense of my father's memory? I couldn't do that. So that's why I've never told Turnbull: he would have killed me. Yesterday, when I went into Bella's room, he had his hands around her throat because she'd kept Taran's birth from him. God knows what he'd have done if he knew the truth about his death.'

'Last night, when we found you in the square with him, and he was talking about the cemetery, what did he mean?'

'There was a rumour at the time that my father had buried Taran there. Branwen told him that, too. It was nonsense, of course, but I could hardly say anything. So if Bella was killed there . . .'

There were footsteps in the corridor and Wyllie put his head round the door. 'He's not in his room.'

Penrose swore under his breath. 'All right. We'll have to organise a thorough search. I'll be out in a second.' He turned back to the room. 'Did anyone see Leyton Turnbull after he left this room last night and before two a.m.?'

'Astrid and I did,' Danny said. 'He came into the garages at around one o'clock and put something in the boot of his car.'

'What on earth were you doing in the garages at that time of night?'

They glanced nervously at Hitchcock. 'I wanted our young friends to get to know each other a bit better, so I arranged for them to be shut in together,' the director said brazenly. '*The*

39 Steps gave me the idea. Everyone said I'd handcuffed Robert and Madeleine together and deliberately misplaced the key, but I didn't; it would have wasted studio time, and studio time is expensive. But garage rental is much cheaper.' He smiled, and Penrose was tempted to wipe it off his face.

'Are there any other tricks that might hinder this investigation? The nun, for example. Who is she?'

Hitchcock shrugged. 'I've no idea.'

'You must know who she is. You invited her to dinner.'

'I paid her. I didn't hire her. Ask David. He found her.'

Archie turned to Franks and raised his eyebrows. 'Well?'

David looked uncomfortable. 'I'd rather not say. She had nothing to do with this.'

'I'll establish that for myself.'

'But she left the village before we finished dinner.'

'No she didn't,' Josephine said. 'I saw her when we were in the Mirror Room. She came from the direction of the headland and walked towards reception. That must have been around nine thirty.'

'And she kept peering at Leyton Turnbull and saying she knew him,' Astrid added. 'It seemed to make him uncomfortable.'

'Who is she?' Penrose demanded again.

'Her name is Joan Sidney. She's a porn star from Kansas.'

Hitchcock's explosion would have been amusing under other circumstances. 'You brought a porn star here without telling me and put her on my payroll? What the hell were you playing at?'

'He didn't mean anything by it, Hitch,' Alma said. 'It's just the sort of gag you'd have played yourself if you'd thought of it.'

For once, her attempts at keeping the peace seemed to fall on deaf ears; Penrose was surprised to see that Hitchcock's anger at the joke – which he personally found funnier than anything the director had attempted all weekend – seemed to stem from a kind of naive embarrassment. 'Where is Miss Sidney now?' he asked, ignoring Spence's smirk.

'I booked her into the Castle overnight. The Deudraeth Castle Hotel,' he explained when the others looked blank. 'It's the building you see on the way in. She's probably left by now, though. She was paid in advance. She always is.'

'I'll go and find out. Stay here until I come back.' Josephine followed him out of the room and walked with him to reception. 'Thanks for your help in there,' he said. 'I don't know how much of all that would have come out without your having heard it first from Bella Hutton.'

'She didn't mention David Franks to me at all, you know. Don't you find that odd?'

'In what way?'

'Well, she talked about the people she loved and the people she hated, and his name didn't come up in either category. I would have expected someone who was close enough to her to know about her cancer to feature quite prominently in the sort of musing she was doing on her life when she spoke to me. She even compared herself to Christine Clay and said that there would be no real grief when she died.'

'They'd obviously drifted apart recently. Franks said as much himself. Perhaps that was it.'

'Yes, perhaps.' Josephine sounded unconvinced. 'Anyway, I don't want to hold you up. I just wanted to let you know that she also talked about leaving all her money to charity. I'm almost certain she was joking, but I thought you should know, and I could hardly say it in there.'

He smiled at her. 'Quite. Anything else to add?'

'Only one thing: it occurred to me that perhaps it was Bella who had come here to settle the score with Leyton Turnbull, not the other way round. She had nothing to lose, after all, and she gave me the impression that she had come here this weekend for a specific reason connected to her family. She told me that I'd helped her make her mind up about something, but she wouldn't tell me what.' He nodded thoughtfully. 'And now you've bled me dry, will you forgive me for not coming back in there with you? I've had enough of all of them.'

'Of course, but don't leave the hotel until we have a better idea of what's going on.'

The receptionist at the Castle told him that Joan Sidney had not officially checked out yet but was nowhere to be found on the premises. He left a message, asking her to contact him immediately on her return, then found a policeman to take formal statements from Hitchcock and his guests. Back in the Mirror Room, everyone was gathered by the French windows, but there was no sign of the director.

'Where has your husband gone, Mrs Hitchcock?' Penrose asked angrily. 'I asked you all to stay here.'

'He's gone to fetch Leyton Turnbull,' Alma said apologetically. 'I spotted him on the lawn outside the Bell Tower just after you'd left the room.'

10

When Leyton Turnbull eventually awoke that morning, he was

horrified to see how late it was. His head hurt and he felt faintly nauseous, but he dragged himself out of bed and straightened his clothes. His trousers were still damp from the rain and his jacket and shirt were splashed with blood and dirt, despite having transferred a good deal of both to the sheets. His raincoat – slung carelessly over a chair by the window – seemed to be missing its belt. There was a jug of water by the bed which he had no recollection of placing there himself, but he was grateful for it: as he drank it down, mouthful after tepid mouthful, tainted by the sour taste of whisky and vomit on his tongue, the events of the night before came gradually back into focus.

It was only a short walk from his room to the Bell Tower. Before going in, he paused on the lawn outside and looked down to the hotel, but there was no one on the terrace yet. It was nearly noon. Bending to avoid scraping his head on the low stonework, he accessed the tower through the nearest of four arched entrances; half a dozen steps led up to a wooden door, then the staircase wound round to the right and became narrower. The musty smell of damp and mould did nothing for his hangover, and, when he reached the fourth level – the one that held the bells – he was glad to emerge into daylight again.

But he was still not high enough. The Bell Tower was the most dramatic flourish that Portmeirion had to offer, a striking landmark on the village's eastern side, and his own gesture needed to be worthy of it. The final two levels of the tower were reached by a ladder; when he had gone as far as he could, he stood at the window and gazed out in wonder. It seemed to him now that he was level with the distant peak of Snowdon, that its grandeur no longer dwarfed him, and, as he looked down, the other buildings of Portmeirion appeared as brightly coloured models built on his past. There were figures on the terrace now, tiny and insignificant, miniature dolls who had lost their power to hurt; up here, he was in control, and the feeling was intoxicating, all the more so for having been absent from his life for so long. He climbed out onto the window ledge to make himself more visible, and the stone felt hot and rough against palms which were soaked with sweat. He waited until he was sure of his balance, then allowed himself to look down; even in that momentary glance, the feeling of being pulled towards the ground was extreme, an insidious lure to self-destruction. Turnbull shook his head, but it only made the sensation worse. Two floors below him, the old chiming turret clock began its greatest effort of the day. The sound startled him and he grabbed at the side walls, feeling his heart beat rapidly in his chest.

And then he saw the house. It seemed to move closer as he looked at it, obscuring everything else on the horizon; he knew it was an illusion, but still it taunted him, daring him to make things right. He felt himself spinning and imagined Gwyneth in his arms; he heard her screams quite clearly, and then the cry of a child – a child who might not have died in violence if he had not been conceived that way. He knew what he had done was wrong, and she had shown him what the consequences would be, but he had loved her, and that was his only defence. At last, he knew what to do. Closing his eyes, he pictured Gwyneth's face and walked out to join his son.

I I

Penrose had left the room to go after Hitchcock, and Danny

took advantage of his absence to draw Astrid to one side, away from the rest of the group. 'Why were you looking at me like that in there? What have I done?'

She met his eye for the first time that morning. 'I don't know, Danny. What *have* you done?'

'You can't think I had anything to do with this? Astrid, for God's sake – you know I'm not capable of that.'

'I don't know what to believe. You unexpectedly bump into a girl who in many respects has ruined your life, and the next morning she turns up raped and strangled. Surely you can't blame me for wondering what exactly *did* happen last night?'

'You know what happened. I was with you.'

'Not all night. You were late to meet me, and you'd changed your clothes. Where did you go for your walk, Danny? You never mentioned it. Did you have a stroll up the coastal path?' She hated the whining sarcasm in her own voice but could not seem to do anything about it, and Danny's silence only made her want to punish him further. 'And Hitchcock was right. You were staring at her all through dinner. You couldn't take your eyes off her.'

'So that's it. You're jealous?'

'Jealous?' She laughed in his face. 'That's not the sort of attention I'm looking for, Danny.'

'I'm sorry. That was a stupid thing to say.' He calmed down and tried to reason with her. 'You know why I was looking at her.'

'I know what you *told* me, but I didn't realise you were a liar until just now. Why did you tell Penrose that Turnbull had made a bet with you about having sex with her? He didn't say anything of the sort, at least not in my hearing. Why would you say he did?'

'Since when did you become his biggest fan?'

'I don't give a damn about Leyton Turnbull. I'm just trying to find out what sort of man I spent the night with.'

'I thought you'd know that by now.'

He winked at her, trying to make her smile, and she marvelled at how quickly the charm that had attracted her to him in the first place had begun to have the opposite effect. 'Aren't you even the slightest bit touched by her death, Danny? By the way she was killed? I was watching the faces in that room while Penrose was telling us what had happened, and everyone else looked shocked or sad or frightened. But not you. You looked guilty, and you couldn't even catch my eye. What are you hiding?' she asked, suddenly afraid of the answer; she had never, in her heart, believed that Danny was responsible for the attack, but she had needed to hear him proclaim his own innocence; now, she was not so sure that he could do so truthfully. 'Did you hurt that girl?'

He nodded. 'Yes. I'm sorry, but I lied to you. She was telling the truth when she said I went too far.' Astrid was so shaken that it took her a moment to relate his confession to the incident in his childhood, not the crime of the night before. 'But I was fifteen years old, Astrid, and it was my first time with a girl. She encouraged me. I thought she was as keen as I was.'

'So that makes it all right?'

'She led me on, then changed her mind at the last minute.'

'Just like I tried to?' At last, the personal resentment that had spurred her anger with Danny was out in the open. She bitterly regretted what she had allowed to happen between them, but there was no going back, and, while she knew that it was cheap and shabby to use Branwen Erley's death as an excuse to turn the shame she felt back onto him, it fitted her new opinion of herself perfectly.

The embarrassment hung in the air between them, and it was Danny who tried to brush it aside. 'You were nervous,' he said. 'That's understandable, but you didn't mean . . .' He tailed off when he saw the expression on her face and tried to take her hand instead, but she flinched at his touch. 'Come on, Astrid, don't be like this. Don't spoil things. We had a wonderful night.'

'Did we?' She undid the top two buttons of her blouse and pulled the silk to one side to show him the livid, purple beginnings of a bruise on her breast. 'That's your trouble, Danny. You always think we're enjoying it far more than we really are.'

It was the final blow to his pride, and he turned away in disgust. 'Jack's right,' he said. 'You do need to grow up. People have to do things they don't like to get on. It's how the world works.'

'And how does going to bed with you help me to get on? You're not a producer or a director. You're a run-of-the-mill juvenile lead who may or may not still have a career in three years' time – just like me.' She put a hand to his cheek and looked at him sadly. 'I wasn't with you to get on, Danny. I was with you because I liked you. I thought you were different, more sensitive than other men. When you were telling me about your father, I really felt sorry for you.'

'Did you?' He laughed, but there was no humour in it. 'Well, maybe that's not the sort of attention *I'm* looking for.'

There was nothing more to say. Astrid started to walk away,

but he caught her arm. 'Are you going to tell Penrose? I haven't done anything wrong, Astrid. If I wanted to kill that girl, I'd hardly have admitted to you that I even knew her.'

'That's really all you care about, isn't it? What I'm going to say, not how I might feel.' She stared at him for a long time, as if trying to make up her mind. 'Neither of us are very nice people, are we Danny? I thought we were, but that sort of sentimentality is just one of the things I lost last night.' Without another word, she turned and went back to join the others.

12

Hitchcock hurried back through the village to the patch of lawn outside his own apartment, determined that – no matter what else Leyton Turnbull was guilty of – he was not going to give Penrose any more scope for criticism by outlining the prank that was supposed to have been played out that day. By the time he got there, the small grass-and-gravel garden was deserted, and he cursed the actor for choosing now to start behaving reliably. He had no choice but to follow Turnbull inside the Bell Tower, and he made swift work of the climb; the ninety-six steps to his top-storey flat in Cromwell Road might be his only concession to exercise, but they were at least effective. As he reached the second level and made for the next flight, a shadow passed across the window.

He stopped, knowing instinctively what had happened but unable or unwilling to believe it. Later, he found it hard to be sure if the sound of Turnbull's body hitting the ground was real or had been conjured purely from his own dread, but it would haunt Hitchcock's dreams for the rest of his life, unshared and unacknowledged. Shaken, he walked reluctantly over to the window. His eyes swept the courtyard below and settled on Turnbull's shattered corpse, unconsciously framing the peculiar arrangement of his limbs against the gravel. A surge of panic welled up inside him but he forced himself to stay calm as he went back down the steps, praying that this might somehow be an illusion, a more elaborate version of the joke he had himself intended to play. But there was no mistake, and he found himself drawn towards the body. The panorama of Portmeirion faded as he moved nearer until, when he was just a few feet from the dead man's face, there was no beauty or sunshine left, only horror. There was blood, so much blood, but he ventured closer still, so transfixed by Turnbull's eyes that nothing else existed: their stare was relentless, accusing, and Hitchcock held them for as long as he could, but eventually they saw too much, and he had to look away.

13

Lettice steered the boat skilfully into shore and Ronnie clambered out. 'Absolutely bloody marvellous!' she said with enthusiasm. 'Who'd have thought the ringside seat would actually be out here?'

'It's certainly a far better view of the Bell Tower than anything you get inland,' her sister agreed, throwing a rope over the landing post and passing Lydia her sun hat.

'We saw the whole thing: the dummy going out of the window, everyone running round like headless chickens.' Josephine tried to interrupt, but Ronnie was in full flight and she had no choice but to let the momentum tire itself out. 'Archie didn't waste any time in getting up there, did he? I bet the look on his face was priceless when he realised that Hitchcock had had the last laugh. I'm not surprised he was fooled: it all looked terribly realistic. Who was the dummy supposed to be? We couldn't quite make that out from a distance.'

Josephine took the oars from Lettice and helped her out of the boat. 'It wasn't *supposed* to be anyone.'

Lydia looked at her sharply. 'What on earth do you mean?'

'It was Leyton Turnbull. Not a dummy, and certainly not a joke. It's been quite a morning while you've been sculling around out here, playing Swallows and Amazons.' They listened, incredulous, as Josephine explained the whole story.

'So you're telling us that Leyton Turnbull murdered them both and then topped himself?' Ronnie asked. 'I wouldn't have thought he had it in him.'

'No, but that's what it looks like. Nobody has said it officially yet, but it's the conclusion that everyone has jumped to.'

'Where's Marta?' Lydia asked. 'Is she all right? It must have been a terrible shock for both of you to discover the girl's body like that.'

If she harboured any feelings of resentment because Marta and Josephine had shared an experience from which she was excluded, she hid them well. 'She's over there with Bridget.' Josephine pointed to the terrace, where the two women were deep in conversation, and wondered if Archie was getting his testimonial. Lydia went to join them and she turned back to Lettice and Ronnie, reluctant to witness any sort of reunion.

'What were you saying yesterday about a matinee idol never being a killer?' Lettice shook her head in disbelief. 'It just shows how wrong you can be, doesn't it?'

'Though in your line of work, we might have hoped for a little more insight,' Ronnie said, then added thoughtfully, 'It seems an awful lot of trouble to go to.'

Josephine laughed, in spite of the situation. 'Trust you to put innocence down to laziness. You make it sound like Leyton Turnbull should be given marks out of ten for effort.'

'I didn't mean that.' Ronnie smiled. 'Although it was a *spectacular* jump. I was just questioning why you would murder two women to protect your reputation and then kill yourself anyway? It's not very logical, is it?'

Nobody answered. To the left of the hotel, Josephine could see two policemen carrying a covered stretcher down the sun-flecked path which led behind the building and out to the road. 'We shouldn't be talking like this,' she said quietly. 'That's the reality of it.' They watched as Bella Hutton's body was loaded into a waiting mortuary van and driven slowly away from Portmeirion for the last time. 'Thank God they've taken her before the press get a whiff of this. There'll be no dignity left for anyone once that happens. She deserved better.' Josephine remembered the stoicism with which the actress had talked of her own death and wondered how long it had taken that courage to desert her when tested by a reality more horrific than any she could possibly have foreseen. 'Come on,' she said, suddenly glad of the Motleys' company. 'Let's go and get a drink.'

14

'I don't understand why he didn't talk to me. I might have been able to help.' David Franks stared down at his uncle's body in disbelief. He had arrived on the scene almost immediately, shortly followed by Spence, and Penrose had not been able to prevent them witnessing the full horror of Turnbull's death. He gave Franks a couple of minutes to compose himself before leading him gently away. 'Did you see what happened?' he asked.

'Yes, but it was all so quick. It's hard to make sense of it. We all went out onto the terrace to see what was going on, and you ran off after Hitch. Turnbull was out of sight by then – he must have gone into the tower. The next time we saw him, he was at one of the windows halfway up, then he vanished again and appeared at the top. That's when I realised what he was going to do.' Spence handed him a cigarette, and he took it gratefully. 'He climbed out onto the ledge, and I started to run, but it was too late.'

'Did you actually see him fall?'

'I did,' Spence said as Franks shook his head. 'He just stepped out into thin air.'

'It wasn't supposed to be like this,' Franks said quietly.

Penrose looked at him. 'What do you mean?'

'It was supposed to be a joke,' he explained reluctantly. 'Hitch and I had it all planned. We were going to set it up to make it look like Turnbull had committed suicide.' He caught the expression on Penrose's face and tried to explain. 'Hitch wanted to see how everyone would react if they thought their behaviour had been partly responsible for a man's death. An experiment in guilt and fear, he called it. Then we found out that Bella had been killed, and everything changed. Hitch would have stopped it but you gathered us all together before he could get to Turnbull.' He took a final pull on his cigarette and ground the butt angrily into the gravel. 'It's my fault. I took part in it, and I involved Turnbull. Hitch would have had anyone. He wasn't bothered who his stooge was. And now he's got his wish: if he wants to know what real guilt looks like, he should come and talk to me.'

'Don't forget it *was* a joke, David,' Spence said. 'You weren't to know that something would happen to make Turnbull want to do it for real. That was his choice.'

'I suppose this means he killed Bella?' Franks asked.

Penrose was too angry to answer him. 'Go back to the hotel and wait,' he said, barely able to keep his temper under control.

'What about Hitch?'

'I need to talk to him before he goes anywhere.' He watched them walk back across Battery Square, then beckoned to a young police constable. 'Is your bloody inspector planning to join us at all today?' he asked.

'I don't know, sir.'

He looked terrified, and Penrose regretted his sarcasm; the boy could not be more than twenty, and the lack of support was not his fault. 'Stay here and make sure no one goes near the body,' he said more kindly. 'I'm going to have a word with Mr Hitchcock, but if anything else happens let me know immediately.'

Hitchcock was waiting on the Watch House balcony. He sat with his back to the Bell Tower, staring blankly out to sea. His face was ashen. 'What the hell is going on here?' Penrose demanded through gritted teeth. There was no answer, so he tried again. 'Would you care to tell me exactly what you had asked Leyton Turnbull to do this morning?'

'Who told you I'd asked him to do anything?'

'Your sidekick.' A scowl passed fleetingly across Hitchcock's face and Penrose guessed that David Franks's next conversation with his boss would not be a comfortable one. 'Thanks to your fun and games, the hotel will look more like a mortuary by lunchtime.'

'Be careful, Chief Inspector,' Hitchcock said, regaining some of his composure. 'I had nothing to do with any of these deaths, and I have very expensive lawyers.'

'You won't be needing them, sir, I can assure you.' Penrose had been so caught up in his frustration with Hitchcock that he had not heard the car draw up outside the Bell Tower. 'I'm Detective Inspector Alan Roberts, and I'll be taking charge of this investigation.'

'Better late than never,' Penrose muttered sarcastically, furious with himself for having chosen that moment to overstep the mark. Roberts was in his late forties, tall and gaunt, with receding dark hair and a weak chin. Like Hitchcock's, his wardrobe made few concessions to the weather, although it was considerably cheaper in cut and quality. His accent, Penrose noticed with surprise, was English rather than Welsh. Without waiting to be asked, he gave the inspector all the relevant details of the case, instinctively restructuring the information that had emerged in a more haphazard fashion throughout the morning, explaining the family connections clearly and succinctly.

'Have you anything to add, sir?' Roberts asked, turning to Hitchcock.

'Only my deepest regrets,' the director said gravely. It had not taken him long to spot that Roberts's allegiance did not sit with his colleague, and he wasted no time in exploiting the fact. 'I was always very fond of Bella, and Turnbull – well, he had his difficult moments but this could have been a new start for him. It was supposed to have been a happy weekend, a prelude to working together, but . . .' He held his hands up to the heavens, as though God himself had conspired to wreck his good intentions. In spite of his resentment, Penrose could only marvel at the performance.

'I'm sorry you've had your stay here spoilt,' Roberts said. 'If you'd like to go down to the hotel now, I'll make sure you're not bothered any further.'

'You've no objection to my wife and I leaving today, I presume? We'd like to get back to London as soon as possible and pick up our daughter.'

'Of course. You're a busy man, and *my* wife would never forgive me if I did anything to delay the next film. When can we expect it?'

'In December, I hope. You must tell me what you think of it when you've seen it.'

'Just one thing before you go, sir.' He got a notebook out of his pocket, and Penrose – who had been watching this display of mutual admiration in astonishment – was relieved to see that Roberts was at least going to ask for details of where Hitchcock could be contacted if there were any further questions. 'I wonder if you'd sign that for the wife?'

'Of course. What's her name?'

'Mildred.' Roberts watched as Hitchcock drew a cartoon and signed it with a flourish. 'I'm embarrassed to admit this to someone like you,' he added, with the lack of self-consciousness that invariably accompanied such a statement, 'but I make a few films myself in my spare time.'

'You mustn't be embarrassed.' Hitchcock handed the notebook back with a smile. 'I dabble in your world. Why shouldn't you dabble in mine?'

Penrose watched as he walked away. The inspector had a brief word with one of his officers, then introduced himself to James Wyllie, who had come up from the hotel. 'Forensics have nearly finished on the girl,' Roberts said. 'They'll be up here as soon as they can. Has anyone examined his room yet?'

'No sir,' Wyllie said. 'I went there about an hour ago to look for him – Chief Inspector Penrose wanted to speak to him – but he wasn't there, and I didn't stay very long.'

'Fine. Show me where it is.'

Penrose turned to go with him, but Roberts held up his hand. 'I'll take over from here. If you'd like to go back to the hotel and wait with everyone, I'll have some news for you in due course.'

As much as he resented being treated like a well-meaning amateur, there was nothing that Penrose could do about it: Roberts was perfectly within his rights to take charge of his own investigation, and, while it was not unusual for Scotland Yard to involve itself in crimes outside London, it had to be at the invitation of the local force. Wyllie, though, seemed to have other ideas. He cleared his throat. 'I've just spoken to the owner, Inspector, and Mr Williams-Ellis would consider it a great favour if you would allow Chief Inspector Penrose access to the enquiries you make,' he said. Penrose suppressed a smile and wondered if the balance of courtesy and firmness in his voice was a professional acquisition or something he had been born with. 'They've been friends for many years, and he would find it very reassuring to know that Penrose will be involved until he can get here himself.'

'I don't care if they're long-lost twins, Mr Wyllie. I won't have an outsider interfering in an investigation on my patch.'

Particularly when it was such a high-profile case and all but solved, Penrose thought cynically; most policemen would consider it a very welcome boost to a flagging career. He considered telling Roberts that he was perfectly capable of earning his own reputation without stealing anyone else's glory, but Wyllie spared him the indignity of fighting for something he did not even want. 'Clough has already cleared it with the Chief Constable, Inspector. Just out of courtesy, you understand. I gather it's perfectly in line with procedure.'

There was a long silence, and Penrose could imagine several of the words with which Roberts would have liked to fill it. In truth, he would have preferred to wash his hands of the case entirely and leave Roberts to deal with what was left of Alfred Hitchcock's ill-fated weekend, but he felt an obligation of friendship to Clough and – although he could not quite explain why – a duty to Branwen Erley, too. She seemed to have paid very dearly for other people's choices, and, alongside the death of two celebrities, hers was the tragedy most likely to be forgotten. 'I'll show you to Government House,' Wyllie said, satisfied that his case had been made beyond further argument. 'It's just next door.'

Turnbull's suite on the top floor of the eighteenth-century-style building consisted of a sitting room, bedroom and small en-suite bathroom. The apartment was uniformly sparse: Turnbull had not bothered to make himself at home, and his suitcase sat untouched on the luggage rack at the bottom of the bed. There were no clothes in the wardrobe, no toothbrush or aftershave in the bathroom, and the bedside table held no books or personal items, just an empty water jug and glass. The only evidence that the actor had spent any time there at all was the state of the sheets and the raincoat in which Penrose had seen him the night before, stained with blood and dirt. 'Looks like he was ready for a sharp exit,' Roberts said. His eye fell on the mackintosh and the empty loops around its waist. 'Does that coat match the belt that was with the girl's body?'

'Yes, it's exactly the same.' Penrose walked over to the fireplace in the sitting room, redundant at this time of year except for a vase of flowers in the hearth. A piece of notepaper had been screwed up and tossed into the grate. He took a handkerchief out of his pocket and carefully picked it up. It was part of a letter, brief and apparently written in haste; the address and first few words were missing, but he read what was left with interest. 'For years I've asked you to tell me what happened to my mother but you've refused even to see me. Well, losing a child doesn't give you the right to keep everyone else apart, and now I've found someone else who can and will give me the information that you won't. I'm meeting Bella Hutton tonight, and she's going to tell me where my mother is. There's nothing you can do to stop it. Everyone deserves to know where they've come from.' The signature was Branwen Erley's.

He handed the note to Roberts. 'I'd call that a fairly conclusive challenge, wouldn't you?' the inspector said, slipping the piece of paper into a bag.

'Odd that there's only part of it, though.' Penrose looked round the room for the rest of the letter but there was nothing; a cursory search through Turnbull's case told him only what the actor had been planning to wear that weekend.

'At least it's the important part.'

'But there's no form of address on it,' Penrose said. 'We can't even be sure that it was for him.'

'Of course it was for him. It was screwed up in his fireplace, and it fits with everything you've told me about Turnbull's past.'

'Not quite everything. David Franks said that Branwen didn't know who he was when she was talking to him. This implies she's known for years.'

'We've only got his word for that.'

'Why would Franks lie?'

Roberts looked at him with the strained patience that a parent gives to a difficult child. 'I meant Turnbull's word. He could tell David Franks anything he liked.'

'And how did Bella Hutton know what had happened to Branwen's mother? She wasn't still with Turnbull when he turned up in the States.'

'Maybe Turnbull told her. Or maybe she didn't know at all but was just saying she did to get the girl off her back. I can't imagine that someone as famous as Bella Hutton took too kindly to being asked about a past she'd left behind and a brother she didn't even like.' That was true, Penrose thought: Bella could have told Branwen anything for a quiet life, and such a promise explained the exchange that Josephine had witnessed on the terrace. 'Anyway,' Roberts continued, 'who else would a letter like that be for?'

Because of the reference to the child, the only other possibility was Gwyneth Draycott, but surely she was unlikely to have known where her husband was planning to take his lover? Penrose cast his mind back to what Franks had said and remembered that, again according to Turnbull's testimony, both he and Branwen had been on the Harlech road yesterday afternoon. Had one or both of them been to see Gwyneth? And if so, how did that explain where the letter had ended up? The scenario raised more questions than it answered, and he dismissed it from his thoughts for the present; there was no point in opening up a conversation with Roberts only to be told that no matter what information Gwyneth might have withheld from Branwen, she had most certainly not raped her.

Instead, he concentrated on something more tangible. Wyllie had not come into the room with them but stood waiting at the door. 'Have you got a sample of Branwen Erley's handwriting?' Penrose asked, ignoring Roberts's sigh.

'Almost certainly. We should still have her original letter of application on file. We keep everything relating to the permanent staff.'

'Good.' Penrose went over to the open window and looked down. The Bell Tower and Watch House gardens had both been sealed off now, and a police photographer was finishing his merciless work with Leyton Turnbull's body. The figure, still dressed in evening clothes and splayed grotesquely on the ground, looked incongruous in the morning sunlight. Penrose wished he had a more reliable witness than Hitchcock to the actor's final moments, but there was no way of knowing now what his state of mind had been when he climbed those steps. 'So what happened to Branwen's mother that Turnbull didn't want people to know about?' he asked, turning back to the room.

Roberts hesitated, and Penrose was almost ashamed of how much satisfaction the moment of doubt gave him. Recovering quickly, the inspector said, 'Impossible to tell after all this time.

They left twenty years ago or more, and she probably changed her name just like he did.'

Penrose waited in vain for him to continue. 'Aren't you even curious?'

'I could be dying to know, but I still wouldn't have the time or the manpower to track down Leyton Turnbull's every move before he got to America when he's lying there dead in front of me. It's not as though there's a case to be made to bring him to justice, is it? And Rhiannon Erley certainly never wanted to be found or she'd have kept in touch with her daughter herself, so does it matter what happened to her?'

'It does if you're going to make it the motive for two very different murders and a suicide.' It wasn't the first time that Penrose had heard a lack of resources used as an excuse not to follow up every line of enquiry; he had used it himself in the past for other crimes when he was sure of the man in custody. But never for murder. Never when there was so much at stake.

'It's not the only motive,' Roberts argued defensively. 'Bella Hutton didn't tell him about his child.'

'Is that really a reason to stab someone forty or fifty times?' Penrose asked. 'You haven't seen her body yet, but her face is mutilated beyond all recognition.'

'And he was seen with Branwen Erley.'

'His explanation for that was feasible, particularly if there turns out to be an abandoned bicycle somewhere along the Harlech road.'

'We'll check, sir,' Roberts said sarcastically, acknowledging Penrose's rank for the first time and not out of respect. 'But whatever we find, there's no getting round the fact that Bella Hutton was slandering him, and he had a track record for rape.'

'You'll check on that too, I presume?'

'If it will make you happy.'

'It's not about making me happy, Inspector, it's about serving justice – and that's justice for everyone, the victims *and* the accused.' He sounded sanctimonious, even to himself; the perfection he was looking for was, he realised, unrealistic, and he stopped himself going any further. There was no logical reason to dispute Roberts' conclusions, and he could not explain why he was fighting them, other than a personal dislike of the inspector's arrogance and a few misgivings which were no less nagging for their improbability. He allowed himself to indulge one more of these before giving up. 'Why would he go to all that trouble only to kill himself?' he asked.

Roberts shrugged, his interest in human nature as probing as ever. 'Remorse perhaps, or resignation. He must have known he'd be caught. Talking of which, have you checked his car yet? You said he was seen in the garages last night.'

'I've hardly had time to . . .'

'Right then, we'll do it now.' He felt inside the pockets of the raincoat and took out a set of keys. 'They must be what we need.'

'I'll take you over,' Wyllie said.

The three men walked across the village square in silence, and Roberts pulled back the garage door. Penrose saw the blood on the bodywork of the Alvis immediately. The car had been driven straight in and its boot was only a couple of feet away from him; bending down to look more closely, he noticed that it was smeared all around the lock, where someone stowing things away had been careless. Roberts took the keys and opened the lid. Inside, there was a set of bloodstained overalls –

the sort mechanics wore – and some gloves, a torch, and a knife with a blade about six inches long, also covered in blood.

'I'll get forensics over here straight away,' Roberts said, 'but I don't think we need their help to tell us what we're looking at.'

Penrose had only seen what he had expected to see, but that in itself made him suspicious. 'I want to go with you when you question Gwyneth Draycott,' he said.

'I won't be questioning Gwyneth Draycott.' Roberts looked at him in astonishment. 'I think she's been through enough, don't you?'

'I think she might be interested to know that her husband's dead.'

'Of course, but we can take care of that. I could hardly ask a detective chief inspector of Scotland Yard to waste his precious time on condolence calls.'

Penrose had lost the appetite to fight a battle that he could not win. 'If you're remotely interested in tying up some loose ends, there's some news on what happened to her son,' he said, wanting at least to be sure that the information was passed on. He outlined what Franks had told him and added: 'You'll want to question him yourself, obviously, but it might give her some shred of comfort to know that the case is nearer to being closed.' He could see from the expression on Roberts' face that it had never truly been open.

15

Even here, on the *Amis Reunis* in the afternoon sun, the chill gloom of the woods was proving hard to shake off. Bridget leant back against the side of the old boat, enjoying the warmth of its wood through the thin cotton of her shirt. It was a relief to close her eyes: the reflection of the light from the brilliant white paper in her lap made it hard to draw for more than a few minutes at a time, and the subject matter she had chosen was hardly conducive to peace. She often turned to her work to exorcise ghosts and had hoped that, by setting down a physical expression of the morning's horror, she might be able to lift the emotional pall that clouded her mind. So far, the effort had been in vain.

'Policeman's widow already?'

She smiled without opening her eyes. 'Just because you spent the night alone, Jack, don't take it out on me.' He sat down next to her and she kissed his cheek. 'It shows what a lucky escape I've had, though, doesn't it? Second fiddle to a corpse would never have suited me, no matter how famous.'

He shook two cigarettes from a packet and looked at her curiously. 'Past tense? Does that mean you've told him?'

'No. I haven't made my mind up yet, and there wouldn't have been time if I had. Things have got a little out of hand round here, haven't they?' The half-finished image lay between them, a composite of memory and fear, and Jack studied it for a long time. 'I know what you're thinking,' Bridget said, 'but sometimes, if you can draw a scream, it loses some of its power.'

'Although it *will* need a certain type of collector.' She smiled, and he pulled her towards him. 'I'm so sorry,' he said. 'It can't have been easy to walk up there and find Bella like that.'

'It wasn't.' Bridget watched the ash burn down on her cigarette, knowing that she did not need to say anything else: Jack was one of the few people who understood something of what she had felt that morning, and it was a relief not to have to explain. 'I'm fine, though. What about you? You seemed a long way away earlier.'

'A long *time* away, perhaps, but I haven't moved far from here. I was thinking about this place and how it used to be. You heard what happened this morning when Archie got us all together?' Bridget nodded. 'I can't believe that was David's father. Everybody was talking about it when I came back here after the war. I think some of the men on the farm had even helped search for the missing boy. I remember going to look for the burnt-out shell of the cottage and finding the dog cemetery. Clough's probably still got the photographs somewhere. I gave them to him when he bought the old house.'

'We used to look for Gypsy graves in those woods when we were kids. Do you remember?'

'Of course I do, but they were far too clever to leave clues for strangers. And it seems a lifetime ago now.'

She resisted the temptation to point out that, if he followed his plans through, there might not be any more years to add. 'You always did love this part of the world.'

'I've always been happy here. There aren't many places you can say that about. It has good memories.'

Bridget let her mind run through a series of images from her youth. 'I can't believe you had to spell it out to me,' she said eventually, shaking her head in embarrassment. 'I felt so stupid. All those years and I never noticed you were in love.' She knew she was about to cross a line, but she did it anyway. 'You can't keep punishing yourself because you lived and he died, you know.'

'Is that what you think I'm doing?' Bridget nodded. 'Perhaps you're right.' She had expected him to be angry, but he refused to rise to the bait. 'Who's to say it would have lasted anyway? These things so rarely do. I suppose that's what makes them precious. If he were still here, we'd probably be as unrecognisable to each other as this shoreline. And that would be worse, I think – much worse.' He grinned at her. 'You and your policeman don't seem to have that problem. Think about that before you destroy it.'

Bridget threw the butt of her cigarette into the water. 'Well, I've punched as low as I know how,' she said, ignoring his last remark, 'and I still haven't managed to change your mind, have I?'

'No, but don't take it personally. A man's got to do and all that.'

He spoke the words with a convincing American accent, every bit the brave pioneer, but Bridget didn't laugh. 'Since when have you worried about that?' she asked. 'Why start now?'

'Don't, Bridget. Let's not go through all that again. It's the right thing to do – for me, anyway. That's all there is to it.'

He took her hand, and Bridget wondered why she suddenly felt so lonely. 'When do you leave?'

'As soon as possible, but I won't go without letting you know. We can have dinner.'

'You mean I get to share your last supper.'

'I'll be fine, Bridget. I'm always fine.'

She hugged him, trying to ignore a sense of foreboding which refused to go away. Over his shoulder, she saw Hitchcock coming towards them across the lawn. 'It looks as though I'm not the only one who's trying to persuade you to do other things with your life,' she said. 'Perhaps he'll have more luck.'

'I doubt it.'

Hitchcock raised his hand and climbed aboard the station-ary vessel with surprising agility. 'I'm sorry to interrupt, Miss Foley, but I need to borrow Jack for a moment. Do you mind?' Bridget shook her head, surprised that the director knew her name. 'Mrs H. and I enjoyed your last exhibition very much,' he said by way of explanation. 'We make a point of never buy-ing a painting unless we both like it – the only time I've ever considered divorce was over a Paul Klee which she refused to have in the house – but in your case we were spoilt for choice.' Her obvious astonishment seemed to amuse Hitchcock. 'I'm not *just* a cheap sensationalist, you know,' he said, winking at her as he led Jack away.

Still smiling, she saw Archie walking down across the sea lawn and went to meet him. 'You look furious,' she said as he bent to kiss her. 'Has something else happened?'

'No, I've just had a run-in with the local police. It seems that everyone is in Alfred Hitchcock's fan club except me. He's caused havoc this weekend, and he's just going to wash his hands of it and walk away.'

'Well, he does have a certain charm.'

Archie looked at her in amazement. 'Not you as well?'

'He's put money in my pocket, Archie, but it's only a profes-sional allegiance.' She nodded to the terrace, where the director was ordering drinks. 'If it makes you feel better, he's in for a dis-appointment now. Hitchcock is about to make Jack an offer he can and will refuse.'

'Is he going to work for another studio? He told me he had plans.'

'No. He might go to America eventually, I suppose, but he's going to fight in Spain first. I can't talk him out of it.'

She was grateful to Archie for refraining from the usual meaningless reassurances about another person's safety. 'And what about you?' he asked instead. 'What are your plans?'

'Back to London for a couple of days, then on to Cambridge.'

There was a silence as each waited for the other to speak. In the end, it was Archie who took the risk. 'We could try this again, away from the film crew.'

'I'd like that. It would be good to talk properly, without any distractions.'

'From what I recall, Cambridge with you was just one distraction after another. That's what I loved about it.'

'Let's meet in London first, Archie.' Worried that she had seemed too eager to deflect him, she added, 'I've got to come up to town a lot over the next few weeks. It would be nice to have something to look forward to apart from work, and I need to check you've got that painting in the right place.' He smiled, and she took his arm as they walked to White Horses.

16

Josephine sat by the hotel pool and watched as Alma Reville hesitated before coming over to her. 'Miss Tey, may I have a word with you?'

'Of course.' Alma seemed relieved by the welcome, but her reticence was unnecessary: it had been a long, restless morning of waiting and thinking, and Josephine was glad of any distraction which kept her mind from the reality of Branwen Erley's body and the imagined horror of Bella's. 'Although I should warn you that it might be detrimental to your health. People have a habit of dying after a heart-to-heart with me.'

She made the comment without thinking, then realised that Alma did not know her well enough to understand that its flippancy was defensive. The director's wife seemed to take the remark in the spirit it was meant, though; Josephine guessed that she was used to black humour, living with Hitchcock. 'It has been a terrible day,' Alma agreed, 'and your conversation with Bella must have made the news of her death even more of a shock. But it's not really a heart-to-heart I want, so I'll take my chances.' She smiled and sat down. 'Hitch and I are going back to London later this afternoon, and, before we go, I wanted to say how much I've enjoyed meeting you.'

The suddenness of the departure surprised Josephine. 'Doesn't your husband want to stay and see all this in action?' she asked, gesturing to the village. 'I've heard how seriously he takes his research, and I would have thought this was a once-in-a-lifetime opportunity. At least, I hope it is.'

'Hitch is not very good at real life,' his wife admitted. 'It's never been his strong point.' She gave Josephine a wry smile. 'And I notice you're taking a back seat, too.'

'I got closer than I ever wanted to this morning,' Josephine said quickly. 'It was a salutary lesson in fact and fiction, and it will be a long time before I need another reminder.'

'Yes, of course. I'm sorry.' The apology was sincerely delivered, and Alma added, 'That was a stupid thing to say, especially as I believe that Hitch's blurring of those boundaries has already led to some tension between him and your friend.'

'Archie knows more about murder than the rest of could understand or bear,' Josephine said, smiling to take some of the edge off her words. 'It's not surprising that there are days when death as entertainment seems a little strange to him, even offensive.'

'Quite, but I hope you won't let any of this affect your decision regarding *A Shilling for Candles*?'

So that was it, Josephine thought: not so much a heart-to-heart as a white flag of diplomacy. 'Of course not,' she said. 'I've made my mind up, and I'm *almost* looking forward to seeing the finished result.' Alma smiled gratefully, and, while she had the upper hand, Josephine took the opportunity to satisfy her curiosity on another subject. 'What was the problem between you and Bella?' she asked. 'I don't know either of you personally, but you seem to me to have had a lot in common: the same strength and determination, the same talent and power, the same joys and worries. That often makes people friends, or at least natural allies, but obviously not you and Bella.'

'The problem was David Franks,' Alma said candidly. 'We demand absolute loyalty and commitment from the people who work for us, and Bella resented the fact that he was prepared to throw his creative lot in with us entirely. That's what she meant by suffocation: she thought that he should spread his wings more widely, and in some respects she probably had a point. He'll be brilliant in his own right one day if he gets the right experience.'

'He must have more experience now than your husband did when he started directing,' Josephine said shrewdly.

'Indeed he does, and I admit that our interests in keeping him with us were not selfless by any means – but neither were Bella's. As David said this morning, it's not easy to see someone you've guided choose advice from elsewhere. More than anything, though, Bella didn't want him to go back to America and she knew we would have asked him to come with us.'

Once again, Bella Hutton's devotion to her nephew sounded unconvincing to Josephine, but she said nothing. She followed Alma's gaze over to the hotel and watched as Franks came out onto the terrace. 'Would have?' she queried.

'Yes.' Alma got up, bringing the conversation to an end. 'If you'll excuse me, there's another apology I need to make. I have a policy of not interfering in my husband's decisions, but I can at least try to clear up after them.' She held out her hand before Josephine could ask for an explanation. 'I'll be in touch with your agent as soon as we've settled back in town, and I sincerely hope that we'll do your book justice.'

Josephine smiled. 'So do I,' she said. In the distance, she saw Archie walking across the lawn from the direction of White Horses. He acknowledged her wave but seemed preoccupied, and she wondered if Bridget had talked to him about whatever was worrying her. 'Is everything all right?' she asked cautiously as he sat down. 'How's Bridget?'

'She's fine,' he said, and she was touched to see how his face lit up at the mention of Bridget's name. 'We've arranged to meet when she's in town next month.'

'I'm glad. I was hoping you weren't going to wait until my sixtieth. Once every twenty years doesn't allow for much conversation.'

He laughed. 'No, I don't suppose it does.'

'So why the frown?' She followed his gaze over to the Bell Tower. 'It's this investigation, isn't it?' Archie nodded. 'Do you know why Turnbull did it?'

'I don't even know *if* he did it.'

'What?' She looked at him in surprise. 'Do you mean that?'

'No, I don't suppose I do, and I'd have a hard job to argue with the evidence,' he admitted. 'Perhaps I just enjoy being on the opposite bench to Detective Inspector Roberts as a point of principle. But there's something about it that I don't understand. I can see that Leyton Turnbull hated Bella Hutton. I understand completely why he found it impossible to forgive her or his wife for keeping the birth of his child from him ...'

'They must have had their reasons.'

'Even so, he missed out on the chance to be someone completely different, and the shock of that realisation might have tipped him over the edge. But there are still so many unanswered questions. Did Bella Hutton know something else that we're not aware of? Where does Branwen Erley fit in, and what happened to her mother? Why did Turnbull kill himself? All that may be completely irrelevant, and murder is never logical, but if it were my case I'd want to know more.'

'Can't you make it your case? Or at least pull some strings to make sure it's done properly?'

'Not really. All the evidence points very clearly to one conclusion; that's partly what bothers me, but I can hardly use it as a reason to go over someone's head. Chief inspectors aren't supposed to be contrary.'

'Are you sure you're not letting the company affect your judgement?' Josephine asked.

'You mean the temptation to arrest Hitchcock and his crew might prove too strong?' He looked a little shamefaced. 'There is an element of that, I suppose. They're all so unpleasant. The sooner we can leave them behind, the better I'll like it.'

Ronnie walked over from the hotel and dragged another

deckchair across to join them. 'The next time I'm having a fucking awful day, I'll think of David Franks,' she said. 'There's always comfort to be found in those worse off.'

'Why? What's happened?'

'Hitchcock's fired him.'

'I thought there was trouble,' Josephine said, remembering the look on Alma's face. 'What did he fire him for?'

'Telling Archie about the stunt they were planning with Leyton Turnbull. I've just been talking to David in reception. That was the last straw, apparently. Hitchcock's furious.'

'He should have thought of that before he set it up,' Archie said. 'He's lucky I didn't charge them all with wasting police time.'

'David's very indignant about the whole thing, naturally. He says he followed Hitchcock's instructions to the letter, and now he's taken the blame for everything.'

'Although hiring an actress for whom *Number Seventeen* is a position rather than the title of a film wasn't the smartest thing to do,' Josephine said. 'Perhaps Alma will manage to smooth things over.'

'Or perhaps he'll decide it's for the best. He told me last night he wanted to strike out on his own.'

'That was probably the champagne talking.'

'Maybe. We'll see.'

'Well, that's me packed.' Lettice sat down and pulled the teapot towards her. 'We could give you a lift, but I'm not sure it would be very comfortable with four of us in the car as well as the luggage.'

'It's all right,' Josephine said quickly. 'Archie and I were going to the Lakes for a couple of days anyway. We'll just lie low here for tonight and head off tomorrow as planned. There's a train to Keswick after breakfast. That's if he's got the small matter of the dog sorted out by then.'

'The dog?' Ronnie asked.

'Bella Hutton's Jack Russell has taken quite a shine to him.'

'I hoped Bridget would be able to take him,' Archie explained, 'but apparently Border Terriers and Jack Russells don't mix, so I'm giving him to Mrs Snipe.'

Archie's housekeeper was notoriously meticulous in her duties, and Josephine looked at him doubtfully. 'Have you told her yet?'

'Of course. She's thrilled. She told me it would be just like having a proper star in the house. I don't know what that says about the rest of us.'

Lydia and Marta walked down the hill from the village, and Lettice waved them over. 'What are you two doing now?' she asked, pouring more tea.

'Waiting for someone to fix the car,' Lydia said wearily. 'Apparently we've got a flat battery. Then it's back to London.'

'We're giving Bridget a lift,' Marta added, winking at Archie. 'It'll give us a chance to get to know her better.'

'Yes, she mentioned it.'

'We never did tell you what she did while we were in Cambridge, did we?' Ronnie said, settling into her story. 'It was the most extraordinary thing. She . . .'

Archie's salvation came in an unlikely form. A man in a dark-brown suit came over to the table and cleared his throat politely. 'Sorry to interrupt you, sir, but I just have a couple of loose ends to tie up.'

'What is it, Inspector Roberts?' Archie asked, and something in his tone made Josephine look at him in surprise. 'This isn't my case, as you pointed out earlier.'

'It's Miss Fox I'm after, actually,' he said. Josephine saw the fear in Marta's eyes as her past came back to haunt her and opened her mouth to object, but the policeman was in no mood to be interrupted. 'My colleague informs me that you've got a criminal record, miss,' he said, making sure that his voice carried across the lawn. 'Accessory to murder, I believe. With that in mind, it's my duty to ask you where you were between the hours of ten last night and two o'clock this morning?'

Archie got up and went over to stand by Marta. 'Don't be so bloody ridiculous, Roberts,' he said quietly. 'You know damned well she had nothing to do with this.'

'Like I said, sir, it's just a formality, but those loose ends do need to be dealt with.'

'It's all right, Archie,' Marta said. 'I was down by the sea until the storm broke, and then I went back to my room.'

'And can anyone confirm that?'

'I can.' Lydia and Josephine looked at each other. If they had planned it, their words could hardly have been more carefully synchronised.

'Both of you?' Roberts raised an eyebrow at Archie. 'What these girls get up to when our backs are turned, eh sir? It shouldn't be allowed.'

Josephine saw Ronnie glance at Lettice, but for once she had the sense to be discreet. In the end, it was Lydia who recovered first. 'We were having a birthday party, Inspector. We didn't know until this morning that it should have been a wake, so I'm sure you'll forgive us for staying up late.'

'You have your answer, Roberts,' Archie said. 'Any more of this and she'll sue you for harassment. I'll make sure of it.'

'Of course, sir. And you were in your room all night?'

Archie glared at him. 'I left my room after dinner and spent the night at White Horses.'

Roberts looked down his guest list. 'With a Miss Foley? Will she confirm that?'

'Of course she'll bloody confirm it.'

'Excellent. You have a safe trip back to London, sir. Oh, and just to put your mind at rest, there's no abandoned bicycle anywhere along the Harlech road. We've checked.'

17

David stood on the old quayside, staring out across the estuary to the island. Alma walked down to speak to him, picking up snatches of conversation from the tables on the terrace, and wondered how he must feel as something so personal was made lurid and sensational by strangers who knew no better than to appropriate his tragedy as their own. He turned round as he heard her approach, but there was no sign of the hostility that she had expected. 'I'm so sorry, David,' she began, seeing little point in prefacing what she had come here to say.

He cut her off with a rueful smile. 'There's no need for you to apologise. He makes his own decisions.'

'True, but that's not what I meant. What happened to your father, everything that's gone on this weekend – I can't even begin to imagine how hurt you must be.'

'I wouldn't want you to.' A flock of wildfowl took off from the sands, twisting and somersaulting in the breeze; when it settled again, the birds' melancholy clamour rose in volume for a few seconds and then died away. She waited patiently for him to continue. 'I can't hate Turnbull for what he's done, you know,' he said eventually. 'Is that wrong of me?'

Alma shrugged. 'I don't think there's a right and a wrong way to feel. Your emotions are your own: don't hold them up for judgement, by me or by anybody else.'

'He was family. I suppose those loyalties are hard to forget.'

'Bella was family too,' Alma reminded him gently.

'In name, yes, but Bella Hutton was never going to be anybody's aunt. That sort of affection just wasn't in her.' His words were spoken as a fact rather than a criticism, but still he felt the need to qualify them. 'Don't get me wrong: Bella did what was best for me, even though it didn't feel like that at the time. She opened more doors than I could ever have dreamt of knocking at, but she never did anything for me out of love, and she never *grew* to love me. We both knew that, and I accepted it.'

'But sometimes you'd have traded the opportunities for the love.'

'Yes. Bella was a star, though, and that life doesn't leave much room for human failings, does it?' Alma shook her head. 'If she couldn't fix something by throwing money at it, then it didn't get fixed.' The first trace of bitterness had entered his voice. 'Do you have any idea how sickening it is to be grateful all the time? Now I'll have to do it for the rest of my life.'

'What do you mean?'

'As soon as the cancer was diagnosed, she told me she was going to leave me a very rich man – so no matter what I achieve off my own bat, it will always be down to the start that Bella Hutton's money gave me.'

'Not necessarily. Whatever the situation was between you, there's no doubt that she believed in you and wanted you to succeed. All right, so it wasn't love – but it *was* respect, and she didn't give that away easily either.' He looked at her gratefully, and she held out her hand. 'Good luck, David. Not that I think you'll need it.'

18

Archie was on his way out of the hotel to fetch Bridget when he heard Marta call his name. 'I've been looking for you everywhere,' she said. 'I wanted to thank you.'

He smiled. 'There's nothing to thank me for. I was about the only person who *didn't* offer you an alibi.'

'Probably just as well: things are complicated enough. But I was talking about earlier. You weren't even aware of what you were doing, but I saw how much you cared about Branwen Erley and everything that had happened to her, and it helped me more than you can ever know.'

'It's part of what I do, Marta. Perhaps the most important part.'

'No. It's part of who you are.' She surprised him by taking his face in her hands and kissing him. 'I've told Bridget she's a lucky woman. Will you let her know we're ready to leave? Someone from the hotel has found us a new battery.'

'So Lydia said. I was just off to White Horses.'

'Do you know where Josephine is?'

'Looking for you.' He nodded to the stairs and left them alone together.

'We're going in a minute,' Marta said. She took Josephine's

hand and led her into the peace of the library. 'I wanted to say goodbye properly. Far too much of today has been public, and I suppose you'll be hidden away in Inverness for months on end now. God knows when I'll see you again.'

'Ronnie and Lettice are launching their autumn collection soon. I thought I might come down for that.'

'But that's in a couple of weeks' time. Lydia was talking about it.'

'I know when it is. And trains do run in August, even in Scotland.' Marta smiled, and Josephine put a hand to her cheek. 'I'm tired of running away, Marta. Let's just see what happens.'

19

The flock of rooks rose as one from the trees and trailed across the sky in loose formation, a shifting, shimmering storm cloud of blue-black. The birds circled the Bell Tower, then descended in rapid, oblique flight, twisting and turning with their wings half closed, and Hitchcock – packing his bags at the Watch House – walked out onto the balcony, mesmerised by their numbers. They had performed the ritual at exactly the same time the night before, and, for a moment, the noise was deafening; the familiar, harsh caw of the flock was punctuated every now and then by one or two birds with a higher-pitched call, and their emphasis suggested to him so many emotions: anger, pleasure, affection, alarm. Everything but regret, and for that he envied them.

Behind him, he heard his wife's footsteps and felt her hand

rest gently on his shoulder. 'The car's waiting, Hitch. Are you ready to leave?'

He turned round, careful not to let his eyes stray to the ground where the telltale signs of his folly refused to be washed away. 'Yes,' he said. 'I'm ready.' Alma smiled and took his hand, and they walked together to the door.

20

Rhiannon stood in the shadows on the landing, hanging back in case Gwyneth was forced to allow the visitor into the house. After a few minutes, she heard the front door close and saw the policeman's image recede through the dusty stained glass over its frame. She waited, peering through the balusters as Gwyneth walked back across the faded hall rug to the stairs, her figure oddly foreshortened by the angle. She seemed to take an age to climb to the top, as if the effort of greeting the world had been too much, and, when she spoke, her voice was low and hesitant – whether from exhaustion or disbelief, Rhiannon could not say. 'It's over,' she whispered, leaning back against the doorframe. 'We're safe.'

PART SIX

SHADOW OF A DOUBT

24 July–13 August 1954, London and Portmeirion

Penrose stared down at the prison photograph of David Franks and remembered Josephine's doubts about him. He should have listened more carefully, although that was true of many things that she had told him during their relationship. At least most of the others only affected him personally; this, he thought, glancing again at the charge sheet, would have been the time to take more notice.

Franks had actually changed very little in the intervening years, but the starkness of the black-and-white image and the absence of that ready smile made him look entirely different. Penrose had seen enough ordinary-looking murderers in his time to know that there was no such thing as the face of a killer, but he guessed that most Americans glancing at their newspaper over the breakfast table would have no trouble in believing that this was a guilty man: there was a blankness in his eyes that suggested a withdrawal from reality and a complete lack of empathy with the world around him – both vital ingredients in the decision to take a life. He picked up Franks's statement again and continued reading, intrigued by the document's tone; perhaps they did things differently across the pond, but these words had an intimacy about them which bore no resemblance to any confession he had ever read.

'That day was significant for us both, I think, because it showed Gwyneth what I might be capable of. She watched Taran so closely over those last few months, sensitive to any trouble and more protective than ever – always knowing, though, that the danger wasn't in the cellar or the water or the woods but somewhere

*far less obvious, somewhere hidden away inside. I watched him,
too, whenever I was with them. It was clear to me that my fate
would always be tied to his. I would flourish as he faded, my life
would begin when his ended, and I felt an overwhelming affection for him because of it – a reverence, almost, which I bore with
a strange mixture of resentment and gratitude.*

*'I suppose it's too easy to read meaning into coincidence, but I
killed Taran a year to the day after she had watched me kill the
dog. I woke him early, while the rest of the house was still sleeping,
and helped him to put his clothes on. There was no problem in
persuading him to come with me: I was the brother he could never have, and he trusted me. That sounds shocking, I suppose, but
does it really make what I did any worse? Ask yourself this: if we
have to die – and I've thought about this a great deal recently, for
obvious reasons – isn't it better to do so at the hands of someone we
love? To him, this was just another adventure, like many we had
had before and – for all he knew – many which were still to come.*

*'The estuary was black and secretive, as it always is in the half-
light of the early morning. I walked down to the quayside, the
child in my arms, and told him to lie quietly in the bottom of the
boat. It was all part of the game to him, and he snuggled down as
good as gold, using my coat as a blanket against the chilliness of
the day. The shoreline was deathly quiet. I dampened the rowlocks
to stop them squeaking and we set off, past the island and across to
the other side, the oars leaving hollows in the water. At the landing stage by the house I let him help me secure the boat, then carried him on my shoulders across the road and up the garden path,
he laughing and pulling my hair, his feet small and vulnerable in
my hands. The house had been closed up for three years or more by
then. Everything about it spoke of neglect, and it sat still and mis-*

trustful in the silence, like an unpopular child wary of sudden attention. We let ourselves in through the kitchen door, and I swung him down onto the floor. He ran off into the house – his family home and birthright, although he would never know it – and I hesitated, aware that if I followed him there was no going back. Even then, I might have changed my mind, but he turned to me and beckoned, and his eagerness seemed to be a strange kind of blessing.

'I killed him in the hallway, at the bottom of the stairs where the first sunlight of a new day catches the corner of the rug. He struggled, and it was a shock to me to find so much strength in a tiny boy. As I held him down, my hands around his throat, my knee in his stomach, pressing him to the floor, I thought about what Gwyneth had suffered to bring him into the world, and I confess – I can say this to you now, certain that the knowledge will never reach her – the memory made me crueller than I needed to be. His death wasn't kind or peaceful. It wasn't mercifully quick. He was a clumsy child, forever hurting himself, but the marks on his face that day were of my making, and there were others that were harder to see. By the time I had finished with him, the hall was bathed in sunlight. I cried – violent, choking sobs, wracking my whole body long after his was still. I have no idea now how long we stayed there. The only other memory I have of that morning is the look on my father's face as I docked the boat back at the quayside. In that one moment, he seemed to see everything that I would become. Perhaps it was my imagination; you would call it the product of a guilty conscience, I suppose. Either way, I was never entirely sure, and very soon it ceased to matter.

'I wonder – if Henry Draycott had understood what he was setting in motion when he raped his wife, would he have stopped *himself? Knowing what I know now, I doubt it. There is no such thing as self-control in moments like that. I was there the very first time he crossed the line, and I remember it clearly. I used to go to the house whenever I could, slipping happily into the role of the child Gwyneth believed she would never have. (There will come a time, I know, when everyone says I was incapable of real affection. That isn't true. For some reason – don't ask me why – it's important to me that you* know *it isn't true.) It was a hot, thundery afternoon, oppressive like that Saturday in Portmeirion. I was supposed to have gone back across the water, but I didn't want to be caught in a storm so I crept back inside to wait until it had passed. They were in his study, and I watched them from the hallway through the narrow crack in the door – the archetypal voyeur, innocent until that first shameful flicker of interest, then complicit in the violence by the very act of witnessing it. I suppose you could say it was the first film I ever saw.*

'Even a weak man can become powerful, and that was Uncle Henry's legacy – what you want, you take. Money. Sex. Influence. Love, too, in a funny sort of way. Think about that before you wipe his slate clean, before you start to feel sorry for him. He had Gwyneth against the wall, and she was screaming at him to stop, threatening him with what would happen if he didn't, but he was beyond all reason. It wasn't about sexual satisfaction. Rape rarely is, although few people understand that. It's about anger. Something switches in you, and the rage pours out, and you want to knock them off their pedestal. Some fight back, some try to talk you out of it but you don't hear a word they say and the more they plead, the more you want to hurt them. When they're scared, you can do anything you want, and the exhilaration is addictive. I knew I'd be caught eventually; I knew my freedom was short-

lived, but still I went on, as if some force inside were controlling me, something stronger than I was. I could never fight it. In that sense, I have so much in common with Gwyneth's little boy.

'But I'm straying from the point. What interests you most is that weekend and why I killed three people in Portmeirion. Every ugly thing we do has a reason, you say, and you're right – but sometimes that reason is simply ugliness. If it would help you to understand, I could say that I killed Bella for her money; I killed her because she forced me to leave somewhere I loved, because I was tired of her meddling in my life, because she had finally realised that you can't keep someone out of trouble if they carry it with them; I could admit that she had begun to see a darkness in me which horrified her, but to which she refused to turn a blind eye; that she had set out on a path which would lead her to an earlier truth, that she was old, that she was dying, that she was in the wrong place at the wrong time; I could tell you that I needed to make Henry Draycott pay for a crime that went unpunished and it was easy to frame him for Bella because everyone knew they were enemies. If I wanted to, I could offer you a different reason for every single time I stuck the knife into her body, and all of them would be true – but it wouldn't be the truth. I killed Bella Hutton – I killed them all, in fact – because I wanted to.

'I return to that place in my mind, you know: I'm there at the end of each day when the last shaft of sunlight disappears and a brooding quiet falls over the cemetery. The image fades more quickly now, no match for this concrete-and-steel cubicle or for the babble of voices along the row, endlessly shouting and bickering because talk is all they have. It's nearly five o'clock, and soon one of them will be gone. Further down the corridor, bolts are slid back against steel, a key is thrust into a lock and a gate swings open.

The man they have come to fetch is three cells down. He can say goodbye to the rest of us or go straight to the room where he'll spend his last night, and he chooses the latter. He can't face our pity. He wants it to be done, and I don't blame him.

'One day soon, of course, it won't be the other man. I try not to think of the wheel that will seal the chamber door or the straps on my wrists or the pungent smell of peach blossom as the fumes invade my body, and I hold on to the peace and the darkness of home. They elude me more often now, those images, but they're still there. They'll always be there.'

Penrose put the sheaf of papers down, disturbed by the insight into Franks's mind, and tried to concentrate on the facts. Detective Doyle was right: the confession to three murders at Portmeirion could not have been more clearly stated, although the only victim actually mentioned by name was Bella Hutton. If Franks had really found a way of killing Leyton Turnbull – Penrose still found it hard to think of Turnbull as Henry Draycott – would his arrogance allow him to be discreet about it? Wouldn't he want to explain how perfectly his plan had been executed? Unless, of course, he was protecting an accomplice: perhaps someone else had been waiting in the Bell Tower to push Turnbull to his death while Franks remained safely visible on the terrace. If so, there was no doubt in Penrose's mind that Franks would delight in taking the truth to his grave.

The other possibility was a third body at Portmeirion that had never been discovered. Was that the twisted purpose of this confession? To taunt the authorities with an unsolved crime? As far as Penrose could see, the only person unaccounted for that weekend was Hitchcock's nun, who seemed to have left her hotel without checking out – but that was no reason to suppose she was dead. He could try to establish what had happened to Joan Sidney, although it would probably be a wild goose chase: he didn't suppose for a moment that a porn star used her real name.

He skimmed through the document again to make sure he hadn't missed anything, then looked through the box that Doyle had left him and took out the other film reel. It was unlabelled, and he began to thread it onto the projector, swearing under his breath at the awkwardness of the process. He managed it at last, but before he had a chance to start the machine, there was a knock at the door. 'Devlin – that was quick. Is there something I should know about our American friend?'

'He doesn't exist, sir.'

Penrose glared at him, as if it were the sergeant's fault that the phrase made no sense. 'What do you mean?'

'There *is* no Detective Tom Doyle with the Los Angeles Police Department, and there never has been. I spoke to someone called Larry Hunter – that's his number – but he didn't know the name, and he didn't recognise the description I gave him of the man who was here.'

'Get on to the Adelphi and . . .'

'I've already done it, sir. Tom Doyle checked out this morning. He arrived late last night, made no calls, took no meals and spoke to no one – as far as they know. He paid his bill in cash.'

'Shit. Didn't they take any personal details from him when he booked in?'

'Oh yes. He gave an LA home address and a telephone number.'

'And?' Penrose asked, his heart sinking.

'It's a poodle parlour.'

'So what the hell is all this about?' Bewildered, he looked down at the materials on his desk – and then it dawned on him. 'How could I have been so bloody stupid?' he exclaimed angrily. 'I should have known the minute Doyle mentioned Hitchcock that this was all some sort of elaborate joke. Well, he's not getting away with it this time. I don't care how famous he is.'

He reached for the telephone, but Devlin stopped him. 'It's not a joke, sir. The LAPD might not have heard of a Detective Tom Doyle, but someone called David Franks *is* on death row for murder. Hunter's sending the files over so you can look at the case in detail, but in the meantime he's given me an overview.'

'Go on.'

'Franks was arrested earlier this year and charged with the murders of twelve women in various cities across America and Canada. The earliest case dates from 1940, and he struck at the rate of roughly one a year. It took a while for the murders to be linked because they were in so many different states, but the women were all killed in the same way – raped, beaten and strangled. It was the papers who dubbed them the cemetery murders. That's where the bodies were dumped each time – in the city's cemeteries. They were left overnight, usually tied up and blindfolded, and laid out on one of the most elaborate memorials.'

'Like a sacrifice,' Penrose said quietly, remembering Bella Hutton's body. 'Who were the victims?'

'All of them were hookers,' Devlin said, and the American slang – repeated verbatim from his informant – jarred with his English accent. 'After Franks was arrested, it emerged that he had been a major player in the porn industry – serious stag films, all very explicit and a lot of them violent. He made a fortune from it, apparently. Most of the victims have been identified as women he used in the films.'

'Used' being the operative word, Penrose thought. 'Anything else?' he asked.

'One of the newspapers did some digging into Franks's past and found out he used to work for Alfred Hitchcock.'

'I bet Hitch was thrilled about that. It must have kept the studio lawyers busy for quite some time.'

'It was played down very quickly, I understand. But not before the same paper had pointed out that some of the murders coincided with the release of a new Hitchcock movie and that the locations of the bodies mirrored the films' settings: New York for *Saboteur* and *Rope*; Santa Rosa for *Shadow of a Doubt*; Vermont for *Spellbound*; Miami for *Notorious*; Washington DC for *Strangers on a Train*, and so on. Hunter was very keen to stress, though, that none of that is official.'

'So how did he explain the *Rear Window* killings?'

'He didn't. He denies they ever took place.'

'What?'

'First he just laughed, and then he got defensive about it.'

'Another Hitchcock fan, no doubt,' Penrose said caustically. He wasn't surprised that Hollywood might try to cover up its links to a serial killer, but none of that explained the confession he had just read or why these materials had found their way to his desk.

'Perhaps. Hunter wants to talk to you about it, and he's asked me to make sure the film reels are sent to him.'

'I think we'll take our time over that. I haven't even looked at them myself yet. So how does he claim that Franks was caught?'

'According to the LAPD, the last victim was found in a cemetery in Quebec City. A vehicle seen parked outside was traced back to Franks.'

'And is there a Quebec film?'

Devlin nodded. '*I Confess*. Quite appropriate, really.' Penrose nodded thoughtfully. 'Franks is at San Quentin, waiting for the gas chamber. The date for his execution has been set for 1 December this year. He hasn't made any attempt to lodge an appeal.'

'Did you ask Hunter about that confession and the murders in Portmeirion?'

'Yes. Franks has bragged about other murders, apparently, but he hasn't made a formal confession for anything other than what's on the original charge sheet. I don't think they're bothered, sir. They can only gas him once.'

Even so, Penrose could think of one person to whom Franks's claims would matter very much indeed. 'I'm going to take a look at this film, but I need you to do some more digging for me. First of all, see if you can trace a woman called Gwyneth Draycott. In 1936, she was living in a house between Portmeirion and Harlech. If she's still alive, I need to talk to her. Then get on to San Quentin and see if they'll give you a list of people with whom Franks has communicated, either by letter or by personal visit.'

'Right away, sir. Anything else?'

Penrose shook his head, then changed his mind. 'Actually, there *is* one more thing: about seven years ago, a woman's body was found in Highgate. That was before you joined us, wasn't it?' Devlin nodded. 'Get the details for me. There's a Hitchcock film set in London.' He remembered going to see it with Josephine – something long and tedious with a courtroom scene; it was loosely based on true crimes and had reminded them both of their conversation with the director over breakfast that day in Portmeirion. 'See if the dates coincide.'

He lowered the blinds again and sat down at his desk. The footage started abruptly with a close-up of a woman's face. She was staring in disbelief at someone out of camera shot, her eyes darting to left and right as she tried to guess his intentions, her fear turning to horror when she realised what was about to happen. As Penrose watched, her breathing quickened in panic, and her mouth opened in a scream. There was a flurry of hands at her throat while she tried to prevent an unseen assailant from tying something around her neck, but he was too quick for her. She twisted her head from side to side, choking for air as the material dug into her skin and squeezed the life from her body. Her hands – well manicured and heavy with rings – continued to claw at the knot, but gradually she lost her strength, and the clawing became a caress, then stopped altogether. She wore a crucifix, and the cord that had been used to strangle her hung down on either side, framing the cross and mocking her faith in any sort of divine protection. For a long time, the camera lingered on her face, her eyes still and lifeless, her tongue protruding grotesquely from her mouth; eventually it panned away and the film stopped as abruptly as it had started, but not before Penrose had glimpsed the outstretched hand of another victim in the background.

Sickened by what he had seen, he had to force himself to watch the footage again and was just rewinding the reel for the fourth time when Devlin returned. 'You were right, sir,' he said. 'The film was called *The Paradine Case* and it came out here around Christmas 1947. Susan Dunn's body was found in Highgate Cemetery on the morning of 28 January by a woman walking her dog. She'd been strangled by her own stocking.'

He handed over the file. 'She wasn't a prostitute, though, was she?' Penrose said, flicking through it to remind himself of the case.

'No, a housewife. Her husband reported her missing the night before. She popped out to get him a bottle of beer and never came back. We didn't find her killer.'

'Perhaps we have now.' He looked down at the image of a woman's body slumped against a gravestone, one stocking around her neck, the other in her mouth, and thought about Branwen Erley. 'Did the prison cooperate?' Devlin passed him a short list of names and Penrose nodded to himself: things were beginning to make more sense.

'And Gwyneth Draycott is still living at the same address. That's her telephone number.'

'Thank you.' Penrose picked up the receiver, then thought better of it. The sort of news he had for Gwyneth Draycott needed to be delivered in person. Everything else could wait.

2

Penrose stayed in Shrewsbury overnight and set out early the next morning for North Wales. It was a relief to be away from London, and he was grateful for any distraction that took his mind off the sadness of the time of year and his anxiety about the future: he had never subscribed to the school of thought that welcomed retirement as an opportunity; almost everything he had wanted in life he had achieved through his work, and, while he knew that the decision to go now, when he would still be missed, was the correct one, there was a part of him that longed to cling to his desk until he was forcibly removed, an embarrassing relic from the old school whose only value was his longevity. He could never have admitted it to those closest to him, but he feared the type of man he might become with no real purpose to his day other than contentment.

The road stretched out ahead of him, a meandering ribbon of grey between fertile green fields, and he shook off his mood and concentrated instead on the pleasures of the journey. Even on a cloudy day like this, when a light drizzle and persistent breeze conspired to undermine all thoughts of summer, he delighted in the subtle variety of the Welsh countryside. The overcast skies could do nothing to rob the hills and valleys of their colour, and Penrose found a sparseness and simplicity in the landscape which made it welcome company.

He bypassed the Portmeirion turning and took the road to Harlech, finally making the journey he had wanted to make all those years ago. As he drove, he considered how best to approach his meeting with Gwyneth Draycott, presuming she agreed to talk to him at all. He had no intention of sharing the harsher details of Taran's murder with her, only the name of the person responsible, and he sensed that the news would bring both comfort and pain: if Franks's words were to be believed in their entirety, there had been a genuine affection between the two of them, something more than a distant relationship through a fractured family, and Gwyneth Draycott's relief in knowing the truth at last was unlikely to temper her sense of betrayal.

The house was harder to find than he expected, and he tried two lanes down to the estuary before locating the right one. He parked the car at the side of the road and took in the reality of something he had only ever seen in miniature. It was a handsome house, one of those solid-looking Victorian structures, built to suggest a quiet but enduring status and given greater authority by its commanding position. Everything about it spoke of care and attention, and Penrose wondered if the tidiness was Gwyneth Draycott's way of restoring some semblance of order to a life scarred by events beyond her control. If he hadn't known what had happened here, he would have said there was an air of peace about the property, and he questioned the wisdom of what he had come to do. Was it really fair to rake over the ashes of forty years in the name of justice, or was he simply playing to Franks's vanity? Before he had made up his mind, the decision was taken out of his hands: a woman was standing at one of the downstairs windows, looking inquisitively at his car, and Penrose had no choice but to get out and explain himself.

She opened the front door before he had a chance to knock. Her dark hair was tinged with grey, and she must have been in her mid-sixties, but it was only her hands and the lines on her neck that gave away her age; her face had a fresh, youthful complexion, and her eyes – an unusually dark shade of blue – were bright and questioning, making it easy to imagine how beautiful she had been as a young woman. Even now, she was still remarkably attractive. 'Mrs Draycott?' Penrose asked.

'Who wants to know?' Her accent was soft, her voice pleasant, but the coolness of the words was unmistakable.

'My name is Archie Penrose. I'm with the Metropolitan Police, and I was staying at Portmeirion eighteen years ago when your husband died. I've recently been given some information which I think you should know about. It relates to him and to your son.'

'Henry Draycott was dead to me long before he had the decency to do it properly,' she said. 'Whatever news you have, you're wasting your time by bringing it here.'

'And your son?' She hesitated, and Penrose guessed that so many years of silence had schooled her against even daring to hope. 'Can I come in, Mrs Draycott? Just for a moment?'

She nodded reluctantly and stood aside to allow him into the hallway. He tried to be discreet as she showed him through to the kitchen, but could not resist a lingering glance over his shoulder towards the bottom of the staircase. Gwyneth Draycott had been living in this house for nearly forty years, oblivious to the violence that had taken place there, walking innocently across that floor several times a day, and the thought horrified him. Whatever else he told her, he was determined to keep that part of the story to himself: there was no sense in turning her refuge into a house of horror; her home was probably the one thing that had kept her sane.

The kitchen smelt of tomatoes and freshly baked bread. He took the chair offered to him while she went over to the stove, resolved, it seemed, not to let him disrupt the course of her day. 'I'm sorry to bring painful memories back after so many years,' he began cautiously, 'but . . .'

'Have you found Taran?'

She asked the question without turning round, but he heard the anxiety in her voice and wished he could offer something more than just a name. 'I'm afraid not.' She walked across to the window, and Penrose gave her a moment to compose herself. 'I'm here because of your nephew, David Franks.' He waited in vain for a response. 'You do remember him?'

'Of course I remember David,' she said, sitting down opposite him, 'but he left here a long time ago and under terrible circumstances. His father was killed because of what happened to Taran, although I expect you know that already.'

'Yes. Did you keep in touch with David after he left?'

'No.' She must have noticed the look of surprise on his face because she added, 'He was upset about leaving, and Bella thought it would be best if he made a clean break.'

'So he didn't visit you when he came to Portmeirion in 1936?' Penrose asked, curious that Franks should claim such affection for Gwyneth Draycott but not take a twenty-minute journey down the road to see her.

'No.' She flushed slightly. 'I thought *you* were here to tell *me* something, Mr Penrose?'

It was a fair point: old habits died hard, but this was supposed to be a mission of mercy, not an interrogation. 'This will come as a shock to you, Mrs Draycott, but David Franks is currently in America awaiting execution. He went back there to live in 1938 and was arrested earlier this year and charged with the murders of twelve women over a fourteen-year period.' Her face was impassive, and Penrose wondered if she already knew of her nephew's arrest. He carried on, interested to see how she would react to news which she could not have come by in any other way, and which was more personal to her. 'I've been shown a document which suggests that it was David Franks and not your husband who murdered Bella Hutton and Branwen Erley in Portmeirion.'

'What sort of document?'

'A letter which he wrote from prison. There's no easy way to say this, but the letter also contains a confession to Taran's murder.' Penrose searched in vain for the reaction he had expected, then continued gently, 'I thought you had a right to know who took your son's life after all these years. It's also right that the people who have taken the blame for David Franks's crimes, officially or not, should have their names cleared.' Still she said nothing, and Penrose found himself watching the second hand of the kitchen clock complete two full circles before he spoke again. 'Forgive me, but you don't seem very . . .'

'Grateful?' It was not the word that Penrose had been about to use, but he realised, on reflection, that it was perhaps more honest. He had wanted to feel that he could bring comfort to a woman whose life had been so senselessly destroyed, but his motives were far from selfless: even if David Franks was made to account for Taran's death, it did not change the fact that Penrose had walked away too easily from the murders at Portmeirion, and Gwyneth Draycott's gratitude would never absolve him from that. 'It's hard for me to explain, Mr Penrose,' she said, 'but it's nearly forty years since Taran died, and the question that haunts me is no longer who, but why. Can you answer that for me? Have you gleaned anything from this letter which might help a mother make more sense of the world?' This time, it was Penrose's turn to remain silent. 'Taran was a happy, beautiful little boy who didn't deserve the fate that God gave him. I don't mean to be rude, but I think it would take a higher authority than yours to put that right.'

'I'm afraid David has given no indication of where Taran's body is,' Penrose said quietly. 'I could ask the American police to press him for the information if it would help you.'

'What good would that really do? Taran suffered enough when he was alive, and I'd rather he was left in peace. Thank you, though. It was kind of you to take the trouble.'

The words were spoken as a dismissal and Penrose stood up to go, feeling oddly flat and thwarted. There were still so many things that he did not understand about Franks's claims, but he reminded himself again that he was not here for his own satisfaction; Gwyneth Draycott had suffered enough, too, and he had no right to pry into her marriage. She was not the accused. As she walked him to the door, there was a noise from upstairs, the sound of something crashing to the floor, and she looked up, startled. 'You don't live alone, Mrs Draycott?' Penrose asked.

'No. My sister joined me here a few years ago. The house is far too big for one person. But she's ill, and I must go to her, unless there's anything else?'

'Just one more thing: did Branwen Erley ever contact you about trying to find her mother?'

She stiffened at the reminder of her husband's adultery. 'No.'

'And you didn't have any contact with your husband during the weekend of his death?'

'Absolutely not.' She shut the door without any further conversation, and he walked over to his car. Looking back at the house, he saw her face appear briefly at one of the upstairs windows, and then the curtains were drawn across, an eloquent closure to his visit. The stretch of water which David Franks had described lay before him, and he stared at the run-down landing stage, imagining the small hands on the rope, the sound of laughter and footsteps as Taran ran up the path towards his death. He shook his head to get rid of the image and concentrated instead on the rugged dignity of the Snowdon line which dominated the horizon opposite. The morning was still sulking, stubbornly bland and grey, but, as he watched, a shaft of sunlight broke tentatively through the cloud and fell on Portmeirion; it seemed to confine itself strictly to the small cluster of buildings, a blessing for Clough's endeavours and an invitation to lay his own ghosts, and Penrose smiled.

Half an hour later, he left his Riley in the car park, paid his five shillings at the gate and joined the throng of day visitors to the village. Walking down the driveway, he could only imagine how frustrating Clough had found the fifteen-year period of war and its aftermath which had prevented him from expanding his vision; with the restrictions now lifted, he seemed to be making up for lost time, and work was already well under way on the new Gate House, a Baroque-style structure designed to straddle the road on the way into the village. The familiar figure of Portmeirion's creator – clad in waistcoat, breeches and long yellow stockings – was standing nearby, overseeing the work, and Penrose raised his hand in greeting. As he made his way round the Piazza, taking the long route down to the hotel, it occurred to him that the gradual evolution of the village had contributed much to its beauty.

From the terrace, he noticed another new addition high up to the right of the village, a round single-storey structure that peered over the clifftop like some sort of wartime lookout post.

Penrose changed his mind about going to the hotel and looked instead for a route up to the building from the shoreline. He found the path eventually and climbed the rock via a series of steep steps, pausing at the top to catch his breath.

'Great minds, Archie.'

He looked up, embarrassed to realise that Marta must have watched his entire ungainly ascent. He had not seen her since before Josephine's death, although they had spoken often on the telephone – stilted, trivial conversations that skirted around their grief but which, in the unspoken solidarity of loss, gave each of them comfort. Her skin was pale and he could see that she had been crying. In middle age, Marta's face had always stayed loyal to its younger beauty – a fact that had simultaneously delighted and infuriated Josephine – but today she looked tired and defeated. 'I don't know why I'm surprised to see you,' he said, 'bearing in mind what the date is.'

'I come here because I don't know what else to do.' It was the first time Archie had heard her acknowledge her despair so openly. He sat down next to her and took her hand. 'I can't forgive her for lying to me, you know. She told me it was nothing serious. She said she'd be back to normal in about a year. A nice simple treatment by tablet, she called it – all so bloody innocent.'

'She told *herself* that, Marta.'

'Since when has an aspirin cured cancer?' He understood her anger too well to reason with it. 'Then she let me go out of the country. Actually, she *encouraged* me to go. I remember her telling me that three months was nothing, when she must have known that it was far too long.' She lit a cigarette, using the diversion to rein in her emotions. 'I read it in the newspaper,' she said, her voice unnaturally calm. 'I picked up the *New York Times*, and there it was.'

'I'm sorry. I wanted to tell you, but I didn't know how to find you.' He thought back to that cold, dreary day in February, when Josephine's sister had telephoned him at Scotland Yard to give him the news, and the hours he had spent calling American hotels, trying to find Marta as a distraction from his own grief. 'She was the only person who knew where you were.'

'I'm not blaming you, Archie. It shouldn't have been down to you.'

'It was a shock to everyone. Johnny sent his dresser out for an evening paper during the interval and read about it then.' Even that announcement was more modest than it should have been, Archie thought; how typical of Josephine to die when the nation was too busy mourning the King to take much notice.

'I'm not John fucking Terry, though, am I? She must have known what that would do to me, and I can't believe she didn't care. I won't believe that.' Marta stood up and walked over to one of the arches that looked out over the estuary. 'I miss her, Archie.' It was a commonplace expression of grief, but its simple truth broke Marta's resolve in a way that all her anger and bitterness had failed to do, and he held her as she cried. 'I've spent half my life missing her, for God's sake. You'd think I'd be used to it by now, but it gets worse every day.'

'I know.'

'Of course you do.' She touched his cheek affectionately, an acknowledgement of the unique bond between them which a shared love had created. 'Did she tell you she was dying?'

It was the question Archie had been waiting for, and he was glad to be able to answer it truthfully. 'No, she didn't tell me.'

He had guessed, though, and Josephine had not denied it, but she had begged him not to tell anyone, and he did as she asked. It was too late now for regrets, and he refused to add to Marta's pain by being honest with her. 'You know how she hated self-pity.'

'It's easy to see the signs when you look back, though, isn't it? She'd make a joke about wanting to lie on the sofa all day, or go to Tagley and be too breathless to use the water pump. Then there was that time when we all went to the Guineas, and she missed a day because she was too tired. Nothing would normally have kept her away from a racetrack. But she always had an excuse, and it was always so damned convincing.'

'Nothing kept her away from going to Suffolk with you,' he reminded her. He remembered how determined Josephine had been to spend that time with Marta and how happy she had been afterwards.

'She always loved it there.'

'Because she associated it with you.' Marta was quiet for a long time. 'If we knew how many last times went on in our lives when we weren't looking, we'd go insane,' he said gently, guessing what she was thinking.

'Am I that transparent?' She smiled. 'I wanted to go again a few weeks later, but she kept putting me off. She blamed it on work, and I knew she was trying to get a book finished, but she usually wrote them so quickly. I couldn't understand why she was being so bloody diligent all of a sudden.'

The words were sad rather than bitter. Archie watched her face as her hand idly traced the shape of one of the scallop shells which lined the inside of the building and wondered, if Josephine could have seen Marta's pain two years after her death, would she have made different decisions? 'If she *had* told you, what would you have done?' he asked.

'Stayed with her. Looked after her.'

'And could you have promised to be strong, to put your own sadness to one side for her sake?' He knew that Marta was too honest to lie, to herself or to him. 'She didn't want you to watch her die, and she couldn't carry your grief on top of everything else. It would have been too much. Selfish or noble – it's always a fine line.'

'And she was right,' Marta admitted. 'I would have made her feel guilty for dying.'

'We all do that to the people we love.'

'You said she died at her sister's?'

'Yes. She came south before Christmas and stayed at her club, then went on to Surrey.'

'She had no time, did she? No time to make a life for herself. Her father had only been gone sixteen months when she died. Why couldn't she have had his bloody genes and not her mother's?'

'You can't think like that – it's not fair to Josephine. Of course she had a life. What else do you call the time she spent with you, everything she achieved with her work . . .' The other people she loved, he had been about to say, but he brushed his most intimate memories to one side, unable yet to cope with them. 'Don't pity her, Marta. Leave that to people who don't know any better. She didn't put her life on hold while she was waiting, and so much has happened in the last twenty years. You have to believe that counts. *I* have to believe it.'

She nodded, and his words seemed to temper her regret a

little. 'I destroyed all her letters, Archie. Every single one of them.'

He looked at her in astonishment. 'Why?'

'Because I was angry with her. I got drunk one night and I sat in front of the fire and burned them one by one. When I woke up the next morning, I couldn't believe what I'd done. Now there's nothing left. Nothing to speak for what we had.'

'There's the drawing you gave her. She wanted you to have it. I told you I'd take care of it until you were ready; perhaps now you are.'

Marta nodded. 'Yes, I'd like to have it, but it's not the same.' He smiled, and she looked at him questioningly. 'What is it?'

'There's a letter attached to it. It's taped to the back. I didn't notice it at first.'

'Why on earth didn't you tell me?'

'Because it would have gone the same way as all the rest, wouldn't it? Whatever Josephine has to say to you, you haven't been in the mood to listen.'

Her tears acknowledged the point, and it was a while before she could speak. 'Thank you, Archie,' she said eventually. 'Have you read it?'

'Of course I haven't read it!'

'I'd have read yours.'

He laughed and stood up. 'Shall we go and get a drink?'

They took the gentler route down to the hotel and sat out on the terrace. 'I never have been brave enough to ask you about Josephine's funeral,' Marta said.

'Just be glad you couldn't get back to England in time.' He thought about that morning – the perfunctory service, the shell-shocked congregation, the sight of Josephine's coffin sliding back into the wall without a single flower on it because that was what she had asked for – and decided to shield Marta from the desperate bleakness of it all. 'There was something surreal about it, as though all the different compartments of her life had come together for the first and last time – her family, her Scottish friends, the theatre contingent; all of us strangers to each other and thinking we knew her best. I met her youngest sister afterwards, and it was as though we were talking about a completely different person.' He closed his eyes, glad to feel the sun on his face. 'I know she hated everything to do with mourning and didn't have any great faith in an afterlife, but I kept wondering if that was really the best we could do. All the beautiful places she loved, and there we stood in Streatham bloody Crematorium.'

'Ovens in the suburb,' Marta said.

'What?'

'I've been reading *A Shilling for Candles* while I've been here. It seemed appropriate, bearing in mind why we all came to Portmeirion in the first place. That's how Grant describes Christine Clay's funeral.' She smiled at him. 'One of the many things that didn't make it to Mr Hitchcock's movie. Do you remember how bewildered she was when she saw it?'

'I know how she felt. I've got a few issues with Hitchcock myself at the moment.'

'Oh? What do you mean?' She listened, astonished, while he told her about his elusive visitor and David Franks's crimes. 'What are you going to do?'

'I haven't made my mind up yet. Franks killed the missing child, too. Do you remember? Leyton Turnbull's son. The little boy who was supposedly abducted by Franks's father?'

Marta nodded. 'Of course I remember. I thought at the time how terrible it must have been for his mother.' Her face clouded over. 'It's unbearable to lose a child in any way, but never to know what really happened . . . I don't know how you would live with that. What did she say when you told her?'

'She hardly reacted at all.'

'You mean she knew already?'

That hadn't been what he meant, but the more he thought about it, the more possible it seemed. 'I was going to suggest that she resented Taran because of the way he was conceived and her hatred for his father.'

'Children aren't tainted in that way, Archie. You love them no matter what. My husband forced me to have sex with him because it was his marital right, just like Gwyneth Draycott's did, but I would have gone to Hell and back for my son. Well, I *did* go to Hell and back for him – you know that better than anyone.'

'So why would she have protected Franks all these years?'

'Hadn't you better go and ask her?'

'I can't intrude with a question like that.'

'Don't you trust your instincts any more? Can you bear not knowing?' His silence gave Marta her answer. She finished her drink and stood up. 'I'll walk you to your car.' They crossed the square and left the village by the tollgate. 'Won't you be glad to retire and leave people to their own misery?' Marta asked.

'To be honest, retirement frightens me to death.'

'Why?'

'Because I don't know what the point will be. Does that sound ridiculous?'

'A little selfish, perhaps, but I think you have enough strong women in your life to set you straight.'

They reached his car and he bent to kiss her. 'Are you sure you want to stay here tonight? You wouldn't rather come back to London with me?'

'No, I want to stay. It's important.' He nodded, understanding what she meant. 'I'll call you as soon as I'm back, though, and come and collect the picture. Good luck with your last case.' His smile must have been unconvincing, because she looked at him with concern and said, 'Remember *The Singing Sands*, Archie?'

'I can't bring myself to read it,' he admitted.

'You should. There's a section where Grant thinks of a list of things to do when he retires.'

'Such as?'

'Oh, messing about in boats. Running a sheep farm.' He started to laugh, but she cut him off. 'And finding time to share his life, to love and be loved.'

He glanced over to the back seat, where the book was lying with a pile of papers. 'And does he retire?'

Marta smiled. 'He's not real, Archie. It's not a real life he's wasting.' She reached into the car and put the book on the seat next to him. 'Perhaps I've read your letter after all. Go and sort your case out, and then go home.'

3

The journey back through Minffordd and across the toll road seemed to take twice as long. Penrose half expected Gwyneth Draycott's door to remain obstinately closed when he knocked again, but she answered almost immediately. 'Mrs Draycott, what I was actually going to say earlier was that you didn't seem very surprised by what I had to say about David Franks.'

The rest of his carefully chosen opening speech was lost in her response. 'Thank God you've come back,' she said, pulling him into the house. 'I was wrong to send you away.'

Penrose saw the panic in her eyes and said calmly, 'You knew that David Franks had killed your son, didn't you?'

'Not *my* son.' He stared at her in confusion. 'I lied to you last time. It's Gwyneth who's ill upstairs. I was only trying to protect her – the habit of a lifetime, I suppose – but she wants to see you.'

'So you're Gwyneth's sister?'

'Not by blood, no, but we were brought up together. I'm Rhiannon.'

'Rhiannon Erley?'

'I don't use that name any more, but yes.' Penrose found it hard to see why Henry Draycott's lover would be caring for his wife; he opened his mouth to ask, but she interrupted him. 'I'll answer all your questions later, but please come and see Gwyneth first. She had a fit while you were here last time, and I don't know how much more her body can take.'

'A fit?'

'Yes. Gwyneth is epileptic. She's very weak now because I can't get her to eat anything, and I don't think she has much time left. She wants to tell you the truth while she still can.'

As he followed her upstairs, Penrose reconsidered Franks's statement in the context of what he had just been told: the assertion that Taran was a child forever hurting himself, submitting to a force stronger than he was; Gwyneth's certainty that the danger was 'somewhere hidden away inside'; a sexual assault which had had such significant consequences – all of these suggested that Taran had shared his mother's illness. He pieced them together with what the local police had said at the time about Gwyneth's family and the suggestion that her son had been better off out of it, and an idea began to form in his mind, one he was reluctant to believe.

The room he was taken to was at the front of the house with a fine view of the island and Portmeirion beyond. It was tastefully furnished but sparse, and dominated by an elaborate dressing table. Penrose's attention was drawn to the collection of photographs that covered its surface. As he stood in the doorway, waiting for an invitation to go to Gwyneth's bedside, he studied the pictorial record of David Franks's life: images of a teenager in America and a young man in London, and pictures of him with Hitchcock and Alma, one in front of a Tudor country house of white stucco and timber, the other on the set of *Blackmail*; several showed him as an older man, either behind a film camera or in the company of an attractive woman, and Penrose wondered if he was looking at any of Franks's victims. Of the twenty or thirty photographs, only one seemed to picture Franks with a member of his family: not Bella or his father, but a blonde little boy of around two, presumably the cousin whom he had killed; from its background, Penrose guessed that it had been taken in the dog cemetery.

Rhiannon noticed him looking at it and beckoned him over to the bed. The window was wide open, allowing a pleasant breeze to blow in off the estuary, but still the room was stale and heavy with the unmistakable smell of sickness. Gwyneth Draycott was lying with her back to him, staring out across the water, and he could see how thin she was from the frail form beneath the sheets. 'I knew someone would come eventually,' she said. Her words were barely more than a whisper, and Penrose moved closer to make it easier for her. 'I'm glad you're here. I began to think it would be too late.' He waited while Rhiannon held some water to her lips; when she continued, her voice was stronger. 'David did what he did because I begged him to. You must understand that. He killed Taran for me because I didn't want my little boy to suffer any more. It was a terrible thing to ask him to do, but he agreed because he loved me and he knew I would never be able to do it myself. I know it was wrong but it was an act of mercy.'

Penrose tried to concentrate on her grief-stricken face, but all he could see was the film his mind had made of Taran's final moments. Her version of her son's death was so far from the stark truth of Franks's confession that he was reluctant to let her continue, but he knew how important it was to her. 'Tell me what happened, Mrs Draycott.'

'Henry was already gone by the time I found out I was pregnant,' she said. 'God forgive me, but I tried everything I could think of to get rid of the baby before it was born. I knew what the risks were, and I didn't want a child of mine to suffer like my brother had, but he – or she, for all I knew – had other ideas. I suppose that heartened me, in a way – to think that the baby might turn out to be tough. I called him Taran because I wanted him to be strong, and he was so beautiful when he was born that it was hard to believe there could be anything wrong. Nothing happened for the first few months, and I began to let myself hope: perhaps Taran had his father's genes. It wasn't something I'd have wanted for him, but it was the lesser of two evils, better than inheriting this sickness from me.'

'Were you looking after him on your own?' Penrose asked, imagining what the strain of watching and waiting must have been like with no one to confide in.

'No. I shut this place up and moved into the old mansion house with Grace during the last weeks of my pregnancy,' she explained. 'I'd never had much time for any of the other Draycotts. They were always a bit above themselves, and they didn't take kindly to Henry walking out with a girl from town, but Grace was a good woman, quiet and kind. She kept herself to herself, and that suited me. She invited me to bring the child up in her house during the early years, where there was help around if I needed it.'

'Because she knew what the situation was with your illness?'

'Because she thought her brother had abandoned his wife and child,' she said, and Penrose was interested in her phrasing of the sentence. 'That's not fair, mind. She did it out of genuine kindness, not because her conscience troubled her, and I confided in her eventually because I knew she wouldn't judge.' She paused to take another sip of water. 'It was a good arrangement for her, too, I think. They were difficult years for everyone, but Grace felt things very deeply, and war saddened her. She hated the reality of what we're all capable of. It was easy for us both to hide away from our worries over there and pretend they didn't exist. They were happy times at first, peaceful – just the three of us, with David and his father spending the summers there and some of the Gypsies passing through now and again. Life was very straightforward.'

'And then Taran's epilepsy began to show itself?' Penrose

asked, gently moving her on. He had known as soon as he saw Gwyneth that Rhiannon had not been exaggerating the seriousness of her illness, and the reliving of her past would only put her under more strain. The woman in front of him had already decided to give up on life, and she was simply waiting for her body to concede defeat; selfishly, Penrose wanted to be able to piece together the whole story at last, while she was still strong enough to give her version.

'It started before his first birthday. We were playing together in the garden and Taran just stopped laughing and stared into space, completely unaware of me or anything else. It only lasted a few seconds, but I knew the signs, and it was enough to make me realise how foolish I'd been to think that everything would be all right. The absences happened regularly after that, several times a week. Then he had his first fit. He was sleepy, and I was putting him to bed one night when his limbs started to jerk. He cried when it was over, as though he knew what it meant and wanted to tell me he was sorry.'

'How did David find out what was happening?'

'He came into the kitchen one day when Taran was having a fit. It happened so suddenly that I forgot to lock the door. Seeing him like that frightened David half to death, I think, but he was so good; he cushioned Taran's head and moved things that he might have hurt himself on. Taran was always very confused afterwards, and David helped me to get him into bed to recover. He was so gentle with him, so grown up. It was as if he finally understood something that had been puzzling him for a long time, and I was grateful to him. You don't expect to look to a fourteen-year-old for strength, do you? But I suppose they grew up quickly then. There were boys as young as David killing and dying in France.'

Hardly for the same reasons, Penrose thought, but he bit his tongue. 'Mrs Draycott, are you sure that you asked David to kill Taran? It wasn't his suggestion?'

'He knew how desperate I was,' she said, and it was hard to tell if she had deliberately avoided the question or was simply answering it in her own way. 'I was more afraid every day of what would happen to Taran because I'd seen it all before in my own family and I knew what the future held for him. I knew it would affect his mind and how people would torment him; I knew they might try to take him away from me and what would happen if they did; and I knew how difficult it would be for me to look after him properly. But, most of all, I knew how unhappy *he* would be, how much *he* would suffer. And it was my fault. I'd allowed it to happen, I'd given him this terrible thing, and it was up to me to make it right, but I didn't know how to do it. Then I was walking in the woods one day and I saw David killing a dog. He told me it had broken its leg, and he was putting it out of its misery – his father had taught him to do it, he said – but it was so quick and so painless, and I wished more than anything that someone would do that for my son. He must have known what I was thinking because he looked at me and nodded. I didn't even have to speak the words. I can't explain the relief I felt to know that there was a way out if things got too bad.'

'And Taran's condition got worse after that?'

She nodded. 'It happened very quickly in the end. David woke him early one morning and took him out. He did that sometimes to give me a break, and Taran loved to be with him.

He had a terrible fit while they were out in the boat. David blamed himself – Taran was always more vulnerable when he was tired or if he had just been woken up – but it wasn't his fault; it could have come at any time, and David was only doing what I'd asked him to do when the moment was right.'

'But he decided when that was, not you.'

'Fate decided,' she insisted, and then, as he looked doubtfully at her, she asked, 'Have you ever seen someone having an epileptic fit?' Penrose nodded. 'Then you'll know it starts with very little warning, and the force of it seems to come from nowhere. Your natural impulse is to hold the person you love until it stops, but you can't because the movements are so violent that you might break an arm or a leg if you try to suppress them. So much strength in such a small body,' she said, unconsciously echoing Franks's words. 'And it gets worse as they get older until it's almost impossible to cope.' Penrose saw the recognition in Rhiannon's face and understood how hard it must be for Gwyneth to accept help when she knew better than anyone what a burden it was, both physically and mentally; no wonder her own death seemed to hold no horror for her. 'Taran was hurting himself that day. There were terrible bruises on his face where he had struck his head against the bottom of the boat, and two of his little fingers were broken from slamming into the wood. David reacted instinctively. It was better that way, I think – better for me not to have known when it was going to happen. I'm not sure I would have had the strength to go through with it.'

Every nerve and fibre in Penrose's body wanted to expose Franks's cruelty and tear the sick, twisted halo from his head, but he held himself back. 'What happened then?' he asked evenly. 'Did David bring Taran's body back?'

'No. He left him somewhere safe and came to fetch me.'

'Where, Mrs Draycott? Where is Taran now?'

He repeated the question, but she ignored it as if it had never been asked, and Penrose guessed that her desire to unburden herself was no match for her determination to ensure that her son's body remained undisturbed. 'He's at peace now,' she said, confirming it as much for herself as for him. 'He wasn't tormented like Edwin. He wasn't hurt or laughed at or punished like a criminal and left to rot . . .'

She was becoming agitated, and Penrose watched as Rhiannon eased her back against the pillows and gently calmed her. 'I'll tell him, Gwyn,' she promised. 'You've said what you needed to say and now you've got to get your strength back. Edwin was her brother,' she explained, turning back to Penrose. 'They were twins, and his epilepsy was very severe. Gwyn was lucky, if you can call it that: she only had mild attacks when she was a kid, and so rarely that she managed to hide it, but Edwin was different. The family was terrified of the stigma. When he was too old for them to keep it quiet, they had him shut away in the Castle. It's a hotel now, but it used to be an asylum.'

'Yes, I know it.'

'I went with Gwyn to visit him once a week. Nobody else from the family would even acknowledge he existed. Not that it did them much good, mind; the gossip round town was disgusting. That place was like a museum for every form of human misery: suicidal, delusional, violent, and a lot like him who were just ill, but there was no difference between them. Some were more trouble than others, that's all. Edwin was one of those. Behind-the-table patients, they used to call them – the ones they thought were going to be most disruptive. I'll never forget the first time we went in there. They'd put him on a chair behind a long table with five or six other patients, backs to the wall, never allowed to speak, and nothing to do except stare and be stared at. If you weren't mad to start with you soon would be.'

Penrose could understand her anger: after the first war, Bridget had made a series of drawings for an anti-war society of former soldiers living in asylums – the victims of society's shame, shut away like criminals simply because their minds could not cope with what they had experienced. He remembered her bitterness at the crudeness of their treatment; drugging, purging and a little light starvation, she had called it, regardless of individual needs. It was the same here: people suffering from epilepsy were not responsible for their actions during or after an attack and were therefore insane according to the legal definition of the word, but an asylum was surely the last place in which they would find the care they needed.

'It would have been humiliating for anyone to be treated like that,' Rhiannon continued, 'but it was only a matter of time before Edwin had a fit up there in front of everyone, like some sort of freak-show entertainment. We were there once when it happened. Everyone was laughing or shouting obscenities at him, and the noise was unbearable. None of the attendants did anything to help. If anything, I think they were grateful for the distraction.'

Penrose glanced at Gwyneth. She had closed her eyes and he could only imagine the pictures she was seeing in her mind. 'What happened to Edwin?' he asked quietly.

'He had a fit one night and hit his head, alone in a cell where they'd put him as a punishment for something. God knows what. He was supposed to be under constant supervision, but he'd been dead for nine hours by the time someone found him.' She took Gwyneth's hand and held it. 'He was just a young man, Mr Penrose, and so sweet-natured. Is it really any wonder that she didn't want that for Taran, that she'd do anything to avoid it?'

Penrose knew that she was pleading with him for her friend's sake, but he doubted that any legal recrimination would be as harsh as the one Gwyneth had given herself. 'It was all right while I was there to protect Taran,' Gwyneth said quietly, as if she had read Penrose's thoughts, 'but I knew they'd take him away if anything happened to me, and I never expected to live a long life. Now, every day I wake up is another day of guilt for the time he could have had, and look what it's all led to.'

'Mrs Draycott, you can't hold yourself responsible for every evil thing that David Franks has ever done,' he said. 'The murders he committed in America are . . .'

The rest of his sentence was lost in the cry of protest from the bed. Gwyneth Draycott clutched desperately at the sheets and tried to sit up. 'Please leave now,' Rhiannon begged, looking at Penrose. 'She needs to rest. She's had so little sleep since she heard about David, and she's more likely to have an attack if she's tired.'

Penrose did as he was asked and waited outside on the landing. Another flight of stairs led up to an attic room, and, through the open door, he caught sight of what looked like a child's nursery. Rhiannon was still occupied with Gwyneth, so he climbed the steps and looked inside. There were toys lying on the floor by the window: stuffed animals, tin soldiers, a wooden Noah's Ark, all the more poignant because this was not the house where Taran had lived, but where he had died. What caught Penrose's attention, however, was a collection of small carved figures, arranged in groups on a long table down one wall. He walked over to look at them more closely and saw that each arrangement represented an everyday scene: a family having a meal, a classroom of children, a woman reading a bedtime story. It was a life lived out in miniature, the story of growing up which every mother took for granted but which had been denied to Gwyneth.

'She's lived in that world more and more these past few years.' Penrose had been too absorbed in what he was looking at to notice Rhiannon's footsteps on the stairs. 'It's as if she can't face reality any more; hardly surprising, I suppose. David made all those figures for her. He was always clever like that.' She picked up one or two of the other toys and tidied them away in a chest. 'David was the perfect son she never had.' She saw his face and tried to explain. 'In Gwyn's eyes, I mean. He was always so full of life – handsome, bright, strong, successful. Everything she had once wished for Taran she saw fulfilled in him. She had watched him grow up, remember. Every summer the Gypsies came back here, he spent more time with her, and he never really wanted to leave. From Gwyneth's point of view, his mother was dead, and it was safe for her to care for him as a son, free from all the fears that tainted her love for her real child. After what happened to Taran, theirs was the ultimate bond, I suppose: you don't share a secret like that without an enormous amount of trust on both sides.'

'Why didn't David stay with Gwyneth after his father was killed?'

'That's what both of them wanted, but Grace didn't think it was safe for him here, and she asked Bella to take him. Looking back, I wonder now if the two of them suspected the truth and got him as far away as they could. Either way, it was the worst possible thing for Gwyneth, and she always resented Bella for taking him from her.'

'What about when he came back to England in the twenties?'

'He lived in London, but he visited Gwyneth all the time, I gather. Grace was dead by then, and Gwyneth had moved back here, but she and David had always kept in touch. Just before the war, when he went to America for the second time, he begged her to go with him. He'd inherited Bella's money, and he offered to move us both out there where we'd be safe, but she wouldn't leave here because of Taran. David saw that as a choice, I think, although if he resented it, he never said.'

'Did she know what he was doing in America?'

'No.' Penrose looked doubtfully at her and she relented a little. 'You saw her reaction earlier when you mentioned it, and it's the same if I try to talk to her. She's in denial, and I suspect she always has been. Every so often, he came back here, and there seemed to be a pattern to his visits: he'd arrive troubled and withdrawn, stay a few weeks and then go back like his old self. My guess is that he came here whenever he had killed, but that's all it is – a guess. He never told me anything, and I would swear that he never spoke to Gwyneth about his crimes either. He didn't need to confess to find peace here. This was always his sanctuary.'

'Somewhere he could come to be forgiven,' Penrose said, trying to keep any note of judgement out of his voice.

'More than that. Somewhere he could come to be loved for what he was, where there was nothing *to* forgive.'

'And you? You're obviously an intelligent woman; was it so easy to turn a blind eye?'

'He frightened me.' She said it with such feeling that Penrose regretted his naivety in even asking the question. 'Particularly towards the end. He was coming back here more often, and I knew he was out of control. He had no affection for me other than as the person who cared for Gwyneth. Would you have challenged him if you were in my shoes, or done anything braver than pray for him to be caught?'

'No, I don't suppose I would.'

She glanced round the attic and gave a shudder. 'I'm sure you have more questions, but do you mind if we go downstairs? I hate this room.'

In truth, Penrose was glad to leave it too. 'Where do you fit into this, Mrs Erley?' he asked bluntly when they were both seated back in the kitchen. She frowned at his use of the name, but said nothing. 'The story is that you ran off with Henry Draycott all those years ago, and yet here you are caring so fondly for his wife. You didn't leave here with him, did you?'

'No.'

'Were you even having an affair with him?'

'He paid me for sex, Mr Penrose. You'll have to decide what you'd like to call that relationship.' She softened, realising perhaps that sarcasm was not the best line to take with so little in her favour; privately, Penrose admired her spirit, although he would never have admitted as much. 'As I said, Gwyneth and I were brought up together. My parents died when I was very young, and hers were kind enough to take me in. We were roughly the same age, and we took to each other straight away. Had we been real sisters, I doubt we would have been closer, and we've stayed friends all our lives.'

'Did she know about your arrangement with her husband?'

'Of course she did. She had always been honest with Henry about what their marriage would be if it went ahead: they would never be husband and wife in the truest sense, and he could never expect children from her, but she would care for him and look after his house and turn a blind eye when he looked for sex elsewhere.'

'And that's where you came in.'

'Yes. It was an arrangement that suited us all for a while. I'd married for what I thought was love when I was very young, but it didn't take me long to discover that he was a bastard and I was a fool. I won't bore you with a list of his qualities except to say that he drank, was handy with his fists and extremely possessive in that one-sided way which comes naturally to so many men.' In spite of the circumstances, Penrose suppressed a smile. 'We lived next door to his family, and sometimes I found it hard to remember whether I'd married him or his mother. My plan was to make enough money to leave him and start again somewhere else, and Gwyneth made sure I was well paid for my services to her husband.'

'So what went wrong?'

'We didn't take into account the fact that Henry loved Gwyneth to the point of obsession. Sex with me – or any other woman, for that matter – was never going to satisfy him in the long term. He would have agreed to anything to marry her, but he always believed that he'd win her round.'

'Hadn't she explained why those conditions were there?'

'Yes, of course. She wouldn't have been able to hide her illness for long in a marriage. One day, when she was sick of Henry trying to persuade her to sleep with him, she took him to the Castle to see what sort of life her brother was living, but even that wasn't enough: Henry couldn't stop himself. He forced her to give him what he wanted, and, once he had crossed that line, he wouldn't stop. It was only a matter of time before she fell pregnant, and she was terrified.'

'Did she know that David had seen it happen?'

'What?' She stared at him in horror.

'It's in his confession.'

'She had no idea. Good God, she'd have died of shame if she'd known; she was reluctant even to tell me, but she was desperate.'

'So what did being desperate lead her to do? Or lead *you* to do? Did you blackmail him?'

She laughed scornfully. 'With what? She was his wife, for God's sake. No man would have blamed him for taking what he was entitled to.' Penrose wanted to argue, but he remembered what Marta had said and knew in his heart that she was right. 'She could have killed him, I suppose, but she wasn't capable of that, so the only way round it was to make him as afraid as she was. It was a way out for both of us.' She avoided his eyes for the first time, and he guessed she was either searching for words or deciding how much to tell him. 'Henry liked his sex on the rough side,' she said eventually. 'I imagine Gwyneth's resistance made things more interesting for him. He was certainly never very considerate with me, and I earned my money. He particularly enjoyed knocking me about or having his hands round my throat. One day, I simply didn't get up. I let him think he'd gone too far.'

'He thought he'd killed you?'

Even as he said it, Penrose doubted his own interpretation of her words, but she nodded. 'I can see what you're thinking; I never thought he'd be that stupid, either. But he panicked, and nobody acts rationally in a situation like that. He was horrified at what he'd done, and he would have agreed to anything to get away with it. Gwyneth made him promise to leave. If he went immediately and swore never to come back, she said she'd hide my body and tell everyone we'd run off together. As you can imagine, it didn't take much consideration. Rightly or wrongly, murder is a capital offence and adultery isn't; he barely stopped to pack a bag.'

'He died thinking he was a killer?' As contemptible as he found Henry Draycott's behaviour, Penrose could not reconcile what had happened to him with his own personal sense of justice. Whatever else he had failed at, Draycott had excelled in the role of scapegoat for the rest of his life, even in his own mind, and David Franks's undertaking at Portmeirion had been made so much easier as a result. Franks had gambled on the human readiness to judge, and he had been right. Rhiannon must have sensed his disapproval because she made no effort to defend what she and Gwyneth had done. 'Who else knew about this?'

'David and his father. I had to leave quickly – it was only a matter of time before Gareth Erley came knocking at the door, demanding to know where Henry Draycott had taken his wife

– and they helped me get away. Tobin was pleased to do it. There was no love lost between him and my husband. The feud was long-standing, and I expect you know how it ended.'

'What about Bella Hutton? Did she know?'

'No. She believed that Henry had run off with me at first. Then Gwyneth got a letter from her, saying she knew what had really happened and that Henry couldn't be allowed to get away with murder. This was back in the thirties, just before Henry died. It wasn't the truth at all, of course. David must have put it into her head.'

'Because he knew that Bella would do something about it and he could use that to destroy them both?' She shrugged. 'Did you know what David was planning to do that weekend, Mrs Erley?'

'No, absolutely not. I hadn't seen him since I left here, and he was still just a boy then. All I knew was that Gwyneth had been in touch to say that it was safe for me to come back – if I wanted to.'

'Safe because Henry and Bella would soon be past caring whether you were dead or alive.'

'I didn't know that,' she repeated calmly. 'I just knew that Gwyneth was getting worse and she needed someone to care for her. I wanted to make up for all the years – all those difficult years with Taran – when I couldn't be there for her.'

'A kind of penance for not being around to stop her making that terrible decision?'

'If you like, yes.'

'So you were back here by the time the murders took place?'

'I came back the following morning.'

What excellent timing, Penrose thought. 'And did you go to

Portmeirion that weekend?' If Henry Draycott had been the third murder victim mentioned in Franks's confession, it was not inconceivable that Rhiannon Erley had been waiting in that Bell Tower to help him on his way while Franks was conspicuous on the terrace. It would have been risky, but she would just have had time to get down the steps and out before he arrived at the scene.

'No. I've *never* been there.'

She had no trouble meeting his eye, and Penrose believed her. 'Did Gwyneth know about the murders in advance?'

Rhiannon hesitated. 'She knew something was up when she saw Henry outside the house. It terrified her – she thought he'd discovered the truth and come back to punish her. She told me that she'd telephoned David at the hotel to find out what was happening and he just told her not to worry. She trusted him to protect her.'

'Don't fool yourself,' Penrose said. 'He settled all his personal scores that weekend: he wiped the slate clean, and organised the evidence accordingly.'

'I can see that now, but I didn't know it then.'

'So when a policeman knocked on Gwyneth's door and told her that her husband had killed two people and then himself, you both took that at face value?'

'Gwyneth would have turned a blind eye to anything after what David did for her,' Rhiannon admitted. 'She loved him unconditionally.'

'And you?' Throughout the interview, Penrose was conscious that Rhiannon Erley had made no reference whatsoever to her daughter. He would have expected her to talk of regret at leaving her child or pleasure at returning, but Branwen seemed to have played no part in any of her mother's choices – and that baffled him. He could not approve of the decisions that Rhiannon had taken, but he understood most of them and sympathised with many; her attitude to Branwen's murder, however, was beyond him. 'Did you love Gwyneth enough to turn a blind eye to the murder of your own daughter?' he asked. 'Franks used her – to set Turnbull up and because he enjoyed it.'

She thought for a long time before answering, but her expression was impossible to read. 'Please don't think I wasn't shocked and upset by Branwen's death,' she said at last, 'but she *wasn't* my daughter. My husband was her father, and she was raised as our child, but I had almost nothing to do with her. Gareth's mother saw to that.'

'So all the time she was looking for you . . .'

'She was looking for the wrong woman, yes. I don't know who her real mother was. There were a number of candidates.'

'Do you know if Branwen sent Gwyneth a letter that weekend?' Penrose asked.

'Yes. It was something else Gwyneth panicked about.'

'Did she give it to David?'

'I don't know. I never saw it, but she told me later that Branwen was threatening to talk to Bella Hutton to find out where I was because her baby had a right to know its grandmother, but obviously I . . .'

'Branwen was pregnant when she died?'

Rhiannon looked at him in surprise. 'Yes. Didn't you know?'

'No,' Penrose said quietly. 'I had no idea.' At the time, he had asked Roberts to send him copies of the post-mortem reports on all the victims, but the inspector had never bothered, and

Penrose had been too busy with his own cases to chase them. So Branwen's unborn child was the third life that Franks had taken that weekend; he would have learnt about her pregnancy when he doctored the letter to incriminate his uncle.

He walked over to the window and looked out at the well-kept garden, stocked with fruit trees, roses and hydrangea. 'Do you know where Taran is buried?' he asked. 'Is he somewhere here?'

'Gwyneth would never tell me,' Rhiannon said, coming over to stand beside him. 'Obviously I've thought about it, and it's possible that his grave is somewhere in the garden. She's left the house to me, and I suppose that would be a way of keeping him safe.'

'But you don't think that's the answer.'

'Why do you want to know?'

'I have no idea, Mrs Erley. It just seems to matter.'

His answer persuaded her to trust him. 'Come with me.' She led him back into the hall and opened the front door. Penrose looked across to Portmeirion and wondered if she was going to tell him that Taran's final resting place was in the dog cemetery or somewhere in the village; in fact, she surprised him by suggesting neither. 'Gwyneth has left instructions in her will that she's to be cremated and her ashes scattered on the island,' she said. 'So that would be my guess.' He followed her gaze and knew instantly that she was right: the island was the perfect burial place, peaceful and solitary, viewed constantly from both sides of the water but never truly seen, and always at the heart of Gwyneth's world. 'Only she and David know for sure, though.'

'You've given your life to her.'

'It may seem like that to you, but loyalty is complicated. From the outside, it's duty; from the inside, it's love.' He nodded, remembering that Josephine had once said something very similar to him. Rhiannon glanced back up the stairs, torn between waiting to see what he was going to do and returning to Gwyneth's bedside. 'I can't expect you not to act on what I've told you. We've broken the law in so many ways, and love and fear don't justify everything.' She must have seen the indecision in his eyes, because she added, 'Gwyneth needs me now, but do what you have to. You know where I'll be when you've decided. I hope, by then, she'll be somewhere much safer.'

She closed the door behind him, and he walked back to the gate. A few yards further up the road there was a bench overlooking the estuary, and he sat down to think, glad to be out of the house. It was just after three o'clock, and Portmeirion had finally lost its exclusive arrangement with the sun; the heat had burnt away the last of the cloud and the whole of the peninsula was bathed in a glorious light. If he didn't know better, he might have been fooled into thinking that the transformation was more than surface-deep, but, in the house behind him, two women were playing out wasted lives surrounded by guilt and fear; and to his right, on an island covered with heather and sweet-smelling gorse, a small boy lay in an unmarked grave. He knew what he should do. He knew what he wanted to do. And he thanked a god he didn't believe in for waiting until now to trouble him with a conflict between the two. He sat there for a long time, thinking back a few years to when Josephine had given him a copy of her new novel, *Brat Farrar*, and they had argued over its ending: he had insisted that the police could never turn a blind eye to such a serious misdemeanour, no matter how sympathetic they were; she had laughed at his earnestness and kissed him, and he could still hear her saying that just because something was real that didn't necessarily make it right. He had had no reply to her then, and he had none now.

Rhiannon's face fell when she saw him back at her door, and he spoke quickly to reassure her. 'I'm only here because there's something you should know, Mrs Erley, and then I'll leave you both in peace. Taran died in this house.' The shock took a moment to register. 'Obviously, that's not something his mother would ever want to hear, but I thought you should know. I don't know what you plan to do with your life once Gwyneth is gone, but it might be time to make a new start.'

Penrose turned to go, but she called him back. 'Why are you doing this?' she asked. 'Why are you being so kind?'

He smiled sadly. 'A friend of mine should have waited to hear the end of this story. We were in Portmeirion together when it started, but it's too late now for me to talk to her about it. The least I can do is make sure that it finishes in a way which would have pleased her.'

Rhiannon was about to say something, but Penrose didn't trust himself to stay any longer. He got into his car and drove away from the house for the last time. As he reached the end of the narrow lane he had to pull over to allow an ambulance to pass, and he realised what she had been going to tell him. In his rear-view mirror, he watched the vehicle make its way down the bumpy track, skirting the potholes as it went, but there were no lights, no warning bell and the lack of urgency could only mean one thing: Gwyneth Draycott was dead. What that said about justice, he could not even begin to work out.

4

The Friday-night crowds in Mayfair fell into different camps: locals and tourists taking a stroll after dinner and asking for nothing more than the splendour of a summer's evening in the capital and those with a more specific purpose, rooted to the pavement outside Claridge's, desperate for a glimpse of the next star to pass through its doors. During the war, the hotel had served as a haven for kings and queens from all over a war-ravaged Europe; these days, its royalty came almost exclusively from Hollywood – less authentic, perhaps, but more popular, and ardent movie fans of all ages were now as regular a feature of the Claridge's façade as its soft red stone and cast-iron balconies. Reluctantly, Penrose took his place alongside them, standing at the corner of Brook Street and Davies Street, waiting impatiently to see at which of the hotel's two entrances Hitchcock's car would stop. The papers had been full of the director's visit to London to promote *Rear Window* – his homecoming, as those still smarting from his Hollywood defection would have it – but Penrose guessed from a quick glance round that most people were here to see Grace Kelly. Press photographers held their cameras ready, fans clutched their magazines, hopeful of a signature, and even Penrose could not remain entirely immune to the sense of occasion. Josephine would have been proud of him.

There was a murmur of excitement as a sleek black car pulled up in Brook Street, and Penrose was pleased to see that he had positioned himself well. Hitchcock got out first without waiting for his chauffeur, and he looked relaxed and happy as he walked round to open the door for his latest leading lady. Other than being a little slimmer and a little greyer, he had hardly changed since those days in Portmeirion – but even from a distance there was an air of success about him, a confidence that exists only in a man at the very top of his game. Grace Kelly emerged from the limousine to a barrage of cheers and whistles: elegant, serene and cool to the point of glacial – like a piece of Dresden china, as one of the magazines had put it. Penrose stared in awe at her perfection, and wondered what Bella Hutton would have made of this new generation of film star; somehow, he thought, she would have approved. Hitchcock and Kelly played up to the cameras, and then, as the actress was whisked off into the hotel, Hitchcock turned back to the car and held out his hand: Alma got out, looking more petite than ever, and smiled up at her husband. The cameras had turned away by the time the director and his wife walked inside together; in Penrose's opinion, they had missed the picture of the night.

He pushed through the crowds and followed the party into the hotel. The art-deco lobby was exquisite, and Penrose smiled to think that the finest British craftsmanship could still compete so effortlessly with all the glamour that Hollywood cared to throw at it. A champagne reception was being held in the film's honour in one of the downstairs suites, and the sound of laughter and celebration made it easy to find. Penrose walked up to the door, but a waiter stepped forward discreetly to stop him. 'I'm sorry, sir, this is private unless you have an invitation?' Instinctively, he reached inside his jacket for his warrant card but found only air. Across the room, he saw that Alma had noticed him. She spoke quietly to her husband, and Hitchcock broke away from the crowd. 'Mr Penrose, how nice to see you again after so long.' He waved the doorman away and ushered Penrose into the room. 'It is "Mr" now, I believe? You've retired?'

Penrose ignored the social niceties: he had not come here to catch up with an old friend. 'I want to talk to you about David Franks.'

'Ah yes. A terrible business, but my association with Mr Franks was very brief, and it all happened a long time ago.'

'Franks wrote to Alma from prison, didn't he?' Hitchcock looked at him sharply, and Penrose experienced the satisfaction that always comes from being underestimated. 'She liked David, and she must have been horrified when she heard what he had done. She wanted to understand, so she sent him a letter to ask why.'

'I hardly think my wife . . .'

Penrose interrupted him. 'You don't need to defend what she did. It's human to look for a reason: evil for evil's sake is too much for most of us to contemplate. And Franks was happy to tell her all about that weekend at Portmeirion because he wanted you to know how clever he'd been. Alma gave him the excuse he needed: to write to you would have been an admission of how important you were to him, but he knew she'd show you the letter. He wanted you to realise that all the time you were blaming him for what went wrong, he was actually a step ahead of you – the organiser, the manipulator, the director. Everything that happened that weekend was planned by him, not by you.'

'I'm afraid I have no idea what you're talking about,' Hitchcock said, recovering his composure.

'There's no point in denying it. The prison records of

Franks's communications are quite clear. What I don't understand is why you sent the letter to me.'

'Don't you?' Hitchcock smiled. 'I'm not admitting anything, Mr Penrose, but if I *had* sent you that letter, it would have been to set the record straight. I can't bear the thought of such a long and distinguished career coming to an end with questions still unanswered.'

'Fine. Then answer this one: what about the killings on your film set? I don't know who you've talked to or what strings you've pulled to keep them quiet, but that's not justice. Those women have died, and their lives have to be accounted for.'

'I agree. Everything has to be accounted for.' He looked defiantly at Penrose, and then his face broke into a smile. 'Come with me.' He walked across the room to a woman in a strapless green evening dress. 'I don't think you've met Miss Sidney? Joan, this is the policeman I was telling you about.'

The woman turned round, and Penrose stared in astonishment at the face he had last seen contorted on the screen in his office, choking in agony with what he had thought were David Franks's hands around her throat. He had watched Joan Sidney die over and over again, and it took him a few seconds to accept the fact that she was alive and well and standing in front of him; then it all fell into place. 'You made that film to get my attention,' he said to Hitchcock. 'You wanted to do the right thing, and you knew something had to be done about the contents of that letter. But why go through this charade?'

'Sometimes it's very hard to admit that you've behaved badly.' He winked and began to walk away. 'But, as I said, I don't know what you're talking about.'

'Apology accepted,' Penrose called after him.

Hitchcock turned back and nodded gravely. 'Keep the Portmeirion films, Archie. Alma and I were both deeply saddened to hear about Miss Tey's death.'

Penrose watched him go and turned to Joan Sidney in embarrassment. 'You must think me very rude, but it took me a moment to recognise you. I've only ever seen you dying or dressed as a nun.' She smiled. 'I left a message for you to get in touch nearly twenty years ago. Do you mind if we talk now?'

'If I've kept you waiting that long, I'm the one who should apologise for being rude.'

'David Franks brought you to Portmeirion. How did you know him?'

'I met him when I was working for Max Hutton. Max and Leyton Turnbull involved him in the seamier side of film-making until Bella found out about it and hauled him back to England. I hadn't seen him for ages, but he got in touch and asked me to come to the Hitchcock weekend. It sounded like fun and turned into a nightmare. I had no idea the joke was going to be quite so vicious, and then the police showed up the next day. I got out of there like a bat out of Hell.'

'What about later on? Did you ever work for Franks when he went back to America to stay?'

'No. I was married by then, and I loved – I love – my husband. The money was great. Actually, the money was sensational, but enough was enough. I didn't want that life any more, and I didn't want Jim and the kids ever to find out what I'd done for a living when I was younger.' She accepted a cigarette and looked at Penrose thoughtfully. 'And I suppose it's easy to say this now, but there was something about David Franks that frightened me. Even in those early days, he wasn't like Turnbull or Max; it wasn't about the profits for him. When I heard what had happened, I wasn't surprised. I was lucky. Other girls weren't.'

'And when did Hitchcock ask you to do a little filming for my benefit?'

'He didn't. He offered me a part in his new movie.' She winked, refusing to rise to the bait. 'That's the trouble with film: you never know when you're going to end up on the cutting-room floor.'

Penrose tried one more time before accepting defeat. 'Is Tom Doyle an actor too? Will I see him in *Rear Window*?'

She smiled. 'It's been nice meeting you, Mr Penrose. Enjoy the film.'

PART SEVEN

YOUNG AND INNOCENT

1 December 1937, London

Josephine stood in the queue outside the Empire in Leicester Square, soaking up the atmosphere of a December night in London. The pavement was packed with people, some hoping to be entertained as she was, others waiting in line for a taxi to take them home from work or out to dinner. The square, which looked nothing by day, never ceased to amaze her with its ability to transform itself in a matter of hours: at lunchtime, when she had passed through on her way back to her club, it had looked haggard and drawn, like someone who had been up for too long; now, against a backdrop of darkness and excitement, the lights shone like jewels, and the mean gardens and unattractive buildings were barely recognisable as belonging to the same place.

'I can't believe we're having to queue for tickets to see *your* film,' Archie said good-naturedly, in a louder voice than was necessary, even above the hubbub.

The people standing close enough to hear him looked round curiously, and Josephine glared at him. 'I knew we should have gone to see this in a fleapit in Clapham,' she said with feeling. 'I only agreed to let you bring me here because you promised we could remain beautifully anonymous.' She glanced up at the enormous lighted billboard above the entrance. 'Anyway, it's not my film: look at the title.'

'Mm. I prefer yours, but at least *Young and Innocent* tells us what we're getting.'

'It could be worse, I suppose. In America they've called it

The Girl Was Young. It must have taken the Hitchcocks hours of pontificating to come up with that one.'

She smiled, daring Archie to reason with her, but he wasn't any more inclined than she was to stand Alfred Hitchcock's corner. 'I don't give a damn what they call it,' he said. 'It's still exciting.'

Josephine put her arm through his and squeezed it affectionately. 'Yes, it is.'

'And I'm not letting you see it anywhere that isn't glamorous.' There was certainly nothing low-key about the Empire, she thought, looking up at the fine Venetian-arched façade which gave only the barest hint of the luxury to be found inside. The owners had wanted a grand movie palace in the American style, and they had got one: the cinema's extravagance was unequalled anywhere else in the country, and Josephine always took an ironic satisfaction in knowing that this epitome of Hollywood idealism – the showplace of the nation, as it was called – had been designed by a Scottish architect.

In true American fashion, the box office was open to the street. 'Where would you like to sit?' Archie asked.

'In the balcony, if you can stretch to three and six.'

'I'll see what I can do.' He paid for the tickets and they went inside. The magnificent double-height foyer was lined with mirrors and dark walnut, and its opulence was almost overpowering: everywhere Josephine looked, she saw crystal chandeliers, rich drapery and ornate Renaissance decoration. 'Are you all right?' Archie asked, seeing her hesitate.

Josephine nodded. 'God knows why I'm so nervous. I haven't

done anything towards this film. Still, it's not every day you have your work trashed in front of thousands of people.'

'You don't know that he's trashed it. Or has Marta said something?'

'I couldn't get anything out of her because she didn't want to spoil it, but she warned me not to expect to recognise too much of the plot.'

'It's a shame she's not free until later.'

Josephine agreed half-heartedly, then admitted, 'I'm actually quite glad it's just the two of us.' He looked at her, and she blushed. 'If it's terrible, I don't want to feel stupid in front of her. Is that ridiculous of me?'

Archie laughed. 'No, it's very human.'

They walked through a luxuriously decorated tea lounge into the auditorium. The circle extended over most of the stalls and its decor echoed the design of the foyer. Josephine had been here several times but the scale of it always took her breath away: the cinema held more than three thousand people, making it bigger than any other picture house, theatre or concert hall in the West End, and she was thrilled to see that there were very few empty seats. 'You've got to hand it to Hitchcock,' she said. 'He knows how to pack them in.'

They sat impatiently through the newsreels. Eventually, the main feature started, and Josephine felt a rush of pride as she saw her name appear on the screen. 'I'd like to have seen it in bigger letters,' Archie whispered, but she was too distracted by the cast list to appreciate his loyalty. 'Where have all my characters gone?' she asked, bewildered. 'The killer's not even in it. And who the hell is Old Will? Or Inspector Kent?'

Archie shrugged, and they watched as the film opened abruptly with a couple having a row against a backdrop of a stormy sea. 'Is that Christine Clay with her husband?' he asked.

'I suppose so.'

'Why has he got a twitch?'

'Your guess is as good as mine.'

'Cornwall looks good, though,' he said lamely.

Josephine stared at the screen, torn between resentment at such a rapid departure from her book and a grudging admiration of the dramatic scene that Hitchcock had created. The storm took her back to Portmeirion, and she was about to say so when the camera lingered broodingly on the man's face, its implications all too obvious. 'But that's not who did it!' she cried indignantly. 'She wasn't killed by her bloody husband.'

Her outburst drew a chorus of resentful tutting from the row behind, and she heard Archie stifle a laugh before he said, 'At least you don't have to worry about it spoiling the book for your readers.'

Reluctant to suffer the ignominy of being thrown out of her own film, Josephine settled back in her seat. For a few minutes, the story reverted to something more familiar as the actress's body was discovered washed up on a beach amid a cloud of screaming gulls, but the respite was short-lived, and she resigned herself to being an outsider in the narrative she had created. The next hour passed quickly in a flurry of Chaplinesque chases and whistle-blowing, interspersed with cleverly filmed model shots and panoramic views of the sunlit Kent countryside with its long, straight roads. It was strange to watch roles which had so clearly been created for some of the guests at Portmeirion and yet to see none of those actors on the screen, and her sense of regret at Bella Hutton's death – which had never entirely left her in the last year – only increased when the story expanded to include Erica's aunt. The performances were good, though; in fact, although she would have been hard pushed to find five direct points of similarity between Hitchcock's story and her own, the essences of the film and the book were not dissimilar.

'Well?' Archie asked as the film finished.

'If it weren't for the credits at the beginning, I'd think I was at the wrong screening,' Josephine said, then gestured towards the people in the audience, happy and smiling as they left the auditorium. 'But I can't argue with that, and there'll always be the book. Let's go and get a drink. I think I need one.'

'You're taking it better than I thought you would,' he said, as they fought their way out into the street.

'If I thought too much about it, I'd be furious,' Josephine admitted. 'But what's the point?'

'Strange how being happy can put things into perspective.'

'Is that what you think this is?'

'You tell me.'

'Well, I suppose that might have something to do with it.'

Lettice and Ronnie were waiting for them by the entrance. 'I thought you were meeting us at the restaurant?' Josephine said, pleased to see them.

'We couldn't wait to see what you thought,' Lettice said, giving her a hug. 'Isn't it marvellous?'

'The dog was excellent,' Josephine said dryly.

'Yes, I thought so too.' The voice was vaguely familiar, and she looked round in surprise. In her pleasure at seeing the Motleys, she hadn't noticed that Ronnie was not on her own.

'David's going to join us for dinner,' she explained. 'He came back early from Kent to celebrate.'

'I wouldn't have thought you'd be in a hurry to see a Hitchcock film,' Archie said.

Franks smiled. 'It took me a while to get over the embarrassment,' he admitted, 'but there's no point in holding a grudge, is there? Anyway, I've got other plans now. In fact, I've just persuaded your cousin to come and see me in America.'

Josephine looked at Ronnie, hoping that her dislike of their unexpected dinner guest didn't show in her face. 'Shall we go?' she suggested. 'We don't want to be late for Rules, and Marta will be waiting.'

They headed for Maiden Lane, and Lettice took Josephine's arm. 'What I really loved about the film was the ending,' she said. Josephine nodded, knowing exactly how she felt. 'I'm so glad they ended up together. You might think of doing that next time you write a book.'

Josephine caught Archie's eye. 'Yes,' she said, smiling. 'Yes, I might.'

Author's Note

Portmeirion was created in 1926 by Clough Williams-Ellis. Over the next fifty years, driven by a passion for the landscape of North West Wales and a unique artchitectural vision, Clough transformed a neglected wilderness into a magical Italianate village, celebrated by *The Times* as 'the last folly of the Western world'. In 1934, shortly after the West End run of her play, *Queen of Scots*, Josephine Tey and a number of her most intimate friends were among many theatrical stars to fall under its spell and find refuge there from the trappings of celebrity; Noel Coward wrote *Blithe Spirit* at Portmeirion in 1941, and John Gielgud, Gerald du Maurier and Alistair Sim were regular visitors. Famous more recently as the setting for George Harrison's fiftieth birthday party and the 1960s television series, *The Prisoner*, Portmeirion is now owned by a charitable trust and is managed by Clough's grandson, Robin Llywelyn. It remains true to its origins: a place of beauty, peace and inspiration, untouched – thankfully – by bloodshed or by film directors with a questionable sense of humour.

The Dog Cemetery, which lies in the woodland beyond Portmeirion village, was created by the house's former tenant, Adelaide Haig, whose son Caton – an authority on Himalayan flowering trees – developed the wild gardens. *Fear in the Sun-*

light is inspired in part by Mrs Haig's compassion and eccentricity, but the Draycotts' story is entirely fictional.

Young and Innocent, based on Josephine Tey's 1936 crime novel, *A Shilling for Candles*, was released in Britain in December 1937. Starring Derrick de Marney as a young man wrongly accused of murdering a famous actress, and Nova Pilbeam in her first adult role, the film was celebrated for its light comic touch, elaborate model work and a spectacular climax in which the camera tracks 145 feet across a crowded dance floor to within inches of the villain's face. It was Hitchcock's own favourite among his British films; 75 years later it stands up to his original estimation of its qualities, anticipating later classics such as *Notorious*, *Marnie* and *North by Northwest*. The director contacted Tey's publisher to enquire if she would collaborate with him on the script, but she declined.

Alfred Hitchcock and Alma Reville moved to Hollywood with their daughter, Patricia, in March 1939, shortly after Hitchcock had completed *Jamaica Inn*. Alma gave up her professional career, but continued to be her husband's closest and most significant collaborator. In 1979, when Hitch was awarded the Life Achievement Award by the American Film Institute, his acceptance speech named only four people: a film editor; a script writer; the mother of his daughter; and 'as fine a cook as ever performed miracles in a domestic kitchen'. All of them were Alma Reville.

Acknowledgements

Portmeirion has become very special to me, and I'm extremely grateful to Robin and Sian Llywelyn for not turning a hair at the prospect of its becoming a playground for a killer. They, their staff and all the people who have written about Portmeirion and its history over the years have helped tremendously in the research for this book. Like many people, I'm indebted to everyone at Portmeirion for preserving the original spirit of a place which is genuinely unlike any other.

I owe a great debt of thanks to George Perry and to the late Anna Massey for sharing their personal memories of Sir Alfred Hitchcock and Alma Reville, and for bringing a very human touch to the legend. Among the many written accounts of Hitchcock's life and career, books by Michael Balcon, Jack Cardiff, Charlotte Chandler, Sidney Gottlieb, Pat Hitchcock O'Connell and Laurent Bouzereau, Patrick McGilligan, Ken Mogg, John Russell Taylor, Donald Spoto and Francois Truffaut have helped to create a comprehensive picture of a complex and fascinating man. Jeanine Basinger's book *Silent Stars*, a brilliant account of early cinema, and Leonard Thompson's memories of the First World War – as told to Ronald Blythe in *Akenfield* – are impossible to forget; I am grateful to both of them.

Walter Donohue's knowledge of Hitchcock and film has

been invaluable, and I hope he knows how much I appreciate his commitment to the series. Thanks, too, to Alex Holroyd and Katherine Armstrong at Faber; to Veronique Baxter, Laura West and David Higham Associates for a brilliant first year; to Mick Wiggins for the beautiful illustrations; and to Sandra Duncan and Dominic White for giving the books such a fabulous audio life.

And my love and thanks, more than ever, to Mandy, for all the conversations, ideas, imagination and insight that have made this book far better than it would otherwise be; to my parents, Ray and Val, and to Michael, Sue and John for everything that they do; to Phyllis, for her continued inspiration and encouragement; and especially to Tilly, who waited to see it finished.